A DIVIDED HERITAGE

PREJUDICE, TRAGEDY AND THE BARBARITY OF WAR

BY THE AUTHOR OF VOYAGE TO VENNING ROAD

MARGARET S GOLDTHORP

PublishNation
www.publishnation.co.uk

Prologue

December 1945

Theo leaned against the deck rail and watched as the English coastline came into view. Soon they would be docking at Liverpool.

He was returning home - or was he? Home was where the heart was, or so the saying went. But he had been longing for the cool green fields of England and they were now within his grasp. And he was eager to see Enid again, and looking forward to being reunited with George and Mary. He wondered if his old school friend, Harry, and his friends from university had all survived the war. And how had Charlie fared? Once he got back to Oxfordshire, he would try to contact everyone. It was four long years since he had last had a letter from England. Some of the men had received mail on rare occasions, but he had not been one of the lucky ones.

The dock area was now clearly visible. He found himself recalling the last time he'd arrived at an English port. Then everything had been new and exciting. He'd been twelve years old, with most of his life still ahead of him and looking forward to whatever the future might bring. He could never have envisaged then how things would turn out.....

~***~

Chapter One

1928

Theo was up on deck early the day they were due to dock at Tilbury. He watched as the shores of southern England began to come into view. He'd heard so much about England from his stepfather and he'd learned a lot about it at school, but until now it had been a strange and remote land. Now he was finally going to find out what it was really like.

His case was already packed and he had nothing to do until they docked, except eat breakfast once it was served. Lessons had been abandoned for today, although Papa had warned that they would recommence for him once they were settled in to their new home and continue until the day before the exam. This was the exam to gain entrance to the local grammar school. Papa's brother, who had booked him in for the exam, had obtained sample papers from previous years and posted them to Malaya before they left. Papa was coaching him, to make sure he passed. Arianna and Enid, his sisters, also had to attend lessons on board the ship; these were taught by a teacher who was going home on leave. They had set sail well before the end of the school term, but were not allowed to get away with an extended summer holiday.

Theo's real father had also been English, but he had come from Yorkshire, not Oxfordshire where Papa had grown up and where they were now heading. Theo had looked at a map of England and seen that Yorkshire was some distance away, in the north of this strangely shaped country. His father had died when he was very small; he retained only a few memories of him, but they were all nice ones. It had taken him almost a year to fully realise that people did not return from heaven, that it was not somewhere you sailed to in a ship, like England. Not long after he'd accepted that his father was gone forever, his stepfather had suggested his surname be

1

changed to Bradshaw, to fit in with the rest of the family, and that Theo call him Papa from now on, as Arianna did, instead of Uncle Jim. Theo had not minded and Jim had said that his real father wouldn't have minded either. Anyway, he'd called his real father Daddy, so the names were different. Jim said that was because he had been born into a more upper-class family than Theo's father.

"Not that that makes me any better than him," he had hastened to add. "It's just that the customs are a bit different."

Jim had gone on leave to England twice in Theo's memory. Once when he was about four and the second time when he was eight. He had not taken his family with him, on the second occasion saying that it would be too disruptive for their schooling, so they had all decamped to his mother's family home for the duration. This had been a bit of a squash, especially the second time with Enid as well. They had all had to sleep in one room and he had shared a bed with Arianna. There were no servants either, and his mother, Alya, was kept busy helping their grandmother with the chores. However, the family had a tiny smallholding, and Theo rather enjoyed helping his grandfather and uncle with the animals. When Jim returned to Klang after seven or eight months' absence, they were able to reoccupy their old home, the Acting District Officer having moved out.

Now, there was a new permanent D.O. in their old home. He had moved in about two weeks before they sailed, so that Jim could show him the ropes. Theo had had to relinquish his bedroom and share with the girls. It was then that the move to England, which had been talked about for ages, finally started to seem real. There was frantic activity in those two weeks; trunks were packed and sent to the dock at Penang, then the rest of their things were packed into cases and bags, which they would carry. Even six year old Enid had a small case. It had felt strange and unreal, as well as sad, saying goodbye to his friends at school, knowing he would probably never see them again, and the farewell with Alya's family had been quite emotional. Their grandmother had hugged them all in turn and entreated them to write often. Theo knew that his mother would make sure that they did.

Arianna appeared beside him at the rail. She was nine and looked very different from her brother. She had black hair and coffee coloured skin, taking after their Malayan mother. Theo and Enid were more like their fathers, being much fairer in colouring, with mid brown hair, and Theo had blue eyes.

"Mama says it's time to come to breakfast," she announced. "Is that England?"

He nodded. "It's the south coast."

"Where's Oxfordshire then?"

"A bit further inland, towards the west. We have to go on a train once we've docked."

By the time they had finished eating, the ship was in the process of docking and they went to fetch their luggage from the cabins. Once they had gone through the disembarkation procedures, Jim told them all to wait while he went to see about having their trunks sent on. This seemed to take a long time and all three children were getting bored and impatient, but eventually he returned and they made their way to the railway station. The train, when it arrived, looked rather different from the trains they were used to in Malaya.

"A lot of things are going to be different, " Jim told them. "This is a north European country. Just wait 'til you experience snow!"

Theo had read about snow in English books. He knew it was white and cold and fell from the sky like rain, but he found it hard to imagine what it looked and felt like.

"It's not as cold as I expected," Alya commented.

Jim laughed. "It's July. One of the warmest months of the year usually. We'll have to get you all some warm clothing before autumn sets in. Luckily you've all got rain gear."

It rained a lot in Malaya, so this was something they were all used to.

They changed trains in London, crossing the capital city in an underground train, which Theo found fascinating. The second train headed for Oxford after leaving London, then meandered through the Oxfordshire countryside until it arrived at the town of Great Pucklington. Despite its name, this was a fairly small town in West Oxfordshire. There they were met by Jim's brother's chauffeur, who introduced himself as Dave. Their cases were piled into the boot of the rather smart car and Alya and the children crammed themselves into the back seat, Enid sitting on Alya's knee. Jim sat in front with

Dave and started to ply him with questions about the estate, the family and the staff.

The children had already been told that they were to live in a cottage on Jim's brother's estate and Jim was to be a part-time assistant estate manager. He had explained that his wages would supplement his colonial service pension and enable them to live quite well, especially with a rent-free house, although his income would not stretch to sending them all to private schools.

The estate was at the edge of a village called Little Pucklington, about three miles from the town. After the car had gone through the wrought iron gates at the entrance, and started making its way through the estate, Jim pointed out the house they would occupy, which he said was about half a mile from the entrance and a similar distance from the main house. The distance to the centre of the village was about three quarters of a mile.

"We're going to the main house first," he said. "Pucklington Manor. We'll have tea with George and Mary, then we'll come down to our new home and settle in."

George was a baronet, they had been told, which meant he was titled gentry. He was called S*ir* George and his wife was *Lady* Mary. Theo had read books which featured the English upper class and he had expected a large house, but the house they drew up in front of appeared enormous. It was even larger than the house in Kuala Lumpur where the Resident of Selangor lived and where Theo and his sisters had once attended a children's party. The children clambered out of the car and wondered aloud to each other whether they would be allowed to explore.

"I'll show you all round very soon," Jim promised.

Alya, alighting from the car, looked up at the imposing mansion and wondered how she was ever going to fit in here. People like her usually only entered such a house by the servants' entrance. She was suddenly very nervous about meeting her in-laws. Sensing this, Jim squeezed her shoulder.

"It'll be fine. Don't worry."

A balding man in his forties, dressed in a black suit, whom Jim addressed as Mr Hughes, had already opened the door.

"Mr Jim!" he exclaimed. "Welcome home!"

Jim shook his hand, asked about his health and that of his wife, then introduced his family. As they all followed him inside, he told them that Mr and Mrs Hughes were the butler and house keeper and 'the ones who really run this place!'

Mrs Hughes, a rather plump lady with a kind face, appeared in the hall and the introductions were repeated. Then they were ushered into the drawing room, a spacious room with a lot of heavy Victorian furniture, comfortable sofas and easy chairs. George rose to greet them. He and his brother shook hands and clapped each other on the back; Jim gave Mary a peck on the cheek. She was a thin woman in her early fifties with dark hair streaked with grey, clipped back in a rather severe style. George looked rather like Jim, Theo thought, with the same jovial expression and thinning, greying fair hair.

"This is my wife, Alya."

"Welcome to Pucklington Manor," Mary said, rather formally.

"These are my daughters, Arianna and Enid, and this is Theo."

After they had all been welcomed and taken seats, a uniformed maid appeared and proceeded to serve tea. There were little sandwiches with the crusts cut off, cakes and pastries. They were all hungry, having had only a small snack on the train for lunch, and tucked in enthusiastically. The maid, a pretty girl in her early twenties called Ivy, poured them all cups of tea.

"You'll find the cottage all ready to move into," Mary said. "It's been refurbished throughout and I've furnished it with pieces from the rooms we no longer use. But if there's anything you don't like, please feel free to make changes - I shan't be offended. And the larder's been stocked with some provisions."

"And we've recently engaged a new maid, Daisy, " George added, "on the basis that she work part-time for you and the rest of the time for us. She can do the heavy cleaning for you and help with the laundry. You can agree how many hours and at what times with Mrs Hughes, once you've settled in."

"I know you were used to a lot of servants in Malaya," Mary said, "but I assume Alya doesn't mind doing the cooking here?"

"Yes, that'll be fine," Jim responded for her. "She's a good cook. And I'll do the gardening and outside jobs - perhaps with some help from Theo."

5

That was the first Theo had heard of it, but didn't really mind.

"And Arianna can help me," Alya added. "It's time she started learning to cook."

Arianna pulled a face.

"I'm having a small luncheon for some of the local ladies in a couple of weeks time," Mary said. "I hope you'll join us, Alya? It will give you the chance to get to know people."

Alya thanked her, but her heart sank. She knew she would be on display to all these white upper-class women and regarded as a curiosity.

After tea, they headed down to their new home. Dave had already delivered the baggage and it was waiting in the small entrance hall. The cottage was quite a good size, with kitchen, scullery, sitting and dining rooms on the ground floor, plus three bedrooms and bathroom above. There was also an attic and a second WC in an outhouse immediately outside the back door.

"That'll be useful in the mornings!" Jim commented. "We can put a paraffin heater inside it in winter."

There were two large bedrooms towards the front of the house and a smaller one at the back, opposite the bathroom.

"That one's yours, Theo," Jim told him, "and you girls can have this one."

The girls' room had windows on two sides and was furnished with twin beds. It was slightly larger than the opposite room, which held a double bed.

They unpacked their things and Alya inspected the larder. It was well stocked and she would not need to go shopping until after the weekend.

"When do our trunks get here?" she asked Jim.

"In a few days. I start work on Monday but I have three afternoons off each week so I can help you sort everything out. And these three can pitch in."

The children went out into the back garden. It was not very large, but it had a lawn, a bench and a rockery at the far end. There was also a shed, which contained garden tools and a couple of strange-looking objects. Jim joined them.

6

"Ah, paraffin heaters!" he exclaimed. "One for the outside lavatory and we can put the other on the landing. The main rooms all have fireplaces, so we'll have coal or log fires in winter."

Theo tried and failed to imagine how cold it must be in winter in order to need fires inside the house.

That evening after supper, Jim expanded on how things would be.

"Your exam is in ten days time, Theo. I'll drive you into town but you can get the bus back. It's held at the boys' grammar school, where you'll be a pupil - provided you pass. I'm sure you will. We just need to do a bit more work on the arithmetic paper, with the pounds, shillings and pence questions - we'll have another lesson tomorrow. You girls will be going to the village school until you're eleven, then you too can take the exam for the grammar school."

"Where will we go if we don't pass it?" Arianna asked.

"There are other schools, but the grammar is the best. If you only just fail, I might be able to pay for you to still attend."

The children were silent, all of them wondering what these new schools were going to be like.

"You won't be starting until the beginning of September," Jim continued. "There're only ten days left until the end of term, so it's not worth you starting now."

This was met with a collective sigh of relief.

"Can we explore the estate?" Theo asked.

"Yes, you can have the run of the place, pretty much, provided you don't disturb the work of the gardeners or the farm staff. And you mustn't run rampage in the formal gardens near the house, nor in the fields containing crops."

"There's a farm, with animals?" Theo asked.

"Yes, some. Cattle, poultry and pigs mostly."

"Can we have a pet?" Enid asked. "A cat or a dog?"

"Not a dog, please!" Alya exclaimed. "I don't like dogs."

"A cat, then?"

"I don't see why not," Jim said, smiling. "I'll ask around to see if there's a litter of kittens expected anywhere."

On Monday, Jim went off to work and Alya set off to the village to do some shopping. She took all three children with her. They would have preferred to continue exploring the estate, as they had done over the weekend, but she insisted.

"I need Theo, and perhaps also Arianna, to help carry the bags and I can't leave you on your own, Enid."

"Papa said we could have stuff delivered," Arianna said.

"Groceries, yes, but we need fresh food as well and a few other things. Anyway, don't you want to see what the village is like? We can take a look at your new school."

The village was fairly small, but it had several shops, including a grocers, greengrocers, butchers, chemist, pub and post office. The latter also sold stationery, sweets and tobacco and the children looked at the sweets displayed in the window. Some were familiar to them, but others were not.

"After we've got everything else, you can go in there and spend some of your pocket money," Alya promised. "Come along now."

In the grocers, where they went first, Alya struggled to make payment with the unfamiliar money. Theo helped her to sort it out, remembering the pounds, shillings and pence arithmetic lessons he'd just had.

"How silly, having the pound divided by twenty and twelve!" Alya exclaimed. "Why couldn't they just divide it by tens?"

The man behind the counter looked at her curiously.

"Where have you come from," he asked.

"Malaya."

"Ah, you'll be Sir George's brother's family. We heard he was coming back."

Outside, Alya asked Theo how much that had all cost in Malayan money. Theo didn't know, but said he might be able to work it out at home with pen and paper, provided he was given the exchange rate.

When they had finished the shopping, having got everything on Alya's list except some spices she needed for Malayan dishes, which she was told she would have to get in town, they did a detour on the way back to look at the village school. As they passed it, the doors opened and children spilled out, heading home for their midday meal. Many of them stared openly at Alya and Arianna and some pointed and giggled.

"How rude," Enid said indignantly.

Arianna said nothing but she was thinking that she had to go to this school next term and she was going to be the only dark face in a sea of white ones. Guessing her thoughts, Alya said consolingly,

"Don't worry, *sayang*. They'll have got used to seeing you around the village by the time you start and you'll no longer be a novelty."

Arianna was not so sure.

When they got home, they found the trunks had been delivered. After lunch, they made a start on the unpacking. When Jim arrived home, he joined in and by suppertime they had most things unpacked, although pictures, ornaments and books still had to be arranged, and a place found for Alya's sewing machine.

"I hope we'll have enough bookshelves," Jim said. "If not, I'll get some wood and make more."

Over supper, Theo asked Jim if he was going to be able to visit his Yorkshire relatives during the summer holidays. His late father had a brother who had been sending Theo Christmas and birthday cards. He had a family and there was one boy cousin the same age as Theo. Jim looked sheepish.

"I've a confession to make about that. When we were packing up, I looked high and low for the letter with their address on, but couldn't find it. And I can't remember it. I think the place name began with 'H' but that's all I can recall. But don't worry, I'll get in touch with the Colonial Office; they should have it on file as his brother was his original next of kin until he married."

Theo nodded. He didn't really mind if meeting his paternal relatives had to wait until half-term or even Christmas; there was no hurry.

The children continued roaming the estate grounds for the next few days. Luckily the dry weather continued to hold. They found a tree house and climbed up into it. It was a bit of a squash with all three of them, but Theo thought it would be a good place to escape to on his own with a book. As they headed home that day, they bumped into a red-haired boy who looked about eleven.

"Hello," he said. "You must be Mr Jim's children. I'm Arthur - my father's the estate manager and I live just over there." He waved a hand vaguely.

"Oh, yes, Papa mentioned you," Theo said. "You're going to the grammar school next term, aren't you?"

"If I've passed the exam. Are you?"

"I hope so - if *I* pass it. I'm taking it next week."

"Well, good luck. Will we be in the same year? How old are you?"

"Twelve, thirteen in November."

"You'll be in year two then. I'll be in the first year. How old are you?" he asked Arianna.

"Nine. We'll be going to the village school. Do you go there? What's it like?"

He shrugged. "It's all right. It'll be nice to have other children to play with on the estate - if you don't mind me joining you sometimes?"

"Of course not! I'll be glad to have another boy for company."

"I've only got sisters too, but they're quite a few years older than me. One's married."

When they got home, Alya said Jim had gone to the pub with Fred, the estate manager, but would be back for supper. She set them to work, laying the table and other minor domestic tasks.

"When's this new maid starting?" Arianna asked.

"On Monday, but she's not here to run after you three. You need to keep your rooms tidy and you can make your own beds during the holidays."

The following Sunday, they went to church in the village, without Alya, who was a Muslim. They had only attended church occasionally in Malaya, but Jim said it would be expected of them here.

"George and Mary go every Sunday - we're supposed to set an example to the village!"

Sitting in the church behind George and Mary, Theo found that he enjoyed listening to the music, but found the sermon boring, and he was annoyed by the stares being directed at Arianna.

"Just ignore them," he whispered to her.

Outside, the vicar shook hands with Jim and said "Hello" to the children.

"Your wife has not come with you?"

10

"She's not a Christian."

"Would she consider converting? Now you are in England. I'd be happy to give her tuition."

"Thanks. I'll ask her."

"Have the children all been christened?"

"Yes, they have."

While they were out, Alya had prepared a traditional English roast lunch with all the trimmings, following the instructions in a cookbook which Mary had thoughtfully supplied.

"Capital!" Jim said, beaming. "Mind you, I'd still like to have curries and Malayan dishes sometimes - I've got used to them."

"I need to go into town for the spices and some other things. The village shops don't stock them."

"Let's go next Saturday then. You and the children need some warmer clothes as well, this nice weather might not last all summer. Then we'll have to go again in September for mid-winter clobber. And perhaps we'll have a trip into Oxford soon."

The following day, Jim drove Theo into town for the exam, saw him inside to meet the invigilator, then left him to it, wishing him good luck. Theo was the only one sitting it that day, the local children having done so earlier. He didn't find it too difficult and just had to hope he had passed.

Over the next couple of weeks the weather varied but was never too cold. The rain, when it came, was lighter than the tropical downpours they were used to. They were invited for lunch and tea at the manor and Jim showed them round the house. A lot of the rooms were closed up and the few they glanced into had dust sheets over the furniture. Enid asked why.

"Well, there's only George and Mary here most of the time now - except when Bertie and Charlie visit, or Isabel." Bertie and Charlie were George and Mary's sons and Isabel was George and Jim's sister. "It saves money not having to clean or heat all the rooms. After my father died there were a lot of death duties to pay and economies had to be made. There are fewer indoor servants now than in my day; just Mr & Mrs Hughes, Daisy and Ivy, Cook, and Millie, the kitchen maid. Dave comes in daily from the village and when he's not driving anyone or looking after the car, he gives Mr. Hughes a hand.

11

Mr and Mrs Hughes live in a cottage on the estate, as Fred does, and Cook and the three maids have rooms on the second floor. The rest of the rooms on that floor are either used for storage or closed."

Theo asked how it was that George was a baronet and had all this - waving his hand expansively - whereas Jim had very little. Jim explained that, in families like his, the title and the estate went to the oldest son. Younger sons had to fend for themselves and daughters had to marry well.

"That's not fair!" Theo exclaimed.

Jim laughed. "Life's not always fair, son. But, having said that, I don't think I drew the short straw. Owning an estate like this isn't a bed of roses; it has to pay for itself and George has a lot of responsibilities. He had no choice in the matter, either - the estate was entailed to the eldest son and that was that. Bertie will inherit when George dies. I, on the other hand, had the world in front of me when I left university and I don't regret my choice to join the Malayan Colonial Service. I've had a good life and enjoyed my work. I was also able to choose who I married - however controversial that choice was! George had to marry someone 'suitable'." He paused then went on: "My parents did try to find me a suitable wife too; on my first long leave back in England I was introduced to one candidate after the other. My father was dead by the time I took my next leave after marrying your mother and having Arianna, but when I told my mother, she was absolutely livid. To her, marrying a native woman and having a mixed race child - and taking on another one to boot - was beyond the pale and she told me no good would come of it."

"I'm glad we didn't have to meet her, then!" Arianna interjected.

Jim continued. "I shall die a happy man, despite her prognosis, and despite never having owned property. Wealth does not bring happiness, Theo. As long as one has enough to live comfortably - as we do - the rest is superfluous. You're lucky because you will inherit nothing and you will make your own way in the world through what's in there." He poked Theo's forehead. "And you will be able to marry whomsoever you choose - provided she also chooses you, of course!"

Alya attended Mary's luncheon for the local ladies and found it rather an ordeal. They were all very polite to her, asking lots of questions about life in Malaya, but she felt as if she were on display and providing them with entertainment. One of them was a leading light in the local Women's Institute and suggested Alya come along to their next meeting and see if she would like to join.

"We do lots of crafts and suchlike and I understand you're a dab hand with a needle."

Over the next couple of weeks, Bertie, accompanied by his wife, Violet, and two small daughters, Charlie, and Isabel all paid visits to the manor. Bertie was a banker and Charlie a lawyer and both worked in London. Charlie was unmarried and his mother asked him about his love life.

"I don't have much time to pursue the ladies, Mama. I've only just started at this firm and I'm still proving myself."

Bertie and Violet's daughters were two and four years old. Arianna and Enid were instructed to take them to the old nursery playroom and amuse them. They did so somewhat reluctantly, but when they got there, they found a rather grand dolls house, which had previously belonged to Isabel, and all four managed to play amicably with it.

Isabel came alone for her visit, her wealthy financier husband being too busy to accompany her. She also lived in London and had three grown-up children. After tea, Theo was in the well-stocked library, returning a book he had borrowed and looking for another one, when Mary and Isabel entered the room. He was hidden from view behind a large bookcase which jutted out into the room and the two ladies thought themselves to be alone.

"Really, I don't know what my brother was thinking of, marrying that woman and bringing her back here. I mean, she's perfectly pleasant and all that, but how is she ever going to fit in?"

"Think yourself lucky you don't have the task of trying to integrate her. I got one of the local ladies to invite her to join the WI, but I don't know how that will turn out."

There was more in the same vein before they eventually left the room and Theo was able to escape. He returned to the drawing room feeling indignant on his mother's behalf and went to sit beside her. She smiled at him, but he said nothing about what he had just heard.

Alya's evening at the WI was not a success. When she returned home, she told Jim emphatically that she was not going again.

"No-one spoke to me except the lady who invited me and Fred's wife, Sarah, and they were busy a lot of the time, organising things. I tried to make conversation with some of the other ladies but they just gave me one word answers and then turned away to talk to other people. I felt like I did at the club in Klang those times you took me along - like I ought not to be there and I'd never be one of them."

Jim sighed. "Perhaps if you persevered? Things might improve."

"No! I don't need those snooty women in my life. I have you and the children, and Sarah is friendly. That's enough for me."

Jim said nothing further but could not help wondering how she would fare when he was dead and gone and the children were grown and left home. He was over twenty years older than Alya. Hopefully, one of the girls would marry someone local and stay nearby.

Theo passed the exam and Jim went with him into town to get his school uniform. Theo was dismayed to find he would have to wear a tie every day. The blazer bore the school motto: ' Per Ardua ad Alta'.

"Do you know what that means?" Jim asked.

"Through hard work to the heights?" Theo guessed.

"That's the gist of it. Work hard and the world's your oyster."

Jim managed to find a family who had a litter of kittens ready to be homed. Two of them were still available and they all went to see them. The one they chose was a black and white male whom they named Felix. He soon became a much loved member of the family.

In late August, Jim and Theo were roped in for the annual cricket match between the estate staff and the village. Theo was a good batsman and also fleet of foot and managed to score the most runs. The estate won the match for the first time in several years, and George clapped Theo on the back and told him he was a great asset to the team.

All too soon, the holidays drew to a close and the prospect of school loomed. All three children became quite nervous, not knowing what to expect at these English schools. This was

14

especially true of Arianna. On the morning of the first day, she was physically sick and Alya worried that she may be coming down with something.

"It's just nerves," Jim said. "If you keep her home today it will only be harder for her, starting after the beginning of term." To Arianna he said, "Don't let all the white faces intimidate you, sweetie; remember you're as good as any of them and probably better than most!" Then he added, looking at his other two children, "Cheer up! Think yourselves lucky to be coming home tonight. I was sent away to school - at the age of eight!"

"That's barbaric!" Alya commented. "And the British are supposed to be so civilised!"

Setting off to catch the bus into town, Theo joined up with Arthur at the point their routes converged. Arthur confessed to being nervous too.

"I'm the only boy from the village school going to the grammar this year. There're two girls who passed but the girls' grammar is separate."

The two girls were already on the bus when it stopped near the estate entrance, having got on in the centre of the village. There were also many other children, of varying ages, some in the grammar school uniforms and the rest in the uniforms of other secondary schools. As the bus wound its way along the country roads to the town, there was a great deal of loud chatter, laughing and banter. One or two of the children looked across at Theo, wondering who he was, but no-one addressed him.

Once at school, Theo was ushered to the headmaster's office and told to wait outside until Mr Warburton was ready to see him. He was joined by a fair-haired boy of about his own age, who introduced himself as Harry Fenton. They fell into conversation and it turned out that Harry was new too, his father having been sent to a different area with his job. Theo told him he'd been living in Malaya.

"Gosh! So you're new to England as well! How old are you?"

"Twelve, nearly thirteen."

"Then we should be in the same year."

They were called in together to see the Head. He was a tall man of about fifty, with heavy-rimmed spectacles.

"Welcome to Pucklington Boys Grammar. I hope you'll be happy here. You will both be in the same form - class A in year two. "

The two boys exchanged pleased glances.

"Fenton, you shouldn't have any trouble with the curriculum as your school in Kent is following a pretty similar one to us. However, you, Bradshaw, will have a bit of catching up to do in some subjects. But don't worry, the teachers will give you all the help you need. I'll take you to your form class for registration. Assembly is finished now."

In their class, they were welcomed by the teacher and told to sit next to each other, near the front. At morning break several boys came up to them, asking where they were from and there was considerable curiosity about Theo's life in Malaya. Generally, the day went well and Theo started to relax. A few boys made disparaging comments about both his and Harry's accents, but most were friendly. In Geography, the teacher announced that, as they had a pupil newly arrived from Malaya, they would have a lesson on the British colonies, focusing particularly on Malaya, and asked Theo to describe various aspects of his life there. Initially embarrassed at being in the spotlight, he soon warmed to his theme and answered questions from the boys. By the time he returned home at the end of the day, he felt that he and Harry were destined to become good friends and school here was going to be all right.

That evening at supper, Theo and Enid, who had also enjoyed her day and made new friends, were competing for their parents' attention, excitedly describing their experiences. Amidst the lively chatter, only Alya noticed that Arianna said very little. Later, she asked her how her day had been. She shrugged.

"All right, I suppose."

Alya could get no more out of her.

~***~

Chapter Two

Arianna hated her new school.

Little Pucklington Primary was divided into three classes, and pupils spent two years in each. Enid was in the junior class and would move up to the middle one next year. Arianna was in the senior class which also had children aged ten and coming up to eleven. There was no streaming and all abilities were taught together. Arianna was bright and had no trouble keeping up with the lessons; the problem was the other pupils, three of the older girls in particular.

At her former school in Klang, there had been many Eurasian pupils, as well as Malayan, Chinese, Indian and a few British, so her light-coffee coloured skin had blended in with everyone else. Here she stuck out like a sore thumb. From the first day she'd been aware of whispering, giggling and pointing and it was not long before this escalated into direct taunts. At break-time, she stood alone in a corner, looking across to the juniors' end of the playground, where Enid was happily playing hopscotch or skipping with other girls, and envied her sister. Goaded into reacting to the comments being made by the other children, she called them ignorant and told them that where she came from many people looked like her, but this just brought forth a chorus of "Well, go back there then!"

On her fourth day, just before the midday break, the teacher tossed the board rubber at one of the older girls, instructing her to clean the board. The teacher then left the room. The girl advanced menacingly towards Arianna, board rubber in hand.

"Let's see if it comes off, shall we?"

There was sniggering from the class although a few looked uneasy. One of the boys said:

"Leave it, Diane!"

She ignored him and, grabbing Arianna by the hair, she swiped the rubber back and forth across her face, several times. It hurt, but the humiliation was worse; Arianna wished the ground would open and swallow her up.

"Oh, look, it *doesn't* come off!   There was laughter from the onlookers.

Diane let go her hair and Arianna was able to escape. She ran outside to where Enid was waiting to walk back with her for their midday meal.

"Come on Ari, we'll have no time to eat anything at this rate!" Then she asked: "What're those white marks on your face?"

"Chalk!" Arianna said, wiping her hand over her face. She told Enid what had just happened.

"What a horrible girl! Are you going to tell the teacher?"

"No, and you are not to tell anyone either. If I tell tales on her, she'll only make it worse for me."

"Has she done other things?"

"She's been calling me names all week, her and her two best mates, Caroline and Elizabeth, and sometimes the others join in."

"I think we should tell Mama."

"I said no! Promise you won't say anything."

Reluctantly, Enid promised.

After that, Diane upped her campaign. No longer content with name calling, she started pushing Arianna whenever they were in a queue, so that she fell against the children ahead of her and incurred their annoyance. Then she gravitated to pinching her arm, pulling her hair, spitting at her and other minor physical assaults, whenever there was no teacher around. When Arianna eventually retaliated in kind, this resulted in the three girls all attacking her at once. She was pushed to the floor, slapped and kicked, until two of the boys came over and pulled them off.

"Leave her alone, she can't help being a wog!"

Arianna ran off to the lavatory and wept bitter tears as she tried to straighten her clothes and hair before the bell rang for class.

Although the others took little or no active part in her abuse, many of them seemed to find it highly entertaining and only one girl was sympathetic to her. She was the same age as Arianna, and her name was Annie. She was quite fat and wore unflattering round spectacles. She confided that she had been the object of Diane's bullying all the previous year. She said nothing when Arianna was being attacked, not wanting to draw the bullies' attention back to

18

herself, but at least she spoke to her and an unsatisfactory friend was better than no friend at all.

At home, Arianna became withdrawn and sullen. She felt resentful towards Alya, blaming her for passing on her Malayan looks. On one occasion, she was downright rude to her mother, earning a slap from Jim, who only rarely hit his children. She burst into tears and ran from the room. Later Alya went into her room and tried to talk to her.

"What is it, *sayang*? Is something wrong at school?"

She very nearly blurted it all out. It was sorely tempting to offload everything on to her mother and have her parents deal with it. But she wasn't sure that would bring an end to it; it might just make everything worse. She also felt ashamed of not being able to deal with it herself and sometimes felt that it must be her fault for being who she was - a freak in this country. So she said nothing.

She contemplated running away. Perhaps she could make her way to a port, stow away on a ship bound for Malaya, and then go and live with her grandparents. But when she considered all the logistics of carrying out this plan, they seemed insurmountable. So she carried on dreading each forthcoming school day from the moment she woke up.

Matters came to a head about four weeks into the term. At afternoon break, Arianna made her way to the girls' lavatories. Diane and her cronies were standing by the washbasins. As she headed for a cubicle, they pounced.

"Oh no you don't!" Diane exclaimed.

"Let me past!"

"No, you're not going in."

"I need the lav!"

"Tough! You'll have to hold on, won't you?"

"Or not," Elizabeth added and they all sniggered.

Arianna gave up, for now, and went outside. Towards the end of break time she saw the three girls come out and head towards the school door. She made a dash for it but found all the cubicles occupied. As she waited, in came Diane and her mates. A girl came out of one cubicle and Arianna grabbed the door, but Diane and Elizabeth held her back.

"Please help me," she pleaded to the girl who had come out and another who had also just emerged. They ignored her. The bell rang for class. Diane and the other two still remained there, blocking her way. The bell rang again.

"We'll have to go now, " Caroline said to Diane. "Or we'll be late."

"Yes, and you're coming with us. Don't want to be late for class, do you?"

They propelled Arianna in front of them, resisting all her attempts to get away.

She sat through the lesson becoming increasingly uncomfortable. She could have raised her hand and asked to leave the room but that would have drawn attention to herself and resulted in sniggers from the class. She was not yet absolutely desperate and thought she could hold on until the end of school and then get out ahead of Diane and her cohorts, as she was seated nearer to the door than they were. Her plan would have worked were it not for the teacher beckoning to her at the end of the lesson.

"I wanted to ask how you were getting on," she asked kindly. "Are you settling in all right?"

Arianna itched to tell her what was happening but didn't dare. She mumbled an answer. The teacher dismissed her, but she had lost precious time and Diane was already on guard in the lavatory. Her need much more urgent now, she tried to fight them off but there were three of them against only one of her and she stood no chance. After several abortive attempts to gain access, Enid appeared in the doorway.

"Come on, Ari, it's home time."

"I need a wee!"

"Well, go then!"

"I can't, they won't let me - they've been stopping me since break."

Enid tried to help her get in but Diane gave the little girl an almighty shove which sent her sprawling. She fell onto her bottom and was not hurt, but Arianna gave up then. She couldn't have her little sister attacked as well.

They headed out of the school gates, Diane and her partners in crime following behind. Arianna was crying by now, her need barely containable.

"I don't think I can make it all the way home!" she wailed.

"You don't have to. Just hold on until we get into the estate and you can go behind those bushes near the entrance."

It was a plan of sorts but Arianna was by no means sure she'd last even that long. As they approached the estate, Enid looked back and saw that the three girls were still behind them, even though they had passed the turn to the village. As they went through the gates, she told Arianna to run and get behind the bushes and she'd try to stop the girls getting in. Arianna hesitated a moment, not wanting to leave Enid at Diane's mercy, then she saw the bus pull up across the main road and spotted Theo getting off. Enid would have support. She dashed the few yards to the bushes and crouched behind, just in time. The relief was tremendous.

Enid closed the gate and confronted Diane.

"You can't come in here!" She pointed at the sign which said that trespassers would be prosecuted. "My father has a gun and he'll shoot you if you come in."

Diane just laughed but then saw Theo approaching. Not wanting to get into an altercation with a boy who was bigger than her, she stepped back and the three of them retreated a few yards. Theo was alone, Arthur having continued on to the village to see a friend. As he came up to the gate he said to Enid,

"Hello. You're later than usual. Where's Ari?"

"Behind the bushes, having a wee!"

"Why didn't she go at school?"

"Because *they* wouldn't let her." She pointed to Diane and the others. "They've been stopping her going all afternoon and she was bursting. And they've been bullying her ever since we started school. I don't know all of it, but they're making her really miserable - she hates school because of them. That dark haired one, Diane, she's the worst."

Theo looked grim. He thrust his satchel and blazer at his sister and strode towards the three girls. They immediately started to run towards the village. Theo ran too. They had a head start on him and might have made it to the relative sanctuary of the village centre before he caught up, had Diane not tripped and fallen headlong. As her friends were helping her to her feet, Theo was upon them. He grabbed Diane's arm and held on.

"Let go of me!"

"Not until you promise to stop bullying my sister."

"I'm not."

"Don't lie. You've been making her life a misery!"

"We were just joking; she's got no sense of humour, that girl."

"You think it's funny to stop her going to the lav all afternoon? You nasty, vicious little bitch! I suppose you were hoping she'd wet herself and then you could all laugh at her. If you don't leave her alone from now on, I will come and find you, along with my mates, and we'll really show you what bullying is. You'll be begging for mercy! Do you understand?"

Diane glared at him but said nothing. Her two friends had retreated to a safe distance. She tried to free her arm but Theo only held it even tighter.

"You're hurting me!"

"Good. I'll be hurting you a whole lot more if you even touch one hair of my sister's head in future. Now, swear that you'll leave her alone."

"All right, I will! Now let go of me."

He released her arm and she ran off, with the other two close behind. He turned and headed back. Both his sisters were now standing at a point from where they had been able to watch the proceedings. Enid giggled.

"You showed her, all right! It's time she got her come-uppance."

"Yes, thanks Theo, but I hope it doesn't make her worse."

"If she doesn't stop, you tell me, and Harry and I will find her and sort her out. Why the hell didn't you say something, Ari? And why didn't you, if you knew what was going on?" he demanded of Enid.

"She made me promise not to tell anyone."

"Don't tell Mama and Papa, Theo. I don't want them to know."

"I don't see why, but all right, I won't mention it."

The next day, which was a Friday, Arianna's three tormentors all kept their distance from her. Annie was amazed.

22

"They never gave me a day off!"

"Don't tell anyone else, but my big brother threatened them. It seems to have worked, for now at least. "

However, when Jim arrived home that evening he looked very annoyed. He bellowed:

"Theo! Come here, now!"

Theo obeyed, wondering what he had done.

"What's this I hear about you having attacked some girl? George has received a complaint from her father."

"I didn't attack her. I just grabbed her arm to stop her running away. I wanted to talk to her."

"Why? Her father said you pushed her over and then held onto her and threatened her. She apparently has injuries to prove it."

"I didn't push her, she fell over, trying to get away from me. And, yes, I did threaten her - I was trying to get her to stop bullying Ari."

Enid and Arianna were standing at the door, listening.

"It's true, Papa. He was helping me. Don't be cross with him. And he didn't push her over, she fell. We were watching and saw it all."

"So what the hell has been going on? Arianna, I want to know all of it, from the beginning!"

Alya had by now also joined them and they all sat down. Arianna started to tell her tale of woe, haltingly at first but then her words gathered momentum and it all tumbled out; all the insults and assaults inflicted on her, all the fear and misery of the past weeks. By the time she had recounted the events of the previous afternoon, she was sobbing bitterly and Alya reached out and gathered her into her arms.

"We can't let this go on!" she said fiercely to her husband.

"Indeed we can't! I'm not having my little girl terrorised. I'll go with George to see that girl's father tomorrow morning and tell him just what his daughter has been up to. You'd better come too, Theo, to give your side of the story. I appreciate you were defending your sister, but these matters are best left to adults to deal with. You should have come to me."

At first, Diane stuck to her story of being attacked by Theo, and denied bullying Arianna.

"We were just teasing her; she can't take a joke!"

"Teasing? Joking?" Jim's voice held suppressed anger. He listed all the incidents Arianna had recounted the previous evening.

"Is this true?" Diane's father demanded of his daughter.

"Well, sort of, but he's making it sound worse than it was...." Her voice tailed off.

"Get out of my sight. You disgust me! I'll deal with you later."

"But Dad......"

"I said, get out. I'm thoroughly ashamed of you!"

To Jim and George, he said: "I can only apologise for her. She'll be punished, you can be sure of that, and it won't happen again. I'll also speak to Elizabeth and Caroline's parents. However, she does have a bruise on her am and a scrape on her knee and two wrongs don't make a right. Your son shouldn't have done what he did."

"She got the scrape falling over, and if she hadn't been pulling away, her arm wouldn't have got bruised," Theo protested.

"That's enough, Theo," Jim reprimanded. To Diane's father, he said, "it won't happen again, he's been told. However, he was trying to defend his sister."

On the way home, George said:

"Of course, none of this would have happened if Arianna didn't look the way she does."

"That's hardly her fault."

George looked to where Theo was walking, a few yards ahead of them, and lowered his voice.

"No, it's yours, brother. You married a native woman, spawned mixed-race offspring and then brought them all back here, to rural Oxfordshire. It wasn't the best decision of your life."

Jim made no reply but a part of him belatedly acknowledged that George had a point. Theo and Enid would fare all right and Alya would cope, but had he condemned Arianna to a lifetime of problems?

However, from then on, things improved for Arianna. Diane and her two friends continued to give her a wide berth, and to Annie's relief they did not revert to bullying her either. In fact they behaved themselves. Once the other girls realised the situation had changed, some of them started being friendly towards Arianna. One told her that many of them had been afraid of crossing Diane before and that was why they hadn't helped her. She did not entirely forgive them, but it was nice to have friends and be able to join in with games in the playground. She started to relax and began to enjoy school. The three bullies left at the end of that school year and Arianna and Annie were not the only ones who were glad to see them go.

Two years later, when she started at the girls' grammar school, she was afraid she might encounter similar problems, but was relieved to find that, after a few days of being on the receiving end of curious stares, everyone seemed to accept her.

~***~

Chapter Three

As autumn drew in, the weather became colder and the children and Alya had to wrap themselves in more layers of clothing than they'd ever worn before. Later on, this included gloves, which the children kept losing. Alya sewed tapes onto Enid's and attached them to her coat sleeves, but told the other two they were old enough to remember to put them in their pockets when they took them off and if they continued to lose them, she would deduct the cost of new ones from their pocket money.

One Saturday in October, they all went to Oxford for the day. They looked round some of the University Colleges and Jim told Theo that his real father had studied here.

"Which college was he at?"

"He wasn't. He was here on a scholarship and in those days scholarship boys mostly lived in digs, because it was cheaper."

Theo liked the idea of living and studying here and the seeds of his later ambition to get into Oxford University were sown that day.

Theo sometimes went to Harry's house after school on a Friday evening and had tea with his family. Alya said they must return the favour and suggested that Harry come to them for a day during half-term. After Harry had accepted the invitation, Theo said rather nervously:

"There's something I need to tell you, before you come."

"What?"

"My mother is Malayan, native Malayan."

"You mean she's black?"

"No, but brownish, Asian. And one of my sisters looks a bit like her - she's darker than me or my other sister."

"Is that the one who was bullied at school?"

"Yes."

"Well, I don't care what colour your mother and sister are. It makes no difference to me."

Theo was relieved. He had worried about Harry's reaction but it seemed there had been no need.

Harry greatly enjoyed his day and envied Theo living in such a place and having the run of the estate.

"Fancy your uncle being a baronet!   My parents will be so impressed!"

"Well, actually he's not really my uncle."

"How come?"

"My father isn't my real father, he's my stepfather. My real father died when I was very small. So Uncle George is my step-uncle."

Harry shrugged. "Uncle, step-uncle, what difference does it make? You're still related to a baronet and you still get to live here!"

After he had gone home, Alya commented what a nice boy he was and Jim agreed. Theo was pleased; it made life easier if your parents liked your friends.

On 2nd November, which was a Friday, it was Theo's thirteenth birthday. Harry came to tea and Alya managed to fit thirteen candles onto the cake, which Theo blew out in one go. On the Saturday after November 5th, there was a large bonfire and firework display in the village, to which they all went, having set off their own sparklers in the garden on Guy Fawkes day itself.

Christmas approached. They had always celebrated it British style in Malaya, but here Father Christmas could actually come down a chimney. Enid still believed in him, but Theo knew the truth and Arianna was wavering. They drew up their wish lists. Theo had asked for a bicycle and was delighted to find one in the hall on Christmas morning.

"How did Santa get that down the chimney?" Enid wondered.

"Oh, he had to knock on the door to deliver that one - just as we were going to bed," Jim said.

"You saw him?" Enid was round-eyed. "Did he look like he does in the pictures?"

"Indeed. A portly, bearded gentleman in a red suit with white trimmings."

"And did you see the sleigh and reindeer?"

"Yes, they were parked at the end of the track."

Arianna looked sceptical and Theo grinned, but Enid believed every word. She got a doll which could cry as her Christmas present and Arianna got a miniature shop, complete with produce and toy money. Even Felix got a toy mouse with a bell on it.

After a traditional Christmas dinner with goose, they went up to the manor for the rest of the day. Charlie was also there, staying with his parents for the holiday period, and the children all liked Charlie - he was fun. They played snakes and ladders, draughts and other board and card games.

On Boxing Day, they awoke to a white world. Enid looked out of the window first and squealed,

"We've got snow!"

Arianna joined her and they both viewed the white blanket with awe. They rushed next door to where Theo was still snoozing and shook him awake.

"Go away, you horrible little girls!" he grumbled.

"It's snowed, Theo - look!"

He did and was similarly transfixed. They all dressed quickly and went outside. Jim joined them and, gathering up a handful of snow, formed it into a ball and threw it at Theo. Soon they were all having a snowball fight which lasted until Alya called them in to breakfast. Returning outside after they had eaten, they were joined by Arthur.

"Let's make a snowman," he suggested.

By the end of the morning they had a fine snowman in the front garden, complete with carrot for nose and buttons for eyes. Jim provided him with an old hat and scarf. After lunch they went round to Arthur's house to make another one there. By the time that was finished, Jim had retrieved two old sledges from the attic at the manor. Arthur fetched his sledge and they all adjourned to a grassy slope on the estate and spent the rest of the afternoon hurtling down it.

By the New Year, the snow had melted and the snowmen were no more.

"It rarely lasts long down here," Jim told his disappointed children. "Not like up north."

Mention of the north of the country made Theo think of Yorkshire and his as yet unknown relatives.

"Did you ever hear from the colonial office with that address in Yorkshire?" he asked Jim.

"Ah. I was rather hoping you'd forgotten about that! They did respond, but apparently they've lost his file, or part of it. They say they've instigated a search and they'll get back to me in due course, but I imagine it won't be high on their list of priorities, and that search order is probably still languishing in someone's in-tray."

Theo was only slightly disappointed. He was a bit curious to see what his father's brother was like and it would have been nice to meet the cousin who was the same age, but it was not hugely important to him.

Alya had been quite pleased at the news when Jim had first told her.

"I'm glad. If he went to see those people up in Yorkshire, they might try to take him away from us."

"Don't be silly," Jim responded. "They couldn't do that. You're his mother and I've adopted him as my son. They'd have no claim on him."

"But he might prefer them to us and want to go and live with them."

"Of course he wouldn't! We're the only family he's ever known and he's happy with us. You're being ridiculous!"

The three children and Alya had already contracted minor colds and coughs, having no immunity to English viruses, and in January they all went down with influenza, starting with Enid and culminating with Alya. Alya managed to nurse Enid through the worst of it before she herself succumbed, but Arianna and Theo were still in the throes of the illness. Daisy was drafted in to do extra hours, to take care of the household chores and some of the nursing while Jim was at work. The children were all off school for two weeks and it was at least three before Alya felt herself again. When home, Jim found himself taking care of a fractious, convalescent six year old and two sick and miserable older children, as well as tending to his bedridden wife.

Helping Theo to take a bath once he started to feel a little better, he noticed that the boy was showing physical signs of starting to become a man and he resolved to have a little chat with him before long about the birds and the bees. With this in mind, when there was

29

a spell of mild, dry weather at the beginning of March, he proposed an afternoon's fishing for just the two of them.

Sitting by the stream on the estate, they cast their lines and Jim launched into his speech on the facts of life. He was quite explicit and also touched on how puberty affected girls and how Theo should behave once he started dating.

"Always treat girls with respect," he warned.

Theo asked some questions, which he answered without prevarication and then said,

"You'll be the best informed boy in your class now! Not many fathers give their sons so much information. My father told us nothing at all. And many girls don't find out anything until their wedding night! Your mother was one of them, and she'll make sure that doesn't happen with your sisters."

After a pause, Theo asked, "Was that with my father? Her first wedding night, I mean."

"No, she was married and widowed before she met your father, all in the space of one year, when she was seventeen." He hesitated, then went on, "That brings me to something else I should say. You mustn't follow your father's example, nor mine for that matter. Babies should only be conceived in wedlock. Your mother and I didn't marry until Arianna was well on the way and your father never married your mother at all."

Theo said nothing and Jim looked sideways at him, trying to read his expression.

"Was that news a bit of a shock to you? I'm sorry, perhaps I shouldn't have been so blunt or maybe I should have waited until you were older to tell you. Are you all right?"

Theo nodded. "I think I sort of knew, at least I wondered. I wasn't sure. I have no memory of them being together; it was you who were always there with Mama and he just visited." Then he added: "This makes me a bastard, doesn't it? "

"That's not a very nice word. But yes, it makes you illegitimate and unfortunately there is a stigma attached to that. There shouldn't be - it's never the child's fault - but there it is. It would be wise of you not to broadcast the fact as you go through life; there's no need for anyone else to know. If I were you, I wouldn't even tell your

30

mate Harry; these things have a habit of getting out even if you swear someone to secrecy."

"Why didn't they marry?"

Jim could have replied that Englishmen in the colonies rarely married their native mistresses and he himself was a glaring exception, but he refrained. There was another reason here, and he thought it might be more palatable to Theo.

"He was already engaged to a woman in England. In 1914 when war broke out they were supposed to be getting wed. The church in Klang was booked - he was the D.O. there then - and all the arrangements made, then she was unable to sail because of ships being requisitioned for the war. Your father couldn't get to England at that time either. No-one knew then how long the war would last. Your mother was widowed by then and her aunt Zainab was cook at the D.O.'s residence, so that's how they met. She says he was always honest about not being able to marry her. When you were about two, towards the end of the war, he managed to get leave, went to England and finally got married."

"To that lady we met once at his graveside, when I was about seven," Theo said. He recalled the somewhat heated exchange between his mother and the other woman. "She didn't know about me until then, did she?"

"No. He always intended to tell her once she got to Malaya, but when the war ended she was expecting a baby so she stayed in England for the birth and then the baby was still-born and she was quite ill afterwards. In the end, she didn't arrive in Malaya until it was too late; your father was already dead, he'd died while she was still at sea."

"Poor lady," Theo said, feeling sudden sympathy for this dimly remembered woman. "What did he die of?"

"He got severe dysentery which caused complications requiring surgery and he didn't survive the operation. It was a sad business; he was only thirty-nine."

Theo was quiet and thoughtful on the way back home and for the rest of the day. Jim had given him a lot to think about and some of it was difficult to take in. He thought about some of the girls he knew from the girls' grammar school, and was both repelled and fascinated

31

at the image in his mind when he envisaged indulging in the activity Jim had described. Then his thoughts turned to the story of the love triangle between his mother, father and the English lady he had encountered on that day in the cemetery.

Alya, meanwhile, was furious with Jim for telling Theo the circumstances of his birth.

"He didn't need to know, not yet anyway. And I should have been the one to tell him."

Jim defended his stance, saying that the way the conversation had gone he would have had to lie to avoid it, and anyway, the boy had a right to know.

Theo had long ago told his mother that he was too big to be tucked up at bedtime and she had respected that, so he was surprised when she came in to his room just after he had got into bed. She sat on the edge of the bed.

"Are you all right, *sayang*? I know what Papa has told you."

He nodded, then asked: "Did you love my real father?"

"Yes, I did. You were a love child - at least on my part."

"But he didn't love you, did he? He loved that woman we met at his grave that time."

"That's true, but he cared about me too and he was always kind and affectionate. We were happy together as long as it lasted and we remained friends after it came to an end. He was pleased when I told him that you were on the way, and once you were born he was quite besotted with you. He adored you and he travelled a long way at weekends so that he could see you." She went on: "You're a lucky boy in many ways; you had two fathers who both loved you and you still have one of them. You know Papa thinks of you as his son, don't you?"

Theo nodded. "I think of him as my father too."

"That's all right then." She kissed him goodnight and left the room.

Over the next few days Theo continued to dwell intermittently on the issues Jim had raised, both in regard to his own rather dubious origins and the rather scary, but at the same time intriguing, world of sex. However, he soon became absorbed again in his day to day life and by the time Arianna's and Enid's birthdays came around   -

within a week of each other in early April - he had pushed those things to the back of his mind.

Arianna was ten and Enid seven and they had a joint birthday party. Several of their friends from the village attended and the sitting room was filled with giggling, squealing and sometimes whining little girls, playing 'pass the parcel' and other games and gorging themselves on jelly and ice-cream until one of them made herself sick. Theo made his escape and spent the rest of the afternoon with Arthur. They both agreed that girls could be more of a bane than a blessing.

~***~

Chapter Four

July 1931

Afterwards, Theo was to remember the events of that fateful Sunday morning as if they had taken place in slow motion.

It was the first weekend of the school holidays and six weeks of glorious freedom stretched ahead of him. The family had a fortnight by the seaside to look forward to and he and Harry had various plans for the rest of the time, some of which involved two girls they were becoming friendly with.

The previous day had passed pleasantly and uneventfully. It had been quite warm and sunny and he and Jim had been working in the garden, putting the finishing touches to a pool they were building by the rockery. They had finally completed it shortly after lunch.

"All it needs now is some fish," Jim said. "We'll go and get some next week."

Alya and Arianna came outside to admire the installation. Enid was in the village visiting one of her friends. They all sat in the garden for a while, Jim and Alya on the bench and Theo and Arianna sprawled on the grass. Afterwards, Theo could no longer remember what was talked about; he just recalled the happy, relaxed family atmosphere.

Shortly after four o'clock, Theo went inside to wash and change and put a few overnight things into a bag, as he was going to Harry's and staying the night there. That evening, they were going to the cinema with Clare and Julia. Clare was a pretty, vivacious blonde and Theo liked her a lot. He was looking forward to being seated next to her in the darkened cinema; perhaps she would allow him to steal a kiss. While he was upstairs, he was vaguely aware that the others had come back inside and that Enid had returned, and he heard some argument going on between Alya and Arianna, in which Jim later intervened, putting an end to it.

He went downstairs and said goodbye to them all.

"Hold on a minute," Jim said and fished in his pocket, producing two florins. "Extra pocket money for helping me with that pool. You've worked hard and I appreciate it."

"Gosh, thanks!"

"You can treat that young lady of yours to an ice-cream out of it. But mind you behave yourself!"

Enid, witnessing the exchange, asked if she too could have extra pocket money.

"Only if you earn it!"

Feeling wealthy, Theo caught the five o'clock bus and made his way to Harry's family home. After tea, the two of them headed to the cinema where they met up with the girls. Theo and Clare did enjoy a lingering kiss while watching the film and he was on cloud nine for the rest of the evening.

Later, after the boys went up to bed - Theo being accommodated on a camp bed in Harry's room - Harry produced a couple of magazines from under the mattress which he'd obtained from an older boy at school and they both pored over the raunchy photos of scantily clad women in suggestive poses. Theo tried to imagine Clare dressed like them, posing for him, but was not really sure if he wanted her to do that.

After breakfast, he said goodbye to Harry and his family and headed home.

Meanwhile, in the early hours of the morning, George had been shaken awake by Mr Hughes.

"Sir George, wake up! Your brother's cottage is on fire!"

"What?!"

"Fred saw smoke and flames from his window. He's phoned the fire brigade and they're on their way, probably there by now."

George was now wide awake and throwing back the bed clothes. Mary, in the other bed, was struggling out of sleep.

"What's happened?"

Mr Hughes repeated what he had just told George.

"Oh, my goodness! What about the family - are they all right?"

"I don't know. Fred and Sarah have gone over there."

George threw on some clothes and left the house. He part walked, part ran the half mile or so distance. When he reached Jim's house, he was appalled at the sight in front of him. Part of the front of the house was in flames, almost up to the roof on one side, the porch had collapsed and the firemen were desperately trying to contain the fire to stop it spreading further.

"Where are the family?" he yelled. "Are they safe?"

"They must have all been asleep when it started. We've got a man and a woman and two young girls out. They've been taken to hospital; the ambulances have just left."

"What about the boy?"

"What boy?"

"There's a fifteen year old boy as well as the two girls."

"We've found no-one else."

"He sleeps in the room at the back, opposite the bathroom."

"Well, the back of the house is relatively unaffected; he should have been able to escape."

"Where is he then?"

One of the firemen went round the back with a ladder. He climbed up and looked through Theo's bedroom window, shining his torch inside.

"There's no-one here and the bed doesn't look as though it's been slept in."

He climbed through the window and disappeared inside. Reappearing, he said there was no-one in the bathroom either. He climbed down and went in through the back door. Coming out again, he said:

"There's no-one there. If he's in the front room on that side, then there'll be no hope for him now and I can't go in there, it's a furnace."

"Perhaps he wasn't at home tonight. I suppose he might have stayed in town with a friend."

"That's most likely the case. If he'd been asleep upstairs, he'd have been able to get out from that back room and a boy of that age could have shinned down the drainpipe. If he'd been awake downstairs when it started, he'd have raised the alarm."

Going back round the front, George spotted Fred.

"Did you see Jim and Alya and the girls before they were taken to hospital?"

"Yes," Fred replied. "But they were all unconscious, except Enid. She was crying and Sarah tried to comfort her. Apparently she was asleep by an open window, which saved her from the worst of the smoke. Sarah's gone to the hospital with them, in the second ambulance with the girls."

"Do you know where Theo is?" George asked.

"No. He doesn't appear to have been at home."

By now the fire had engulfed all the front half of the house. The windows were blown out and flames were coming up through the roof. But there were signs that the firemen were beginning to get the fire under control; the remains of the porch were blackened and charred but the flames were out there.

"Looks like it started just behind the front door," one of the firemen said. "In the entrance hall. Then it quickly spread to the front room on that side - probably the door was open - and through the ceiling to the rooms above. Too early to say what caused it. The police will be here as soon as possible after it gets light and they'll be investigating."

As there was nothing more he could do there, George returned home. Mary met him at the door.

"Are they safe? How bad is it?"

He told her what he knew. "I'm going to phone the hospital. Sarah's there with them; perhaps I'll be able to speak to her too."

When he eventually got through to one of the doctors who had treated them, he was told that Jim and Alya could not be saved. Jim had died in the ambulance and Alya shortly after arrival.

"The older of the two girls is in a critical condition; we are keeping her heavily sedated for now. The younger one will recover; she seems to have breathed in much less smoke. However, she was very distressed and asking for her mother, so we gave her a mild sedative and she's now sleeping. We've not told her about her parents. I recommend that she stays here a further night so we can keep an eye on her, but she should be able to return home tomorrow - assuming she has somewhere to go?"

"Yes, she does. I'm her uncle and she'll come home with us."

"We need someone to formally identify the bodies. Would you be able to do that, sir?"

"Yes. We'll come in this afternoon to see the two girls and I'll do it then." He then asked to speak to Sarah, but was told she had left and was on her way back.

He relayed the gist of the doctor's words to Mary and then sat down heavily and put his head in his hands. She sat beside him and put an arm around his shoulders.

"I'm so very sorry, dear."

George didn't answer. He was trying to come to terms with the fact of his only brother's death. They had not always seen eye to eye - far from it - but they had nevertheless remained pals. Although Jim had been away for many years in Malaya, he had always spent his leaves at the manor and since his return to England three years ago, George had enjoyed having him nearby and working with him on the estate. He knew he would miss him dreadfully. But for now there were things to do and three orphaned children to deal with.

"I don't know where the hell Theo is," he told his wife, "but if he's just stayed the night in town he'll be back sometime this morning."

"And he'll come back to..... that!" Mary said.

"Yes, I need to get back down there before he arrives, although Fred is sticking around there for a while and I doubt he'll be back before mid morning."

As Theo rounded the bend in the road which brought their house into view in the distance, he could see there was something very wrong. The house looked strange, a different shape at the front and darker in colour and there were people milling around outside. There were also vehicles parked in front, beside Jim's car, and with a jolt he saw the red of a fire engine and recognised another as a police car. He had read in books the phrases ' his blood ran cold' and 'his heart was in his mouth' but only now did he appreciate what they really meant. He broke into a run, panic rising inside him.

"Is that your missing boy?" one of the policemen said to Fred, pointing down the track.

Fred turned and saw Theo. "Yes!" He turned to Arthur who had joined him by then. "Run up to the manor and fetch Sir George!"

As Theo neared the house, he took in the blackened and shattered facade of what had been their home. He smelled the acrid smell of smoke and saw fragments of ash swirling round in the breeze.

"Where are they?" he yelled at Fred. "Where are my parents and sisters?"

"They were taken to hospital in the early hours. We didn't know where you were, so we couldn't contact you."

"They knew; why didn't you ask them?"

"They were unconscious, except Enid and she was very distressed."

"Are they all right now?"

Fred hesitated. He knew from Sarah what the situation was, but how was he going to break it to the lad?

Theo repeated his question, yelling it this time, panic in his voice.

"Enid is recovering, she will be discharged in a day or two. Arianna is still very ill...."

"And Mama and Papa?"

Fred put his hands on Theo's shoulders. "I'm so very sorry, son, but I'm afraid they didn't make it."

Theo stared at him. "You mean they're.... dead?"

Fred nodded.

Theo suddenly felt cold and clammy. He could sense his heart beating very fast and his breathing became laboured. He started to shiver and felt light headed. He swayed slightly.

"Sit down, lad," Fred said, gently pushing him down onto the grassy bank in front of the house. "You've had a terrible shock."

This couldn't be happening, Theo thought. He must be in the middle of a terrible nightmare and he'd wake up soon. He closed his eyes but when he opened them again, the scene was unchanged. He couldn't get his head around the fact that his parents were dead. They had always been there; he was unable to envisage a world without them. Perhaps it was a mistake, perhaps they were still in the hospital and Fred had got it wrong. He clung to that thought.

George arrived on the scene. His questioning look at Fred was answered with a nod. He crouched down beside Theo and took hold of his hand.

"I'm so very sorry. It's a terrible business."

Theo stared at him blankly.

"Let's get you up to the house."

He stood up and then held out a hand to Theo, pulling him to his feet. Fred picked up Theo's bag and jacket from where he had dropped them and handed them to George.

They entered the manor by the kitchen entrance and George passed Theo over to the care of Mrs Hughes and Cook. By now, all the staff knew what had happened.

"Make him some hot sweet tea. Lots of sugar. He's had a nasty shock."

"You poor lamb!" Cook said, enfolding Theo in a massive bear hug. "Come and sit down."

He was handed a cup of tea. It tasted extremely sweet and he grimaced.

"It's good for you, drink it down now."

After a while he stopped shivering and his heartbeat slowed. Reality was starting to sink in. This was no dream, nor was it a mistake.

"How ill is Arianna?" he asked. "Will she die too?"

"I don't know, dear," Mrs Hughes answered, "but the doctors will be doing all they can. I'm sure she'll pull through."

Mary appeared at the kitchen door and told Cook that they would forgo the usual roast Sunday lunch and just have a light meal.

"Very good, milady."

Turning to Theo, Mary said: "If you've finished your tea, dear, why don't you come upstairs?"

He followed her up the stairs and into the drawing room. George was there.

"Ah, Theo. Are you feeling a little better now?"

Theo nodded, assuming he meant physically.

"After lunch we'll go to the hospital and see Enid and Arianna. They want to keep Enid in another night, so we won't be able to bring her home with us today, and Arianna is being kept under sedation, so she will be in for longer."

"Will she be all right?"

"Let's hope so. She breathed in more smoke than Enid and her lungs will need to heal."

When they sat down to lunch, Theo didn't think he could eat a thing, but once cajoled by Mary into trying a few mouthfuls, his teenage boy's appetite revived to some degree.

Dave drove them all to the hospital. Arianna was in a side room off the main ward. She was lying on her back, very still, hooked up to various bits of equipment with tubes coming in and out of her. Her black hair fanned over the white pillow. Theo touched her cheek.

"Don't die, Ari," he murmured. "Please don't die!"

They found Enid awake and sitting up in bed. Her face lit up when she saw them, then fell again when she realised there was no-one else with them.

"Where're Mama and Papa? I want Mama! And where's Ari? They said she's in here too, but they won't let me see her."

"We've just been in to see her," Mary said. "She's still asleep; she needs to rest."

"And Mama and Papa?"

"Enid, dear, you need to be a very brave little girl. I'm afraid your Mama and Papa have gone to heaven. They're with the angels now, but they'll be looking down on you and watching over you."

For a moment or two Enid stared at her uncomprehendingly. Then she let out a piercing scream.

"Nooooo! They can't be dead, they can't be, no, no, no!" She burst into tears.

Mary reached out to her but she turned away from her and flung herself against Theo, on the other side of the bed.

"Say it's not true, Theo! It's not true, is it?!"

She pounded his chest with her fists. He gently took hold of her hands, then put his arms around her, as she cried heartbrokenly.

George turned to Mary and muttered in an undertone. "I'd better go downstairs now. I'll be back shortly."

Enid's sobs were wracking her small body, her tears soaking Theo's shirt, and her breath was coming in laboured gasps. Tears were now also rolling down Theo's cheeks. Helpless in the face of all this raw emotion, Mary went in search of a nurse.

Down in the morgue, George looked sadly at his brother's still, lifeless body and then at Alya's.

41

"Yes, that's my brother, James Bradshaw, and his wife, Alya."

He was told there would have to be a post mortem and also an inquest, although it would probably just be opened and adjourned. After that, the death certificates could be issued and the bodies released for burial.

Back in the ward, he found Enid still clinging to her brother, although her sobs had quietened. A nurse had brought in a hot sweet drink but Mary had failed to persuade her to drink it.

"Perhaps we should go now and leave them here together for a little while," George suggested to Mary. She nodded.

To Theo he said: "You can get the bus back, can't you?"

"Yes."

George fished in his pocket and produced half a crown. "That should cover the fare. Keep the change. But don't stay too long, she'll need to rest."

To Enid he said: "We'll be taking you home tomorrow, dear. The doctors want to keep an eye on you here one more night."

Enid raised her head long enough to wail: "I haven't got a home any more. It's all burnt down!"

"To our home, I mean, to the manor."

After they had gone, Enid eventually mopped her face and blew her nose, then asked Theo where exactly Arianna was.

"Just down the corridor."

"Can I go and see her?"

"I don't see why not."

Seeing her sister lying there, neither moving nor speaking, with tubes and equipment everywhere, caused Enid's tears to well up again. As she took hold of Arianna's hand, Theo thought he saw her eyelids flicker. He took hold of her other hand.

"Ari," he said in a low tone, "can you hear us? It's Theo and Enid."

There was no reply but her eyelids flickered again.

"Do you think she knows we're here?" Enid whispered.

"I don't know, maybe."

A nurse entered. "What are you two doing here? Out, now!"

"She's our sister!"

"And she needs to rest. Now say goodbye and go."

They both kissed her goodbye and her eyelids seemed to flicker once again.

"Get better quick, Ari," Enid entreated.

When they returned to the main ward, another nurse said Theo should leave now.

"Your sister needs to rest."

"I've been resting all day," Enid protested. "Please let him stay a bit longer."

"All right, another half hour and that's it."

When she had gone, Enid asked about the house: "Is it all burnt down?"

"The front part is badly damaged. The porch is more or less gone."

Enid was quiet for a few minutes, tears welling up once more. Then she asked:

"What about Felix?"

Felix. Theo had forgotten all about him.

"I don't know. Hopefully he'll have escaped in time and he'll turn up later."

"Or he might have burnt!"

"I bet he'll have got out. He'll turn up, I'm sure."

But he wasn't sure; maybe Felix would turn out to be yet another casualty of the fire.

Walking to the bus stop, Theo passed a newsagent. The local evening paper had just come out and a poster announced the main headline: 'Fire at Pucklington Manor estate.' He stopped. A kind of morbid fascination compelled him to go in and buy a copy of the paper. The article was on the front page. He threw the remainder of the paper into the nearest waste bin, folded up the page and put it in his pocket. He read it on the bus. It recounted the events of the previous night, stating that a man in his fifties and a woman in her thirties had perished in the fire while two young girls were presently in hospital, one critical. A further member of the household, an older boy, had not been at home the night of the fire. The family were believed to be related to the owner of the manor, Sir George Bradshaw. The cause of the fire was still unknown but investigations were ongoing. There was more, about the response of the fire service

43

and the police, and Theo skimmed through it. Then a paragraph at the end jumped out at him.

'This tragedy has left three children orphaned and homeless. It is believed that the two girls are the nieces of Sir George and will therefore presumably be taken in by him, but the future of the boy is less certain as he is understood not to be a blood relative of the baronet.'

Up to that point, Theo had given no thought to his future. Grief for his parents and concern for his sisters had driven everything else from his mind. He wondered how the journalist had obtained his information; it was not widely known that he was not Jim's son. Perhaps some of the staff at the manor had been gossiping. Was the paper merely speculating for the sake of spicing up the article or had someone actually said that his future was in doubt?

By now the bus had reached the village. Theo screwed up the page and threw it into the bin by the bus stop, but he could not rid his mind of it so easily. Reluctant to go straight up to the manor, he made his way to the stream and sat on the grassy bank, his back against a tree. Grief was welling up inside him, along with a growing anger. How had the fire happened? Whose fault was it? Or was it just a terrible accident? Nothing in his young life so far had prepared him for this. He had known nothing but love and security and it had all been whipped away in an instant. He didn't know how to deal with the pain and rage which were tearing him apart. Not only were his parents gone and he would never see them again, but perhaps Arianna would die too and Enid would be brought up by George and Mary, while he might be turned out to fend for himself; his childhood gone forever, along with his dreams for the future.

Misery and anger overwhelming him, he let out a long low howl, like a wounded animal, then turned and drove his fist against the tree trunk. For a moment, physical pain took over from the mental anguish and was somehow more bearable, and he slammed his hand against the tree again and again until it was bruised and bleeding. Then he let the grief escape and cried until he could cry no more.

Arriving back at the manor, having bathed his face in the stream and wrapped his handkerchief around his still bleeding hand, he encountered George in the hall.

"Ah, there you are, we were wondering where you'd got to."

George took in his red, swollen eyes and then noticed his hand.

"What have you done to yourself?"

"I hit a tree."

Mary had appeared in the hall. "What on earth did you do that for?"

George seemed to understand. "Pity you couldn't have found something softer to take your feelings out on," he said kindly. "Go and see Mrs Hughes and get it bathed and dressed properly."

Down in the kitchen, Mrs Hughes clucked over his injuries.

"You silly boy! I'll put some ointment on it, but it's still going to throb for hours."

"I suppose you were trying to block out the pain inside with pain on the outside," Mr Hughes observed shrewdly.

"Something like that."

The evening paper had arrived at the manor. George and Mary both gave the article on the front page a cursory glance, but did not read it. Some of the staff did, however, and it was a subject of discussion over their supper.

"Surely they'll take him in too," Daisy said.

Her eyes were red with crying. She'd known Alya better than any of them. They'd become friends as they worked together on the household chores at the cottage and she knew she would miss her terribly.

Theo had supper with George and Mary. Earlier, Mrs Hughes had shown him the room she'd made up for him in the nursery wing. She told him that two other rooms, one next door to Theo's and one opposite, would be made up for the girls when they came out of hospital. They would be on their own in that part of the house and would have a bathroom to themselves. She had also found him a clean shirt which had belonged to Charlie and wasn't too bad a fit. He saw that his jacket and overnight bag were in the room.

"I assume you have pyjamas, toothbrush and so on in there?" she asked and he nodded.

"There's one small bit of good news. The fire investigators say your room is pretty undamaged and tomorrow Dave and Mr Hughes will be allowed in through the back door to pack up your things and bring them over here. Your clothes might need to be aired to get rid of the smell of smoke, but that won't take long. They should also be able to bring over most of the girls' clothes - apparently they were in a heavy oak chest at the back end of their room. Daisy said that both girls' dresses were in there."

After supper, exhaustion started to set in. Sitting in the drawing room, his eyes were starting to close and Mary suggested he go up to bed.

"We won't be long after you. We've been up since the early hours."

"Yes, it's been one hell of a day," George said. "Undoubtedly the worst one of your young life, Theo, but perhaps things will look less bleak in the morning."

"My parents will still be dead!" Theo said bitterly.

"That's true, of course, but after a good night's sleep you may be better equipped to cope with it."

Despite his tiredness, sleep took a long time to come to Theo, but once it did, he slept like a log until mid-morning.

~***~

Chapter Five

When Theo woke the next day, at first he didn't realise where he was. Then the events of the previous day flooded back into his memory, and a black depression settled on him. He wanted to bury his head back under the bedclothes and seek the oblivion of sleep once more. He might have done just that, were it not for his full bladder directing him to the bathroom. Once up, he decided he might as well get washed and dressed and go downstairs.

He expected breakfast to be long over, as it was past ten o'clock, and thought he would have to go to the kitchen to get anything to eat, but he put his head round the dining room door anyway and found George still there, finishing his coffee and reading a newspaper.

"Morning, Theo. Sleep well?"

"Yes, thanks."

"Help yourself to whatever you want. There's bacon and so on keeping warm on the sideboard. We haven't been up that long."

When Theo had nearly finished eating, George folded his newspaper and stood up.

"We'll collect Enid from the hospital this morning and get an update on Arianna. I assume you'll want to come with us?"

"Yes, of course."

"We'll leave in about half an hour then."

When Dave brought the car round, he also brought something else.

"Enid's bear!" Theo exclaimed. "Basil!"

"It's just been rescued from the cottage, along with most of your things and the girls' clothes. I thought you might want to take it to the hospital to welcome Miss Enid."

"I'm glad to see him too," Theo said. "He was mine before he was Enid's."

The bear's fur smelled smoky but he was undamaged. Enid always had him on her bed.

Dave turned to George. "Sir, we've also recovered a small fireproof cabinet, which probably contains family papers. It's locked, but I expect you could get it open without too much trouble if we don't find the key."

"The key's on the key ring which hangs in the hall," Theo said. He wondered if the keys would have melted in the heat. He added, "Were you able to rescue any of the family photos?"

"Not yet. Where were they kept?"

"In the living room." As he said it, he realised what the answer would be. That room was probably pretty much destroyed.

"I doubt they'll be salvageable then," Dave said gently. "But there was one photo in a frame in your room."

That was Theo's only photo of his real father. He was glad that he would still have it, but given the choice, he would rather have had a family photo with Mama and Papa.

George said, "We've got a lot of photos of you all which Jim sent from Malaya, and some more recent ones which we took at Christmas time. You and the girls can have some of them."

"Thanks."

At the hospital, the doctor told them that Arianna had been brought out of sedation.

"She's still very weak and her lung function is somewhat impaired. That will improve gradually, although there may be a very slight long-term weakness. We'll keep her in a few more days, but you should be able to take her home at the end of the week. Then I'll see her again in about six weeks - perhaps just before the end of the school holidays, then I can assess what, if any, physical education she will be able to do next term. Meanwhile, she should avoid strenuous exercise, as she would quickly become breathless. She's asking for her mother, but we thought it best to leave telling her to you."

Arianna was sitting propped up on pillows. She smiled when she saw them but her eyes were searching beyond them.

"Where are Mama and Papa?" Her voice was very husky.

Before Mary could launch into her speech about heaven and angels, Theo clasped Arianna's hand and said gently,

"They didn't survive the fire, Ari."

"You mean they're...... dead?"

"Yes."

48

For a few moments she didn't react. Then her face crumpled and tears ran down her cheeks. Mary reached out with her handkerchief and wiped them away.

"We'll take you home with us, to the manor, in a few days time," she said. "Enid's coming back with us today and Theo is already there. You will all have rooms near to each other in the nursery wing."

The only thing Arianna really absorbed from this was the reference to Enid.

"Can I see Enid?"

"Yes, of course. We'll go and get her."

They found Enid sitting on the edge of the bed, dressed and ready to go. The hospital staff had found a dress for her which had probably come from some charity collection. It was mud-coloured cotton, very plain, and far too long for her. It was a far cry from the pretty dresses Alya had always made for her daughters. Her hair had been scraped back tightly and tied into two plaited pigtails which stuck out from either side of her head. She looked like an orphaned waif, Theo thought. But that's what she is, we all are.

Theo held out the bear.

"Basil!" she exclaimed, her eyes lighting up. She hugged the bear to her.

"Enid, Arianna is awake now and you can go and see her," George said.

She jumped off the bed and ran ahead of them down the corridor. The two girls hugged each other tightly, both of them crying.

After what seemed a very short time, a nurse came in and said that Arianna must now get some rest.

"Theo and Enid can come back tomorrow," George promised.

When Theo kissed her goodbye, she clung to his hand.

"What's going to happen to us?" she asked in her rasping voice.

"Like Aunt Mary said, we'll all be staying at the manor."

"Is our house all burnt down?"

"Part of it is."

"Did Mama and Papa feel anything, did they suffer?"

"I don't think so. I think they died while they were still asleep."

He hoped that was true.

49

That seemed to comfort her a little and she let go of his hand.

"I'll see you tomorrow," he said, trying to inject a cheerful note into his voice, which fooled neither of them. She managed a wan smile.

After lunch, Theo and Enid were left to their own devices. Enid had been given the room next to Theo's, the slightly larger one opposite was to be Arianna's. Mrs Hughes had exclaimed at the sight of the dress Enid wore.

"Where on earth did they get that from! You'll be glad to know that your frocks have been rescued and are being aired right now, so tomorrow you'll be able to get rid of that one!"

Looking out of the landing window, they could see all their clothes airing in the courtyard. Luckily it was a dry day. Theo's books and other things had already been delivered to his room, and someone had even put his books up on the shelves, although rather haphazardly. Theo started to rearrange them. Meanwhile, Enid had pulled out her plaits and let her hair fall loose. Alya usually partly pinned it back for her, but without hairpins she could not effect this style herself. She held out the ribbons, which had been used to tie the plaits, to Theo and asked him to tie her hair back with them. He did the best he could.

Then she said, "Let's walk down to our house and see what it looks like now."

"Are you sure you want to see it? You'll find it upsetting."

"Everything's upsetting! I can't get any more miserable than I already am!"

Theo supposed that was true. He didn't really want to see the house again in its fire damaged state, but it would be difficult to avoid it forever, so he may as well get used to it. Besides, if he didn't go with her, she would go on her own and he felt an older brother's obligation to keep an eye on her, to try to somehow mitigate the effect that the death of their parents was having on her.

They made it outside without anyone asking where they were going. As the blackened semi-ruin of their home came into view, Enid took a sharp intake of breath.

"Oh, look at it!" she wailed. "Our poor house."

Theo felt a deep penetrating sadness at the sight. Their lovely, happy home, reduced to this shell. He saw that the tiles were missing from the roof at one side and the rafters were visible. As they approached, they saw that fire investigators were still working there, picking through the rubble.

"What are you two doing here?" one of them asked sharply.

"We live here - or rather we did," Theo answered.

"Right, well, I'm very sorry for what's happened, but you can't come inside, it's not safe."

"Can we go round the back, into the garden?"

"Yes, all right. But don't go in through the back door either. The house looks more normal at that side, but it could still be dangerous."

The garden at least looked more or less as it had before, apart from the firemen's boots having churned up Jim's carefully tended lawn. Theo looked sadly at the pond he and Papa had only just finished; now it would never have fish swimming in it. They sat on the bench, looking towards the rear facade of the house, which didn't look too bad.

"The fire was all at the front then," Enid said.

"Seems so; they said my room was undamaged."

The fire must have gone right up through the roof on the porch side, Theo thought, through the room where their parents slept. He hoped that they really had died in their sleep, that they had not tried to fight their way through the flames and died in agony. He tried to banish the image which had come into his mind.

As the two of them sat there, each lost in their own sad thoughts, they suddenly saw a black and white furry shape streaking across the lawn towards them.

"Felix!" Enid shrieked. "Oh, Felix, you're alive!"

She ran to the cat and caught him up in her arms. Theo joined her and stroked Felix's fur. He smelled faintly of smoke but appeared unhurt. The cat seemed delighted to see them and purred loudly, licking Enid's face and Theo's hand. Enid covered his head with kisses. They sat back on the bench and Felix settled himself comfortably in Enid's lap, still purring.

"He must be hungry and thirsty," she said.

51

"Oh, he'll have found a mouse or two and he'll have drunk from the stream."

"Do you think they'll let us keep him at the manor?"

"Let's hope so. He'll have to get on with old Humphrey, though."

Humphrey was the resident manor cat. He was a very old, rather fat, ginger tomcat who ruled the roost in the kitchen.

They headed back to the manor, Enid carrying Felix so he could not run off. George was outside the door, in conversation with Fred.

"I see you've found your cat!"

"Can we keep him here, Uncle George?" Enid asked anxiously, her eyes pleading.

"Yes, of course. Take him down to the kitchen and get him fed and watered. And introduce him to Humphrey!"

At the sight of Felix, Daisy exclaimed, "Oh, he did get out in time! That's wonderful." She stroked his fur.

"Uncle George says we can keep him here."

Felix was struggling to get free and Enid lowered him to the floor. He attempted to run back outside, but Daisy quickly shut the door. He sat in front of it and mewed.

"This is your new home, Felix," Enid told him. "We all live here now, except Mama and Papa, who've gone to live in heaven."

Cook filled a bowl with cat food and another with milk and Enid picked Felix up again and took him to the food. He ate hungrily and then lapped up the milk.

"Now you have to be introduced to Humphrey," she told him.

Humphrey had been watching the interloper from his basket in the far corner of the room. Enid carried Felix over there and held on to him as he tried to escape. The staff and Theo watched in amusement as she put Felix's right paw against Humphrey's right paw and told them they had to shake paws and be friends. Humphrey glared and Felix struggled to escape Enid's hold.

"Let him go," Cook said. "They'll get used to each other eventually. And if Felix runs off, he'll be back when he's hungry, now he knows he gets fed here."

Millie had found a cardboard box, cut one side off and lined it with a piece of old blanket.

"Here, Felix, this is your bed."

52

She put it on the far side of the kitchen, well away from Humphrey. Enid carried Felix over to it and put him in. After circling round a few times, he settled down to have a nap.

Meanwhile, Dave had broken the padlock on Jim's document cabinet and George looked through the contents. All the essential family papers were there, including passports, birth certificates, bank documents and a copy of Jim's will. George took out the will and bank papers, to take to his solicitor, and replaced the rest, first noting the name of Theo's biological father from his birth certificate. It would be a starting point for tracing his relatives in Yorkshire.

At the staff supper that evening, Daisy asked Mrs Hughes if her hours and wages would now be reduced as she was no longer working at the cottage.

"Will I only have half a job?"

"I've been thinking about that and I've got to speak to Lady Mary. I think we'll need you full-time here, now that we have three extra people to look after. I don't see why you can't become a nursery maid to the children - clean their rooms, deal with their laundry, look after their clothes and so on. Miss Enid is still young enough to need some supervision in the morning and at bedtime and they'll all need waking in time for school once term starts again."

Mary later agreed with that proposal and Daisy became established in her new role as nursery maid cum parlour maid.

The next day, Tuesday, George informed Theo that the post-mortem had been completed and a report issued.

"It confirms that they died of smoke inhalation."

"So they wouldn't have known anything, would have died in their sleep?"

George wasn't sure about that. The report detailed burns to Jim's hands and feet. But he knew what Theo and his sisters needed to hear.

"That's right, they didn't suffer at all, thank goodness. There's an inquest scheduled for tomorrow morning, which will almost certainly just be opened and adjourned, pending further police enquiries. Then they'll issue the death certificates and we can make the funeral arrangements. So on Thursday morning I'll go to the registrar to

53

register the deaths and then onto the undertaker, and in the afternoon I'll be going to see the vicar about the funeral service."

"Can I come too? To see the vicar, I mean?"

"Yes, if you want to."

That afternoon, Theo and Enid returned to the hospital and gave Arianna the good news that they had found Felix. Her eyes lit up.

"Oh, that's marvellous! I was just wondering about him."

Theo recounted Enid's attempts to get him to make friends with Humphrey and she laughed, then started coughing.

"Are you all right? Shall I get a nurse?" Theo asked anxiously.

"No, I'm fine. It's stopped now." Her voice was still hoarse but less so than the previous day. "Since when have you become such a mother hen?" she added lightly.

"Since we nearly lost you!"

Mrs Hughes had given them a box of chocolates to take to the hospital. "For Arianna, from all the staff, and tell her we wish her a speedy recovery." Theo and Enid were perched either side of her on the bed and all three were dipping into the chocolates which were open on her lap.

"Hey, you two greedy pigs! You're eating most of them and they were meant for me!"

"Well, no-one brought me any sweets when I was in here," Enid declared.

"You weren't in long enough, were you?"

The trivial, everyday sibling squabble made Theo smile at its sheer normality. They would be all right, the three of them, as long as they had each other.

On Thursday afternoon, Theo accompanied George to the village church. After the vicar had expressed his condolences, he looked at his calendar and asked George if Monday would be an acceptable date.

"Yes, that will be fine." Arianna would be out of hospital on Friday and she would have the weekend to convalesce.

As the discussion about the service and the burial progressed, Theo realised that his mother would not be buried in the family plot with Jim but would have a separate grave. He supposed that didn't matter too much. Then the vicar paused and said hesitantly that,

54

actually, the bishop would probably not allow her to be buried in the churchyard at all as she was a Muslim and that really she should have a Muslim funeral service too.

"I'm not sure where the nearest Muslim cemetery is. I know there is a large one at Woking in Surrey, but there may be one nearer. I'll have to make enquiries. I believe there's a mosque at Oxford, where you may be able to hold the service. The rites and customs of the Islamic religion are very different from ours, as you will appreciate, but I regret that I'm not familiar with the detail."

Theo listened to this with mounting horror. Woking was many miles away; he and his sisters would not be able to visit very often, if at all, and his mother would want to be buried near her husband. Jim would want that too. And a service in a mosque? What would that be like? His mother was only a Muslim by birth anyway, she had never gone to a mosque, either in Malaya or here, as far as Theo was aware. She had no interest in religion.

"She wasn't a practising Muslim," Theo said, and then added, "and she was planning to convert to Christianity. She'd been reading books and talking about it to my father." Warming to his fabricated theme, he went on, "In fact, she'd said only a few days before she died that she was going to come to church with us on the Sunday and speak to you about taking instruction in the Christian faith. So, if she hadn't died, she'd have been starting the process of conversion by now."

He waited with bated breath for the vicar's response.

"Really? Well, this puts a different complexion on the matter. In that case, I'm sure I can persuade the bishop to agree to a Christian burial here and we can include her in the service on Monday."

After they had agreed the order of service and chosen hymns, George and Theo shook hands with the vicar and left. On the walk back to the manor, George said, "that wasn't true, was it, about your mother planning to convert?"

"No," Theo admitted. "But it is true that she wasn't a practising Muslim; she never went to a mosque as far as I knew."

"You know that lying is wrong," George said in a stern tone. "And lying to a man of the cloth is particularly reprehensible."

Theo felt miserable. Was George going to return and tell the vicar it was a lie?

Then George grinned and slapped him on the back.

"Top marks for quick thinking, though! It certainly did the trick!"

On Friday morning, Mary collected Arianna from hospital, taking her own, now aired, clothes along so she did not have to wear a charity dress. After lunch, Mary suggested that she take a little rest in her room.

"You mustn't exert yourself too much yet."

Theo and Enid followed her upstairs.

"Do you want to sleep?" Theo asked.

"No, I don't. Come and keep me company."

They all sprawled on Arianna's bed, which was a small double, Enid curled up at her side and Theo lying across the bottom of the bed. They hadn't been there very long before they heard mewing outside the door. Theo opened it and Felix ran in. He had been out of the house when Arianna arrived back. He was not supposed to come into bedrooms but Enid had already contravened this rule by showing him the way up to their wing and he had spent at least one night curled up at the foot of her bed. Felix leapt up onto the bed, purring madly, licked and nuzzled Arianna's legs and hands and then curled up contentedly on her lap. She stroked his soft fur, tears in her eyes.

"I'm so glad he didn't die, although I suppose it seems silly to care about a cat when we've lost Mama and Papa."

The next day, at breakfast, Arianna announced that she was going to go for a short walk.

"Is that wise, dear?" Mary asked.

"The doctor said I should take moderate exercise and get fresh air into my lungs, and gradually build up my strength. I won't go far."

"Well, all right. But Theo must go with you, just in case."

Once outside, she said she wanted to see their house. Unsurprised, Theo resigned himself to yet another painful visit to the sad ruin of their former home. As the front facade came into view, Arianna winced.

"It's even worse than I imagined."

There was no-one there to tell them not to go inside and Theo tried the back door. It was locked but he still had his key and it was in his pocket.

"You'd better stay outside until I've made sure it's safe," he said to his sister.

The kitchen was smoke-blackened but everything seemed intact. There were two cups on the draining board, which had probably been his parents' last night-time cups of cocoa. The scene was unbearably sad and he felt tears pricking the back of his eyelids. He went across to the door leading into the hall and peered through. The far end, by the front door, was more or less demolished and he could scarcely recognise the area. He took a few steps forward and felt scrunching under his feet. Ash coated the floor and there was still an acrid smell of smoke. He made his way to the door to the living room, which was now just an opening, the door itself gone, and peered inside. Everything was destroyed and the room was unrecognisable. He could see the bare iron frames of what must have been their sofa and easy chairs, but all the wood and upholstery, all the pictures, ornaments and books, had disintegrated into charred debris. The ceiling had collapsed and he could see the blackened joists of the floor above. He heard Arianna's footsteps behind him.

"No, don't come in here!"

But it was too late, she was behind him, seeing what he had seen.

"Oh, my God!"

"Let's get back outside."

He steered her in front of him to the back door. They passed what had once been their staircase, now a pile of rubble in a gaping hole. They could not have gone upstairs had they wanted to. Theo supposed Dave had got into the back upper floor by means of a ladder, when he had collected their things. Outside, he locked the door and they went to sit on the bench. They were both crying and Arianna was shaking. He put his arm around her. For a long time neither of them spoke, then Arianna said,

"Do you think Uncle George will have it rebuilt?"

"I don't know. Does it matter? We will never live here again."

57

"Maybe we could, when we're older, when you are old enough to be a householder and in charge of us. How old would you have to be?"

"I don't know. Probably twenty-one." It was a ridiculous fantasy and they both knew it.

She continued, " But I suppose we wouldn't want that, not really, not without Mama and Papa. And we'd have to do all our own housework, we wouldn't be able to afford a maid!"

"Yes, I suppose one good thing about living at the manor is that everything is done for us, like in Malaya. We don't have to help with anything at all."

"I'd lay a thousand tables, wash a thousand dishes and make a thousand beds if it would only bring Mama and Papa back," Arianna declared passionately.

"So would I."

After lunch, George said he was going to the funeral parlour to view the bodies in their coffins and pay his last respects.

"I'd like to come too," Theo said.

"Are you sure? You might find it upsetting."

"Yes, I'm sure. I need to see them and say goodbye."

Arianna asked if she and Enid could come too, but George said no, they were too young.

As they entered the room where the bodies were laid out in their open caskets, Theo felt a fluttering of apprehension, no longer sure he wanted to do this. George went first to Jim's coffin and Theo steeled himself to look at his mother. She looked like a waxwork, an effigy of herself. He suddenly missed her live presence with a searing intensity of need which made his chest constrict. He knew he had grown apart from her in recent years. That was partly the natural result of being a boy and growing older, but, in a flash of self-awareness, he knew that it was also because Alya was not English and had only a basic level of education. He hadn't felt able to talk to her about things he'd learned at school or books he had read, the way he could with Jim. He bitterly regretted this now.

"I'm sorry, Mama," he whispered, and then added, "I love you." He wished he had told her that when she was still alive.

If George had heard him, he said nothing, but came over and put his hand briefly on his shoulder. Theo went over to his stepfather's coffin and said goodbye.

"You couldn't have been a better father," he murmured. "I was so lucky you married Mama."

Back at the manor, when Arianna asked how he had got on, he said, "It's not them, it's just their bodies. Their souls are gone."

~***~

Chapter Six

The day of the funeral dawned cool and overcast. The previous evening, Isobel, Bertie and Charlie had all arrived to stay the night, and Daisy had pressed and laid out Theo's best dark suit and the darkest, plainest dresses she could find from the girls' wardrobes.

"We only wear those in winter," Arianna told her.

"Well, without a coat they'll be fine. Your summer frocks are all too bright coloured."

The children travelled to the church in the official car, behind the hearse, along with George and Mary. The three guests followed behind, driven by Dave. The staff all walked to the church, after they had finished preparing a buffet lunch for the mourners to return to.

Theo got through the service without breaking down only by distancing himself emotionally from the proceedings. As they followed the coffins down the aisle he stared rigidly straight ahead so as not to meet the sympathetic eyes of anyone he knew. He refused to let the music enter into his soul and closed his ears to the words, although he was dimly aware that the vicar's eulogy was mostly about Jim, with very little said about his mother. He could hear Enid's muffled sobs from the pew in front and was aware of Arianna's silent tears at his side, but was determined not to do the same. Boys don't cry, not in public. The final hymn, 'Abide with Me', threatened to penetrate his armour, but he managed to resist its onslaught.

Outside the church, he saw Harry with his parents and also Clare. Mrs Fenton clasped him in a maternal embrace which was almost his undoing.

"Come and see us soon," she said.

Clare reached up and kissed him on the cheek. That kiss would have put him in seventh heaven just over a week ago, but now he could not allow himself to react. He managed to smile at her but did not trust himself to speak.

His strategy eventually failed him at his mother's graveside. As his throat constricted, his face contorted and tears ran down his cheeks, he felt a comforting hand on his shoulder and a large handkerchief being pressed into his hand.

"A stiff upper lip isn't required from you today," Charlie murmured in his ear.

Blinded by tears, he heard the vicar intone the words...*earth to earth, ashes to ashes, dust to dust, in sure and certain hope of resurrection to eternal life.....* He just hoped that there really was an after-life and one day he would meet his mother again.

Back at the manor, it seemed as though half the congregation had returned. Most of them were strangers to Theo and his sisters, but they recognised one man who made his way towards them.

"Theo! And Arianna and Enid! My, how you've all grown! Do you remember me?"

They did. His name was Walter and he was a good friend of Jim's, who had been based in Kuala Lumpur during their last few years in Malaya and been a frequent visitor to Klang. Theo had sometimes gone fishing with the two of them.

"I retired back to England a couple of months ago and last week I telephoned Jim to arrange a get together. My call was redirected here and I was given the dreadful news. How are you all coping?"

They shrugged, not really knowing how to answer. Walter was joined by his wife, Mildred.

"You poor dears! I'm so very sorry for your terrible loss," she gushed.

Some further, rather stilted conversation followed, then Mildred said they really must go and mingle with the other guests. As if it were a party, Theo thought. Walter fished in his pocket and brought forth a card.

"Here's our address and telephone number," he said. "We live in London. If you're ever there, please do look us up and if you need anything at all, either now or in the future, please don't hesitate to get in touch."

Theo took the card, thanked him and put it in his pocket.

The dining and drawing rooms were packed full of people, standing with drinks and plates in their hands and making animated conversation. Food was laid out in the dining room, but there was a throng in front of it and the children would have had to keep asking people to move in order to get through, so by tacit agreement they all gave up and headed upstairs.

"We can go down to the kitchen later and get something to eat," Arianna said, and then added, "Are you going to keep that card?"

"Might as well. You never know. I quite liked him."

"Yes, he was all right, but I was never keen on her."

"I thought she was nice," Enid said.

"She was, to you, but she had a different attitude to Mama and me, she was....." She sought for the right word.

"Condescending?" Theo suggested.

"Yes, that's it. She looked down on us in a sort of gracious way - being nice to the natives, you know!" She mimicked Mildred's cut-glass accent and they all laughed.

They lounged on Arianna's bed, making desultory conversation and after a while, they heard footsteps along the corridor.

"Where are you all?" they heard Charlie say.

"In here." Theo poked his head through the doorway and saw that Charlie was laden with a large tray.

"I've brought you all sustenance!"

He had put together a selection from the buffet and also some soft drinks.

"It's all finger food, so you don't need knives and forks. Tuck in."

As they ate, Theo asked Charlie who all those people downstairs were.

"I think a lot of them are old friends of Uncle Jim's from school and university and the rest are friends of my parents."

During the conversation which ensued, Arianna mentioned that they'd been supposed to be going to the seaside on Saturday for two weeks.

"It was all booked and everything," she said sadly.

"Is that so?" Charlie said nothing more, but looked thoughtful.

That evening, after everyone had departed, including Charlie, Bertie and Isobel, George said,

"I believe that a holiday at the seaside was booked as from next Saturday. Jim did mention it but I'd forgotten, so I haven't yet cancelled the hotel. Charlie has suggested that he take the three of you for the first week and we only cancel the second. He'd booked a week off work anyway, as it happens, and he was planning to come here, but he'd be happy to go to Burnham on Sea instead. What do you think to that?"

Three broad grins said it all.

"Right, that's settled then. I'll phone Charlie later on. Meanwhile can any of you remember the name of the hotel to save me phoning round all of them in the town?"

Luckily, Theo could.

On Saturday, Charlie picked them up in his car and they drove to Burnham on Sea. The hotel was a fairly modest one but it had everything they needed. A double, a twin and a single room had been booked and Charlie took the double. There were sinks in the rooms, a bathroom opposite, and guests' lounge and dining rooms downstairs. The booking included breakfast and dinner but not lunch.

"We'll try different cafes," Charlie said, "and perhaps have a picnic on the beach if the weather picks up."

The weather did pick up and they spent quite a lot of time on the beach and in the sea. Charlie bought Enid a bucket and spade and he had brought two cricket bats with him for himself and Theo. There were quite a few games of beach cricket going on and they joined in. They also all played miniature golf and crazy golf, which were not too strenuous for Arianna, and spent time on the pier with the amusements. Charlie was determined to give them a good time, as an antidote to the last terrible two weeks, and he succeeded. There was just one slightly jarring note, of which only Theo was aware. He had just come out of the sea, leaving the girls splashing about in the shallows, and was making his way to their deckchairs, when he saw Charlie in conversation with a dark-haired, rather swarthy young man. Their conversation seemed rather intense, although Theo could not catch the words, only the tone, but when Charlie saw Theo approaching, he seemed to cut it off short. As he came up to them, Theo heard the other man say, "See you later then."

"Who was that?" he asked.

Charlie shrugged. "Just some chap, making conversation."

That evening, after the girls had gone up to bed, Charlie suggested Theo do the same.

"I'm going to go for a short stroll before I turn in."

Theo normally slept like a log but for some reason he woke in the early hours and after a few minutes he heard Charlie unlocking the door to his room, which was next to his. He looked at the clock and saw that it was nearly three in the morning. Had Charlie only just returned from that walk? Or had he just been across the landing to the bathroom? Sounds from the room indicated he was getting undressed and putting things away and then he heard him go across to the bathroom and return. It was about ten minutes before silence resumed. He said nothing to Charlie the next morning, nor to the girls, and pushed the incident to the back of his mind, but events a few years later would reawaken that memory.

Upon their return home, the following Saturday, George informed Theo that a letter had arrived from Malaya, addressed to Alya.

"I opened it, but it's all written in Malay. Can you take a look at it?"

Theo read it quickly. It was from their grandparents, who were blissfully unaware of what had happened. He looked up.

"It's from our grandparents. We should have told them, I should have written," he said guiltily. He'd forgotten all about them.

"No, it's my fault, not yours. I should have thought of them and sent a telegram. I'd better do that now and then follow it up with a letter."

"They can't read English. It will have to be in Malay."

"Well, that won't work for a telegram. In that case, I'll just send a letter."

He dictated a formal letter of condolence with apologies for the delay and Theo translated it. He also wrote a letter from himself, writing from the heart, expressing his grief and shock, and Arianna added a couple of paragraphs at the end. Enid had forgotten most of her written Malay, having had less than a year of school there before they left, but she told Theo what she wanted to say and he wrote it down.

A day or two later, when Enid was bemoaning the loss of her dolls and toys, Mary pointed out that there was a cupboard full of toys in the old playroom, where they had previously found the dolls' house, and she could play with anything she wanted. They all rummaged through it and as well as dolls and other toys, found a

64

rather splendid train set, which, when set up by Theo, took up almost half the room. They also found that the library was well stocked with children's books as well as the classics which Theo had already discovered and borrowed. Some of them were quite old fashioned, dating from when Isobel, Jim and George were children, but Arianna found she rather enjoyed them.

George also produced a selection of family photographs, as he had promised, and they each chose one to be framed and kept in their rooms.

On the Wednesday following their return from holiday, George took a phone call from the police in Great Pucklington. They wanted to interview Theo and said he should have an adult with him as he was under age.

"Why? And when?"

"Just some routine questions about the house, where things were kept and so on. And this afternoon preferably."

George frowned. "I have an appointment with my bank manager this afternoon and it's rather important. Is it acceptable if my chauffeur is the adult who comes with him? He can drop me off at the bank and they can come on to the station."

"That would be fine, Sir. It's just routine."

Theo was only slightly apprehensive when he and Dave entered the police station. They were shown to an interview room where two plain clothes policemen joined them, introducing themselves as a Detective Inspector and a Sergeant. The rather stern-faced inspector did all the talking and the young sergeant merely took notes. He began by asking Theo whether there were paraffin heaters in the house and if so where they were kept. Theo told him.

"There wasn't one in the downstairs hall?"

Theo shook his head.

"Would they have been in use at the time of the fire?"

"No, we haven't used them for a couple of months, not since the weather got milder."

"Where was the supply of paraffin kept?"

"In a can, in the shed."

"Do you know if this can would have been full?"

Theo thought for a moment. "it should have been fairly full. Papa filled it up at Whitsun and we've hardly used the heaters since."

"Are you sure about that?"

"Yes, I remember, because when he came back with it, he asked me to take it to the shed."

"So you knew there was a full can in there?"

"Yes." Theo wondered where this was leading.

The inspector changed tack. " Get on well with your father, did you?"

"Yes."

"He wasn't your natural father, though, was he?"

"No. My real father died when I was very small."

"Do you remember him?"

"Yes, a bit. I was nearly four when he died."

"Did you resent your stepfather taking his place?"

"No."

"No? Your father has died, this strange man comes into your house, taking over his role. Surely you must have been upset at that?"

"No. It wasn't like that. My father and mother were no longer together, as far back as I remember, and my stepfather was already there. My real father visited at weekends."

The inspector raised his eyebrows at this unusual arrangement, then fixed Theo with a steely gaze.

"So, you and your stepfather got on well, had a good relationship?"

"Yes, I've already said."

"Never a cross word, all sweetness and light, was it?"

"Well, no, of course not! We were a normal family! But we were basically a happy one and I got on with my stepfather better than most of my school friends seem to get on with their real fathers. He was like a father to me and he always treated me like his own son." His voice caught slightly.

"So, how come we have a witness who overheard an argument through an open window at your house late that Saturday afternoon, with a man's voice raised in anger, shouting?"

66

Theo looked bewildered. "Well, that wasn't anything to do with me and I don't remember anything like that. I left at about quarter to five anyway."

"This was earlier than that, around four fifteen."

Theo suddenly remembered what he had heard from upstairs. "Arianna, my sister, was having an argument with our mother around that time. I was upstairs but I heard their raised voices and then I heard my father intervene and put an end to it. He raised his voice but he wasn't shouting, just speaking firmly."

The inspector looked sceptical, but changed course.

"You left at quarter to five, you say?"

"Yes, thereabouts. I caught the five o'clock bus."

"Do you have a bike?"

"Yes."

"Where is it?"

"In the shed." Reminded of its existence, Theo made a mental note to go and retrieve it.

"Why didn't you go into town by bike?"

"Because we were meeting some girls, so I was wearing my best clothes, and it might have rained."

"When you got off the bus, where did you go?"

"To my mate, Harry's, first, then we went to the cinema to meet the girls, and afterwards back to Harry's and I stayed the night there."

"Full name and address of this Harry?

Theo supplied it.

"There all night, were you? And his family can confirm that?"

"Yes." Theo was becoming increasingly anxious as to where all this was leading.

The inspector decided to enlighten him.

"You see, the fire investigators have concluded that the fire at your home was definitely started deliberately. We are looking at arson here."

Dave took a sharp intake of breath.

The inspector continued. "Significant traces of paraffin were found in the entrance hall. It is believed that rags were soaked in paraffin, set alight and pushed through the letter box, possibly using a long pole so they would go further inside. Such a pole, charred at the edges, was found some distance away, along with an empty paraffin can. And there was no such can in the shed. Nor was there a bike in there."

Theo was in shock, absorbing this information. Someone had deliberately targeted them? Who? Why? A surge of anger rose up in him. Someone had murdered his parents!

The inspector was watching his face carefully. "This is news to you?"

"Yes, of course it is." His voice was shaky. "If it's true, it's terrible. My parents were murdered! Who would do that to us?"

"You tell me."

"What do you mean?"

"Well, you say you got on well with your stepfather, that the argument wasn't with you and that you were in town all night, but as yet we have no proof of any of that. You may well be eliminated from our enquiries in due course, but at present you would appear to be a potential suspect."

Dave started to protest, but was silenced. The inspector leaned forward and adopted a more conciliatory tone.

"Perhaps you only intended the fire as a prank, not expecting it to have the disastrous consequences it did. Perhaps you just meant to cause your parents annoyance and inconvenience or give them a fright, in order to get your own back for some grievance, and it got out of hand. Is that how it was?"

Theo was rendered temporarily speechless. Anger, fear and grief were coursing through him in equal measure and they were making a hard knot in his throat. When he found his voice, he said shakily:

"I would never, ever have done anything so reckless and stupid, endangering the lives of my family, whom I loved, no matter what grievance I might have had. And I didn't have any! I left home that afternoon feeling happy, looking forward to the evening and to the holidays, and my father had just given me extra pocket money for helping him build a pool in the garden."

"Any witness to that?"

"Yes, my sister, Enid."

The inspector checked his notes. "I thought she was in the village? We have a statement from a family there that she was playing with their daughter that afternoon."

"Yes, but she was back by then. This was at about twenty to five, just as I was leaving."

"Well, we can ask her, and we can ask your other sister about the argument, but I daresay both of them will say anything necessary to protect you. They've lost their parents, they won't want to lose their big brother too."

"They're not liars! They'll tell you the truth."

"Hmm. We'll also interview the Fenton family and check your alibi. Make sure that there's no way you could have sneaked out after everyone was asleep and biked home and back."

Theo stared at him. "I've already told you, I went on the bus, I didn't have the bike. And Fred and the firemen can confirm that I returned to the house on foot on Sunday morning."

"Well, the bike is not in the shed, where you say it was kept. You could have left it in town and returned on the bus or dumped it somewhere en route."

"Why on earth would I do that?!"

"To give the impression you didn't have transport to return on during the night. However, it's also conceivable that you simply walked there and back in the early hours. A boy your age could cover the distance in less than an hour each way." Before Theo could say anything, he continued, "I understand you have a history of behaving aggressively. A couple of years ago I believe there was an incident with a girl in the village - you apparently attacked her."

"I did *not* attack her! She was bullying my sister and I was trying to get her to stop. It was all sorted out!"

The inspector merely shrugged. Theo gazed at him in disbelief. This was a nightmare. He didn't know what else he could say, but felt he had to continue to protest his innocence, try to convince this man.

"Everything I've told you is true. I did not start that fire, would never have even thought of it, and I couldn't have done it because I wasn't there. I love my family and now my parents are dead, I am grieving for them, and you are accusing me of killing them!"

He couldn't continue without breaking down and he was not going to give these policemen the satisfaction of seeing him cry.

Dave put in, "This is all nonsense. The boy was in town as he said and his friend will confirm it. I can confirm that they were a happy, close family; I knew them all well, especially Mr Jim. We had a pint in the pub quite often and he always spoke fondly and proudly of Theo and referred to him as his son, his boy. You're upsetting and scaring the lad for no reason and I don't think Sir George will be too pleased when he hears how you've been interrogating him."

The inspector made no comment except to say, "This interview is finished. We'll be checking everything out and we'll get back to you. You may well be cleared of any suspicion by our further enquiries, but if there is still doubt, we may need to take matters further."

"What does that mean?" Dave asked.

"It might mean a further interview, this time under caution. Now you may go."

Outside, Dave patted Theo's back. "Don't worry, lad, this is a storm in a teacup. Your alibi will clear you. Come on, let's go and pick up Sir George and tell him about this."

"Do you mind if I go back under my own steam? I'd like to walk a bit, clear my head and be on my own. I can get the bus back."

"All right. But don't worry, it will all blow over. Don't go thinking you're going to be clapped in jail!"

Theo walked slowly to the bus stop, his mind churning. He'd heard of people being framed for crimes they had not committed - was that going to happen to him? He tried to tell himself that it wouldn't; of course the Fentons would confirm he was there all night and could not have left without their knowing. But perhaps they were all heavy sleepers and could not be sure of that? Surely Harry at least would be adamant he'd have heard Theo get up, they were in the same room. He should have told the inspector that, he realised belatedly. Then his mind focused on the fire, deliberately, cold-bloodedly started. Who could have done that? Who hated them that much? Or was it purely random, some drunks on the rampage, any house would do? But why would anyone be in the estate grounds at night? It wasn't a short cut to anywhere.

70

He continued on the bus until the village and made his way into the churchyard. He sat on the edge of his mother's grave.

"You know I didn't do it, don't you, Mama? he said out loud. "I wish you could haunt that policeman and tell him I didn't!"

A flash of rage shot through him. His parents were here, in this graveyard, because of some criminal, some maniac. It had not been a tragic accident, an act of God, it had been malicious intent, murder. If they ever caught the culprits, he hoped they would be hanged.

Meanwhile, Dave had relayed the gist of the interview to George and then driven him to the police station. After demanding to see the inspector, George launched into a furious tirade.

"How dare you give a fifteen year old boy the third degree like that? A boy who's just lost his parents. Your theory as to his guilt is hare-brained to say the least. And why didn't you tell me you'd discovered it was arson? I'm the owner of the property and the next of kin to the deceased; I should have been the first to know. Instead you pretend that you are just going to ask some routine questions - a blatant lie!"

He paused to draw breath and the inspector put in: "I wanted the element of surprise, wanted to see the boy's reaction."

George continued, "As to the supposed evidence of the missing bike, that bike is in one of the outhouses at the manor. Fred brought it up a while ago, I just forgot to tell Theo."

The sergeant put his head round the door.

"Sir, I've just got back from the Fentons." He looked uncertainly at Sir George.

"Yes? Spit it out. What did they say?"

"Mrs Fenton says that she's an extremely light sleeper and their door has heavy iron bolts across it which make a loud scraping noise when moved. She's adamant no-one could have left the house without her hearing. And the boy, Harry, says that Theo was happy at home, had no issues with his parents and he says that he too would have woken up had Theo left; they were sleeping in the same room."

"Right, thank you, sergeant." Turning to George, he said. "Well the boy seems to be in the clear. You can tell him he's no longer a possible suspect."

George got up to leave. "That's assuming I can find him. Apparently he's gone off somewhere. If anything's happened to him, if he's done something stupid, like run away, I'll be holding you personally responsible! And I hope you're now going to go out and find the criminals who really did this! See that you keep me informed."

Theo was unaware of just how long he'd been in the graveyard until he heard footsteps approaching and looked up to see Arianna coming towards him.

"I thought I might find you here. Everyone's worried about you, you've been gone ages. It's all sorted out now. The police have spoken to Harry and his mother, and Uncle George told them that your bike was brought up to the manor. You're officially cleared of being involved and Uncle George apparently gave that policeman a piece of his mind."

Theo absorbed this information with relief.

"Did you think you were going to be thrown into jail?" she asked, sitting down beside him.

"It had crossed my mind."

"More than crossed it, I think!"

"But it's still not all right, Ari. The fire was started deliberately. Someone wanted to burn our house down and didn't care who died. Who would do that to us?"

"Perhaps it was some strangers, maybe drunks, who had no idea who lived there? Maybe it was a dare or something and it got out of hand?"

"Perhaps, but who would be wandering through our estate at night? The road doesn't lead anywhere."

She had no answer to that and didn't want to dwell on it. She got to her feet and held out her hand to her brother.

"Come on, let's go home. It's nearly supper time."

~***~

Chapter Seven

Theo was dreaming that he was in a smoke filled corridor. He was trying to get to his parents to rescue them, but when he opened the door, he met a wall of flame. Through the flames he could see them reaching out to him, entreating, but he couldn't get to them. He awoke sweating, with his heart racing.

There was a tap on the bedroom door and Arianna's voice asking if he was all right. He didn't immediately answer so she came in and sat on the side of the bed.

"You were yelling out loud. Was it a bad dream?"

He nodded and told her the gist of it.

"If I had been there that night, perhaps I could have saved them. They said that the fire didn't reach my room, only the smoke. If I had woken up in time I could have phoned the fire service and warned the rest of you and maybe Mama and Papa would have got out before it was too late."

"You can't think like that, Theo. You weren't there and it's not your fault. You're just torturing yourself."

He supposed she was right, but the dream refused to be forgotten and his thoughts kept returning to it.

Both Arianna and Theo had grown up fast in the last few weeks and now seemed mature for their years, but the tragedy seemed to have the opposite effect on Enid. She retreated further into childhood, playing with dolls and toys more than she had prior to the fire, and Basil the bear not only resided on her bed, but was cuddled close at night. She wanted Theo to come and read her a story before she went to sleep, even though she was perfectly capable of reading them herself. She would often follow her brother or sister around the house and also outside, as if she were subconsciously afraid of losing them too. They teasingly called her their little shadow. All three missed their parents keenly, but Enid yearned for her mother with a primal need. As first Theo and then Arianna had grown and become more independent, Alya had concentrated her mothering on her youngest child, and Enid craved the attention and physical affection she had been used to. Mary's cool, brisk manner was a stark contrast to Alya's gentle, loving nature, and although Daisy and Mrs Hughes were kind and took care of her needs, they were too busy to spend much time with her. She was encouraged to go into the village again and visit her friends and this did seem to help, not least because her friends' mothers tended to make a fuss of the poor little orphan.

During the remaining two weeks of the school holiday, Arianna and Theo both took trips into town to see their friends. Theo and Harry met up with Clare and Julia and went for a walk in the park. Theo and Clare let the other two go on ahead while they sat on a bench. Clare was unusually quiet and Theo asked her why.

"I'm not sure what to say to you. I feel for you, I really do, but I don't know if you want to talk about it and I'm afraid of saying the wrong thing."

"Just be your normal self and say whatever you think. You don't need to tread on eggshells around me."

She leaned against him and put her head on his shoulder. He put his arm around her and kissed her on the lips. She responded and they kissed and cuddled for a while. He unbuttoned her blouse and stroked and kissed the top of her small breasts. Emboldened by her acquiescence, he started to slide his hand up her skirt, but she pushed it away.

"No, not there."

"Sorry."

"It's all right." She kissed him again to show she wasn't annoyed. "I do really like you a lot," she said earnestly.

"Likewise!"

At that point, Harry and Julia returned and Clare hastily buttoned up her blouse.

After they had said goodbye to the girls and were heading to Harry's home for tea, Harry commented that Theo seemed to be getting further with Clare than he was with Julia and perhaps it was a pity he hadn't lost a parent as it seemed to gain sympathy with the girls! Theo stopped in his tracks and stared at him in disbelief.

"What a bloody stupid, vile, childish thing to say!" he exploded.

"All right, keep your hair on. It was only a joke, I didn't mean it!"

"You should never joke about things like that. Do you have any idea what it feels like, what me and my sisters are going through?"

"I'm sorry, all right? Forget I said it. You're right, it was stupid. It's just that Julia hardly even lets me kiss her and I saw you two getting really cosy on that bench!"

As the school holidays were drawing to a close and Daisy was busy checking Theo's and Arianna's school uniforms and letting down hems, Mary buttonholed George.

"Have you made any decision yet, about the children's futures?"

"What do you mean?"

"Well, it goes without saying that we keep Enid here and bring her up as we would a daughter, but I can't help wondering if Arianna might be happier in the longer term if she returned to Malaya and went to live with her grandparents. I'm sure they would be delighted to have her. And Theo does have relatives in Yorkshire, if we could find them."

George stared at her in disbelief. "You can't be seriously suggesting that we separate them, after they've just lost their parents? It would be the height of cruelty! And sending Arianna to Malaya? Thousands of miles from her sister and brother - she might never see them again! And, apart from anything else, by all accounts her grandparents' house is pretty basic, she's used to better and she's at an age when that sort of thing matters to a girl. No, there's no way I would ever agree to that. And I owe it to my dead brother to raise his children."

"I wasn't suggesting that we should do anything right now, but perhaps next year? However, I take your point about Malaya, perhaps that wasn't a good idea, I just thought she might fit in better there."

"She fits in fine here now," George said shortly. "She's happy at the grammar school and doing well. She stays here, is that understood? I don't want to hear another word about Malaya!"

"All right, agreed. But what about Theo? You must have thought about contacting his Yorkshire relatives? They are more closely related to him than we are, bearing in mind he isn't Jim's natural son."

"Jim adopted him, gave him his name. But, yes, I had thought about looking for them. I don't think Jim tried very hard. But only so that he could make their acquaintance, visit them."

"But they might want him to go and live with them. They would have a valid claim on him. Don't we have an obligation to give them the option?"

"Meaning you hope they *do* want him to live there!"

"Well it wouldn't be so terrible, would it? Yorkshire isn't thousands of miles away and he could visit his sisters in the holidays."

"You're very keen to get rid of him - and Arianna too. Don't think I don't know why Enid is the only one you want to keep. You can't replace *her* you know."

Mary flushed. "I'm not trying to. But if they are all to stay here until they are grown up, you will have to increase my household budget. We've already incurred the extra cost of half a maid's wages, and those three have voracious appetites, especially Theo - he eats more than you do - not to mention the cost of clothing them. Daisy tells me that she's now let down Arianna's gymslips and Theo's school trousers as far as they will go. They'll need new ones next term. Luckily Enid can wear Arianna's dresses as she grows out of them, but it's still a significant cost."

"We'll manage. I'll divert some more estate funds to the household. I'm saving Jim's wages, provided Fred can continue to manage on his own."

"And Theo's relatives?"

"You don't give up, do you? I'll talk to him, see what else he knows about them. At the moment I only have his father's name from his birth certificate."

George broached the subject as they were finishing lunch the next day.

"Theo, what do you know about your real father's family in Yorkshire? Names? Place they lived?"

Alarm bells rang in Theo's brain. Why did George want to know? He remembered the newspaper article - was he going to be sent to Yorkshire? Reluctantly, he gave George the first names of his aunt and uncle, their youngest son and their daughter.

"There were two or three other cousins, older boys, but I can't remember their names. They only signed the first few cards."

"And the place name?"

"Papa thought it began with an 'H'. I can't remember."

George fetched an atlas and looked at the map of Yorkshire. He sighed.

"There are loads of places beginning with 'H'. He shut the atlas.

"The thing is, Theo, these relatives are actually closer kin to you than we are. We really should try to find them now that you are orphaned."

"Yes, and they may want to give you a home with them," Mary interjected.

George glared at her. Enid and Arianna looked horror struck and Enid burst out,

"No! He can't go up there to live. We need him here! Don't send him away, please!" Her eyes filled with tears.

"Now look what you've done!" George said furiously to Mary. To the children he said. "Nothing is decided. They may well be content with him just visiting every now and then. What do *you* think about contacting them, Theo?"

Theo felt that his future hung in the balance. Trying to choose his words carefully, he said,

"Well, of course I'd like to meet them one day, but I don't know them and I don't want to go to live with strangers, leave my sisters, and have to change schools and make new friends." Another thought struck him. "And perhaps they wouldn't be able to afford to keep me at school. I know I'm old enough to leave and get a job, but I wanted to go to university provided I can win a scholarship." His voice starting to crack a little, he added, "I've lost my parents, I don't want to lose everyone and everything else. If you let me stay here until I finish school, I can work on the estate in the holidays and at weekends and earn my keep."

George looked at him thoughtfully for a minute or two, then said,

"Right, well, that's pretty clear. I'll tell you what we'll do: I'll apply to become your legal guardian. I'll phone my solicitor this afternoon and set things in motion. And we'll wait until that's gone through before we try to find your family, then they won't be able to

77

disturb the status quo, you can just visit them in the holidays. And you don't have to earn your keep! However, I understand you're quite good at gardening and if you do want to help out a little during the Easter and summer holidays, you can earn yourself some extra pocket money."

Theo felt as if a load had been lifted from him, a load which had been lingering at the back of his mind ever since he had read that newspaper article. Relief made his voice wobbly.

"Thank you, thank you," was all he could manage to say.

The following day, shortly before supper, two policemen arrived. Mr Hughes showed them into the drawing room where the whole family were congregated. Theo recognised the two detectives who had grilled him earlier. Once they were seated and offered tea, George asked what progress had been made with the investigation.

"I assume that's why you're here?"

"Yes, sir. We've made an arrest. Three young men."

"Well? Who are they? Why did they do it?"

The Inspector looked towards Arianna and Enid and said hesitantly,

"Perhaps the two young ladies should withdraw? Some of the detail is not very pleasant."

"Enid, Arianna, leave us please."

Arianna opened her mouth to protest then shut it again. Theo would tell them all about it afterwards.

Once the door had closed behind them, the Inspector launched into his tale.

"One of the men is from the village. He lodges with a family there and works on a farm a couple of miles away. The other two are his cousins, from Oxford, who were visiting him that weekend. One of the two Oxford men has pleaded guilty to arson and manslaughter but denies murder. He says the fire got out of hand and it was only his intention to cause a fright, not hurt or kill anyone. The other two deny all charges relating to the fire but admit they left him outside the cottage after they had all three daubed some unpleasant words on the front door, using chalk they'd picked up at the pub - the landlord uses it to mark special offers on the blackboard."

"What words?"

"They made reference to the Malayan lady, sir, indicating, not very politely, that she wasn't welcome here and should return to her own country. Of course, by the time anyone reached the cottage, that door was almost completely incinerated and the wording obliterated. The three of them had been drinking all evening and were rather the worse for wear - the pub landlord confirms that. The two Oxford men were feeling aggrieved because one of them had recently lost his job and believed this was because of Indian immigrants being given employment at lower wages. Apparently, the chap from the village then said that they had immigrants there and he was asked to show them where they lived. I understand that part of the conversation took place outside the pub after closing time, but the landlord has made a witness statement confirming what he heard of their earlier talk. It was this which led us to question the chap from the village. After they'd defaced the cottage door, two of them returned to the village but the other stayed and prowled around for a while. He was the one who had lost his job. He went into the shed, which was apparently unlocked, and found the paraffin, along with matches, an old broom handle and some rags, and this gave him the idea. The alcohol he'd imbibed was exacerbating his sense of grievance, causing him to feel hatred towards anyone who was not English and in his view had no right to be here."

"He should be charged with murder!" George exclaimed, and Mary murmured agreement.

"And he may yet be. That's still to be decided by officers above my level. But a sentence for arson and manslaughter will still be a very long one."

"And the other two?"

"They will be charged with lesser offences, which will still carry a prison term. They say they had no idea what he was planning and that may be true, but they still left him there, issued no warning, and even when the news of the fire broke, did not report him. When he eventually returned to the village, he probably reeked of paraffin but the other two say they were asleep and did not notice anything. They also say they never connected the fire with him, but I find that quite incredible, as would a jury. I daresay those two will eventually plead

79

guilty to being accessories before and after the fact, so we should avoid a trial - unless, of course, it is decided to prosecute the third man for murder. Otherwise, they will just be referred for sentencing in due course."

"What about the people this man lodged with?" Mary asked. "Did they not notice anything untoward which they should have reported?"

"They were away that weekend. By the time they returned on Sunday evening, the two Oxford men were gone."

The Inspector rose to his feet and his sergeant closed his notebook and did likewise.

"Unless you have any further questions, sir, we'll leave you to mull this over. At least you have the consolation of knowing that we have caught the culprits and they will face justice. We'll continue to keep you informed of progress in the case."

Theo's mind was churning, digesting this information and the chain of events which had led to his parents' deaths. He felt a searing hatred towards this man, he wanted to be let at him with a gun or a knife, he wanted to kill him. When the detectives had been shown out, he burst out:

"He should be hanged!"

"I incline to agree," Mary said, and George nodded.

"I feel the same, but we will have to accept the final decision of the police. If it does go to trial, a jury may still find him not guilty of murder."

Over supper, the girls were given an expurgated version of events. After Enid had gone to bed, Arianna asked some searching questions, not content with such a brief summary, and George ended up telling her the whole story. Like Theo, she was filled with impotent rage, and neither of them slept well that night.

Arianna's hospital check up was on the Friday morning before school started again. On Thursday evening at supper she asked Mary if they could go shopping afterwards as her school satchel and all its contents had been destroyed in the fire and she would need replacements by Monday.

"Now you tell me! At the last minute."

"Sorry, but I've only just thought about it."

Their appointment was scheduled for 10.30 a.m. but the doctor was exceptionally busy that morning and it was over an hour later before they were seen. After testing Arianna's lung function and asking her various questions, the doctor said he was very satisfied with her progress and she would be pleased to know that she would be able to do some PE during the coming term.

"However, you'll need to refrain from the most strenuous sports. I'll give you a letter to take to your teacher."

"Is hockey considered too strenuous?" Arianna asked.

"I'm afraid so. Do you enjoy hockey?"

"No, I hate it! I'll be glad of a term free of it!"

They had to wait for the letter to be typed and signed and by the time they left the hospital it was lunchtime. Mary found a payphone and let the manor know that they would not be back for lunch.

"We'll get some lunch at Harding's," she said to Arianna, "and do your shopping afterwards."

Harding's was the town's department shore, which boasted a restaurant on its top floor. Arianna looked around her as they entered; it was all very smart, with plush carpet, tables covered with crisp white cloths and potted plants dotted around the perimeter. The menu looked mouth watering too.

"Can I order anything I want?" she asked.

Mary smiled and said yes, within reason.

After three years in rural England, Arianna was used to being stared at and hardly noticed it, but Mary soon became irritated by the stares and whispers of two elderly ladies at the next table. Leaning towards them, she said, in her most imperious tone,

"Is there anything I can do for you ladies? You seem very interested in us."

They both looked very embarrassed and murmured an apology. Arianna giggled and whispered,

"That put them in their place!"

Mary had asked Arianna to make a list of everything she needed to get and while they were waiting for their meal to be served, she asked to see it. Scanning the items, she asked,

"What's a protractor?"

"You use it in geometry, for measuring angles."

81

"Oh, right."

"Didn't you have one when you were at school?"

"No. I didn't study geometry, in fact not mathematics at all, just arithmetic and bookkeeping. "

"Bookkeeping sounds more useful than algebra and geometry," Arianna commented. "Where did you go to school?"

"I was educated at home with a governess until I was about twelve and then I was sent to a small private girls' school. We didn't do a lot of the subjects which Bertie and Charlie did at their school and which you and Theo are doing now, but I think I learned all I needed to know."

"Yes, we learn a lot of stuff we'll probably never use; take Latin, for example - it's a dead language!"

Mary smiled and returned to the list.

"The last item was surely not in your satchel," she commented drily. " New brassieres."

"Well, I didn't want to mention it last night in front of Uncle George, but mine are getting too small for me and Mama had said that we'd go and get new ones in the holidays."

A wave of sadness swept over her as it often did when she thought of her mother. She should be going shopping with her, not Aunt Mary.

"Right. They have a good lingerie department here, so we'll get those first after lunch."

By the end of the afternoon, they had everything, including two very pretty, lace-edged bras, and Arianna felt that she'd got to know her rather cool and remote aunt a little better.

~***~

Chapter Eight

As the school term progressed and the children settled back into normal life, their natural youthful exuberance - dampened by sadness during the summer - gradually reasserted itself. They had been on their best behaviour at the manor during the holidays, partly because they lacked any inclination towards mischief and partly because they were unsure of the boundaries where George and Mary - particularly Mary - were concerned. They soon learned.

Fooling around in the drawing room one wet Saturday afternoon, Arianna and Enid managed to knock over a vase and break it. Such a misdemeanour would probably have just earned them a scolding from Alya, but Mary gave them each a slap and sent them to bed without any supper. Theo later sneaked them up something to eat.

Shortly afterwards, Theo incurred George's ire when he and Arthur were playing cricket rather too near to the garden area and Theo managed to hit the ball straight through one of the glass panes of the greenhouse. George told him sternly that sixpence a week would be deducted from his pocket money until the new pane was paid for.

George had said that they were welcome to invite their friends over on occasion at weekends and one Saturday both Harry and Arianna's friend Rosa came to lunch. Afterwards they were joined by Arthur and one of Enid's friends and they all played hide and seek amongst the many closed rooms, sometimes hiding under the dustsheets which covered the furniture. Looking for Enid, whose turn it was to hide, Rosa managed to lose her way and went into Mary and George's bedroom by mistake, where Mary was engaged in trying on her winter outfits.

"What are you doing here?" she asked sharply.

"Sorry, I was looking for Enid, she's hiding."

"Well, you won't find her in here and this part of the house is out of bounds for games."

Later, Rosa asked Arianna, "Is she a bit of an ogre, your aunt?"

"She can be rather sharp-tongued, but she's not too bad underneath. She's very different from my mother though, and a lot stricter."

On another weekend, Theo invited Clare over and, under the pretext of showing her round the house, took her upstairs and into one of the unused bedrooms, where he removed the dustsheet from the bed. They kissed and cuddled for a while, becoming a little more intimate than before. Theo thought he might be falling in love with her.

Theo and Arianna usually did their homework in the library, seated at a large table. One evening, Arianna finished hers first and wandered around the library browsing the book collection. She came across some photograph albums and started leafing through them.

"Hey, Theo, come and look at this."

"Just a minute, I need to finish this essay."

When he had finished, he went to see what she was looking at. She showed him a photo of Charlie and Bertie as small boys with a girl seated between them. The inscription below said: 'Bertie, age 7, Alice, 4 and Charlie, 2.'

"Who's Alice?" she asked.

Theo shrugged. "Could be anyone. Maybe a cousin; what about what's-her-name, Aunt Isobel's daughter?"

"She's called Daphne, not Alice and she's younger than Charlie."

"Well, it could be a friend's child who was visiting."

"But it isn't just this one photo. There are loads before this, including her as a baby with Aunt Mary. Look!"

Theo looked. It was true. The mysterious Alice appeared at various stages of development from a babe in arms to four years old. Then the pictures of her stopped and it was just Bertie and Charlie. There was a gap too. After the one of her at four years old, the next photo showed Bertie aged nine and Charlie aged four.

"Are you thinking what I'm thinking?" Arianna asked.

"Yes, it looks as if they had a daughter, doesn't it? Between Bertie and Charlie. I wonder what happened to her?"

"She must have died."

They were interrupted by Mary entering the library.

"Have you two finished your homework yet?" Then she added sharply, "What are you looking at?"

"Sorry," Arianna said. "We didn't know they were private."

Mary looked flustered. "They're not, but it would have been polite of you to have asked."

"Sorry," Arianna said again. "Can I just ask you, who Alice is?"

There was a brief silence. Theo watched Mary's face and saw conflicting emotions flit cross it.

"She was our daughter. Between Bertie and Charlie in age. She died when she was four years old."

"How sad!" Arianna said, "I'm so sorry."

Theo murmured agreement and then asked, "How did she die? Was it an accident?"

"No. She contracted a fever on the brain. It was very sudden and very quick." She paused. "Charlie has no memory of her, but Bertie does."

"How terrible," Arianna said, feeling sympathy for her aunt. "You must have been devastated."

"Yes, well, it's a long time ago now. Getting on for 30 years. Life goes on for those left behind, as you two are finding out. Now, if you've finished your homework, I came in here to read in peace. You can look at the rest of the photo albums another time; I don't mind you looking at them."

They picked up their books and left the room.

"Well, that explains a few things," Arianna said, as they headed upstairs.

"What does it explain?"

"Why she's like she is, so unapproachable and sort of held in."

"Repressed?"

"Yes, that's a good word. And it explains why Enid is her favourite."

"Is she? And why does it?"

"Come on, Theo, you must have noticed."

"Well, Enid gets more attention from her than we do, but I assumed that's because she's the youngest and she's still such a child."

85

"That might be part of it, but I bet she's planning to make a genteel English lady out of her and marry her off to some wealthy young man, like she would have with Alice. She might even present her as a debutante! She can't do that with me - can you just imagine it! - and you're a boy; she's got two of them already!"

"You're letting your imagination run away with you!"

"I don't think so. You'll see. I bet she'd have liked to have got rid of us. I'm sure she was behind that idea to send you to Yorkshire."

On their next visit to the graveyard, they took a closer look at the family plot where Jim was buried and found Alice's inscription:

'Alice Mary Bradshaw. 1899-1903. Dearly beloved daughter of Sir George and Lady Mary and sister of Albert and Charles.'

"You're her replacement," Arianna said to Enid.

"What do you mean?"

"Shut up, Ari!" Theo said. "Don't fill her head with your fanciful theories!"

Probate was granted on Jim's will and George outlined the terms of it to the children.

"He only had a modest nest egg and none of you are going to be rich, but when you reach the age of twenty-one, you will each inherit one third of his estate. Meanwhile, it will be invested by his trustees, who are myself and his solicitor. His savings were mostly in cash and I think we will keep it that way, bearing in mind the American stock market crash and the recession. Once you receive your small lump sums, it will be up to you what you decide to do with them, although I will be happy to provide advice. In Theo's case, it could give him a helping hand when embarking on a career, following university, and for you girls it could provide you with a small dowry upon marriage."

"You're assuming we're going to get married," Arianna commented.

"Well, girls usually do, but if you decide to concentrate on a career, it will provide you with a little bit of security to fall back on. However, as I said, it is not going to make you wealthy. The total estate is only £900 now and it remains to be seen by how much it will grow. You won't be able to sit back and live on it."

Nevertheless, it sounded an enormous amount of money to Theo. He would have £300! He was grateful to Jim for leaving him the same amount as the girls and felt a fresh stab of grief for him.

At the end of October, the three arsonists were sentenced. It had been decided not to pursue a charge of murder against the main perpetrator and he was sentenced to twenty years for arson and manslaughter. The other two pled guilty to being accessories and received eight years each.

"Just twenty years for our parents' lives!" Theo commented bitterly. "Mama was only thirty-five, she'd barely lived half her life and Papa would have had another fifteen years at least ahead of him. This chap's young, he'll be free when he's still in his forties."

"Yes, well, they don't work it out like that, more's the pity," George replied. "There are set maximum terms. I feel as you do, that it isn't nearly enough punishment, but we have to accept it and get on with our lives. There's nothing to be gained by feeling bitter, bitterness just eats away at you."

Getting on with their lives, however, was easier said than done, at least in the short term, thanks to the press. Now that the case was no longer *sub judice*, the local papers had a field day and the story was also picked up by several nationals, including those delivered to the manor. One of them had a spread on the front page. The sentencing had taken place on the Friday morning of the children's half term week and the news broke first in the local evening papers, followed up on the Saturday by both locals and nationals, with discussion arising from the case continuing unabated in the Sunday nationals. Not only were the details of the fire rehashed, with pictures of the ruined cottage - including some taken of the interior - but the background and motivation of the criminals was also gone into, leading to a general discussion on the issue of immigration. Some papers also did lengthy and detailed articles on the background of the victim family. One of them took a 'Prince and Pauper' theme, describing the convention-flouting love affair between the Harrow and Cambridge educated son of a baronet, and an Asian peasant girl, who already had a small son fathered out of wedlock by another Englishman.

Theo groaned when he read that; so much for keeping quiet about his ignominious birth! Arianna was so incensed by one of the articles on immigration (which took the view that all persons of colour should be banished to their homeland forthwith) that she penned a letter to the paper, signing it with a flourish, 'A. E. Bradshaw, age 12'. Enid viewed the photographs of the interior of their former home with shock, having not previously seen inside as her brother and sister had, and wept bitterly.

By the time they returned to school on the Monday - which was Theo's 16th birthday - local gossip was at its peak. At Enid's village school, everyone was already well aware that she was one of the orphans referred to and children of her age did not take much notice of their parents' discussions on items in the news, so she did not suffer too much from the notoriety, but it was a different matter for Theo and Arianna. Boys of Theo's age and older often joined in such discussions at home, as did the older girls at Arianna's school. By the end of that day, Theo had got used to coming up to a group of boys having an animated discussion, only for them to fall silent upon his arrival and look embarrassed. Although the papers had stopped short of actually naming the three children, their ages and genders were given and most of Theo's fellow pupils were well aware that he was the boy referred to. In Arianna's case, it was blatantly obvious that she was one of the two girls and, for the first time since coming to the grammar school, she was on the receiving end of some spiteful comments, to the effect that she did not belong in England. Luckily, her friends rallied round her and provided support and she was able to hold her head up high and rise above it.

After school on the following day, as the older pupils of the two grammar schools mingled in the area between them, Clare came up to Theo and, sounding serious, said she needed to talk to him.

"Can we go for a walk in the park?"

He was glad of the chance of a short time in her company, hoping for a sympathetic ear. On the way, he caught sight of Arianna heading for the bus stop and called to her that he'd be on a later bus. She gave a wave of acknowledgement. In the park, Clare was very quiet at first and then burst out:

"We have to stop seeing each other!"

He stopped in his tracks, dismayed. "Why?"

"My father won't let us go out together any more. He says we can still be friends in a large group, but we can't be alone together and not even go out in a four with Harry and Julia."

"But why not?"

"Because you're mixed race. He says you've got black blood in you."

"But you already knew that I'm half Malayan. You were at the funeral."

"No, I didn't actually. Harry told Julia that Arianna is your half-sister, so I thought the Malayan lady was your stepmother. And that's what I told Dad. But that newspaper article made it clear that she was your mother. I suppose I should have realised; your skin has a slight golden tinge even in winter - it's one of the things I really like about you. The article also says your birth was illegitimate, but Dad did say he could have overlooked that. But he won't accept me going out with a boy who is half Asian."

Theo digested all this but said nothing. What could he say?

She went on: "I don't care two hoots that you're half Asian and illegitimate - none of that matters to me. But I couldn't persuade him to change his mind; he just got angry when I tried."

Her first statement gave him a glimmer of hope.

"Couldn't we continue to meet in secret?"

She shook her head. "He'd find out. This is such a small town and he knows everyone. And then there'd be hell to pay. I'm scared of him when he's really angry; he used to beat my brother with a belt when he crossed him."

Theo knew Clare's brother was now in his early twenties and had left home.

Sounding thoroughly miserable, she continued: "I don't want to end it. I will really, really miss you. And I'm so sorry to have to do this to you now, with all that you've gone through, losing your parents and everything."

Suddenly angry and wanting to hurt back, he retorted: "You think this compares with that? No-one can ever replace my mother and father, but girls like you are two a penny!"

With that, he turned on his heels and left. By the time he reached the bus stop he was already regretting his outburst. On the way home, he thought about what life would be like without her. He wasn't sure whether or not he was in love with her, he didn't know exactly what that was supposed to feel like. He only knew she had been a bright light in his life for the last six months or so, that he always looked forward to seeing her, found her extremely attractive and loved to kiss and cuddle her - even though it always left him wanting more. He also felt in tune with her mentally, they could talk to each other easily. Was that love? The thought of never being able to touch her again, smell her scent, feel her lips on his, left him feeling bleak and bereft. He should not have been nasty to her. It wasn't her fault, it was her bigoted father, and she was scared of him. He decided he would write her a letter of apology.

Arriving home, he changed out of his school uniform and headed down to the kitchen, where the children were always served milk and biscuits or cake on their return from school. Arianna was just finishing hers. Cook cut him a large slice of the remains of his birthday cake.

"Has it been better at school today?" she asked him. "Gossip dying down, is it?"

"A bit."

"It was better for me," Arianna said. "No-one made any nasty remarks."

"They want stringing up, those journalists," Cook declared. "You'd think they'd take more care with the stuff they write, more account of people's feelings, especially where there's children involved."

At supper, Mary asked Theo if he wanted to invite some friends over for tea on Saturday, by way of a belated birthday celebration.

"I know you had your presents and a cake yesterday, but your birthday's been a bit marred by the fall-out from those wretched newspaper articles and I don't think you had a very happy day at school. Would you like to ask Harry and Arthur and Clare? Cook can easily bake you another cake."

"Thanks, that would be nice. But I'll only have Harry and Arthur, not Clare."

George raised his eyebrows. "Has there been a falling out?"

"Not exactly."

"What happened this afternoon?" Arianna asked.

Theo sighed, he was going to have to tell them. "Her father's forbidden her to see me anymore. He now knows I'm mixed race and he doesn't want his daughter associating with a boy who's half Asian."

There was a brief silence, then Mary said brightly, "Well, never mind, dear, you're a bit young to be getting seriously involved with a girl anyway."

George agreed and added, "There're plenty of fish in the sea - or rather pretty girls at the grammar school! You can play the field a bit now."

Theo had no inclination to do that yet. "I think I'll give girls a miss for a while."

"Good idea!" George said heartily. "Concentrate on your studies. You've got your school certificate in the summer."

Later on, when he and Arianna were doing their homework, he asked her if she'd deliver a letter to Clare at school the next day.

"Why? What's the point in writing to her?"

"I was nasty to her at the end and it wasn't fair. I was just angry and wanted to hurt her back, but it wasn't her fault. I want to apologise so there's no bad feeling between us and we can still be on friendly terms when there's a group of us together. She's still Harry's girlfriend's best friend."

"Well, she's in the fifth year and I'm in the second, so our paths don't cross much."

"But you could go and find her at break time, couldn't you?"

"I suppose so. Provided you help me with my maths homework tonight."

"Deal!"

The next day, at afternoon break, Theo and Harry heard a group of boys from 5B talking loudly about the issues arising from the arson case in the corridor ahead of them. As they came up to them, most of the boys fell silent, but one of them, Bruce Smith, whom Theo had never liked much, carried on regardless. Looking directly at Theo, he said:

"Of course, if his father hadn't brought his black whore back to England, none of it would have happened."

All the anger Theo had suppressed, against the arsonists, the journalists and Clare's father, rose to the surface and added to the sudden fury he felt at this boy's cruel and ugly remark. A red mist formed in his brain and his fist shot out, connecting satisfyingly with Bruce's nose. Blood spurted from it. For a moment, Bruce looked surprised, then he lunged at Theo. The next minute they were on the floor, scrapping, and a crowd was forming around them. Then they heard the stentorian voice of one of the masters.

"Stop this at once!" he thundered. "Smith, Bradshaw, get up now!"

"Bradshaw started it, sir, " one of the 5B boys said.

"Only because Smith made a nasty remark about Bradshaw's dead mother, sir," Harry countered.

"Smith, go and get yourself cleaned up and then report to the Headmaster's office. Bradshaw, you come with me to the Head, now."

The Headmaster gave Theo a long, measured look and told him that fighting was always punished by caning, no matter what extenuating circumstances there were.

"I understand that you were provoked by a particularly unpleasant slur against your late mother, but part of growing up is to learn to deal with such things in a civilised, adult way. You're an intelligent, articulate boy, you could have responded with a verbal put-down."

Theo couldn't help thinking that supposedly civilised adults still got themselves and their countries into wars. Out loud, he said,

"I just couldn't think of anything right then, sir. Everything that's happened lately, it all merged in my head and I just reacted instinctively."

The Head sighed. "I'm aware of all that you've been through these last few months, Bradshaw, but I can't condone fighting under any circumstances and I can't make an exception to the rules. I'm going to have to cane you and I'll also be giving you a letter to take home to your guardian - your uncle, isn't it? Be sure you give it to him, I will check. Now, bend over and lower your trousers."

As he arrived back at the manor, George was also just coming indoors. Theo handed him the letter.

"From the headmaster."

"What's it about? What have you been up to?"

"I got into a fight and I've been caned."

"Is that so? Well come into my study while I read it. You'd better sit in the soft chair!"

When he had read the letter, George looked steadily at Theo, who tried to read his expression. Was he going to be angry or not?

"What exactly did this boy say?"

"Doesn't it say in the letter?"

"Not in so many words, no."

Theo repeated the exact words Bruce had used.

"Well, I daresay at your age and in your circumstances, I might well have lashed out with a fist. Did you cause injury?"

"Yes, his nose bled."

"Well, I expect you're pleased about that! But you'd better give this boy a wide berth from now on and for God's sake don't let yourself react to remarks like that again. Persistent fighting could get you suspended or even expelled and you don't want that, do you?"

"No."

"React with words, not your fist, or just walk on by and ignore the comment. Remember, violence rarely resolves anything."

~***~

Chapter Nine

Arianna's letter was printed in the paper on the following Sunday. George read it out at the breakfast table and he and Mary congratulated her on a well-written letter.

A week or so later, a letter arrived from Alya's parents in Malaya. Letters took about six weeks each way, so they had not expected a reply any sooner. There was a brief formal reply to George, which Theo translated for him, and a much longer one addressed to the children. After expressing their shock and grief, they implored their grandchildren not to lose contact with them, nor forget the Malayan part of their heritage.

' You are living in a big, posh house now and living the life of the English upper class, but your family here still love you and you are all we have left of our daughter. We hope that we will see you again one day. Please speak Malay amongst yourselves, so you do not forget your mother's language, and if any of you ever consider returning to Malaya when you are grown up, you will always have a home with us.'

"I might even take them up on that," Arianna commented. "When I'm twenty-one."

"Really?" Theo said, surprised.

"Yes, why not? I might fit in better there, have more chance of finding a husband - if I decide I want one, of course! I might prefer to have a career."

"You could pick a career which could take you back to Malaya; they need nurses and teachers."

"Good idea. And you could do what Papa did and join the Malayan civil service."

"Perhaps. It's a possibility."

"We should speak Malay more amongst ourselves. It has the added advantage that no-one else understands it, so we can use it when we don't want anyone else to know what we're saying!"

Enid, who had been listening to their exchange, said, " Well, I don't want to go back to Malaya and I don't want you two to go either. I would really miss you."

"Cheer up," Theo said. "It's not going to happen for years and years - if at all."

"Yes, and you'll be married to some rich man by then," Arianna added.

Theo was missing Clare a great deal and thought she was probably feeling the same. They often saw each other from afar at the end of the school day and their eyes met with expressions of longing and yearning. Now that they were unable to be together, their desire for one another was intensified.

One evening at the end of November, Arianna brought home a letter, which she handed to Theo.

"For you, from Clare."

He opened it eagerly. She wrote how much she was missing him and said she'd had second thoughts about meeting in secret.

'Perhaps it could work, if we are very careful and aren't seen together in this town. Maybe we could take buses or bike to nearby towns and villages where no-one knows us? We would have to keep it quiet from most people, just tell Julia and Harry so they can give us alibis and Arianna so she can pass messages between us. Can you meet me tomorrow after school, in that wooded area behind the cricket pavilion in the park? No-one goes there this time of year. I'll be there waiting for you anyway and I hope you can come. Then we can talk about it.'

Arianna was hovering.

"What does it say?"

He told her the gist of it. "It's a pity I already told Uncle George and Aunt Mary that it's over and why. They'd never believe me if I said her father had changed his mind, so I shall have to keep it from them or they might tell him. And don't tell Enid; she might just let something slip."

When he rounded the corner of the cricket pavilion and saw her standing there amongst the trees, his heart gave a lurch. As he came up to her he couldn't resist reaching out and taking her in his arms. She snuggled against him and they held onto each other tightly.

"I've sooooo missed you," she said.

"Me too. Let's do it, let's meet in secret."

The winter weather did not lend itself too well to secret meetings between two teenagers with only limited pocket money. A couple of times a week they met after school behind the pavilion, but both had to head home after about half an hour or questions would be asked. Their thick winter clothes precluded much intimacy, but they kissed and hugged and pressed their bodies tightly against each other. On Saturday afternoons, they usually managed a few hours together in a town a few miles away. They found a cheap and cheerful cafe where they could sit in the warm, nursing one cup of tea each, holding hands and touching each other furtively under the table. They would find a spot in a far corner where they could have some privacy. Theo was by now sure that he was in love with her and told her so.

"I love you too," she responded, smiling in delight that he felt the same.

What had previously been a gentle, tender, tentative coming together of two young people embarking on their first relationship, hesitantly exploring their sexuality, now became much more intense, urgent and passionate. The forbidden nature of their love increased their desire. They likened themselves to famous fictional romantic couples; they were Romeo and Juliet or Heathcliff and Cathy.

"Or Anna Karenina and Count Vronsky!" said Clare, who was in the middle of reading Tolstoy's book.

" I sincerely hope that you don't follow in Anna's footsteps," Theo said drily.

"What do you mean?"

"You haven't read to the end of the book yet, have you?!"

They made plans for the spring and summer when the weather would be warmer and they could take picnics out into the countryside and have whole Saturdays together. Neither looked ahead to the end of their time at school and how they would maintain their relationship beyond that. That was too far ahead to worry about.

Meanwhile, Christmas was looming on the horizon. Enid, who was quite artistic, was busy making her Christmas cards. Arianna and Theo, who were not, reluctantly also made theirs as it was less of a drain on their pocket money than buying them. Enid's put theirs to shame and for once she could lord it over her older siblings. George and Mary, keenly aware that the first Christmas without their parents would be difficult for them, made an effort to make everything as festive as possible. Enid still just about believed in Santa Claus and George asked her for her list of requests so that he could "post it to him." He asked the other two if they wanted anything in particular; Theo asked for money so that he could buy what he wanted and Arianna, who was becoming fashion conscious, asked for a new dress. Mary said they would go shopping before Christmas but the dress would then be wrapped and put under the tree. The weekend before Christmas, they all went into town and saw a pantomime, which made the children laugh more than they had for a long time.

The schools broke up the day before Christmas Eve and they were then on holiday until just after the New Year. Theo and Clare would have to be apart for both the Christmas weekend and the following one, but arranged to meet on the Wednesday in between. Charlie arrived on Christmas Eve, with a large bag of presents which he added to the pile already under the tree. That evening, they all attended a carol service in the local church and returned there for the service on Christmas day morning. On their return home, George distributed gifts and the customary bonuses to the staff before they started preparing the lunch. Once that was served, they had their own downstairs. The family pulled crackers, wore the silly hats which came out of them and read out the jokes. Charlie also kept them entertained with jokes and anecdotes of his own. Nevertheless, underneath all the jollity, there was an undercurrent of sadness; even when they were excitedly opening their presents, their memories returned to last year in the cottage with their parents.

On the day after Boxing Day, when Charlie had gone back to London, George dropped a bombshell on Enid.

"I've left this until after Christmas to tell you, Enid, as you might be a little upset initially. You won't be returning to the village school next week, you're going to a private girls' school a few miles away. There's no direct bus, so Dave will drive you there each morning and collect you at the end of the day. Your school uniform has been ordered and is now ready to be tried on, and your aunt will take you to the shop tomorrow, so that any adjustments needed can be made in time. It's a very nice school, there's a brochure here you can take a look at."

He produced a glossy brochure from underneath the newspapers on the coffee table. His words were met with a short silence, then Enid asked, panic in her voice,

"Why? Why do I have to go there? Why can't I stay at the village school where all my friends are? I won't know anyone at that school!"

"Because it's not really appropriate for you to continue to attend the village school for another eighteen months, now that you are living here, at the manor. Most of the children of my estate workers go there."

"But what about Theo and Arianna? Do they have to change schools too? Some of the children from the village go there. Arthur goes to Theo's school."

"Arthur is the son of my estate manager, a very senior member of staff, so that's entirely different. Theo and Arianna will stay where they are; they are doing well at the grammar schools. Anyway, I can't afford to send all three of you to private schools and you are the one who will benefit most."

Theo and Arianna breathed silent sighs of relief.

George continued, "You'd have been changing schools anyway in a year and a half's time. This just brings it forward. You won't have to change again; this school takes pupils from age eight to eighteen."

"But then I'd have been going with some of the others in my class, and Arianna is there. I wouldn't have been on my own."

"You're assuming you would have passed the exam for the grammar school, but I'm afraid your headmaster thinks it unlikely. You're not as academically inclined as your brother and sister. Nothing wrong with that, everyone's different, and your talents lie elsewhere. You are very good at drawing and crafts, needlework and so on. This new school will nurture those talents at the same time as giving you a good broad education. You can still see your friends in the village at weekends, but you'll soon make new friends. You're a sociable little girl, you won't find it difficult."

Enid just looked at him, eyes brimming, face a picture of misery.

"Here, take a look at the brochure, you can see what a lovely place it is."

Enid took it from him, gave it a cursory glance, then hurled it across the room. It made brief contact with a china ornament, which wobbled precariously but luckily did not fall. There was a stunned silence, during which Theo and Arianna held their breath, and then Mary said angrily,

"Go and pick that up, right now!

Enid collected the brochure from where it had fallen and put it back on the table.

"If you behave like a toddler having a tantrum again, you'll get your bottom spanked. And if you'd broken that ornament, you would be being spanked right now! Now, go to your room and don't come back until you're in a more reasonable frame of mind!"

She burst into tears and ran out of the room.

George sighed and handed the brochure to Theo.

"Can you two have a look at this and then, when she's calmed down, try to convince her that it's a nice school where she'll be happy once she's settled in? She'll listen to you. It's in her own best interests to start there with a more positive attitude."

Theo nodded. He could see the sense in that. He took the brochure and he and Arianna followed their sister upstairs.

"Fancy Enid throwing that thing!" Arianna commented on their way up. "It's not like her."

"No, rather more your style than hers!"

She aimed a swipe at him, which he dodged.

They found Enid in her room, sitting on the bed with her head in her hands, sobbing as if her heart would break. They sat either side of her and each put an arm around her.

"Don't take on so, *sayang*," Theo said. "It's really not the end of the world."

His use of the Malay endearment reminded her forcibly of her mother and she just cried harder.

"You'll soon settle in," Arianna said. "I was terrified when I started at the grammar, but it was fine and I soon made friends."

"Yes, and you made friends straight away when you started at the village school," Theo pointed out. "It was Ari who had a problem, not you."

Arianna leafed through the brochure. "It does look really nice; look, there's even a swimming pool!" She held the brochure out in front of her sister.

Eventually Enid calmed down, dried her eyes and blew her nose. Theo and Arianna turned the pages of the brochure, holding it between them and in front of Enid, so that she couldn't help but see it.

"Everything looks new and smart, " Theo observed. "Different from the rotten old desks we have at the boys' grammar!"

"They can afford to have new things, when they're charging fees. I wonder how much it's costing Uncle George? There're no prices in here. You know, you're privileged, Enid. We aren't going to go to posh private schools!"

"You can go instead of me then," she retorted.

"Uncle George wouldn't allow that, would he? You're the chosen one!"

"Why didn't either of you say anything? You could have taken my side down there!"

"What would have been the point?" Theo asked. "They wouldn't have taken any notice of us. They're in charge and what they say goes."

"Anyway, I bet you like this school once you're settled in, you'll see," Arianna added.

On Monday morning she cut a forlorn figure, despite her smart green uniform, as she waited in the hall for Dave to bring the car round, along with Aunt Mary who was taking her in on the first day. As she and Theo left to get their bus, Arianna gave her sister a quick hug.

"You'll be fine, don't worry."

Theo pecked her on the cheek. "Good luck!"

She was full of trepidation as Mary marched her down what seemed like endless corridors to the Headmistress' office. However, as everyone had predicted, her first day at the new school turned out not to be so awful after all. She found the teachers welcoming and the other girls friendly and she returned home feeling much more relaxed.

"Told you so!" Arianna said.

One Saturday at the end of February, Clare returned home at about five o'clock, after an afternoon with Theo. She was met in the hallway by her father, who had an ominous look on his face.

"Where have you been?" he asked sternly.

"At Julia's, like I told you."

The ringing blow to the side of her face took her unawares and she staggered back.

"Liar! I've seen Julia, out shopping with her mother. Now, where have you really been?"

He got it all out of her eventually, interspersed with a few more slaps.

"We love each other, Dad," she sobbed. "Please let us stay together."

"Over my dead body! He's half Asian and I'm not having that, I told you before. Nothing good ever came of a mixed race relationship. And you're too young to get serious with anyone. We should never have allowed you to go out alone with a boy, not at your age. Love! You don't know the meaning of the word! From now on, you stay home Saturdays and you come straight home from school every night. Is that clear?"

She nodded miserably. Her face was smarting from his blows and she could feel her eye swelling up.

"Right. I'm going up to Pucklington Manor, right now, to make sure that boy stays away from you. I shall tell his uncle what's been going on behind my back and make it clear I won't stand for it. And your mother can take you to the doctor next week, make sure you're still a virgin and not expecting."

"There's no need for that," she protested. " We never went that far."

Clare wasn't entirely sure exactly how virginity was lost and babies conceived, but she knew it involved a much more momentous act than they had ever indulged in.

"You'd better not have!"

Clare had no way of warning Theo of the imminent arrival of her irate father as they were not on the telephone and her mother refused to allow her out to use a phone box. He arrived at the manor just as the family were about to be served their evening meal. Mr Hughes put his head round the dining room door and announced that there was a Mr. Harris at the door, demanding to see both Sir George and Theo. Theo paled. Clare's father! He must have found out. He nervously followed George out to the hall.

"Yes? What can we do for you?" George asked.

"You can keep that boy away from my daughter!"

"And your daughter is..?"

"Clare. You've met her, I know she came here once to lunch. That was before I knew the truth about him, who his mother was. After that, I told her she couldn't see him anymore, but they've carried on meeting behind my back."

"Is this true?" George demanded of Theo.

He nodded and said defiantly. "We love each other, it's not fair to keep us apart."

George rolled his eyes in exasperation. To Mr Harris he said, "I had no idea, but now that I do know I'll see that he keeps away from her. I don't agree with your reason for not wanting her to associate with him, but I accept your right as a father to decide."

But Clare's father hadn't quite finished.

"We're taking her to the doctors' next week, to make sure she's still intact. If she isn't, you won't have heard the last of this."

For a moment, Theo didn't realise what he meant, then it dawned on him.

"Of course she's still a virgin, we both are! There's no need to put her through that."

"That's for me to decide. Now, you stay away from her from now on!"

"As I've already said, I'll make sure that he does," George said coldly. "Now, if you've finished, we'd like to have our evening meal."

George refused to discuss the matter until they had finished eating, then told Theo to come with him to his study.

"What the hell did you think you were playing at?" he said furiously.

"We love each other. We were miserable apart, so we started meeting again."

"Just like that, totally disregarding her father's wishes?"

"He's being unreasonable, he's just a nasty bigot!"

"That's not for you to judge. He's her father and has control over her until she's adult. If he objects to you being mixed race, then that's something you just have to accept. I'm afraid that's the legacy your parents bestowed on you and you'll have to learn to live with it. And I certainly hope she is still a virgin, or there'll be hell to pay!"

"Of course she is! I wouldn't be so stupid as to risk getting her pregnant. Besides, we never had the opportunity and she wouldn't have let me anyway!"

"Right, well, make sure you stay well away from her from now on. And to make that easier for you, you're grounded for the rest of this term. You come straight home after school and you spend the weekends here on the estate. You've got Arthur for company and I don't mind your mate Harry coming over, but no girls! Is that understood?"

Theo nodded miserably. "If I can't see her, then I don't care what I do, where I spend my spare time."

George softened his tone slightly. "You think you're in love, Theo, but you're only sixteen. You don't really know what love is. You're probably confusing it with physical attraction. You get hard when you're with her and you think that's love. It's not, it's just lust!"

Theo flushed, embarrassed. "It's not just that, that's only part of it. We're in tune with each other, we care for each other, we're soul-mates!"

George shook his head and gave up. "Well, you'll have to forget about her now, like it or not. If that man re-appears on my doorstep, I won't be letting you off so lightly!"

He headed for the door and opened it to see Arianna scurrying off down the corridor.

"Were you listening at the door?" he called after her, in a stern tone.

She turned, looking guilty.

"Did you know about this secret liaison?"

"No, she didn't," Theo said quickly, not wanting to get her into trouble.

"Yes, I did!" Arianna said defiantly. " I passed messages between them. Her father's a horrible man, keeping them apart just because Theo's half Malayan!"

"Well, you're not to pass on any more messages, is that clear?"

"Yes."

"Now, get out of my sight, the pair of you!"

Recounting the whole episode to Mary later, George commented,

"It's a pity those grammar schools are right next door to each other. It's asking for trouble! When Jim and I were at school - and Bertie and Charlie too - there were no girls within miles, so there was no temptation."

"We'll have to keep an eye on Arianna in a couple of years' time," Mary observed. "Especially as she's showing signs of becoming a real beauty. She gets her colouring from Alya but her features are classically English. In fact she reminds me a bit of that lady in the painting in the corridor outside our room."

"Great-aunt Agnes? Now she was reputed to be a notorious society beauty who took many lovers!'"

"At least we've now got Enid safely away from boys, until we're ready to introduce her to some suitable young men."

George agreed. However, they were both overlooking a potential future candidate for Enid's affections who was quite close to home.

On Monday, after school, Arianna reported to Theo that Clare was sporting a black eye.

"Her father hit her."

"So he's a vicious bully as well as a bigot!" Theo felt impotent anger at being unable to protect the girl he loved.

"She says to tell you goodbye, but that she loves you and she'll never forget you."

"Can you tell her the same back?"

"I already did!"

About a month later, just after the Easter break and a week before her thirteenth birthday, it was Arianna's turn to experience a traumatic event. She went to the toilet in her afternoon break at school and was horrified to find her underwear soaked in blood. Where had it come from? She couldn't see any wounds on her skin. What was the matter with her? Was she going to bleed to death? Not knowing whether it had stopped or not, she stuffed toilet paper into her knickers in an attempt to absorb the flow. The paper was quite hard and it felt very uncomfortable. Then she remembered she had gymnastics next lesson and would have to get changed in front of all the other girls. She panicked. What was she going to do? She went to the sink to wash her hands. She'd got some of the blood on her hands and the water ran red. Two sixth form girls, talking by the sinks, noticed.

"You're bleeding," one said. "Have you hurt your hand?"

"No, it's fine."

"There's blood on your leg, too," the other girl commented.

Arianna looked down. It was true; she hadn't noticed that. And the top of her white sock also had a bloodstain on it.

"You've got the curse, haven't you?" one of the girls said, sympathetically.

Arianna just looked at her, bewildered.

"Is it your first time? It was a shock to me too, even though my mother warned me."

"I've got gym next lesson," Arianna burst out. "What am I going to do?"

"Go and see the nurse. She'll sort you out and she'll get you excused."

Arianna did as the girl suggested. The nurse was quite brisk and matter of fact about it.

"Nothing to worry about, you're not dying! I suppose your mother didn't warn you? It'll happen every month from now on and last a few days. It's a nuisance but it's something we ladies just have to put up with."

She produced a bulky pad in some sort of cotton material with tapes either end of it.

"I don't have a belt here to lend you, but I expect your mother will have one. Meanwhile you'll have to use these safety pins to secure it. Pop into the toilet now and put it on. Then I suggest you go straight home. I'll let your teacher know."

Arianna did as she was bid. It felt strange and bulky. When she came out, the nurse said,

"All fixed? Good. Off you go home now, see your mother."

Arianna found her voice. "I don't have a mother any more, she's dead!"

"Oh, I'm sorry, dear, I didn't know."

Arianna remembered that this nurse was new last term.

"Who looks after you then, is it just your father?"

"He's dead too. I live with my uncle and aunt."

"Oh, well, your auntie will sort you out and explain everything."

Arianna could not imagine approaching Aunt Mary about such a matter. She would go and see Daisy instead, she decided on the way home. She remembered that her mother had said they would have 'a little talk soon' a few weeks before she had died. Was that about this? Why did women have to go through this every month? What was the point of it? She now also had a dull ache low down in her abdomen, adding to her discomfort.

Arriving at the manor, she entered by the kitchen entrance. Cook and Millie were there.

"Where's Daisy?" she asked.

"It's her half day off," Cook replied. "She's gone to see her family so she won't be back until mid evening. Why are you home so early?"

"The nurse sent me home."

"Are you feeling ill?" Cook asked, concern in her voice.

Suddenly, it was all overwhelming. She blurted it all out in one long sentence.

"I'm bleeding down below, my underwear's all blood stained and she says it's going to happen every month and she gave me this horrible pad thing to wear and she said my mother would sort everything out, but she's dead, and oh, I want Mama!" She burst into tears.

"Oh dear, oh dear!" Cook exclaimed. Wiping her hands on her apron, she folded Arianna into her arms. "There, there, don't take on so, dearie. It's perfectly natural, happens to all of us. You get used to dealing with it."

Mrs Hughes appeared and took in the scene.

"What's going on? Arianna, what's the matter?"

"She's started with the curse," Millie said.

"Oh, right. Yes, of course, she's nearly thirteen, isn't she?   We should have thought to warn her, then it wouldn't have been a shock."

"It's not up to us, is it? " Cook said. "That's her ladyship's job."

When Arianna had stopped crying, she repeated her tale of woe to Mrs. Hughes.

"Right then, let's get you properly sorted out."

She left the room and returned with a pile of towelling pads and a contraption which looked a bit like a suspender belt.

"These are washable pads. They were Lady Mary's but she doesn't need them anymore, she's gone through the change."

"What's the change?"

"When a woman stops bleeding every month. Happens when you're about fifty."

Fifty! She was going to have to put up with this until then!

Mrs Hughes went on, "You can get disposable ones now which will be easier for you at school. I'll ask Lady Mary if she'll authorise my buying you some."

She showed Arianna how to attach the pads to the belt and also gave her a brown paper bag.

"You can take a clean one to school in this and then bring the used one back in it for laundering. I suggest that you remember today's date and a few days before the month is up, start taking one to school, so you're prepared. Now, off you go upstairs and wash and change, and bring your bloodstained laundry down for us to soak."

When she returned downstairs, a glass of milk and a large slice of fruitcake were waiting for her. As she ate, she asked Mrs Hughes why women had to bleed every month.

"It's got to do with making babies. Your body sort of prepares itself for the arrival of a baby inside you and when one doesn't materialise, you bleed. I don't know the exact biology of it. I daresay you might learn something about that at school later on."

Arianna digested this. "But how would a baby get inside?"

"Well, that's something it's not my place to tell you about and you don't really need to know until you're older and thinking about getting married."

Enid appeared in the kitchen.

"You're home early," she said.

"She was feeling a bit under the weather," Mrs Hughes said, "so the nurse sent her home."

"Are you better now?"

Arianna nodded. She wouldn't tell her little sister about this, not yet. She'd make sure she knew about it in good time before it happened to her, but meanwhile it was kinder to leave her in blissful ignorance.

After she went back up to her room, she had a visit from her aunt.

"I'm so sorry, dear. I should have talked to you about this earlier, told you what to expect. It was very remiss of me."

"It's all right."

"No, it isn't. You were frightened and upset and that could have been prevented. Anyway, I've told Mrs Hughes she can buy you disposable pads, so she'll get you some tomorrow and keep you supplied every month."

"Thanks." Then she dared to ask, "Aunt Mary, how are babies made?"

"You don't need to know about that yet. Time enough when you're engaged to be married. I promise I'll tell you before your wedding night."

Arianna had to be content with that, for now.

~***~

Chapter Ten

September 1934

Theo was busy packing to go to university. He had passed his higher school certificate with flying colours and had won a scholarship to Keble college at Oxford, to read history. At first, he had thought he might not be able to go, as his scholarship was only for tuition, not living costs, his guardian's wealth being taken into account, and students at Oxford were not allowed to have jobs while there. He had asked George if he could have a loan from his trust fund, but to his delight George had offered to pay him a term-time allowance instead.

"I can offset it against tax, so it won't cost me the full amount," he said in response to Theo's heartfelt thanks, "and I'll be saving the cost of your food here! Besides, it's my fault that you're not getting the full scholarship; had you been assessed on Jim's income, you probably would have."

Daisy had offered to help him with his packing, but he had declined, knowing how busy she was since Ivy had left to get married. Ivy had not been replaced by another live-in maid but only by a part-time cleaning lady from the village, Daisy taking on the rest of her duties in return for an increase in wages. On Daisy's days off, it was now Arianna and Enid's job to lay the table for meals and clear away afterwards, for which they had both received a small increase in pocket money.

Theo was now the proud owner of a car, which had been a combined eighteenth birthday and Christmas present from George and Mary. It was several years old, but Dave had brought it up to scratch and he had also given Theo driving lessons. By late January, he had been pronounced capable of driving alone and, after a few solo spins to gain confidence, he had taken his sisters for a day out.

He found having a car scored him points with the girls and Harry had also benefited as the car seated four people.

Harry and Julia had gone their separate ways shortly after the demise of Theo and Clare's relationship, Harry having become tired of her rationing of physical contact.

"I obviously don't expect her to allow me to go all the way," he said to Theo, "and anyway I'd be too scared of getting her pregnant, but it's frustrating not getting any further than a few kisses."

Theo had dated a few girls since Clare but none had lasted long. He saw her occasionally from a distance and, although it no longer hurt, he still had a small soft spot for her.

Harry had now gone off to teacher training college in Bristol and they had said their goodbyes a few days before he left, promising to write to each other.

Over the last couple of years, Theo and his sisters had become used to living at the manor and being without their parents and it now seemed the norm. Time had worked its healing process. Long periods went by without them thinking of their parents and their former home, but every now and then there would be a sudden, bittersweet reminder of their loss. They all sometimes had dreams in which one or both of their parents were still alive. Recounting one such dream to her siblings, Enid said sadly,

"It seemed so real. I could actually feel her when she hugged me."

Their cottage had not been rebuilt and they all avoided going past the sad ruin with its boarded up windows and doors.

Now that he was about to leave home for the first time, Theo reflected that they would all have eventually grown up and left in the normal course of events and would only have seen their parents at intervals. And Jim and Alya would gradually have aged and eventually died. Nothing stayed the same forever. Jim would probably have been the first to die and Alya would have been left alone in a country which was not hers and which did not exactly welcome her. He wondered idly if she would then have returned to Malaya. Probably not, as she would not have wanted to be so far away from her children and, possibly also by then, grandchildren.

Arianna came in and sprawled on Theo's bed.

"I wish you weren't going," she said, "I'm really going to miss you. Who am I going to argue with?"

"Enid?"

"You know Enid's no good at arguing. She just either agrees with you or walks away."

"Perhaps she has the right idea, being less confrontational."

"Meaning I'm too confrontational, I suppose."

"You said it!"

"Well, I think you have to stand up for what you think and what you feel is right."

"Up to a point, yes," Theo conceded.

She changed the subject. "And how am I going to go out and have fun and meet boys, without you to escort me there and back and supposedly chaperone me in between? They won't let me go into town on my own in the evenings. It's not fair, you had a lot more freedom than me when you were my age!"

"Benefits of being a boy."

"It doesn't make sense."

"Yes, it does. Girls have to be more careful or some boys might take advantage. They are just protecting you, Ari."

And not without reason, he thought, recalling some of the comments he'd overheard from some of his fellow pupils. Arianna had blossomed into a stunning, sultry beauty who had half the sixth form boys lusting after her. Theo had heard some remarks which were less than respectful, to put it mildly, and he'd had to have words with those making them and warn them off. He'd let it be known that anyone harassing his sister would have him to deal with, but now he would not be around for half the year and many of those he'd warned had also now left school and been replaced by the next sixth form intake.

Out loud, he said, "Never mind, Oxford terms are much shorter than your school terms and I'll be home over a month at Christmas and Easter and three months in the summer. We'll go into town again some evenings then, and you can go off with your friends and meet me when it's time to go home, like we did before, so long as you still promise not to go off alone with any boys."

Arianna smiled to herself. Theo didn't know it but she had gone off alone with a boy on a few occasions. Nothing untoward had happened, they had only kissed and she didn't understand what all the fuss was about, but it was better to keep it quiet.

That evening after supper, when they were all relaxing in the drawing room, George said thoughtfully, "You know, Theo, it would be wise not to mention that you are half Asian to people at Oxford. That sort of thing does not always go down too well with everyone and it would be best to play safe. There's no need for anyone to know."

Before Theo could respond, Arianna said, "You mean he should deny his heritage and also deny our lovely mother!"

"He wouldn't be denying anything, no-one is actually going to ask him. He'd just not be volunteering the information."

"And when he's asked about his family?"

"He can still talk about them at length if he wants to, just not mention that his mother was a native Malayan."

"If he talks about Mama without mentioning that, then he'd be leaving out a large part of who she was, he'd be describing another person. And, he'd be kowtowing to all those people, like those arsonists and that awful Mr Harris and the journalist who wrote that article, who think that Asian people are somehow inferior to white British people."

"You can't lump the journalist and Mr Harris in with the arsonists," George protested, "they are not criminals. Mr Harris just didn't want his daughter to be in a mixed race relationship. An awful lot of people, from all sectors of society, would agree with that, like it or not. My own mother nearly had an apoplectic fit when your father came home and told her he'd married your mother, fathered you and taken on Theo. If she'd still been mistress here, she'd have thrown him out. She never came to terms with it."

"What did you think about it, when Papa told you?" Enid asked.

"I accepted the situation and I wasn't going to disown my brother over it, but I thought it an unwise move on his part."

"Do you still?" Theo asked.

There was a pause, then George said slowly, "I can no longer judge it objectively, now that I know you all. You are part of my family and I've grown extremely fond of you all."

Arianna snorted. "That's a real politician's answer, Uncle George."

"Maybe, but it's the only answer you're going to get."

Theo said slowly, "I agree with Ari that I ought not to have to keep it quiet and it's society's attitudes which need to change, but they won't change overnight, if ever, and one man, or one woman, can't change them. I want to fit in at Oxford, so I won't be shouting my mixed race status from the rooftops, but if I am asked searching questions I won't tell a bare-faced lie. And if I make some really close friends, I may eventually tell them."

"That sounds like a reasonable compromise," Mary commented. "And bear in mind, Theo, that your mother would want you to be happy and I'm sure she would understand. However, I believe there are quite a few women at Oxford nowadays and if you should meet a girl whom you wish to marry, you must tell her. Any children you might have may possibly be darker skinned than you are; these things often skip a generation."

Arianna laughed. "You won't be able to pretend to be pure white then, Theo, will you?!"

He left on the Saturday morning before term was due to start. His car loaded up with a small trunk on the back seat and suitcases in the boot, he took his leave of his family and also the staff, who were all gathered on the drive to see him off. His sisters both hugged him tightly.

"Write often," Enid entreated. "We want to hear all about it."

"Yes, and if you do have the odd Sunday without much on, you'll be welcome back here for Sunday lunch," Mary said. "Just let us know."

He pecked her on the cheek, shook George's hand heartily, then got into the driving seat. In his rear mirror, he could see them all waving until he had turned the bend in the road.

It all seemed very strange and bewildering at first. It took him a few days to find his way around everywhere and even longer to get used to the terminology. Even the terms had special names; he was now in the Michaelmas term, which would be followed by Hilary and Trinity. He discovered that a *battel* was your bill for food and rent each term, a blue was a sports award, the library was called the Bodleian, a senior member of college was a Fellow, Formal Hall was a college dinner, and the JCR was the junior common room. He got into the habit of referring to the grassy areas between the college buildings as the quads and the college gatekeeper as the porter. He also soon realised that the porter was both security guard and counsellor and that it was a good idea to cultivate his goodwill. He was slightly surprised to find that curfews were in place and he would not have quite the unrestricted freedom he had vaguely anticipated. He was also required to wear a dark suit and tie for all lectures and tutorials. Most of the tutorials took place in college, but the lectures were for everyone at the university studying the same subject.

Keble college had a large intake from grammar schools and Theo soon made some like-minded friends. The rooms there were arranged along corridors, rather than around staircases as was the case in most of the other colleges. His study-bedroom was spacious and well appointed, with a bathroom just down the corridor. Board included three meals a day in the college dining room and a laundry service. Students congregated in the common room and the bar in the evenings and there were also numerous clubs and societies you could join. Theo signed up initially for the debating society, the history club, a political discussion group and the music society. He then added membership of the dancing club, after he had been advised that it was a good place to meet girls. In the spring, he would later join the cricket club and also the rowing club, as a novice.

There were only four female colleges, so men still greatly outnumbered women. Demand for their company at dances and other social events was high. There were some women at Theo's lectures, but they tended to all sit together. Some of the male undergraduates regarded these women as blue-stockings and preferred to seek the companionship of the sisters and friends of students whose homes were in or near Oxford.

Theo had to attend several lectures each week as well as regular tutorials and had to complete weekly or twice-weekly essays, for

114

which research at the library was required. There were also some seminars and study circles. However, he still had some spare time and no shortage of social events to fill it. In fact, he soon found he had to be quite disciplined in order to get the work done on time and not get sidetracked.

There were quite a few Indian students, particularly at Brasenose college, and some were reading history. Theo became friendly with one called Rajeev Singh. This resulted in raised eyebrows from some of his fellow Englishmen, as the English and Indian communities did not normally mix, but Theo pointed out that he had spent the first twelve years of his life in Malaya, and he had had Indian friends there. There was also just starting to be a significant intake of Jewish students from Germany, whose families had fled the oppression of Hitler's regime.

Keble had a strong affiliation to the Anglican church and, to Theo's dismay, undergraduates were expected to attend the college chapel regularly. Many of them turned up for Sunday Matins nursing hangovers. In his first few weeks, Theo imbibed more alcohol than he ever had in his life before. Apart from regular socialising in the bar and the local alehouses, some of the japes and pranks carried out, particularly against the freshmen, involved drinking copious amounts of some form of alcohol by way of a forfeit. After being the victim of one such incident, Theo had to throw up in the gutter on his way back to college. After a while, he realised that he would have to limit his drinking, not only because he was tired of feeling ill the next day, but also because he would otherwise use up his allowance before the end of term. He then did what he should have done in the beginning and divided up the remains of his allowance by the number of weeks left in term and only allowed himself to spend that sum.

One Saturday evening towards the end of October, Theo and several of his Keble friends went on a trip to London with a number of second and third year students. They were taken to various clubs and bars and then ended up at what they were told was a private club but later realised must have been a brothel. Theo lost his virginity to a young, quite pretty girl, although, as he was fairly drunk by then, his memory of some of the details was rather vague. In the cold light

115

of the next morning, he wondered why she had to earn her living that way and felt rather sad for her.

Since the start of term, he had had his eye on a pretty brunette who attended the history lectures, but had not yet got beyond smiling at her from a distance. His chance to get into conversation with her came one day when she tripped on her way out of the lecture room and dropped the pile of books and papers she was holding. Providentially, Theo was just behind her and he hastened to gather them up.

"Thanks very much," she said, as he carefully placed the pile back in her arms.

He introduced himself. "I'm Theo."

"Susan."

"Which college are you in?"

"Somerville. And you?"

"Keble."

The conversation might have ended there, as she started to turn away from him and made to head off. He hastily took the plunge.

"Would you like to go for a drink sometime?"

To his delight, she agreed.

He found out that she came from the Midlands and her father was a wealthy industrialist.

"He doesn't really think that women need a university degree, but he's prepared to indulge me," she told Theo. "I just wanted to spread my wings a bit, have a career for a while and see more of life before I settle down and get married."

She told him that she was an only child and her mother had died when she was twelve.

"My mother's dead too, and my father as well. But I have two sisters, both younger than me. We live with our aunt and uncle now."

"How old were you all when your parents died?"

"I was fifteen, my sisters twelve and nine."

"Did they die together?"

"Yes."

"Was it an accident?"

"It was a fire. A house fire. Our home was burnt down by arsonists."

"That's terrible!" she exclaimed and put a sympathetic hand on his.

The evening sped by for Theo, until at about twenty to ten she looked at her watch and said she'd have to be getting back to college, as their curfew was 10pm.

"That's early! Our gate closes at midnight."

"I know. You chaps have much more freedom than we do."

He walked her back to Somerville and dared to kiss her on the cheek. She kissed him back.

"Would you like to go to the cinema next week?" he asked. " I believe there's a film on starring Cary Grant."

"Oh, I like him! Yes please! But we'll have to go to the early showing because of this stupid curfew."

They continued to see each other at regular intervals. Neither of them were allowed to entertain the opposite sex in their rooms, so all their meetings were in public places and they had to grab the opportunity to kiss and caress each other whenever they could have a degree of privacy, usually on the way back to her college, under cover of darkness, or in Theo's car on Sunday afternoons when they took a spin outside the city. Her eager responses to his overtures gave him hope that she returned his feelings in equal measure. She was in the Somerville dancing club and, when there was a dance involving both colleges, they danced together almost exclusively, which earned Theo some ribbing afterwards from his friends.

There was just one jarring note, when she came across him talking to Rajeev Singh outside the lecture hall. After Rajeev had left, she said,

"Why do you bother with him?"

"Why shouldn't I?"

"Because he's Indian. They're not the same as us."

"They are human beings, Susan, and he's a thoroughly nice chap, I like him."

"I suppose it's because you lived in Malaya as a child. I expect you got used to associating with people like him," she said lightly, and dropped the subject.

He wondered how she would react when he told her he was mixed race. He would have to eventually, if their relationship continued.

Before the term came to an end, Theo made some enquiries about his birth father's time at Oxford. He ascertained that the students who lived outside college were members of a society called St. Catherine's, which served as a sort of substitute college for them. This society had premises in the High Street and he paid them a visit. They had archives with information on former students and he discovered that, like him, his father had been a member of the history and debating clubs, and had also been in the rowing team. There was a photograph of him with his fellow rowers. He also found his home address, which was in a place called Huddersfield. Was this the place beginning with H where his uncle still lived? It rang no bells with Theo when he tried to envisage the address on top of the occasional letters he'd received as a child. Next of kin was given as his mother and she would probably be dead now - in fact she almost certainly was or he would have heard from her as well as his uncle. But perhaps her other son still lived in Huddersfield? He noted down the address, resolving to go there one day and see if he could find his relatives. George's enquiries had soon ground to a halt. He had told Theo that, as his father's surname was a common one in Yorkshire, visiting all the towns beginning with an H and checking the electoral rolls seemed the only way to find out anything and the cost of employing an enquiry agent to do that would be prohibitive.

The address of his father's lodgings in Oxford was also in the records and Theo went to look at it from the outside. He stood in the street of tall terraced houses and looked up at the windows, wondering which room had housed his father for those four years. Theo was now around the same age as his father was when he was in his first term at Oxford and he felt the pull of kinship with him. He wondered what it was like to be a grammar school boy at Oxford in those days; there would have been far fewer of them and perhaps they were cold-shouldered by the public school chaps, a bit like the Indians were now?

As the term drew to a close and Theo and Susan faced being apart for over a month, they exchanged addresses so they could write to each other and send Xmas cards.

"Have you a photo of yourself I could have?" she asked.

"No, not here, but I could send you one. Will you send me one too?"

She nodded. "I'll really miss you."

"Me too."

They exchanged a long, lingering kiss.

She looked more closely at his address. "What's it like where you live? The house sounds rather grand - Pucklington Manor!"

He briefly described the house and the estate.

"It sounds lovely! We have quite a large house but it's not old; Father had it built when I was a baby. Is your uncle a lord of the manor or something?"

"He's a baronet, actually."

"Really? Gosh, my father will be impressed! But how come you went to a grammar school and not a public school?"

"Well, my father wasn't wealthy and I was already established at the grammar school when we went to live at the manor. My youngest sister now goes to a private girls' school, though."

At their final meeting, the night before leaving, they found a secluded spot in the grounds of Keble and indulged in a passionate exchange of kisses and caresses.

"I've never felt like this before," she whispered. "I can't wait until January when we're together again!"

"Neither can I."

~***~

Chapter Eleven

It seemed very quiet and peaceful back at the manor. Enid, Arianna and Arthur were all still at school; their terms would not end until much nearer Christmas, and Harry's college had not yet broken up. Theo was almost broke, having spent nearly all his allowance, so he asked George if he could do a paid job for a few days on the estate and was put to work digging new flower beds. The cash he earned enabled him to spend an evening with some of his former school friends who were now working. They all seemed to have plenty of money to splash around, despite having to hand over some of their wages to their parents for their keep.

On his second Saturday at home, he and Arianna headed into town in the evening, to meet separately with some of their friends. They had been instructed to be back home by eleven so Theo told her to meet him by the car at twenty to. When she had not appeared by ten to, he set off in search of her. Spotting some of her friends obviously heading home, he asked them where she was. They exchanged uneasy looks between them and then Rosa answered,

"She went off with a boy who was talking to us earlier."

"What boy?"

Rosa looked uncomfortable. "I don't know who he is. He's older than us, at least your age, but he was really taken with Ari, paying her compliments and so on."

Theo's heart sank. What had his sister got herself into? He silently cursed her for being stupid and naive.

"Do you have any idea where they went?"

She shook her head and they went on their way. Theo wondered what to do now. If he went home without her there would be hell to pay; he was supposed to be keeping an eye on her all evening. He looked at his watch, it was now past eleven. Damn Arianna! She had landed them both in trouble for being late. They would have to think of a convincing excuse. As the time ticked by he started to get really worried. Ari had a watch, she would know what time it was, was something or someone preventing her joining him? Perhaps he should go to the police, but that would land them both in the hottest of hot water with Uncle George.

Then he saw her, running madly towards him. As she drew nearer, he saw how dishevelled she was. Her hair was flying loose, her coat undone despite the cold, and it looked as though her blouse was hanging open. When she reached him, she was gasping for breath and unable to speak. Her lungs still had a residual weakness from the fire and she could not run as fast or as far as other girls her age. He grabbed her by the shoulders and waited until her breathing eased before saying angrily,

"Where the hell have you been? Do you know what time it is? We're both for it now!"

"Don't be mad at me, Theo. I'm sorry, but it's not all my fault." He realised she was crying.

"So what happened? I know you went off somewhere with a much older boy, breaking your promise, so how is it not your fault?"

"Yes, that part of it is, I admit, but I thought he was really nice, he was saying lovely things and he promised to walk me back in time. He said he was taking me to this place where a friend of his worked, but after we'd walked quite far, he suddenly pulled me into this dark alley and shoved me up against a wall. Then he started trying to take my clothes off. I was trying to stop him but he just ripped open my blouse and then he pushed my skirt up and tried to get my knickers down and he undid his trousers and..... oh, Theo, I was so scared!"

"How did you get away?"

"I brought my knee up and caught him between the legs. He yelled out and let go of me for long enough for me to grab my bag and start running. At first he came after me but he must have given up before I got back to the town centre. I heard him yell after me that it was no good me saving myself for my wedding night because no white man would ever want to marry me."

"The bastard! Who is he, do you know him?"

She shook her head. "His name's Ed, that's all I know."

"So you went off with a complete stranger, several years older than you, just because he was flattering you. You stupid, gullible idiot! I suppose we should really go to the police and report him, but if we do that, Uncle George will know that we spent the evening apart and we'll be in even more trouble."

By now they were back at the car.

"You'd better tidy yourself up on the way back, you look a wreck, and we'd better think of a good excuse for being so late."

"Please stop shouting at me, Theo."

He looked at her. It would be more like Ari to simply shout back. She must be quite shaken by her experience. He said nothing more for the time being and started the car.

Arianna had lost most of her hair pins but managed to comb her hair back and secure it with those she had left. She dried her eyes and fastened her coat over her torn blouse. Replacing her comb in her bag, she said,

"I suppose we could say I lost something out of my bag, my purse maybe, and we spent some time looking for it in the dark?"

"All right. But make it convincing."

As they neared Little Pucklington, she said in a small voice, "I won't have a baby, will I?"

"Jesus, Ari, he didn't get that far did he?"

"I'm not sure."

"What do you mean, you're not sure? You know how babies are made, don't you?"

"Well, sort of, but not exactly. I've heard things at school but I'm not sure what's true and what isn't. In biology the teacher skipped over that bit and when I asked Aunt Mary how babies were made she said I didn't need to know until I was engaged to be married."

Theo rolled his eyes. "Well, at the rate you're going, Ari, that's going to be too bloody late! Just how far did he get?"

She told him.

"No, you won't get pregnant from that," he said, relieved, and told her in a few blunt, explicit words what else would need to have happened.

Arriving back at the manor, Theo used his key in the kitchen door and was relieved to find it unbolted. He shot the bolts after them and they tiptoed out of the kitchen and up the back stairs. Reaching the turn in the stairs, they saw George standing at the top, arms folded, with a grim expression on his face.

"What time do you call this? It's nearly midnight."

"Sorry, Uncle George," Arianna said meekly. "It's my fault. I lost my purse out of my bag and it took us ages to find it. We had to retrace our steps along several streets and search in the dark."

She stayed one step behind Theo, partly in his shadow, and George noticed nothing untoward in her appearance.

"How did you manage to lose it?"

"My bag had fallen open, I think I hadn't closed it properly."

"Well, you should be more careful in future. Get yourselves to bed now."

He strode off. Once he was out of earshot, she whispered.

"Well, we got away with it."

Theo made no reply, except to say a curt goodnight, went into his room and closed the door.

The next morning, when they got back from church, Enid, who was becoming a keen cook, went down to the kitchen to help with the lunch and Arianna followed Theo into the library, where there was a roaring fire.

"Are you still mad at me?" she asked.

"A bit. I can't afford to get into Uncle George's bad books; he might stop my allowance and then I would have to leave Oxford."

"That's all you care about, isn't it? Your precious future. You don't care that I was attacked."

"Don't be silly, of course I care, but you did rather ask for it."

"Yes, maybe I was foolish, and I've learned my lesson, but I really frightened and upset last night, and it was such a relief to see you, you were like a safe haven, my big brother, but all you did was yell at me."

Theo felt a tiny twinge of remorse, but was reluctant to back down. "Did you expect me to be so glad you were safe that I'd forget you'd broken your promise and caused us to be late? I was doing you a favour, taking you into town, and the curfew was because of you - I could have stayed out later had I been on my own - and now you're trying to put me in the wrong."

"I've said I'm sorry. It won't happen again."

"Too right it won't. I'm not covering for you anymore. I either won't take you into town at all, or you can stay with me when we get

123

there. Some of your friends can join us if they want to. I don't suppose my unattached friends will mind the company of a few fifth form girls."

She didn't protest but said sadly, "He was really nice to me at first, that Ed. He said I was beautiful, that I set his heart on fire. He made me feel special. No-one's ever said things like that to me before."

Theo snorted. "It wasn't his heart you set on fire, it was another part of his anatomy! Look, Sis, you *are* beautiful. Half the boys at school fancy you, but that means you have to be careful. You were nearly raped last night. Some boys, men, will say anything to get what they want, although few will resort to violence."

"I suppose that's all any white man will ever want from me; like he said, no-one will want to marry me."

"I'm sure that's not true. There'll be someone for you one day."

"I doubt it. I'm a misfit. And no-one really cares about me. Aunt Mary favours Enid and Uncle George prefers you. I'm just an embarrassment, a dark-skinned niece who they have to explain away to their visitors. I did think that at least I was loved and valued by you and Enid, but now I don't think you care at all and she probably prefers her friends at that posh school."

"That's not true! Enid and I both love you dearly, despite how infuriating you can be at times! And Uncle George and Aunt Mary do care. Where's all this come from, Ari?"

She shrugged. " It's just the way I feel."

He stared at her, not knowing what to say, his anger now entirely dissipated.

"Perhaps I was a bit harsh last night, I could have been kinder," he conceded. "You'd just had a dreadful experience."

After a moment's pause, she said, "Maybe I don't actually want to get married anyway. I didn't much like the sound of what you described last night."

"I put it rather bluntly, I'm sorry. That's just the mechanics of the final act, the end stage of making love. It starts with kisses and cuddles and then caressing each other's bodies and by the time you get to that stage, you'll want it, especially if you really love the man, and you won't marry someone you don't love, will you? And if he

124

loves you, he'll want to give you pleasure. I've heard it can hurt a bit for a girl the first time but then it's fine after that. It's a pity there isn't a married woman you can talk to. I expect Mama would have spoken to you by now, just as Papa did with me."

"Have you ever done it?"

He wasn't going to tell her about the prostitute, so he shook his head.

"Of course not, no nice girl would let me go all the way, and you mustn't let any boy either. You don't want to become an unmarried mother, do you? When you're a bit older they'll let you have boyfriends - although I expect they'll want to vet them first! - but it will be up to you to put the brakes on."

Christmas arrived and with it, Charlie. Mary questioned him again about his love life.

"Why is it that you've never brought a girl home for us to meet?"

"Because there's no-one special, Mama. I know a lot of girls and I go out with some of them from time to time but if I suggested to one of them that she come home with me and meet my parents, she might get the wrong idea and think I was going to pop the question."

"Would that be such a terrible thing?" George enquired. "You're getting on a bit now, son, well over thirty. Time to think about settling down."

"I don't think I'm the settling down type. I like my freedom."

"Well, you can't go on being a bachelor forever. Besides, as Bertie and Violet have only managed to produce daughters, we're relying on you to supply us with a grandson. And there's the succession to think of; the estate is entailed to the eldest male heir. Our granddaughters can't inherit."

"That's unfair," Arianna interjected.

"Perhaps, but that's how it is. Let's not get into a discussion about women's rights, please Arianna. It's a good job you weren't around when the suffragettes were protesting, I expect you'd have wanted to join in!"

Looking at Charlie, Theo had the impression he was hiding something. He suddenly wondered if Charlie had a married lover? It would make sense. He couldn't bring such a lady home and anyway she'd be spending bank holidays with her family. It could also explain that night in Burnham on Sea when Charlie had returned in the early hours. Perhaps his lady friend had come to spend a night in another hotel and he was visiting her there?

When he caught Charlie alone in the library, he said jocularly, "I think I've guessed your secret!"

Charlie's face paled. "What secret?" he asked warily.

"You're having an affair with a married woman, aren't you?"

There was a brief silence, then Charlie smiled and said, "Yes, I am, but for God's sake don't tell my parents. To say they wouldn't approve would be an understatement."

"I wouldn't dream of it, don't worry. How long has it been going on?"

"A while."

"Did she come to the seaside that time, when we were on holiday? Is that where you were when you came back so late? I was awake and heard you."

"Yes, that's right. She stayed a night in a nearby hotel."

"Is she ever going to leave her husband, get a divorce and be free to marry you?"

"Perhaps, one day. Look, Theo, please don't breathe a word of this to anyone, not even your sisters. I don't want it getting out, it could have repercussions for her as well."

"Don't worry, my lips are sealed."

~***~

Chapter Twelve

Returning to Oxford in January, Theo and Susan had a rapturous reunion. She told him that her holiday had been quite dull, with mainly her father and her aunt for company. Her aunt - her father's spinster sister - had lived with them since her mother died.

"No reunions with your school friends?"

"Yes, one. I have one friend who doesn't live too far away and she came for a visit. But the others are spread around the country, and abroad. My best friend lives up in the north of Scotland. That's the trouble with going to boarding school. I expect your friends are all local?"

"Yes, except those I had in Malaya, but I've lost touch with them now."

He told her briefly about Arianna's brush with a fate worse than death, leaving out most of the sexual detail and not referring to his sister's colouring.

"How dreadful! Poor girl. Is she all right now?"

"Seems to be. She's quite resilient."

Their relationship continued apace for the rest of the term. They spent time together whenever their work schedules and other social commitments allowed. She belonged to the Somerville debating society and there was a joint debate with Keble one evening. Luckily they both took the same side in the debate, which concerned the Nazi regime in Germany, so there was no disagreement between them. So far, they had not really had any arguments, but both were aware that this idyllic state could not continue forever. She didn't much like his friendship with Rajeev Singh but, after her initial comment, she kept her opinion to herself, not wanting to cause a row.

By mid February, Theo was sure he had fallen in love with her and she was the girl he would eventually ask to marry him. One evening, when they were having a lingering goodnight kiss in the grounds of Somerville, he told her that he loved her. She responded with delight and told him she felt the same. Emboldened by this, he said,

"I'm not in a position yet to propose marriage, and we're probably too young, but I can see us marrying one day, when we've got our degrees and embarked on our chosen careers."

"So can I! And having children."

"Yes, of course."

Her mentioning children reminded him of Mary's comment that any children he fathered may be darker skinned than he was. He would have to tell her the truth about his ethnicity before they became engaged. Should he say something now? No, better to wait until she loved him more deeply and then she would be more likely to accept the situation.

Near the end of term, she asked him if he would like to come to her home for a few days during the Easter vacation. She had mentioned to her father that she had a special boyfriend and he wanted to meet him.

"To vet me, you mean!"

"Well, partly, I suppose, but he won't be able to find fault, will he?"

Theo was not so sure about that.

They agreed he would return home first, spend a week or so with his family, and then drive up to her home, which was near Birmingham. Easter that year was towards the end of the vacation, so it would be before the bank holiday.

When he got home and told George and Mary of his plans, Mary said that they must reciprocate and invite Susan to stay with them during the summer break.

"I'll do a formal letter of invitation for you to take with you," she said.

That will be decision time, Theo thought ruefully. I'll have to tell her about my Malayan mother before she meets Arianna.

Susan had provided instructions for the last stage of the journey, after he left the main roads, and he had no trouble finding her address. He drew up in front of a large modern house, having entered the grounds through wrought iron gates and driven along a short drive. Susan must have been watching for him, as she came running outside almost immediately. They embraced. Inside, his bag was taken by a manservant and he was shown up to his room. After a quick freshen up and having unpacked, he returned downstairs and was ushered into a spacious drawing room. Susan was there with a burly, grey-haired man in his fifties, who rose to greet him.

"Theo Bradshaw, I presume?"

"Yes, sir."

"I'm Mr Hardacre, Susan's father. Do sit down. Drink?"

Theo accepted a small dry sherry.

"I trust you had a good journey?"

"Yes, thank you."

"So, Theo, is your first name short for something? Theodore perhaps?"

"Yes, but no-one ever calls me that."

"I understand your uncle is a lord of the manor and a baronet."

"Yes, sir."

"So, you have aristocratic blood in your veins!"

"Well, no, not really. He's my step-uncle and my guardian, but not my uncle by blood. His brother, the man I think of as my father, was actually my stepfather. He adopted me, but he was not my natural father."

"Oh, that's disappointing. However, I suppose you are still well-connected. Does your uncle have sons?"

"Yes, two."

"No chance of you inheriting the land and the title then!"

"No, none at all."

The conversation shifted to other topics and the evening passed pleasantly enough. At dinner, Theo was introduced to Miss Winifred Hardacre, Susan's aunt, who came across as a rather prim and proper lady. When they said their goodnights and Theo went up to bed, he hoped Susan would come to his room and was delighted when she appeared after a few minutes.

"I think Father quite likes you," she said.

"Good."

He reached out and took her in his arms. They kissed passionately and he drew her down onto the bed. She snuggled against him, but said regretfully,

"I can't stay long. If Father or Aunt Winifred knew I was here, I'd be in trouble. Young ladies do not go into young gentlemen's rooms!" The last sentence was uttered in a mock prim tone, obviously intended to mimic her aunt, and she giggled.

Disappointed, Theo bid her goodnight.

The next day, Susan showed him round the local area. They lived on the outskirts of a small town where her father had his main factory. She pointed out the building from the outside.

"What's made in there?"

"Machinery parts," she replied, rather vaguely. "All very dull, but it's made Father rich and allows me to go to Oxford."

Theo had assumed the issue of his antecedents had been put to bed the previous evening, but after dinner that night, Mr Hardacre started to ask Theo further questions. He began with enquiries about Oxford and Keble college, touched on his likely future after graduation and then switched to his background.

"I do like to know the pedigree of Susan's suitors, " he said, rather pompously. "I had thought you were a baronet's nephew, but as that is not the case, I wonder if you'd mind telling me something about your real father?"

"Well, he died when I was very small. He was in the Malayan Civil Service like my stepfather."

"Yes, Susan said you'd spent your early years in Malaya. What else do you know about him?"

"He was from Yorkshire and he went to Oxford university, like me."

"Which college?"

"He lived outside college, in digs. He was there on a full scholarship, and they often did that, as it was cheaper."

"So he must have been from a very ordinary family."

"I believe so."

"What about your mother?"

This was dangerous ground. "What do you want to know?"

"Her background. Where her family are from."

130

"She was born in Malaya. Her family lived there."

"Was her father also in the colonial service?"

"No. Her family have a farm."

"A large farm? A plantation?"

"Not exactly."

"Well, how big is it? How many acres?"

Theo shrugged. "I don't know how many acres exactly. It's a reasonable size." As he spoke, a mental image of his grandparents' tiny plot of rented land and their small basic cottage came into his head and he almost laughed.

"So, how long would it take to walk across their land, from one side to the other?"

Less than two minutes, Theo thought wryly. Out loud he said, "I've no idea, I've never timed myself walking across it!"

"How long had the family been settled in Malaya?"

"I'm not sure. Several generations, I believe."

"Are they British, or Dutch?"

Theo hesitated, wondering what to say. Either answer would be a direct lie.

"Surely you know that! Why am I getting the distinct impression that you are hiding something?"

Theo gave up dissembling. To hell with it!   "They are Malays."

"Native Malay? Asian?"

"Yes."

Mr Hardacre sat back in his chair and surveyed Theo. "So, your mother was an Asian lady. She must have been quite a beauty to have ensnared not one but two Englishmen into marriage. I always thought that men working in the colonies very rarely married their native mistresses. Or, was she actually married to your natural father?"

Theo said nothing.

"So, you are illegitimate as well as half Asian. Were she and the man you refer to as your stepfather legally married at least?"

"Yes."

"And he adopted you, so I suppose you are partly legitimised. However, far from being the nephew of a respected Oxfordshire baronet, as I was led to believe, you are actually the bastard son of an working-class Yorkshireman and a Malayan whore!"

Theo saw red. "Don't call my mother a whore!"

Mr Hardacre ignored him and went on, "Needless to say, I cannot regard you as a suitable consort for my daughter. If your relationship were to continue into marriage you might be presenting me with brown-skinned grandchildren. That I could not tolerate. You are lucky to look the way you do, but the Asian blood will doubtless come out in the next generation. Your friendship with Susan must therefore cease forthwith, and I think it best that you return home in the morning."

With that, he got up and left the room, followed closely by his sister, who had contributed nothing to the conversation. Susan had said nothing either and Theo now looked across at her. Her eyes were downcast.

"Susan?"

"You should have told me!" she said in a low voice.

"I intended to, but the time never seemed right. I would have told you, before I asked you to marry me. Does it make a difference to you? Is this the end for us or shall we continue to meet at Oxford regardless? He won't know if you don't tell him, and when you are twenty-one you won't need his permission to marry."

"What's the point, when there can be no future in it?" she said miserably. "We can never marry now. I can't have brown babies!"

"At most, they might be pale coffee coloured. Would that really be so terrible?"

"Yes, it would, to me."

"Then I suppose there's nothing more to be said." He added bitterly, "You know, it's people like you and your father who caused the death of my parents."

"What on earth do you mean?"

"The fire at our home was caused by racially motivated arsonists. They targeted us deliberately, because of my mother."

"That's terrible, but you can't think we are like them. We'd never do anything like that!"

"No, but it's the same underlying attitude. Can't you see that?" He stood up. "I'll go and pack and leave here tonight."

"It's gone eleven. You won't get home until well into the early hours."

"So be it. I'm not staying another night under this roof, with you and your bigoted father. You obviously share his views, he's brought you up well!"

Theo was about half an hour into his journey before his anger evaporated and gave way to misery and depression. At first he told himself he was well rid of Mr Hardacre as a potential father-in-law, the pompous, arrogant snob. And that tight-lipped sister of his. How did Susan stand living with the pair of them? Then he remembered how much in love he'd been with Susan, he couldn't just switch his feelings off. He still loved her, damn it! And was this always going to happen? Every time he lost his heart to a girl, his hopes would be dashed and his heart broken as soon as his true identity was discovered. Perhaps he should follow Charlie's example and seek out a married lover, an older woman who was disillusioned with her marriage and out of love with her husband but who had no intention of divorcing. With children not under consideration, his mixed race status would matter less. Did he want children? He supposed he did, in the longer term, but it was not an issue as yet. And with a married woman he would be able to have sex. Perhaps he should also think about joining the colonial service after he'd got his degree. Go back to Malaya. He realised that English girls there and their families would have the same attitude to the Asian part of his heritage, but there were plenty of Eurasians. People like him, products of liaisons between the ruling English *Tuans* and the native girls.

Luckily, he had filled the car up with petrol the previous day, so he did not splutter to a halt with an empty tank. There were no petrol stations open at this time of night. There was also very little traffic and he made good time, arriving back at the manor not long after 1.30 am. He turned his key in the lock of the kitchen door but when he pushed the door, it remained shut. Of course, no-one was expecting him and the door was bolted from the inside. He should have thought of that and telephoned before he left, but he had just wanted to get the hell out of that house. If he rang the bell on the main door, it would wake up the whole household and he would not be popular, to put it mildly. He also didn't want to face questions tonight, he just wanted to get to bed. Enid's room faced the courtyard at the back but Arianna's window was at the side. If he threw pebbles up at it, perhaps he could wake her and she could come down and let him in. He found a few small stones and tried it. No luck. If he used a larger stone, he might break the window. Then he realised that her window was open a couple of inches at the bottom and also that the adjacent tree had grown branches which reached across underneath the window sill. He could climb up and gain access.

After extracting his toothbrush from his bag, he placed the bag back in the boot of the car. He could retrieve it in the morning. Climbing the tree was not too difficult and he was soon standing on the branch which ran immediately below the sill. He just had to hope it would bear his weight. He pushed up the window and started to heave himself inside. As he parted the curtains and poked his head through, he saw Arianna sitting bolt upright in bed, her mouth forming a frightened 'O'.

"Don't scream, Ari," he whispered urgently. "It's only me."

As he levered himself headfirst through the opening and landed in an ungainly heap on the floor, Arianna found her voice.

"What on earth are you doing, Theo? You gave me such a fright!"

"I climbed up the tree. The door was bolted and I didn't fancy waking everyone up by ringing the bell."

As he spoke, he picked himself up off the floor and sat on her bed.

"So you wake me instead and nearly give me a heart attack," she said, crossly. "I thought you were a burglar!"

"Sorry!"

"So why are you back so soon? What happened?"

He gave her a summarised account of his interrogation by Susan's father, finishing by saying,

"So, he won't tolerate having brown grandchildren and she doesn't want to give birth to brown babies. I was told to leave in the morning, but I wasn't going to stay another night in that house. And don't you dare say it serves me right for not being honest from the beginning!"

"I wasn't going to. I'm sorry, Theo. You were in love with her, weren't you?"

"I still am."

"But you're better off out of it if that's the way she thinks."

"I daresay, but that doesn't stop it hurting."

Theo slept late the next morning. George and Mary had seen his car outside and Arianna told them at breakfast the gist of what had had happened.

"If Theo can climb up that tree and get into your room, then so can a burglar," George commented. "We'd better get it pruned."

"Poor Theo," Enid said. "He doesn't have much luck in love, does he?"

And neither will you or I, Arianna thought.

Theo had lunch with George and Mary, the girls having gone to school. They made sympathetic responses to his tale of woe, but afterwards George said to Mary in private,

"Jim, and Theo's natural father, never thought beyond the end of their noses when they fathered those children. They gave no thought to the long term consequences of the divided heritage they bestowed upon them, which would mean they fit into neither world."

"It wasn't the end of their noses they didn't think beyond," Mary said drily. "It was a much lower body part!"

"Really, Lady Mary, that's not a remark one would expect to hear from a gentlewoman!" George replied, laughing.

~***~

Chapter Thirteen

Back at Oxford after Easter, for the Trinity term, Theo decided to concentrate on his studies, bearing in mind the end of year exams, and give girls a wide berth for a while. Susan reverted to sitting with the other women on the far side of the lecture hall and they simply ignored each other. Theo felt a stab of pain and longing whenever he saw her and couldn't help wondering if she felt the same. Several of Theo's friends commented on the situation and asked what had happened.

"You were all over each other last term," one said.

"We just decided we weren't suited," Theo replied. He should have left it there, but made the mistake of adding, "and her father took rather a dislike to me when I visited and she's very much under his influence."

"So what happened exactly?" one friend asked curiously. "You're not the type a parent would normally dislike; nice, polite young man is how my mother would probably describe you! Did you get drunk and throw up all over his expensive carpet, or something?"

"Or maybe he got caught sneaking out of Susan's bedroom," another added.

Into the laughter which followed these conjectures, Theo said dismissively that he'd done nothing and refused to be drawn into any further discussion. Let them speculate!

However, when Rajeev Singh asked him the same question, he decided to tell him the truth.

"Her father found out that I'm half Asian; my mother was Malayan."

"Really? One would never guess from your looks, although I suppose you do have the skin tone which normally goes with darker hair and brown eyes."

"I'd be grateful if you didn't broadcast it, it might not go down too well with a lot of people here."

"I can imagine! Don't worry, I'll keep quiet."

About half way through the term, another Saturday trip to London was arranged, by way of a final fling before they got their heads down to prepare for their exams. Towards the end of the evening they decided to try one further club, which none of them were familiar with.

"It looks private," one student commented.

"Well, if it is, they just won't let us in," another pointed out. "We can but try."

There was no doorman in sight and no-one prevented them from pushing open the inner door. They entered a fairly large room, with a dance floor surrounded by tables and seating, and a bar at the far end. They looked around.

"This is weird," one student said, "It's all men, no women."

They all looked towards the dance floor, where men were dancing together and at the sides of the room where men were sitting close together in couples.

"It's a queers' club!" one of Theo's friends said in disgust. "Let's get the hell out!"

As he spoke, the doorman appeared and asked if they were members.

"No, we're not, and we don't want to be," someone answered. "We're just leaving."

They turned to go, but not before Theo's gaze had alighted upon one of the men on the dance floor. Shocked, he stood stock-still, staring, and as he did so, Charlie raised his head from his partner's shoulder and met Theo's eyes.

"Come on, Theo," one of his friends said impatiently. "What are you looking at? Fancy one of these chaps, do you?!"

"No, of course not." He turned and followed the others outside.

After that, one of the party looked at his watch and said they'd better head to the station as, if they missed the next train, they'd not get back before the gate was closed. Theo followed them, but did not join in their raucous laughter and ribald comments about the men in the club. His head was reeling. So this was Charlie's secret, there was no married lover - not a female one anyway. Charlie must have admitted to that to put him off the scent. Homosexuality was illegal; Charlie was risking imprisonment if caught, and the end of his career as a lawyer. And Theo could barely dare to dwell on George's likely reaction if he found out. Theo didn't understand how men could be inclined that way and under normal circumstances would have joined in with his comrades' condemnation, but this was Charlie! His cousin, who had always been such a good companion and who had been so kind to him and his sisters after the funeral. He remembered the seaside holiday, which would not have happened without Charlie and which had started the three of them on the healing process. How could he be disgusted at Charlie? He was quiet most of the way back but luckily no-one particularly noticed.

Meanwhile, Charlie was in a panic.

"That was my cousin!" he told the man he was with.

"Do you think he'll blab?"

"Don't know."

He spent a sleepless night and rose early. He had to get to Theo before he told anyone and beg him to keep his secret. He'd go to Oxford to see him. Then he realised he didn't know which college Theo was at, he'd been told once, but had forgotten. He'd have to phone home and steer the conversation around to that without arousing suspicion.

Mr Hughes answered the phone. "The family are all at church, Mr Charlie. They've just left."

Damn! He'd forgotten about church.

"There's just Miss Arianna here. She has a cold and Lady Mary thought it best she stay home, to play safe, with her weak lungs you know."

Relieved, Charlie asked to speak to her. She would know her brother's college. After some polite preamble, during which he commiserated with her on her cold and she told him it wasn't too bad and at least it had got her out of boring church, he brought the conversation around to how Theo was doing at Oxford.

"He's at Christ Church college, isn't he? I know someone there."

"No, he's at Keble."

Keble, of course. He remembered now. He brought the conversation to a close as soon as he could and rang off.

Charlie had a car, garaged not far from his flat, but thought the journey might be quicker by train so took a taxi to Paddington. At

Keble, he asked the porter which room Theo occupied, explaining he was his cousin. He took the stairs to the first floor two at a time and walked hastily along the corridor, hoping Theo would still be there, so he didn't have to go searching for him in the communal areas of the college.

A bleary-eyed and unshaven Theo answered the door. He had slept late and skipped chapel.

"Charlie."

"I think you know why I'm here."

"Yes. Come in."

Theo's room reminded Charlie of the room he'd occupied when at Cambridge. It was there that he'd first become sure about his sexual orientation, although there'd been indications of it when he was still at school. At Cambridge, he'd experienced his first relationship and his course in life was set; always to be part of a minority operating in the shadows, constantly hiding the truth, pretending.

"I suppose you've come to ask me not to say anything. You could have saved yourself a journey."

Renewed panic gripped Charlie. Was Theo determined to tell, was that what he meant?

But Theo continued, "I've no intention of saying a word to anyone. Your secret's safe with me."

Relief flooded through him and he sat down heavily.

"Thanks. Thanks very much. It's vital that no-one finds out."

"Yes, I can just imagine Uncle George's reaction!"

"He'd probably disown me and so would my brother. But it's not just them. You know that what I do, how I live, is against the law. If I were exposed, I could go to jail and it would be the end of my career as a lawyer."

"I realise all that. Don't worry, Charlie."

"And what about you? Do I disgust you?"

"You could never do that," Theo replied gently. "I confess I was surprised and shocked, in fact I was awake for hours thinking about it, and I admit I find what you do difficult to understand and perhaps even rather abhorrent, but you are still you, still cousin Charlie, who's always been such good company and so kind to me and my sisters."

139

"So, we're still friends?"

"Of course."

"Have you had any breakfast?"

"No."

"Let's go and get some brunch then. I haven't eaten much either. Get shaved and dressed and we'll find a cafe - my treat."

While they were waiting for their order of full English breakfasts to arrive, Charlie thanked him again for being willing to keep his secret and not condemning him.

"Well, I've got secrets myself."

"Really?"

"I've kept it quiet here that I'm half Asian and also illegitimate."

"Are you? Illegitimate, I mean. I didn't know that."

"My real father never married my mother."

"Well, if your secrets did get out, at least they won't land you in jail."

"No, but they lost me two girlfriends, whom I really cared about, when their fathers found out. One when I was at school, and one just a couple of months ago."

"That's a shame. There's far too much prejudice in this world. People are too quick to condemn those who don't fit into the established mould." He added with a grin, "Perhaps it's a pity you don't bat for our side; we don't worry too much about our partners' backgrounds and we don't have to consider a chap's suitability as a spouse!"

Theo grinned back. "Afraid I'm only attracted to girls!"

Their meals arrived. As they tucked in, Theo said, "I suppose you said you had a married lover to put me off the scent."

"Well, it was you who came up with that idea. And it was true at the time, although my lover was not female."

"Did he, or an earlier lover, come to Burnham on Sea that time?"

"No, that was a chap I met on the beach."

Theo remembered the man he'd seen. "Had you only just met that day?"

"Yes. Things often develop quicker with us. We don't usually court each other to the extent you do with girls and we don't have to

140

worry about unwanted pregnancies!" After a short pause, he added, "I expect you're still a virgin."

"No, actually, I'm not." He told Charlie about the prostitute. "And that's something I'd rather you didn't pass on to your father!"

"Ah yes, a fresher's initiation. I wouldn't be surprised if Papa had that too in his time! I had a similar experience in my first term at Cambridge."

"Did you? Could you, er...."

"Perform? Yes, I managed it, but only by thinking about a man!"

Their conversation was interrupted by a man in his forties who stopped by their table, and greeted Charlie.

"I thought it was you. What're you doing in Oxford?"

"Visiting my cousin here." He introduced Theo to the man, whose name was Howard.

"Ah, your cousin, right."

The two men exchanged a few more pleasantries and then Howard went on his way.

"Is he one of your lot?" Theo asked.

"If by 'my lot' you mean a homosexual, yes he is."

"Did he think I might be one of your lovers?"

"Possibly, until I put him right."

"Is he one of your ex lovers?"

"No. We don't all have relationships with each other, Theo, any more than you go out with all the girls you meet!"

Theo gave this some thought, then said, "but it's not exactly the same, is it? I mean, most people are heterosexual so obviously we choose our mates from a wide pool, but you are part of a tiny minority."

" A minority, yes, but a much larger one than you think. You'd be surprised at how many of us there are. You probably know quite a few here at Oxford, but of course they can't be open about it. There are also many married men who are inclined the same way as me."

"Really? Why on earth did they marry?"

"For respectability, or because of family pressure, and so on. And some are bisexual and some don't realise their true natures until after they're married."

"So they have to live a lie."

"We all live a lie." Then he added, "and don't forget the women. A smaller minority, I daresay, but at least for them it's not illegal, just condemned by society."

Theo said, remembering one of his social history lectures, "There was a famous lesbian at the beginning of the last century, a landowner in Yorkshire. She lived openly with her lover and flouted convention."

"Really?"

After a moment or two, Theo asked, "Have you ever been in love or is it always just sex?"

"I've been in love. We have the same feelings as heterosexuals, they are just directed towards our own gender."

"You're all going against the bible, though, aren't you? It's a sin, isn't it?"

"Depends on your interpretation. And remember, the bible was written by men, not God. And it was God who made us this way."

Theo thought about that for a few minutes, then said, "Whether or not it's a sin in the religious sense, I don't think it should be illegal. You're not harming anyone, are you? It's not as if you're going around molesting choirboys!"

"You'd be surprised at how many people think that we all do that! Perhaps one day society will become enlightened enough to decriminalise homosexuality between consenting adults in private, but I doubt it will happen in my lifetime."

~***~

Chapter Fourteen

After that eventful weekend, Theo got down to studying for his exams and passed with good grades. Then it was the long summer vacation. There was a labouring job going on the estate for a couple of weeks and Theo took it, to earn himself some holiday cash. George paid him the same wage he would have paid to any casual labourer, without asking him to contribute to his keep from it, and Theo felt slightly guilty that he was doing for pocket money a job which would normally have provided the sole income for a whole family. He was developing a social conscience, fuelled by the debates and discussions in his Oxford clubs as well as by his social history studies. He was well aware that he led a privileged life, especially since coming to live at the manor. Although the depression which followed the Wall Street crash had hit much harder in the north of the country than the south, he was still aware from the newspapers and radio news bulletins of the continuing unemployment and resultant poverty in those regions. Even in Oxfordshire, the wages for agricultural labourers seemed very low; Theo didn't know how they managed to pay rent and feed a family on the sum he was now earning.

By the time the schools and Harry's college broke up, Theo's job had come to an end and he was free to spend time with Harry and Arthur. Harry now had a girlfriend in Bristol who was due to visit him for a week during the summer holidays. From the way he spoke about her, Theo guessed that Harry had finally fallen in love. He was happy for him, but also slightly envious. Arthur had now finished with school, having just taken his Higher Certificate, and was due to start at agricultural college in September. The idea was that, when he finished his course, he would become an assistant estate manager, working with his father, and eventually take over from him when he retired. So his future was all mapped out, Theo thought, as was Harry's, who would become a teacher at the end of next year. Theo was still unsure about what he would do when he finished at Oxford. He knew he didn't want to teach. Historical research was one option, but it would mean further studying first and he would have to finance that himself from the money Jim had left him. Another option was joining the colonial service, and there were also other things he could look into. He told himself he still had two years to decide, no need to worry about it yet.

Arianna, on the other hand, was already giving thought to her long term future. She had just taken her school certificate, and assuming she passed, as predicted, had the option of continuing into the sixth form if she wished. However, she and Mary had looked into a two year course at a college in a neighbouring town which taught office skills and business administration. They brought the brochure home for George to see and the matter was discussed after supper one evening.

"That course is supposed to be one of the best in the country of its type, and would give me the skills and qualifications I need to get an office job anywhere," Arianna declared. "And I only need school cert as an entry qualification."

"But are you sure that's what you want?" George asked. "Why not do your higher cert first and then, if you still want an office based career, you can go on to do this course afterwards. Completing sixth form and getting the higher cert would give you more options."

"But that means four more years studying instead of two, and I already know I won't want to go to university, nor train as a teacher, nor anything else I can think of which requires the higher certificate."

"But you might change your mind about that."

"I don't think so."

"It's a very good course, George," Mary said, "and the college is very nice. The principal showed us round. She'd have to change buses in town but the times fit in well and her journey would only be about twenty minutes longer."

"What do you think, Theo?" George asked.

"Me? It's not up to me, is it? It's Ari's life."

"Nevertheless, you are her older brother and I'm sure she'd value your opinion."

Theo doubted that, but said, "Well, it does look like a very good course. If she wants to work in an office and make her way in the business world, it seems ideal. With their diploma, she should surely get an office job very easily and she could then work her way up to a more senior level."

"Exactly what I think," Mary said.

"No-one's asked me my opinion!" Enid chipped in.

"Well, what do you think, dear?" Mary asked.

"I think that Ari usually knows her own mind and, if she says she wants this now, I don't think that will change."

"We do need to apply and reserve a provisional place without delay," Mary said. "It's a very sought-after course. It will be subject to her passing school certificate, but I'm sure she will."

George agreed, and the application was made. When he and Mary were alone, he commented that, once Arianna married, it wouldn't matter much what qualifications she had. Mary's response was that Arianna may well have problems in finding a husband because of her skin colour and it was best that she was well equipped to earn her own living.

The rest of the summer passed uneventfully and Theo found it rather dull at times. After Harry's girlfriend, Dorothy, returned to Bristol, he found himself a job in a shop for the rest of his holidays, so was only free evenings and Sundays. Most of Theo's other schoolmates who were at college or university also had holiday jobs and Arthur spent some of his weekdays helping his father on the estate, by way of work experience. Theo did a few more odd days labouring or gardening on the estate and otherwise took walks, read and spent time with his sisters when they were not out with their friends. The three of them went for a few trips out in Theo's car, including full days to Bath and Stonehenge, along with Arthur. They also took a trip to London on the train, accompanied by Mary, and met Charlie and Bertie for lunch. The last time Arianna and Enid had been in London had been with their parents the Easter before they died, so there was some nostalgia expressed as they revisited some of the tourist landmarks they'd first seen with them. Mary pointed out the house in Eaton Square which had at one time been owned by the Bradshaw family.

"Why was it sold?" Arianna asked.

"To pay death duties after George's father died. It was also becoming a luxury the income from the estate could no longer afford to maintain. We didn't use it a lot, but it was nice to have it. However, when I want to spend a few days in London now, I can stay with either Isobel and Frank or Bertie and Violet."

At the beginning of September, Enid returned to school and Arianna started at her new college. She was quite nervous that first morning, suddenly regretting not staying on at school instead where she knew everyone. Predictably, she was the only non-white girl at the college, but there were a handful of Indian boys doing business administration courses. She was the recipient of many admiring glances from the boys in her business admin classes, which earned her a few bitchy remarks from some of the girls, but most of them were friendly. By the time she'd been there a few weeks, she had made a couple of particular friends, Phyllis and Irene, who were in her shorthand and typing classes. She enjoyed all the lessons and was glad she had made the choice she had.

It was towards the end of November when a bombshell fell on the family. Theo was in his room writing an essay when the porter came to tell him he had a telephone call.

"Your sister, she said. Anna?"

"Arianna. I wonder what she wants?"

He followed the porter back downstairs, to the communal telephone, with some trepidation. Ari had never phoned him here before. Had Mary or George been taken ill?

"All hell's broken loose here!" she said without preamble. "Charlie's been arrested. Uncle George is in a furious temper, we daren't go near him, and Aunt Mary's really upset. He's been charged with buggery and gross indecency. I asked Mr Hughes what buggery meant and he said 'sodomy', so we looked that up in the dictionary and it said..."

Theo interrupted her. "I know what it means, Ari."

"Right. You don't sound all that surprised."

"Well, I knew about Charlie's inclinations."

"You never said."

"It wasn't my secret to tell and he asked me not to say anything to anyone. I only found out by accident, not long ago; I saw him in London one evening."

"With a man?"

"Yes."

"Well, Uncle George is going around saying that Charlie's no longer his son, he's disowning him, and I gather Bertie's taking the same attitude, but Aunt Mary says he's still her son and she's going to London to see him tomorrow. He's out on bail apparently, but there's a trial date set for just after Christmas. He's been suspended from his job until then."

"Poor Charlie. Ask Aunt Mary to let him know that I'll come to see him on Saturday."

"Oh, good. When you see him, give him our love. Enid and I don't care what he's done, he's still our cousin Charlie."

Theo found Charlie in a very morose mood.

"You're the only male relative who's prepared to give me the time of day," he said. "Papa and Bertie have disowned me, Uncle Frank put the phone down on me, and when I phoned cousin Michael at work, he couldn't end the call fast enough and said he'd rather I didn't phone again. He and I were childhood playmates; there's only a few months age gap between us."

He sounded bitter and Theo couldn't blame him.

He went on, "and it's not only the family. My colleagues want nothing to do with me, ditto most of my heterosexual friends, and friends who are like me are afraid to be seen with me in case people suspect the truth about them!"

"How did you come to be arrested?"

"You obviously haven't read the Pucklington papers!"

"No, I'm still at Oxford."

"It's splashed all over the front pages of the local papers and the London evening one has a piece inside. One of the chaps arrested with me is quite big in the city; I think Uncle Frank and Bertie know him quite well. That'll be someone else for them to cut dead! Anyway, we were at a private party at this chap's house and a few of us had adjourned to the bedrooms with our partners - and that's when the police raided us. They must have had a tip-off. I was literally caught in the act, so I really have no defence. There were four of us in that situation and we've all been arrested and charged. They couldn't really prove anything against the others, as they weren't caught in compromising positions, although I believe some charges are being levied against our host."

"Ari said a trial date's been set for after Christmas?"

"Yes. Thursday 2nd January."

There was a short silence, then Charlie said, "Sorry, Theo, you've come all this way and I'm being lousy company."

"Well, I didn't expect you to be brimming with joy! And I came to offer you my support, not to have fun."

"You're a good chap. I've always liked you. And I'm glad you're now grown up. I think I'm going to need your friendship."

"Well, you've got it. And my sisters both send their love and support. They don't care what you've done."

Charlie smiled. "That's nice. But do they really understand what I'm charged with?"

"I think so, more or less. They looked the words up in the dictionary!"

Charlie laughed, then said, "it's nearly lunchtime. I'd rather not go out to eat, if you don't mind. There're some press hovering around."

"Yes, I saw them on my way in. They asked me which flat I was going to, but I just ignored them."

"I've got a few supplies in the larder. How are your cooking skills?"

"Non-existent."

"Mine are pretty basic, but I've got eggs and I can rustle up a couple of omelettes. And there's bread and tomatoes. Will that do you?"

"That's fine."

Theo chopped the tomatoes, cut the bread and laid the table, while Charlie cooked the omelettes. Over lunch, they chatted about other things and he left Charlie in a slightly less melancholic frame of mind than when he'd arrived.

Shortly after that, it was the end of the Michaelmas term and Theo returned to the manor for the holidays. George refused to speak about Charlie at all and told Theo not to mention his name in his presence, but Mary thanked him for going to see him.

"He's going to need all the friends he can get."

The atmosphere at Christmas was subdued. Everyone was acutely aware of Charlie's absence and the reason for it but no-one dared mention his name. George was overheard saying angrily to Mary that he now had only one son and his name was Bertie.

"That pervert is no child of mine!"

Theo wondered at how unforgiving George was being towards Charlie. Whilst it was true that George was a bit more straitlaced than Jim, Theo had never found him to be unduly rigid about other things. Why was this something he simply could not accept? Surely a parent's love for their child should be unconditional? Mary's was proving so, why not George's?

Mary and Theo attended the trial. Arianna and Enid asked to go too, but George refused to allow it, saying it was no place for impressionable young girls. The defence barrister did his best, but there was no disputing the evidence of the police officers who had caught the men in *flagrante delicto* and they were all four found guilty. Sentencing was carried out the following week and they were all sentenced to one year in prison.

"It could have been worse," the defence lawyer said to Mary. "He could have got up to two years."

On the train on the way home, Mary struggled to hold back tears.

"How's he going to bear being in jail?" she asked. "They're such terrible places and he'll be in with violent men. He's always been such a gentle, sweet-natured boy!"

Theo wondered that too. He'd also heard that men of Charlie's persuasion were treated worse than most by the other prisoners.

After they returned home, he could hear Mary and George arguing in the drawing room. She sounded to be crying but was receiving scant comfort from her husband. Theo retreated into the library with Enid, who had just returned from school, and they were later joined by Arianna.

"Can we go and visit him in prison?" she asked.

"I expect anyone can go, but I think you have to get a permit."

"Uncle George will never let us go," Enid said.

"Well, he doesn't need to know, does he? " Arianna answered. "If Theo goes one Saturday, when he's back at university, you and I can tell Uncle George we're going shopping in Oxford, meet Theo there and he can drive us all to the prison."

So that's what they did. Mary had signed the consent form they required as they were all under age, but upon arrival a stern-faced prison warden said that Enid was not allowed to come in without a parent or guardian present as she was under sixteen.

"I'm her brother. Can I not act as her guardian?" Theo asked.

"No, you're under twenty-one."

Enid said she'd wait in the car.

They were shocked at the sight of Charlie who was sporting a black eye and a cut and swollen lip. He managed a lopsided smile.

"It's good to see you."

"Enid came with us but they won't let her come in as she's under sixteen."

"I'm surprised my father allowed you girls to come at all."

"He didn't." Arianna told him how they'd managed it.

He smiled. "Well I hope you don't get into trouble on my account."

"Never mind us," Theo said. "How are you getting on? What happened to your face?"

"Someone took a dislike to me. Happens a lot in here."

Arianna said, "Aunt Mary seemed really upset when she came home from visiting you last week."

Charlie sighed. "Yes, I know, and I didn't tell her everything and I didn't have this face then either. This place is a hell-hole, and men like me get given a particularly hard time. I'm just going to have to grit my teeth and count the days until I get out. Not that life will be much fun afterwards. I've been sacked from my job and struck off as a lawyer. Mama's going to arrange for my flat to be let so at least the mortgage will be paid and she says there'll be some surplus which I can use to tide me over when I get out, but if I don't find some sort of job soon....." His voice tailed off.

Arianna reached out a sympathetic hand to his, but the prison officer immediately barked, "No touching!"

"Don't despair, Charlie," Theo said. "Something will surely crop up."

On the drive back to Oxford, Enid wondered if their Papa would have taken the same hard line as Uncle George. Theo had wondered that too.

"Maybe he'd have stopped short of disowning him. After all, he flouted convention in marrying Mama. Although I suppose that's what most men would consider a normal sin!"

Charlie survived his year in jail, although it changed him. He was never again quite the happy-go-lucky character he'd been before. He was released slightly early, at the beginning of December 1936. Luck was on his side in the choice of release date as it coincided with the day the news broke of the abdication of King Edward VIII and the newspapers were crammed full with the details of his romance with the American divorcee, Wallis Simpson. Charlie's release only warranted a tiny inside paragraph in the Pucklington papers and was not mentioned at all in the London ones. He moved back into his flat but he was unemployed and without any source of income. He applied for numerous jobs with firms requiring someone with a legal background, but his term in jail was difficult to cover up as was the reason for it. Over and over again he did not get past the interview stage. Then Theo had the germ of an idea. He said nothing to Charlie at first, as it was a long shot, but he'd remembered that Jim's friend, Walter, who had given him his card at the funeral, had a legal background and had worked in the courts in Kuala Lumpur. He recalled Jim once asking his advice regarding a case he was dealing with as a magistrate in Klang, when the three of them were out fishing. He only remembered the conversation because the circumstances of the case had struck him, as an eleven year old boy, as being rather amusing. He telephoned Walter and they met for lunch one Saturday.

"It's good to see you," Walter said. "And how are your sisters?"

Theo brought him up to date on their lives and then asked how Walter and Mildred were enjoying retirement.

"Ah, well, I'm not totally retired. I have a part-time consultancy role." He mentioned the name of the firm, which meant nothing to Theo.

"Are there any other similar jobs going there?"

Walter raised his eyebrows. "For yourself? You've several more months to go at Oxford, haven't you, and you're studying history, not law."

"No, it's not for me." He told Walter all about Charlie's predicament.

"I see," Walter said thoughtfully. "Can't his family help him? I believe his brother and uncle both work in the city, I met them at the funeral."

"They've both disowned him, as has his father."

"Right. Well, I can't say I'm surprised. Why have you not done the same? You're not inclined the same way, are you?"

"No, I'm not! But he's my cousin and my friend and it's not for me to judge him. And he was always especially good to me and my sisters." He told Walter about the seaside holiday after the funeral. "That holiday started us on the healing process. We were floundering in grief, didn't know what to do with ourselves, especially Enid, and he did it purely out of the kindness of his heart."

"Right, well, he sounds like a nice chap, sexual orientation apart! Give me his contact details and I'll get in touch with him, find out his qualifications and experience and see what I can do. Can't promise anything, mind."

He was as good as his word, met up with Charlie and a week or two later got him an interview with the firm he worked for.

"They know about your jail term, so you don't have to worry about that. Just convince them you can do the job."

A few days later, Theo got a phone call from Charlie, telling him he now had a job, in the same company and same department as Walter.

"I know I have you to thank for this, as well as him. I can't tell you how grateful I am. I'm forever in your debt."

~***~

152

Chapter Fifteen

Theo graduated with a first class degree in the summer of 1937. George, Mary, Enid and Arianna all attended the graduation ceremony. Susan was also graduating and he saw her, her father and aunt all looking across at Arianna. He'd never discovered just how many people she'd told about the reason for their break-up, but when he'd asked one of the other girls at his history lectures for a date, she'd turned him down flat and the same thing had happened with a girl from Somerville. Despite that, he had still managed to date some female students over the last two years, although he had not fallen in love again.

During his last term at Oxford, he'd finally decided that he wanted to join the colonial service. He'd put Malaya as his first choice on the application form, and, as he spoke the language and had spent his early years there, it was a foregone conclusion that he would be offered his first choice. Despite his knowledge of the country, he was still required to study for a year at the London School of Oriental and African Studies, starting in September. The colonial office would be paying for his tuition, but he had to finance his term-time living costs from the money Jim had left him, which had been transferred to him the previous November, following his twenty-first birthday. When he asked Charlie's advice about cheap lodgings in London, Charlie offered him his spare room, rent free.

"Just pay your share of food and bills while you're there," he said. "Mind you, the neighbours will probably think you're one of my lovers, so be prepared for some disapproving looks!"

During the second week of the summer vacation, he went up to Yorkshire to see what he could discover about his natural father's relatives. He booked a couple of nights at an inn in Huddersfield and travelled up by train. The next morning he set off for the Almondbury area of the town, as indicated by the address he'd found at St. Catherine's, but that particular street did not appear to exist. A map he'd obtained from a local stationer's shop did not show it. Perplexed, he went into a nearby pub, which was on the edge of what looked like wasteland, and asked the landlord if he knew where that address was.

"Those houses were all knocked down many years ago. Slum clearance. They were just over there." He indicated the area of wasteland. "The area's scheduled for redevelopment but nowt's happened yet. The council's got no money for owt like that now, what with the depression an' all. Pity, as there's plenty of men round here in dire need of the work. Were you looking for someone in particular?"

Theo told him his uncle's name. "Do you know of him?"

"No, doesn't ring a bell, although that's a common surname round these parts. But old Bill over there might be able to help you. He's lived round here for years and he was re-housed from one of the streets they demolished. Buy him a pint and I expect he'll tell you all he knows."

Bill was a grey-haired, wrinkled man who could have been any age from sixty to eighty. He looked at the name and address Theo had written down.

"Aye, that were the street next to mine and I knew a family o' that name. Many years ago now, before the war. A widow wi' two boys. They were clever lads, didn't leave school at twelve and go into the factories like most of 'em round here. The younger one even went on to university, which were practically unheard of then in these parts. Then he got a job abroad somewhere; never saw him again. She died suddenly not long after that, bleed on the brain I think it was, and t'other son got married about six months later. Then they moved away. He had a job in a shop in town, and they offered him a manager's job in another branch."

"Do you know where he moved to? Or which shop it was?"

The old man shook his head. "Nah, not sure I ever knew that and if I did, I've long forgotten. Why do you want to know?"

Theo explained that the younger son had been his father and he was now trying to find his uncle.

"Where was it he went off to, somewhere out East wasn't it?"

"Malaya."

"How come you don't know where his brother ended up? Your Dad never tell you?"

154

Theo briefly explained.

Bill chuckled. "So the dirty dog had it off with a native girl, did he! So much for his fancy education!"

As Bill could tell him no more, Theo thanked him and took his leave. He went into the town centre and looked at various shops there, but he had no way of telling which one his uncle had once worked in. He went into a couple which looked as though they may have branches in other towns and asked if the name rang a bell, but no-one remembered anyone of that name working there. It was simply too long ago. Disappointed, he gave up and returned home the next day.

Harry was now working as a teacher in Bristol but came home to visit his parents for a couple of weeks in the summer holidays. He was now engaged to Dorothy and their wedding was planned for September the following year.

"Will you be my best man?" he asked Theo.

"I'd love to, but it probably won't be possible. I'll most likely be sailing to Malaya before September."

"That's a pity. How often will you come home on leave?"

"About every four years, for six months at a time."

"Well, make sure you come and visit us then."

Arthur had just finished agricultural college and was now working with his father on the estate. When Theo did some odd days work in the estate grounds, he found himself taking instructions from Arthur, which they both found a rather novel situation. Theo reflected that, by the time he came home on leave following his first tour of duty in Malaya, Arthur would probably be the estate manager, as Fred and Sarah were planning to retire to the coast in a few years time.

Enid would be embarking on her last year of school in September, and she was then planning to go to art college for at least a year. She was becoming an accomplished painter and her watercolours were displayed around the manor. Theo and Arianna each had one in their rooms.

Arianna finished college at the beginning of July and found herself a job at the largest bank in Great Pucklington. She was due to start at the beginning of August. For nearly a year, she had been courting one of the Indian students she had met at college, whose name was Sanjay. He had been duly vetted by George and Mary and reluctantly approved, as they could find no fault with him apart from his nationality.

One evening in July, she came home much earlier than expected and in floods of tears. She ran straight upstairs, seeking the privacy of her room, but bumped into Theo who was just heading downstairs.

"Hey, Ari, what on earth's the matter?"

She could scarcely speak for crying, but after a couple of minutes managed to sob, "It's all over with Sanjay!"

Theo followed her into her room and they sat on the bed. She poured it all out. It turned out Sanjay had been promised since his early teens to a girl in India, the daughter of friends of his parents. An arranged marriage. She was due to come over to England shortly and their wedding was planned for September, so his parents had insisted that his and Arianna's friendship must now come to an end.

"He never told you about this before?"

She shook her head. "He never said a word! He said tonight that he'd hoped to back out of it, but when he suggested that to his parents they hit the roof and said it would bring shame on the girl and her family, and they would never be able to hold their heads up again. They said if he broke off the engagement they'd throw him out and disown him and all the Indian community would ostracise him. So he chose them over me!"

"Oh, Ari, I'm so sorry! He shouldn't have led you on, he should have told you the truth at the beginning, then you wouldn't have let yourself fall for him. I feel tempted to go there and punch him on the nose!"

"Don't you dare, Theo! That wouldn't solve anything, anyway." She started crying again. "I really loved him, I thought he was the one and we'd get married one day!"

When George, Mary and Enid were told, George said he felt inclined to go to see the boy's father and express his displeasure.

"His parents were complicit in keeping this from Arianna, they showed no consideration for her feelings."

"Please don't, Uncle George. There's no point."

156

Enid gave her a hug, said it was his loss, and there would be bound to be lots of nice young men at the bank.

"I don't want anyone else, I only want Sanjay! And anyway, no white man is going to ask me out!"

A few weeks later, she started her new job. She was still miserable and depressed and said she didn't care whether or not she enjoyed the job. She looked very smart and businesslike that morning, in her dark grey skirt and jacket, with a high necked white blouse, a stark contrast to the colourful dresses she usually wore. She set off for the bus stop with the family's good luck wishes ringing in her ears. On the bus, she started to feel nervous and had to steel herself to walk through the staff door at the rear of the bank. She wasn't surprised to be on the receiving end of stares from those of the staff who had no idea that the new girl was not white, but once they'd got over their initial shock, most of them were friendly and showed her the ropes. She was engaged as a bookkeeper, but was also expected to do some shorthand and typing. Most of her immediate colleagues were girls, the men being in the more senior positions. She recognised a couple of the girls from school, they'd been in the year above her. By the time she'd been there a few weeks, she felt settled and reasonably happy with the work, and at least it took her mind off the loss of Sanjay.

George had merely grunted when he was told that Theo would be staying at Charlie's flat while in London, and he never referred to it subsequently. Theo enjoyed his year there, and found he gained more from the course than he had expected. Even the Malay language lessons were not a complete waste of time as English had become his primary language and his previously fluent Malay was now a little rusty. His knowledge of the country was also ten years out of date and from a child's perspective. Three of his fellow students were also destined to be cadets in the Malayan Civil Service and they would all be sailing out together. By the time the course ended in June 1938, their sailing date of Thursday 25th August had been booked. They had all been issued with a list of items to obtain before they left, a standard list for those going to work in the tropics. Some of the things seemed unnecessary to Theo, recalling his early years there, but he supposed he would no longer be acclimatised to the tropics and had better play safe.

He was back at the manor and starting to make his preparations when, in early July, Arianna dropped her bombshell on the family.

"I want to return to Malaya too," she announced after supper one evening.

"What?!" George exclaimed.

"I wrote to our grandparents asking if it's all right to come and live with them, at least initially, and they've written back saying they'd love me to come."

"But why?" Mary asked, "and what about your job at the bank? You're doing well there and you have the chance to work your way up the ladder."

"It's given me a year's work experience, which, added to my qualifications and English education, will enable me to get a decent job in any of the British government offices there. They employ a lot of Eurasians in support roles, I remember there were some in Papa's office."

"But why do you want to up sticks and go there? Is it because Theo's going?"

"No. That's a bonus, having my brother in the same country, but I would want to go anyway. I had this idea years ago, but I shelved it when I met Sanjay. If it had worked out with him then I would be staying here, but it didn't. There're other people like me there, Eurasians with English fathers and Malayan mothers and coffee coloured skin. I will fit in much better there than I do here."

"And how do you propose to pay for your fare," George asked.

"Well, I've saved some money from my wages, but if it's not enough, could you arrange to let me have a loan from my trust fund?"

"It seems to have escaped your notice that you can't go yet without our consent," George said. "You're only nineteen and until you're twenty-one you're under my guardianship."

Before Arianna could reply, Mary added, "And have you thought it through about living at your grandparents' home? From what I heard from Jim, their place is pretty basic. You've been used to living here, with your own room and a nice bathroom and servants making your meals and doing your laundry and cleaning. You'll have none of that with them."

"Well, it's true that it will be much less luxurious and I'll have to do more for myself, but that won't do me any harm, will it? If I stayed here and did eventually get married it would be unlikely that I'd have servants, so I'd have to get used to doing housework sooner or later. And I have done domestic science at school and I used to help Mama a bit, so I'm not totally useless domestically. And their home is not as bad as you think. It's better than it used to be. They rented some more land, expanded the farm and the landlord extended the cottage. There's a couple of extra rooms and an improved bathroom. Uncle Khalid took some photos and they sent copies. They say I'll have my own room." She paused and then went on, "Please let me go, Uncle George. Ideally, I'd like to sail on the same ship as Theo, but if it's booked up then I'll have to go on a later one. Either way, I need to get it arranged so I know when I'm going and then I can give in my notice in at the bank and make preparations."

Enid had been listening to all this with mounting apprehension. "Please tell her she can't go, Uncle George, not yet anyway. I'll be left on my own here and I'll really, really miss her!"

"I'm sorry Enid, I'll really miss you too. But I need to do this. Please don't try to stand in my way. In a few years time you will get married and probably move away, but it won't be so easy for me, not here." Then she added, "I may be officially underage, but lots of girls my age leave home to get married and start having children. Rosa is engaged and getting married in the spring."

"That's very different," George said. "They have husbands to look after them. You're proposing to strike out on your own, thousands of miles away from most of your family. And Theo will be posted to many different places, just as Jim was, and will probably not be anywhere near you most of the time."

"But I have Mama's family there. Not just our grandparents but also uncles and aunts and cousins."

George sighed. "Well, let us think about it. I'll let you know in a few days time. And, if I do decide to let you go, then yes, I'll lend you the rest of the fare."

"Thank you!"

"I haven't agreed yet. Your aunt and I will discuss it, and we'll also speak to Theo. By the way, you haven't yet said a word, Theo. Did you know about this?"

He shook his head. He was busy thinking about how this development would affect him. The colonial service had no idea he was Eurasian; there had been no space on the application form for mother's nationality, and no-one had asked him at the interview. His three colleagues had no idea either and he preferred it to stay that way. He would have to make sure that Ari did not drop him in it. He tackled her about it the next day, when they were alone.

"Ari, if you're coming out with me, then I need you to keep quiet about me being half Asian. The colonial service don't know and neither do my colleagues. I can introduce you as my half-sister and they will assume........."

"That the white parent is the one we share!" she finished for him.

"Exactly."

There was a short pause before she said, "So, you're still denying your heritage and our mother, pretending to be someone other than you are, and now you're proposing to demean me in the process! You'll be making me out to be the illegitimate one when it's actually you who are the bastard! And you'll be claiming my birthright as yours, pretending you were born into the English upper class, when it's actually only courtesy of *my* father that you've had this upbringing! If he hadn't adopted you, you'd probably have had to live with our grandparents until we came to England and then you'd have been sent up to Yorkshire, where your father was apparently raised in a slum!"

He winced. "You're overreacting. I'm not doing any of those things, I'm just not making it obvious that I'm half Asian. I can't help what they assume, can I? And you are my half-sister, so that's not a lie."

"We've never been just half-siblings to each other, as you well know. You're the same to me as Enid is. But perhaps it's a pity that Papa took you on; if we hadn't been brought up together, you wouldn't feel like my brother and I wouldn't feel like you're betraying me now!" She paused briefly, then added, "You don't want me to come to Malaya, do you? You don't want me there."

160

"That's not true. I'm glad you're coming."

"Well, you've a funny way of showing it!"

He sighed. "I'm just trying to do what's necessary to fit in. Surely you can see that? But, if it upsets you so much, then I'll tell my colleagues the truth and hope they don't treat me differently because of it. You know as well as I do just how prejudiced people can be."

"Yes, and I don't have the option of avoiding it!" But her anger had subsided and she also belatedly realised she needed him on her side to support her case with George and Mary. "I suppose I understand why you're doing it. And I don't want to make your life difficult. I won't blow your cover, I promise. But, in return, will you please try to convince Uncle George to let me go?"

"Yes, of course I will," he said, relieved.

George did agree and they also found that there was still a berth available on Theo's ship. Arianna would be sharing a cabin with a young English nurse. She handed in her notice at the bank and asked them to give her a written reference to take with her. Then she started to make her preparations, including shopping for more hot weather dresses and speaking Malay with Theo whenever they had the opportunity.

~***~

161

Chapter Sixteen

Dave drove them all to Southampton on the 25th August. George, Mary and Enid all came along to see them off. One of their trunks was in the boot of the car, along with their cases, and the other had to be strapped to the roof.

"It won't fall off, will it?" Arianna asked anxiously. "It would be a disaster if I arrived there with none of my clothes!"

At the docks, emotions ran high. Enid was in floods of tears as she hugged her sister and brother goodbye. Arianna was also crying and Theo had to blink hard. Mary and George were not given to lavish displays of emotion but Mary's eyes were suspiciously bright and George kept clearing his throat. Mary had come a long way since wanting to offload Theo and Arianna and she knew she was going to miss them.

"Don't forget," George said to Arianna, "if you're not happy there, just get in touch and I'll send you the money for the return fare. You'll always have a home with us."

To Theo he added, "We look forward to having you back with us for your leave in four years time."

Theo spotted his three colleagues elsewhere on the dock, also saying good bye to their families. He had had telephone conversations with all of them in the run up to their departure date, so they all knew that his Eurasian half-sister would be accompanying him. He'd taken pains to point out that the two of them had been brought up together and she was as much an English lady as any white girl. He didn't want them to treat her with any less respect because of the colour of her skin.

Theo was sharing a cabin with Edward, one of his colleagues. As they unpacked, Edward said,

"I saw you on the dock, with your sister. You never mentioned how gorgeous she is!" His open, boyish face radiated enthusiasm.

Theo merely smiled, but hoped that a shipboard romance was not going to be on the cards. Edward could be posted anywhere in Malaya and the Straits Settlements, as could he.

Meanwhile, Arianna was making the acquaintance of her cabin mate, Emma, and her two nursing colleagues, Shirley and Jean, who were in the adjacent cabin. They were all in their early twenties. Arianna was inured to the expressions of surprise and shock she normally encountered when white people first set eyes on her, but she had to admit that these three hid their reactions very well. She was warmly welcomed into their circle and by the end of the voyage they were all firm friends. The three nurses were all going to be working at the former European hospital, now called Bungsar hospital, in Kuala Lumpur, so they would not be far from Arianna in Klang.

That evening, at dinner, the four young men shared a table with the three nurses and Arianna and that became the pattern most nights. Afterwards, there was dancing and Edward immediately asked Arianna to dance. They made a striking couple on the dance floor, Edward's blonde hair contrasting with Arianna's sultry beauty.

"I think he's a bit smitten with your sister," one of the other men, Ralph, commented.

"Well, she's certainly quite a beauty," Laurence added.

And a liability! Theo thought. He would have to keep an eye out, make sure none of these men overstepped the mark. The sooner he could offload responsibility for her onto their grandparents, the better.

Later, Theo, Ralph and Laurence partnered the three nurses in the dancing but did not dance with any one of them exclusively. They were all pretty, vivacious girls and good company but neither the three men nor the girls were looking for anything more than companionship and fun.

A close friendship did develop between Edward and Arianna and Theo often came across them together around the ship. However, Arianna told him that Edward was always the perfect gentleman and anyway she was not yet ready for another romance; they were simply friends.

When they docked at Colombo, the sights, sounds and smells of the East formed a bewildering maelstrom. The heat and humidity also hit them like a sledgehammer, and Theo and Arianna found it just as oppressive and enervating as the others did. After ten years in

England, they were no longer acclimatised to the tropics and would have to readjust.

They docked in Penang at the end of September. This was the port from which they had sailed to England and they had expected to recognise it, but their childhood memories were hard to reconcile with the bustling, chaotic, present-day reality of the busy port. After redirecting their trunks, they all took the ferry across to the mainland and boarded the train for Kuala Lumpur. On the long rail journey, they played cards, read and chatted intermittently. Arianna kept looking out of the window for familiar scenes but found none. She was acutely aware that at the end of this train journey she was going to be on her own in this now unfamiliar country, heading for Klang on the last leg of her journey. Would she even recognise her relatives, or would they seem like strangers? Would Klang seem familiar at least? Surely it would; that was where they had lived and spent most of their time.

Becoming aware that Arianna was unusually quiet, Theo asked her in a low voice if she was getting nervous. She nodded.

"You'll be fine. Once you see Grandma and Grandpa and Uncle Khalid and the others, it will be as if you never went away."

"I hope so. Can you come with me to Klang?"

"No, sorry. We won't reach Kuala Lumpur until late afternoon and I'll have to go straight to the government offices with the others. But I'll see you to the platform the Klang train departs from."

"When will you come to visit? Grandma's bound to ask."

He shrugged. "Depends on where I'm posted initially. If I'm staying in KL for a bit, then I'll come over at the weekend, otherwise I'll write and let you know where I'm based."

At the imposing, Moorish-style Kuala Lumpur railway station, they all said their goodbyes. The three nurses and Arianna had already exchanged addresses and Arianna had also given hers to Edward.

"Hope to see you girls at the Selangor Club," Laurence said to the nurses. "I believe that's where everyone goes to socialise."

"That's if we're staying in KL," Ralph reminded him. "We might not be."

"We'll be back at some point. Everyone goes back and forth from the capital, don't they?"

Edward raised Arianna's hand to his lips and kissed it. "I hope to see you again soon."

Theo asked the three men to wait a few minutes while he saw Arianna to the right platform for the Klang train. One was just coming in and he hoisted her case onto it. She shut the door and then leaned out of the window.

"I hope Uncle Khalid is at the station. I can't carry this case all the way to their house."

"He said he'd meet every likely train until you arrived. Don't worry. He'll either be there or you won't have long to wait."

She waved as the train pulled out and he waved back. She watched her last link with home disappear from view, then found herself a seat, feeling tense and apprehensive and very alone.

Theo returned to join his friends. They headed out of the station and took a moment to take in the sights and sounds of central Kuala Lumpur.

"Does it look familiar?" Edward asked Theo.

"A bit. But I didn't come here all that often."

They had a map and the government offices were walking distance from the station. They soon found themselves staring up at another grand Moorish-style building, opposite a large green, called a *padang*, which was bordered on the other side by the famous Selangor Club.

"Where's the place we'll be staying?" Ralph asked Edward, who had the map.

"About half a mile away in that direction." He waved his arm towards the far side of the *padang*.

"Short distance to get to work then, if we'll be based here."

"Some of us will be," Laurence put in. "But if we're going to be here for some time, it might be worth renting a house together."

Reporting for duty at the designated office, they found that Theo and Laurence were to stay in the capital until the end of the year at least, but Ralph was to head south to Seremban the next day and Edward north to Taiping. That night they all stayed at the cadets' mess, where they were served an evening meal in the communal dining room by the Chinese houseboy and met a few others who were also staying there. Their rooms were small, but adequate. All of them except Theo expressed some shock at the sanitation arrangements; the Shanghai jar system of washing still prevailed, where you ladled water over yourself from an enormous earthenware jar, and the lavatory was of the thunderbox variety. Many buildings still had these arrangements, although the houses of the more senior officials had been updated, one of the other men staying there told them.

"I suppose we could stay here if we're going to be moving on early next year," Laurence commented to Theo. "I expect we wouldn't be able to afford a place with better facilities." Theo agreed.

The next morning, Edward gave Theo a letter to take to Arianna. "Just giving her my address."

After breakfast, Theo and Laurence said farewell to the other two, who were not leaving for another hour or so, and headed to work. They were allocated to different sections; Theo was in the Treasury. The work seemed strange at first and very different from anything he had previously experienced, but he gradually got used to it. He knew he would be gaining experience in many different aspects of colonial government over the next four years, including the law courts in one or more of the state capitals and out in the rural districts where one dealt with anything which cropped up. He remembered Jim saying that he preferred to be in the districts than at the secretariats and Theo thought he might find he felt the same, but it was early days yet.

When Arianna arrived in Klang, Uncle Khalid was waiting, along with his pony and trap, and she did recognise him. He enveloped her in a massive bear-hug and swung her feet off the ground.

"Arianna! My, what a lovely young lady you've become! Is this all your luggage?"

"My trunk's being sent on." She spoke in Malay as he had done and was glad she'd been practising with Theo before she left.

As they made their way out of the station and across the bridge, she recognised a lot of the buildings, but as they continued onwards at the other side of the river, she found the landscape changed.

166

"There're a lot more buildings than I remember. Surely this bit was open countryside before?"

"Yes, there's been quite a lot of building going on. That's why we grabbed an extra bit of land while we still could."

When they arrived, the house was crammed full of people. Nearly all her relatives seemed to have gathered to welcome her. Her grandmother hugged her tightly and wept tears of joy.

"My Alya's little girl! I had despaired of ever seeing any of you again. And Theo is here too. When are we going to see him?"

"As soon as he can. He doesn't know yet where he'll be based."

"Let me show you to your room. It's in the new part of the house."

The living room was much as Arianna remembered it but now a door at the far end led into the new extension. Her bedroom was cheerfully decorated, with a colourful bedspread and pictures on the walls. There was the usual mosquito net around the bed and a bowl and pitcher stood on the chest of drawers.

"Come and see our smart new bathroom!" her grandmother said proudly.

It was the same room as before, but instead of the rough concrete walls and floor of Arianna's memory, it was now smoothly tiled and the floor sloped down to the drainage hole. The Shanghai jar system still prevailed, and when she went to use the lavatory she found it was still an outside privy, or thunderbox as the British dubbed them, albeit a smarter one with a polished wooden seat. However, she had expected that - the District Officer's house they had lived in had sported the same sanitation system - and she had resigned herself to it. In any case you wouldn't want to take an English hot bath in this climate.

She returned to the main room and reacquainted herself with her aunts, uncles and cousins. Cousins who had been small children when she left were now teenagers and those who had been in their teens were now grown up and married, some with children of their own. After an hour or so, the visitors left to return to their own homes and she was left with her grandparents and Khalid. Khalid was their eldest son, who had never married and who worked the small farm with his father, nowadays doing the lion's share of the work as the older man was getting on a bit. Both her grandparents were looking much older, Arianna thought. Her grandmother's hair was now completely white. She tried to work out how old they must be. Alya would have been forty-two, and Khalid and one of his sisters were a few years older, so she concluded they were probably well into their sixties.

Theo arrived on Saturday morning. He received the same enthusiastic welcome as Arianna had, although without the rest of the extended family as he had not been definitely expected.

"So, you are now one of the British *Tuans*, " Khalid said, laughing.

His grandfather asked if the colonial service knew he had a Malayan mother. Theo shook his head.

"Did you lie, or did they not ask?"

"They didn't ask."

After an hour or so, he set off to do the rounds of the nearby houses where his aunts and uncles lived. Arianna accompanied him. On the way to the first dwelling, he fished in his pocket and produced Edward's letter. She read it quickly.

"He's gone to Taiping and Ralph's gone to Seremban. Me and Laurence will be in KL until the end of the year, maybe a bit longer."

"What's your job like?"

"I'm in the Treasury. Actually, you'd probably be better at it than me, with your banking experience, but I'm starting to get the hang of things."

"Are you working with Laurence?"

"No, he's in Planning."

"I like him better than Ralph."

"Actually, so do I. In a way, I'm quite glad Ralph's gone off to Seremban. His tendency to make sarcastic comments gets a bit much at times."

"Edward's the nicest one though. He says he'll be in touch as soon as he's back in KL and he'll take me out to dinner." Then she added, "Which one of the nurses did you like best?"

"I like them all, as friends."

After Theo had seen most of the rest of their relatives, they headed back to the farm. Arianna suddenly said,

"I nearly forgot to tell you. I've got a job interview on Monday."

"Gosh, that's quick!"

"Well, Aunt Rania works at the D.O's residence and she knew there was a vacancy for a clerk at the district offices, so she put my name forward."

"Well, good luck. I'll keep my fingers crossed for you, although I'm sure you'll get it. They won't have many applicants who've been educated in England and worked at an English bank."

She did get the job and she started the following Monday. It didn't take her long to get used to the work, which was not difficult, and to become friendly with the rest of the staff. Apart from the D.O. himself, they were all Eurasians or Malays, including the Assistant D.O. Some of these posts were still filled by English cadets on their first tour of duty, but the natives were increasingly taking over at that level. On her way to work each morning, she walked past the D.O.'s residence, her former home, and one evening she did a detour on the way back and passed her former school. As she gradually explored the town, she found many familiar landmarks, including the Royal Klang Club which her father had regularly frequented, but she also found a lot of changes; ten years was a long time in the life of a Malayan town.

In early November, Emma, Jean and Shirley moved out of the nurses home and rented a house together. They held a house-warming party, to which Theo, Laurence and Arianna were all invited. Theo was chatting to Shirley when he noticed a raven-haired white girl on the other side of the room, talking to Arianna. There was something about her which he found quite arresting and, as soon as he could, he made his way over to her. By then, Arianna had moved away and she was alone. He introduced himself.

"Hello, I'm Theo. I came over on the same ship as our hostesses. Are you a nurse too?"

She confirmed that she was, and told him her name was Natalia. They found a couple of vacant chairs in the corner and sat down. She spoke fluent English, but with a slight accent. Theo wondered if she was of Spanish or Italian extraction, as her colouring suggested southern European, but when he asked her that, she told him she was Eurasian.

"Half Malay and half English. My father was English."

"Same here!" He was delighted not to have to pretend.

"I thought you'd just come from England?"

He explained. She told him her father had returned to England when she was six and she had never seen or heard from him again. She was now twenty-two, just a few months younger than Theo.

"He had me baptised a Christian and left money for English schooling, and that was it. My mother later married a Malayan and I have three younger half-brothers. We all live here, in Kuala Lumpur."

Theo gave her a summary of his rather different life story and pointed out Arianna, across the room.

"Oh, yes. I was talking to her earlier. You and she look very different! You look even more European than I do, you've even got blue eyes."

It wasn't quite love at first sight, but there was an instant chemistry between them and, by the end of the evening, Theo knew she was going to be someone special in his life. He asked if he could walk her home.

"It'll be out of your way, if you're living at the cadets' place."

"I don't mind."

They said goodnight to their hostesses and to Arianna, who was staying the night there. Most of the rest of the guests had already left, including Laurence. Her home was in a street to the north-east of the city centre and about a mile away.

"May I kiss you goodnight?" he asked when they arrived outside her door.

Their kiss was a long, lingering one. He asked if he could take her out to dinner and they arranged an evening in a few days time. She worked shifts at the hospital but was on days at present. He walked the mile or so back to his residence with a spring in his step.

Their relationship developed fast. After only a few dates, Theo realised that he had fallen head over heels in love, much more so than ever before. His feelings for Claire and Susan now paled into insignificance beside this all-consuming passion, this blending of souls. And she was like him, she too had a divided heritage. With her the two halves of his identity, so often at war, merged into one.

170

He did not have to hide any part of himself, he could be who he truly was, without reservation. And his love was reciprocated in full measure. It was scarcely necessary for them to tell each other of their love, although they did, frequently. It was evident in every softly spoken word, every tender gesture and in the passion of their kisses and caresses.

They had no opportunity to be alone together indoors. There was always someone else around at the cadets' mess and it was forbidden to take the opposite sex into one's room. Natalia lived with her family, except when she was on night duty, when she slept at the nurses home, where male friends were also banned. At weekends, when she was not working, they took walks in the Lake Gardens and could sometimes find a secluded spot, but this being Malaya, sooner or later a rain shower would dampen their ardour and they would run, laughing, for shelter.

On Christmas day, Theo, Natalia, Laurence, Arianna and Emma all attended the festivities at the Selangor Club. Jean and Shirley were on duty and would have their Christmas *tiffin* at the hospital, but would join them all later. Neither Theo and Arianna's maternal relatives nor Natalia's family celebrated Christmas.

"What did you do as a child?" Theo asked her. "Didn't you get any presents or anything?"

"Not really, but we did do a nativity play at school, and sang carols, and there was a lucky dip, so I always had one present, and, until he left, I remember my father bringing me a gift on Christmas Eve."

There were very few Eurasians at the club, except amongst the staff. Arianna received some cold looks from some of the older women, particularly when they became aware that their husbands were looking admiringly across at her. One woman barged into her, seemingly deliberately, and then told her angrily to look where she was going. Arianna bit back her instinctive retort; better not to make a scene.

"The prejudice is worse here than in England," she said to Theo as she sat down again.

"Take no notice of them," Emma said. "They're just jealous because their husbands fancy you!"

171

After Christmas, Theo was told he would be transferred to Kuala Kubu Bahru as an Assistant District Officer at the end of January. He had been dreading the news of a transfer as he could have been sent a long way from the capital and Natalia, but Kuala Kubu Bahru was only about thirty miles north of Kuala Lumpur and accessible by train. He was told he would probably stay there about six months. The job came with a small two-bedroom bungalow, built on stilts in the traditional style.

"You could come to visit on your free weekends," he said to Natalia, "and stay over."

"That would be wonderful, but I'll have to tell my mother that I'm working night shifts and staying at the hospital; she'd never allow me to stay alone with you. She'd think it would ruin my reputation, even if we didn't do anything!"

By then, Theo had met her family and had a meal with them and she had also come with him to Klang. Both families seemed to approve of their courtship. Arianna and Natalia had also hit it off from the beginning and were now good friends.

Kuala Kubu Bahru was an attractive small town, surrounded by a green belt of countryside. It had been built in the 1920s near to the original mining town of Kuala Kubu, which had been substantially destroyed by a flood from a burst dam in the 1880s. The District Officer, Henry, was an easy-going chap in his late thirties, married to a pretty blonde, Gertrude, who was at least ten years his junior.

"You'll find the social life a bit limited here," he said, "but if you play chess, I'd be glad to have a game with you some evenings."

Theo did. Jim had taught him and he had occasionally played with George or Charlie and also at Oxford. When he had got to know Henry, he mentioned that he had a girlfriend who was a nurse in the capital.

"Is it all right if she stays over sometimes at weekends, in the guest room in my bungalow?"

Henry smiled. "Yes, of course, but be aware that servants gossip, so make sure she does stay in the guest room, ostensibly anyway!" He added, "You'll have to bring her over for dinner one evening when she's here."

Theo wrote to Natalia, letting her know the good news and asking her to phone him from the hospital when she had the chance. Her family were not on the phone at home; the same applied to his relatives in Klang.

He found he enjoyed the work better than being in the Treasury. It was extremely varied and involved spending a lot of time outside the office, around the district. Amongst other things, they adjudicated in planning and boundary disputes and served as magistrates. The district office was smaller than the one in Klang, where Arianna worked, having only a handful of staff, and the club where the Europeans congregated was quite small. As Henry had said, social activities were a bit sparse compared with those laid on at the Selangor Club, but there was cricket and tennis and Theo enjoyed both.

After he'd been there a few weeks, Natalia came to stay. She arrived on the Friday evening as she had the whole weekend off. They had a rapturous reunion and then went over to the D.O.'s house for dinner with Henry and Gertrude. Before they set off, he warned her that the colonial service were unaware that he was Eurasian, and asked her not to let that slip in front of Henry. To his relief, she took that in her stride and did not react as Arianna had.

Back in Theo's bungalow at the end of the evening, Natalia went into the guest room to deposit her bag and wrap, and Theo followed. The servants had already departed to their quarters. He took her in his arms and very soon they were lying on the bed. As he undid her brassiere and fondled her breasts, he murmured,

"Stop me from going too far, won't you? I love you and want you so much, I'm not sure I'll be capable of putting the brakes on myself."

She nodded, but it wasn't long before they were both naked and the desire to consummate their love became irresistible. Afterwards, as they cuddled together, passion briefly sated, he asked,

"Did I hurt you?"

"A little, but it was worth it! Was it your first time too?"

He never wanted to lie to her. "No, but it was only the once and I was rather drunk. It was nothing compared to this, with you. You've just transported me to heaven!"

She laughed. "I don't think heaven came into it much. We've just committed the sin of fornication. If we were Catholics we'd have to go to confession!"

Her words brought him down to earth and he remembered the possible repercussions.

"If we have made a baby, we'll get married. I'm not supposed to, during the first tour of duty, but they'd just have to lump it, in the circumstances."

"We should be all right. It's a very safe time of the month."

"Is that why you didn't stop me?"

"I don't think I would have anyway. By then I was past caring, I wanted you so much."

"We'd better be more careful in future, or perhaps I can use something. I'm not sure where I would get them here and I don't like to ask Henry, seeing as he's my boss!"

"No need. I'll go to the clinic at the hospital next week and get fitted for a cap. You're supposed to be married but I'll just say I'm engaged and about to be wed."

He looked at her thoughtfully. "We could make that true, the engaged bit I mean."

"Is that a proposal, Theo Bradshaw?!"

"Yes, I suppose it is!"

"Then do it properly!"

So he got down on one knee at the side of the bed, completely naked.

"Natalia, my darling, my dearest love, I love you truly, madly, deeply and I want to spend the rest of my life with you. Will you please do me the honour of becoming my wife?"

"Yes, of course I will!"

He climbed back on the bed and they made love again, this time slowly and languorously, exploring, kissing and caressing each other's bodies, finally coming together when they could hold back no longer.

The next day, she got her period and told him it was all right, there would be no baby this time. They started to make plans for their eventual marriage in about four years time.

"We could marry in Kuala Lumpur just before I go on leave and then you can come with me to England and we could have a blessing in the church there, so the rest of my family can celebrate with us. Have you got a passport?"

She shook her head. "I've never been outside Malaya."

"We'll have to sort that then; perhaps we'll have to do it quickly after the wedding so it's in your married name. I'll make enquiries."

They carried on discussing their future, cocooned in their own little bubble of happiness. However, they were ignoring the storm clouds which were gathering over Europe.

The Munich agreement, signed by Hitler and Chamberlain in September 1938, which allowed Hitler to annexe the Sudetenland in exchange for a guarantee of no further territorial claims, had been proclaimed by Chamberlain on his return to England as ensuring 'Peace in our Time.' But, in March 1939, Hitler invaded Czechoslovakia and Britain started to re-arm and introduce conscription, at the same time issuing assurances to Poland. When on 1st September 1939 Hitler invaded Poland, Chamberlain issued an ultimatum, which was ignored. On 3rd September, Britain and France declared war on Germany and the second major conflict of the twentieth century had begun.

~***~

Chapter Seventeen

When war was declared, Enid wondered firstly how it was going to affect her and secondly what would happen to Theo and Arianna. Malaya was not yet involved, but perhaps Theo would return home to enlist? In that case, presumably his future wife would accompany him, but would Arianna come too? She waited eagerly for their next letters to arrive.

After she had returned home from seeing them off, she had been sunk in the depths of misery for a week or two, missing Arianna especially, as they had never been apart before. But once she had started at art college, she gradually became absorbed in her activities there and with making new friends. At weekends, she started seeking out Arthur's company more often. For the last couple of years, she had secretly held a candle for him, but he seemed to see her as merely Theo and Arianna's baby sister and of little account. Perhaps now he would start to see her as a person in her own right, a young woman. He was five years her senior, but that was not a big age gap once you were grown up. Look at the age difference between Mama and Papa!

In the early autumn of 1939, evacuation of children from the major cities to the countryside commenced. Little Pucklington received its quota of child refugees from London's east end and one Saturday afternoon they were all assembled in the village hall, waiting for the various families in the village with a spare room to choose one of them. Mary despatched Enid to pick one, as she had a social engagement that afternoon.

"I daresay a girl might be easier, but if you can get an older boy, who could help out on the estate at weekends, that would be useful. I'll leave it to you; just one, mind, we don't want an army of children running around."

Even though we have plenty of room, Enid thought. Ours is by far the largest house in the village.

She arrived rather late, Mary having mistaken the time, and most of the children had already been taken. There were just three left, a boy who looked about eleven or twelve and two younger girls.

"Ah, Miss Bradshaw!" the woman who was acting as billeting officer exclaimed briskly. "We've been waiting for you or your aunt. These three are one family and the boy is insisting they must stay together or he'll take his sisters back home. He says that was his instruction from his mother. You have plenty of room for them all at the manor, no-one else in the village can take three."

"But Aunt Mary said to only pick one!"

"Well, if you don't mind my saying so, that's a rather selfish attitude, when you have such a large house and a staff of servants. This is wartime and everyone has to pull together and do their bit."

Enid wondered if she would have dared to say that to Aunt Mary's face. Now she was in a quandary. She couldn't let these poor children return to London to have bombs dropped on them, but on the other hand, she'd get the sharp edge of Mary's tongue if she brought them all back with her.

"What're your names and ages?" she asked the boy.

"I'm Wilfred and I'm eleven, this is Sarah, she's eight, and Annie, she's five."

Almost the same family structure as ours, Enid thought. This could be Theo, Ari and me. How would we be feeling if we'd had to leave our parents and come to a remote place to live with strangers? She knew the answer to that, remembering only too well how they'd felt after the fire, and at least they'd already known their aunt and uncle and were somewhat older.

Sarah piped up, " Please take us with you, Miss. I'd like to live in a big house and we won't be any trouble."

The little one, Annie, started to cry. "I want to go home. I want my Mummy!"

Enid knew just how she felt and her heart melted. She put her arm around the little girl.

"I bet you do, but we'll look after you, and I expect it won't be long before you can go back home and your Mummy and Daddy will be able to visit sometimes."

"So, you're taking them, then?" the billeting officer put in.

"Yes. My aunt will be furious but I can't turn them away. This could have been me, my sister and brother."

She shepherded them out of the hall, carrying the smallest girl's case for her, and they made their way through the estate to Pucklington Manor.

"Cor blimey!" Wilfred exclaimed in awe, "You do have a big house, don't you!"

"Well, it's not mine, I just live here. My uncle owns it."

She ushered them inside and told them to wait in the hall for a moment. George was on his own in the drawing room.

"Is Aunt Mary not back yet?"

"No. Have you picked a child? Where is he, or her?"

"They're in the hall, there're three of them!"

"What!"

Enid explained the situation. George scratched his head.

"Well, I suppose you didn't have much option. At least the boy can help a bit on the estate. We're going to be short of casual labour soon when conscription kicks in. But you'll have to help look after the little girls; Daisy and Mrs Hughes can't do everything. You'd better take them down to the kitchen for now, get them something to eat and drink, and see Mrs Hughes. She's only made up one room so far, perhaps you can give her a hand to get them all settled. Meanwhile, I'll try to smooth things over with your aunt when she gets back!"

Aunt Mary had quite a lot to say on the subject when Enid next encountered her, despite George's smoothing over, but she accepted that she couldn't send them back.

"We'll just have to make the best of it," she said to Mrs. Hughes. "After all, this is wartime. In the first war, part of this house became a sanatorium."

"if you don't mind my saying so, milady, you had a lot more domestic staff then!"

"I know, and I know it won't be easy, but you're a genius at organisation, Mrs Hughes, I'm sure you'll cope."

Recounting that conversation to Cook later, Mrs Hughes said, "She thinks flattery will get her everywhere, but it doesn't get me a new pair of legs, does it?"

As it turned out, the three children were not too much trouble. They seemed to have been well brought up and had reasonable manners, which Enid later heard was not the case with all of the refugees. They ate their meals in the kitchen with the staff, who gradually became rather fond of them and they all attended the village school. Sarah helped Annie to dress in the morning and Wilfred shared the pocket money George gave him, for helping on the estate, with his sisters.

Rationing was gradually brought in, starting with petrol. There was only enough for the farm vehicles, so Dave was made redundant. As he would shortly be conscripted anyway, he decided to enlist. They heard later that he was maintaining army vehicles and rather enjoying himself. The car languished in the garage alongside Theo's for the rest of the war.

Ration books were issued to all the family, the resident staff and the evacuees. Mrs Hughes' shopping trips became a more arduous process and also much lengthier because of the queues. Cook had to become more inventive with her menus and her job was not made any easier by Mary, who kept forgetting the restrictions of rationing when issuing orders for meals. Her memory was starting to deteriorate, although she was only in her mid sixties. Mr and Mrs Hughes and Cook were all now well into their fifties and grumbled frequently about the wartime privations which were making their lives harder.

Daisy's young man was conscripted and for a few days she was inconsolable, but they still planned to marry in a year or so, whether the war was over or not. She started saving her clothing coupons towards her wedding dress. A few months into the war, Millie decided to take a job in a munitions factory and gave in her notice. As Enid was going to be needed more and more at home, she decided that art college was a luxury in wartime and reluctantly left at the end of the spring term. The college was to fold within the year anyway, once the mainly young, male staff were conscripted. At times, she felt rather resentful towards her sister and brother for taking themselves off to the other side of the world, leaving her to deal with ageing relatives, diminishing staff and refugee children.

More of the estate land had to be laid to crops to feed the nation, and Arthur and the full-time farm staff found they were in reserved occupations as agricultural workers, so would not be conscripted.

Enid was very relieved that Arthur would not be sent to fight. Later on, they were allocated a couple of land girls, who also took up residence in the house. Enid herself later joined the Women's Voluntary Service branch in Great Pucklington and found herself taking orders from the woman who had acted as billeting officer.

In January 1940, Sarah, Arthur's mother, died. She had not been well for a few months and had been seeing doctors and having tests for a few weeks in the run up to Christmas. Cancer of the womb was diagnosed. She went into hospital for an operation in early January and never came out. Her family were devastated. Arthur's two older, married sisters were staying at the cottage for a while, but after the funeral they had to get back to their families. Fred and Sarah had been planning to retire to the seaside in the early spring, they had bought a little cottage near to Fred's sister, and Arthur was due to take over as Estate Manager. A week or so after the funeral, Fred told Arthur he was still going to go.

"Are you sure, Dad? You could always stay on here with me after I've taken over. All your friends are round here."

"No, lad, you'll marry one day and this will be a home for your wife and family. I'll be better off living near Rose."

Although Fred and Arthur were both grieving, Fred seemed to internalise his feelings and was reluctant to talk to Arthur about his mother. Arthur turned to Enid to unburden himself, knowing she would understand what he was going through.

"I miss her so much. She was just always *there!"* he said miserably. "You know what it feels like, don't you? You were so young when your parents died, I don't know how you coped."

"I don't think I did cope. I just stumbled through it, with help from Theo and Ari."

"They were young, too. I never really talked to Theo about it; I didn't know if he wanted to and I didn't want to upset him."

"We talked to each other. We all became closer after the fire."

"My sisters are so much older than me; ten and twelve years. And they've got their husbands and children."

Enid wanted to put her arms around him and hug him close, but she refrained. It might scare him off. So she just let him talk and reminisce about his mother and it seemed to help.

180

One evening in late April they were both sitting in front of the fire in the living room of Arthur's cottage. Fred had recently departed for Eastbourne and Arthur was missing his company. Knowing this, Enid had started popping over some evenings after supper. They were chatting about this and that, then Arthur suddenly reached out and took hold of her hand. Looking into her eyes, he said earnestly,

"You're a really lovely person, aren't you? Sweet inside as well as pretty on the outside! I've never properly appreciated you before now."

She blushed. " You're a pretty nice person yourself, and handsome with it!"

Arthur had not reached the age of twenty-three without dating a few girls, but he had never been serious about any of them. He had secretly lusted after Arianna for a while, when he'd been about eighteen and she sixteen, but he suddenly realised that he'd been overlooking the girl who was just right for him. She was so much younger, until recently he had always thought of her as a child, but she was now eighteen. He leaned towards her and touched her cheek tenderly.

"Would you be angry if I kissed you?"

She shook her head. His kiss was gentle and tentative and she initially responded in like manner, but feelings were coursing through her which she had never experienced before, delicious, exciting feelings. Soon she was sitting on his knee and they were kissing passionately. Then Arthur came to his senses and called a halt.

"What are we doing?! This can never be. You're my employer's niece."

"So what? There's no law against it!"

"Your uncle would never agree to us being together, I may even get the sack if he finds out I'm paying court to you."

"I don't think so. He won't want to lose you. He says you're a marvellous estate manager, in some ways even better than your father because you're applying all the new things you've learnt at college and you're saving the estate money. He's always singing your praises! And he'd want me to be happy."

"He'd never let us marry."

Enid felt a surge of joy. He was thinking of marriage!

"You're seeing obstacles where there aren't any. He may need some time to get used to the idea of us together, but when he does he'll realise it's ideal. It would keep you here and he won't ever have to look for a new estate manager - which would be a tall order in wartime - and it would keep me here too, near to them. They're both getting on a bit, Aunt Mary is starting to have memory problems, and they are starting to rely on me much more." She added, "You know, at one time Aunt Mary was talking about taking me to London to do a season as a debutante when I was eighteen, with a view to finding me a wealthy husband, but that won't happen now, with a war on, and anyway it would have been pointless as just one mention of my Malayan mother would cause a potential suitor to run a mile!" She paused for breath then went on, " I think we should just let them see that we have become close friends and let them slowly come round to the idea that we may become more than that. If they do object, we just need to threaten to elope and then they'd lose both of us; they won't want that. And remember, I'm not their daughter, only their niece. They'll be less concerned about class and status for me, even if those divisions weren't already starting to fall apart, which they are."

"Yes, war is a great leveller!" Arthur put in.

"And they let Arianna go off to Malaya when she was only nineteen, so they can hardly justify not letting me make my own choices in life too."

"You're making a convincing case! We'll just take it slowly for a while, then. You also need to be sure this is what you want, you're still very young."

"It is what I want. I started to have feelings for you a while ago."

As she said it, she wondered if she should have admitted that, should she be playing harder to get? However, Arthur smiled and reached for her again.

"Well, I seem to have fallen in love with you, Enid Bradshaw, so we're going to have to work it out somehow."

~***~

Chapter Eighteen

Meanwhile, back in Malaya, the war still seemed rather remote. When war had been declared, Theo and his colleagues had wondered if they should return to England and enlist, but the edict had soon come down from on high that they should all remain in their posts; Malaya still had to be ruled and may also have to be defended at a later date. It was recommended that all the younger men join the Malayan Volunteers, which were similar to the British Territorials.

Just before the outbreak of war, Theo had been posted to Seremban, to work in the secretariat there. After a couple of weeks living in the cadets' mess he found a room in a house share with two colleagues, which meant that Natalia could join him there on her free weekends and stay over. Seremban was a similar distance from the capital as Kuala Kubu Bahru. However, being in the Volunteers meant he often had military training and exercises at weekends, which ate into their time together.

"If we were married, we wouldn't have this problem," he said to her. "You'd be here all the time. Now it's wartime, I daresay I could get permission to marry, especially as you're already in the country and they don't have to pay for a passage from England."

"That would be wonderful, darling, but what about my job? I don't want to give up nursing yet, not until we start having babies."

"Couldn't you get a transfer to the hospital here?"

"Yes, probably, but how long will you be here? I can't keep chopping and changing every few months."

Theo didn't know, but shortly after that conversation, he was told he would be transferred to Kuala Lumpur in the early spring of 1940, to work in the law courts , and that post would be for at least a year. He applied for dispensation to marry during his first tour of duty, which was granted, and as soon as he arrived back in the capital, they started planning their wedding. St Mary's church in the centre of the city was booked for a Saturday in early June and they also reserved one of the private rooms at the Selangor club for their reception. Theo requested to be allocated married quarters by the time they returned from honeymoon. Natalia asked Arianna to be one of her two bridesmaids, the other being a friend from school, and Theo asked Edward to be his best man.

Edward had been posted to the capital a few months earlier and Arianna had recently obtained a job at the government offices, in the treasury department, and was now sharing a house with Emma and Shirley, replacing Jean who had transferred to the new Alexandra hospital in Singapore. Arianna and Edward were now officially courting and Edward asked Theo if he was all right with that.

"It's got nothing to do with me," Theo said, amused. "I'm not her guardian and anyway she's now twenty-one."

"I know that, but she doesn't have a father and her guardian is in England. I want to do things right and you are her older brother."

"Well, you have my blessing! But what would your family think about you courting a mixed race girl?"

"I daresay it might cause a few raised eyebrows, but my family can't dictate who I go out with, and if I should decide to ask her to marry me at a later date, and she accepts, then they'll just have to like it or lump it."

"So your intentions are entirely honourable then? You would be prepared to marry her if things work out between you?"

"Yes, but I haven't asked her yet, so don't say anything, will you? I don't want to rush into anything and I don't want to frighten her off if she's not thinking about marriage yet."

As Edward was now visiting Klang sometimes with Arianna, Theo thought it was time to come clean about his ethnicity before his grandparents let something slip which made it obvious.

"I don't know if Ari's told you - I asked her to keep it quiet when we came here - but I may as well tell you now that I'm Eurasian too."

"Are you? No, she didn't say. So are you actually full siblings?"

"No, still half. We share a Malayan mother but have different British fathers. However, her father adopted me and brought me up. I'd rather you didn't spread it around, if you don't mind. The colonial office don't know - no-one ever asked me my mother's nationality - and I don't want it getting to the ears of the top brass, it might affect my chances of promotion."

184

"Yes, they're a lot of stuffed shirts aren't they? Don't worry, I'll keep it quiet. Does Laurence know?"

"No, but I don't mind if you tell him, as long as he doesn't spread it around either. He's coming to the wedding and my Malayan relatives will be there."

Theo was enjoying the work at the law courts. He had experienced a flavour of what was involved when acting as a magistrate in Kuala Kubu Bahru, but here in the capital the cases were more serious. Qualified lawyers were in charge, but he had quite a bit of involvement in court and found the proceedings fascinating. One case concerned a Chinese criminal gang who had murdered several members of a rival gang. When the trial was over, he recounted the details to Natalia.

"I'm glad you weren't the one who sentenced them to death. Their gang mates might try to get their revenge!" she said, not entirely in jest.

Their wedding day dawned dry and bright and the weather stayed fair for most of the day. Standing by the altar with Edward, Theo watched his bride walking down the aisle towards him, on her stepfather's arm, wearing a simple but elegant white dress and a wide brimmed hat, and thought his heart might burst with love. She looked incredibly beautiful; he could hardly believe his luck that she had agreed to be his wife. When her procession reached the altar, Arianna grinned and winked at her brother as she took Natalia's bouquet from her, guessing how emotionally overwhelmed he was.

After they had said their vows and the service was over, they stood at the entrance to the church for photographs. Laurence - who had travelled to the wedding from Taiping - was a keen and quite expert photographer and had offered to take their pictures. Theo beckoned to his grandparents to be in one of the photos, which also featured Natalia's mother and stepfather.

"Oh, no, you don't want us in your pictures," his grandfather said.

"Yes, I do. I don't have parents anymore and my guardians are in England so you two are the obvious candidates for this one."

They reluctantly came to stand beside him and the photo was a perfect balance of light and dark skins.

However, when they were about to adjourn to the Selangor Club, both Theo's grandparents and Natalia's parents hung back, saying that the club was no place for the likes of them and they would say goodbye now.

"No, you must come!" Natalia said to her mother. "You're my mother, I can't not have you there! We're in a private room, you won't be in the main part of the club with strangers staring, it'll just be us."

Her parents eventually reluctantly agreed to come for a short time, not wanting to upset their daughter on her wedding day, but Theo's grandparents remained adamant. They would feel too out of place in that bastion of British rule. Khalid said he would come for a short time and one of his sisters and her husband agreed to accompany him, but Theo's grandfather said they were too old to change their ways.

"We've come into a Christian church to see you married, and we wish you all the happiness in the world, Theo, but that club is no place for us. We didn't go to the Klang club either, when Jim married your mother all those years ago, we just attended the actual ceremony."

Theo had been at that wedding but as he had been only three, his memories were vague and he could not have said whether his grandparents were there at all. He had to accept their decision, but felt a bit sad.

They were to spend their honeymoon in Fraser's Hill, one of the hill stations used by the Europeans for holidays, where the air was cooler and fresher. Theo's boss had arranged for a hired car to take them there, by way of a wedding present, and it was decorated with the usual tin cans and 'Just Married' slogan.

"I'm so happy for you, *sayang*. Have a lovely time!" Arianna said to her brother.

To Natalia, she said, "I'm so glad we're sisters now. I miss my sister in England terribly, but now I've got one here too!"

"And I never had a sister and always wanted one!"

"Well, now you've got two," Theo said. "You'll meet Enid one day, when we can get to England on leave."

On the way, in the car, Natalia asked, "What's Enid like? In personality, I mean. I know what she looks like from your photos."

"She's sweet-natured, amenable, gets on with everyone. She's also a talented artist. She was at art college, but my last letter from her said she's had to give that up because of the war."

"That's a shame!"

"She can't wait to meet you. She'll be really disappointed to have missed our wedding."

They spent their two week honeymoon in a haze of bliss. Being together all day, every day, with no time constraints, making love whenever the mood took them, seemed like heaven. By the time they returned to Kuala Lumpur, they were more in love than ever. Their new house was ready and waiting for them and they were welcomed by their Malayan houseboy and Chinese cook. Theo had already become used to being a *Tuan*, but for Natalia, being a *Mem* was a novelty and also slightly daunting.

"Do I have to give the servants instructions?" she asked Theo, when they were alone.

"My experience is that they mostly do everything themselves and just get on with it, but that might be more the case in a bachelor household. They'll ask what you want with regard to meals and so on and you just tell them. Don't worry, sweetheart, you'll soon get the hang of it. We obviously have to give Cook money for shopping, but I'll take care of that, and I'll pay their wages and the rent."

"Well, as I'm still working, I should pay half," she declared. "Let me know the household budget and I'll pay my share."

"Not half. I earn more than you and girls spend more on clothes and stuff, but you can contribute if you want to. Anyway, whatever cash I have left at the end of the month will go into a savings account for our joint future." He added, "I also have some money in a bank in England, my share of our father's small estate, and if we ever return there to live, it should provide a deposit to buy a small house."

"Do you want to go back to England one day, permanently I mean?"

"I don't know. Perhaps when we're older? We can talk about it then. You'll have been with me to England on leave several times by then and you'll know if you want to live there or not. If you really don't, then we can grow old here instead!"

"I suppose having servants is second nature to you," she commented a bit later. "You've always had them; in a D.O's residence here, then in an English manor house. I don't suppose you've ever had to do anything for yourself, have you?"

"Not true!" Theo protested. "The first three years in England we lived in a small house on my uncle's estate and we only had a part-time maid to help Mama with the heavy cleaning and laundry. We all had to pitch in a bit weekends and holidays; make our beds, lay tables, help wash up and so on. And Ari helped Mama with the cooking sometimes and I helped Papa with the outside jobs and gardening. I actually got quite good at gardening! And, I worked outside on the estate land quite a bit during my university holidays."

"So, you're not totally spoiled, then! I won't have to wait on you hand and foot if we end up in that little house in England."

"No, but I'll presumably be the sole breadwinner by then and you'll be home with our children, so I suppose the lion's share of the indoor domestic jobs will fall to you. It's the way of the world, isn't it?"

"A world ruled by men," she commented lightly.

"Now you're sounding like Ari!"

He wondered briefly if they were going to have their first argument, but then she smiled and said,

"I'm only teasing you. I won't mind looking after you if you're bringing home the bacon. What do you think you would do for a living if we do return to England?"

"I've no idea. It's a long time in the future and I haven't thought about it. But I imagine experience in colonial government would be a good background for many jobs, the civil service or local government maybe."

The following weekend, they did their first bout of entertaining, inviting Arianna and Edward to dinner. The conversation was mainly about the progress of the war. Just before their wedding, Churchill's 'we'll fight them on the beaches....' speech had been broadcast on the radio, following the fall of France and the evacuation from Dunkirk, and news had just reached them of the

188

occupation of the Channel Islands and Italy's entrance into the war on the side of the Nazis. Enid's letters had updated Theo and Arianna on the war as it concerned rural England, as had Edward's letters from his family in Surrey. Since arriving in the capital, Theo and Edward had both transferred to the Selangor battalion of the Volunteers, but they did not really think they would ever have to fight and reassured Natalia and Arianna that they were in no danger.

From late August, news of the London blitz started to reach them, followed by Coventry and other cities in the autumn. It all made for sobering reflection and much discussion at the Selangor Club, but it was still thought that Malaya was unlikely to be attacked, even though the government was aware of the growing threat from Japan. It was also believed that any threat would come from the sea, therefore naval defences were top priority.

Arianna was starting to fall in love with Edward. At first she had tried not to do that, thinking that Edward was unlikely to ever marry a mixed race girl, but when she voiced that concern to Theo, he hinted that Edward was his own man and unlikely to be influenced by his family in such matters.

"Did he actually say so?"

"Well, sort of. I can't give away any confidences, Ari, but he's not just playing with your affections, I assure you. He won't be another Sanjay."

Edward was always the perfect gentleman when they dated and had never yet suggested that they should sleep together. It would have been perfectly possible for her to stay over in his room in the house he shared with three colleagues or for him to stay in her room at Emma and Shirley's home; none of their housemates would have batted an eyelid, regarding it as none of their business. Such freedom was intoxicating to Arianna, but also made her nervous. If she did sleep with him, would he think she was not a nice girl and therefore not marriage material? She spoke to Emma and Shirley about it.

"Has he suggested it?" Emma asked.

"No."

"Well, don't make the first move. Wait for him to do that and see how you feel about it. If you really want to, then make sure he takes precautions - you don't want to fall pregnant! But if you're not ready, then don't. If he loves you, he'll respect your decision."

"But, if I did, would he think I was easy and lose respect for me?"

"You're a virgin, aren't you?" Shirley asked.

"Yes."

"Well, it's unlikely he'd think you easy then, if he's the first. But you'd probably be better waiting until he's asked you to marry him and put a ring on your finger. Just tell him you're saving yourself for the man you'll eventually marry. That might even propel him into proposing!"

Arianna wanted to ask them if they were still virgins, but decided that would be too nosy. She knew that Theo and Natalia had slept together before they were even engaged; Natalia had confided that to her, and it had not put Theo off! She wondered whether to consult her brother and get a male viewpoint, but Edward was his friend and it might put him in an awkward position.

When she was with Edward and they were kissing and caressing each other, she found desire coursing through her and wanted more. She had had similar feelings with Sanjay, but they had never had the opportunity to be alone together indoors. She didn't want to put Edward off by appearing too forward, so she took her housemates' advice and held off, waiting for him to make the first move. However, in the early New Year of 1941, he was sent to Brunei for eight months, to cover absence on leave, so their relationship became long distance and conducted mainly by letter. His letters, though, became increasingly passionate and she responded in kind.

In April 1941, Theo was transferred to Singapore, to work in the Governor's office, and Natalia obtained a transfer to the Alexandra Hospital, where Jean now worked. Singapore was a much coveted posting with government officers, and Theo's colleagues told him enviously that he was a lucky beggar to get sent there so early in his career. The island had attractive houses, wide streets, bustling shops and parks and a lavish social life centred on Raffles hotel.

At the end of their lengthy train journey they arrived at the imposing white art-deco station in Keppel Road, with its vast hall decorated with murals. Their allocated bungalow was in Mount

Rosie Road, an exclusive area, and Natalia exclaimed in delight at her first sight of it.

"Our house in KL was nice, but this is wonderful!"

Their new home was red roofed, with white walls and a balcony, surrounded by manicured lawns and separated from its neighbours by lush foliage. Inside, the rooms were spacious and tastefully furnished and, best of all, it sported an English-style bathroom. Natalia was round eyed as she viewed the large bath and flush WC - such luxury!

"We can fit both of us in that bath," Theo said, grinning, putting his arms around her from behind and pressing against her.

They were welcomed by their Chinese indoor servants, Wong-Han and Wong-Lian, who were a married couple. By 1941, Singapore had a larger Chinese population than Malayan. They soon discovered that Lian was an excellent cook.

They both had a couple of days to settle in before they started their new jobs and they explored the town. They found the Kampong Glam area, with its grid of narrow lanes around a picturesque mosque, and St Andrews cathedral, just off the Padang which also served as a cricket ground with the cricket club at the far end. They wandered into the Singapore Club and added themselves to its membership, paying their subscriptions there and then. Then they checked out Raffles and had a drink at the famous long bar.

"I believe they have lots of dinner parties here," Theo said. "I think we're going to have fun on this island!"

They found the base station for the rickshaws which abounded there, located Theo's offices at the Empress Place Building and viewed Alexandra hospital from outside. After that, they wandered down to the river and then spent some time in the harbour area. As they looked at the vessels moored there, Theo commented,

"If this damn war is over by next autumn, I can take my first long leave and we'll sail from here to England on one of the large liners. That's an experience in itself, my love. It's like a five week long luxury cruise!"

Natalia smiled and slipped her hand into his, but she couldn't help feeling a twinge of apprehension about going to England and staying with Theo's upper class family. She felt more at home with his native Malay relatives.

The Europeans in Malaya and Singapore were by now much more aware of the serious threat posed by Japan, but official statements were still making light of Japan's military capability and overstating that of the British. In Singapore especially, people still did not believe they would ever be invaded; their defences were supposed to be inviolate, Singapore was an impregnable fortress. Although preparations for war were now being stepped up and some rationing and tax increases had been brought in, these were still viewed as precautions only. The Europeans in Singapore continued to live their carefree lives, immersed in a world of parties and glamour, 'fiddling while Rome burnt', as one English army officer later put it.

On the Monday morning, Theo and Natalia breakfasted early and set off for work. The Wongs were surprised to find that their *Mem* was going to work too; they were used to their *Tuans'* wives being ladies of leisure, breakfasting in bed, then lunching with friends at the club or at Raffles.

Arriving at his offices, it was not long before Theo was introduced to the Governor, Sir Shenton Thomas. He was quite low down the pecking order of the Governor's staff, however, and did not have much future contact with him. He found the work amenable and not too taxing and his colleagues friendly.

Natalia found herself reunited with Jean almost immediately, as they were on the same ward and the same shift that week. The hospital was much more modern than the one in Kuala Lumpur. She enjoyed her first day immensely and hoped that Theo's posting here would be a lengthy one, lasting at least until he could take his leave.

They soon got into the swing of their social life, although Natalia's evening and night shifts sometimes prevented her from attending functions with Theo. After one such evening, when he had been asked several times where his lovely wife was, he ventured to suggest that she should give up work and become a lady of leisure like most of the other wives.

"I can afford to keep you."

"I don't want to be kept! I like my job and I want to continue doing it until we start having children, and I'd rather leave starting a

192

family until this war is over and we know we are safe. We're still young, we have plenty of time. Until then, I don't want to lead an aimless life, being a lady who lunches, I want to do a useful job."

"But there's charity work you can do, for the war effort and so on."

"No, Theo! I'm not leaving nursing!"

Her eyes flashed fire and it was the nearest they'd come yet to a serious argument. Not wanting it to escalate into one, he dropped the matter.

In the early summer, both Theo and Arianna received letters from Enid, telling them of her engagement to Arthur. George and Mary had been dubious at first about their developing relationship, but had gradually come round to the idea, as Enid had predicted, and when Arthur had sought George's permission to marry his niece, it had been forthcoming, although they had been asked to wait another year before they married. The wedding was set to take place in May 1942.

"Well, that's another of us with her future settled," Theo commented to Natalia. "It just leaves Arianna to get herself sorted."

"I expect she and Edward will marry eventually," Natalia said. "They seem to be growing closer."

In June and July 1941, the war was brought closer to home when Theo's Singapore battalion of the Volunteers was mobilised full time. Office work was left to the older men and the native staff, while the young men attended parades, did training exercises and helped to prepare Singapore's defences. In August, things returned to more or less normal, but the war now seemed less remote and the threat from Japan was looming nearer. In September, two practice blackouts were conducted. Nevertheless, their lives and the social round continued much as before, despite the ever increasing Allied military presence on the island. The officers from the regular army were allowed to use the various clubs without paying subscriptions, which caused a degree of resentment, but their presence also instilled a sense of security amongst the residents. There was still no panic, even when the volunteers were again mobilised full time from 1st December.

However, in the very early hours of Monday 8th December 1941, the Japanese army landed at Kota Bahru in Kelantan state in North East Malaya. A few hours later, Japanese aircraft bombed Singapore, attacking the airfields, Raffles Place and also the Chinese quarter. The war was now a harsh reality and lives were to change forever.

~***~

Chapter Nineteen

Theo and Natalia were woken at 4.15 am on 8th December by the sound of air raid sirens, followed within a few minutes by the bombing. They looked out of the window and saw the night sky lit up in the town below by the fires from the bombs.

"Oh, God, it's started, the Japs are here!" Natalia said, panic in her voice.

He held her close. "It's only air raids, they've not landed yet."

But they had, as they heard later that day on the radio. The broadcaster also announced the bombing of Pearl Harbour, which would now bring America into the war.

Once they were awake, Theo realised that he would have to report to his unit without delay, as they would be needed to assist the emergency services with the aftermath. Natalia had been due a day off, but she also dressed hastily in her white uniform.

"They'll need all hands on deck at the hospital," she said. "There're bound to be a lot of casualties."

Lian was also awake and she made them a quick breakfast before they left.

"I understand the bombs landed on the airfields and one on Raffles Place," she said, "and also in the Chinese quarter. We will go down there shortly to check that our relatives are unharmed."

Theo marvelled at the way servants always got information quicker than anyone else, it was like a sort of bush telegraph.

"I hope your family will be all right," Natalia said.

The main casualties were soldiers from an Indian regiment of the army, stationed in Singapore. Sixty-one were killed and more than seven hundred injured. Further air raids followed about a week later on RAF Tegah and again at the end of December on Singapore town. More would follow in the New Year, including a daylight raid. Each time, the hospitals were overflowing with casualties and Natalia had to work overtime. Theo was also on duty most evenings and they became like ships passing in the night. When they were able to spend a brief period of time together, their talk was all about the war and its implications.

The Japanese were advancing rapidly down the Malayan peninsula. After they had taken the northern airfields, Georgetown was bombed into submission on 11th December and Penang fell on the 19th, its European residents being evacuated by train and ship. Ipoh and Taiping were bombed on 17th and 18th December and finally fell to the Japanese just after Christmas. The Allied army withdrew over the Perak river to Kampar and the battle of Kampar took place between 30th December and 2nd January. After the fall of Penang, the Japanese took over the radio station there and started broadcasting propaganda. On the Eastern side of Malaya it was a similar story and Europeans were evacuated to Kuala Lipis by 18th December.

The British continued retreating. The Volunteers were now merged into the regular army and many of them were bewildered by the continuous orders to retreat, retreat.

"Why are we leaving? We could have held them here, we could have fought them," was a constant refrain.

The Volunteers found that their local knowledge of the people and the terrain was largely ignored by the British officers, and they were used mainly for secondary tasks such as digging trenches. Some of their better guns were taken from them and they were left with inferior equipment.

As the news worsened, and the invaders got nearer and nearer to Kuala Lumpur, which had already been bombed at the end of December, Theo became increasingly worried about his sister. After several abortive attempts, he eventually managed to get through to her by telephone.

"Ari, if KL looks at all likely to fall to the Japs, you must get out. Go to Klang and lie low there. Pretend to be wholly Malayan, hide your British passport and change your surname to theirs. You're dark skinned enough to get away with it. If the Japs take over at the government offices and you're still there, you'll be interned. You're on record there as a Bradshaw and they have details of your life in England."

"Yes, I know. Edward's told me the same thing."

Edward had been back in the capital since October and, like Theo, he had been mobilised full-time since the beginning of December.

"His battalion is busy defending KL," Arianna continued, "so hopefully the Japs won't succeed in taking it."

"I wouldn't hold my breath, the way things have been going so far. I don't know what the British military top brass are playing at, they seem to be just giving up on our country, as though it's not worth fighting for." His tone was bitter. "Ari, I don't want to have to worry about you as well as Nat. Please promise me you'll get out in good time."

"Yes, I promise. Take care of yourselves, won't you? I understand you've had air raids there but the Japs won't be able to invade Singapore, will they?"

Theo was no longer sure about that. Singapore had an excellent naval base but no permanent fleet. The idea was that a fleet would be despatched from elsewhere if required, to make its way there at all speed. Two battleships had arrived in early December but no air cover for them and they had been sunk by the enemy on 10th December. Defences were being built up on the south side of the island, assuming the Japanese would approach by sea, but what if they came all the way down the peninsula and over the causeway?

To Arianna, he just said, suddenly feeling very emotional, "I love you, Ari. Keep yourself safe and we'll meet up again when this is all over."

"I love you too, *sayang.* Give my love to Nat."

The next major battle, at Slim River, was fought and lost on 7th January, by which time Klang had effectively been taken over by the Japanese, after they had landed at Port Swettenham, threatening the capital from the west as well as the north. Orders were given for the Europeans to be evacuated from Kuala Lumpur. Edward's unit was being sent to Port Swettenham, as a prelude to retreating south along the coast. Before he left, he went to find Arianna and found her at home packing.

"You're leaving, good. I'll escort you to Klang as I'm heading to the port, make sure you get to your relatives safely. There are still trains running."

She didn't answer immediately, just put her arms round his neck and held onto him tightly. He looked exhausted.

"What's happening with you?"

"We've got orders to retreat along the coast. That's all we ever do, retreat, even when we could have dug in and fought them. They've just given up. At this rate we'll end up in Singapore."

"If you do, will you get to see Theo?"

"I expect so. He's in the Singapore battalion and we'll probably all merge. But, Ari, there's no time to waste. Finish your packing quickly. You'll have to leave your trunk, you can only take what we can carry."

"I left it at grandpa's house anyway. I just have two cases. Can you carry one for me?"

"Yes, of course."

She put the last of her things into the smaller case and closed it.

"Ready?"

"Yes. Oh, Edward, I wish we'd had more time together and I wish we'd been together totally."

He knew exactly what she meant. "So do I, darling."

They kissed passionately, desperately, pressing their bodies tightly together. Then he reluctantly released her.

"Come on. We have to go."

The train journey was uneventful; they met no Japanese soldiers and the carriages were strangely empty. The Europeans were heading directly south, Emma and Shirley amongst them, and the native population were staying home.

When they reached her grandparents' house, he said he couldn't stay, he was already going to be late rejoining his unit.

"Wait for me, won't you, my love? This war can't last forever and when it's all over, we can be together again. This is not the time to propose, but I love you very much and I want you to be my wife one day."

"I love you too and I want that more than anything!"

After one final intense embrace, he abruptly pulled away and she watched him walking back towards the river, tears obscuring her view of him.

In Singapore, later in January, Theo and Natalia managed to spend a rare evening and night together, and Theo broached what had been on his mind for a while.

"Nat, if the worst comes to the worst, all of Malaya falls and Singapore is being invaded, you must get out. Evacuations by ship have already started. Get to England if you can, but, failing that, to Australia and wait the war out there. I've written out my family's address and telephone number; I suggest you memorise it, it's easy to remember. If you can get to them, they'll give you a home for the duration, and you could even get a nursing job at the local hospital. If you're stuck in Australia, try to contact my uncle; he'll send you the money for the passage to England, assuming ships are still sailing there. Tell him I'll repay him after the war from my trust fund money. Meanwhile, I've drawn out what spare cash I have here; take it." He handed her an envelope.

"I've also got some money in the bank."

"Then withdraw it."

"But, what about my family in KL? I can't just desert them. And if I got back there, I could hide out with them."

"You wouldn't make it back there. KL is occupied now and the front line is well south of there. And it wouldn't be easy for you to hide out with them, you look too European. Your family will be all right, the Japs won't be issuing reprisals against the Malays, they'll need the native labour to keep the country going."

"I don't want to go anywhere without you. Can't you leave too?"

"How can I? I'm a soldier now, I have to fight until the end, then I'll become a prisoner of war if we lose. I can't desert."

"You're a volunteer, not with the regular army."

"And we were all conscripted last year, you know that."

"So, you are going to fight the Japs when they arrive, risk being killed!"

"Yes, I have no alternative."

Her face suddenly crumpled. "I can't bear it, I can't bear the thought of you being killed or injured."

He wrapped his arms around her. "I'll try not to be!"

199

"Well, just don't try to be a bloody hero! Don't do anything more then you have to, don't put yourself in danger when you don't need to. Promise me!"

She was crying in earnest now and he held her tightly, stroking her hair. Then they made love, slowly but with desperate intensity, each of them trying to become a part of the other, to lose their beings in each other, to merge their souls. Eventually, emotionally spent and physically exhausted, they fell asleep in each other's arms.

Meanwhile, the Japanese advance and the Allied retreat was continuing relentlessly southwards, towards Johore. On January 29th, Johore Bahru was evacuated and blitzed. The European civilian refugees from Malaya were now all pouring across the causeway, filling every available home and hostelry in Singapore. Some stayed with friends, some dossed down in the clubs. Many had to sleep in corridors and on balconies. By 31st January the whole of the Malayan peninsula was in the hands of the Japanese. When the last of the retreating regiments had crossed the causeway, Australian troops blew it up, on the last night in January.

The army started to commandeer houses in Singapore, to billet the troops. Edward and Laurence both made their way to Theo's home of their own volition. Neither Theo nor Natalia were there, but the Wongs made them welcome. Edward eventually caught up with Theo a day or two later when his unit was despatched to help the Singapore battalion with the shoring up of the defences on the north side of the island. He told him that Arianna was now safely in Klang.

"That's a relief. Thanks for helping her."

"No thanks required. She's the lady I'm going to marry once this nightmare is over."

"You've proposed?"

"Not formally, but we've declared our feelings for each other and she feels the same. I'll become your brother-in-law."

Theo clapped him on the back. "Couldn't wish for a better one, old chap."

Among the refugees were Emma and Shirley. They made their way to Alexandra hospital, where they were welcomed onto the staff, given bunks in the nurses' home and reunited with Jean and Natalia.

Singapore's population was now immensely swollen, with all the refugees and army personnel. Air raids in the second half of January and into February caused an average of two thousand casualties a day, stretching the hospitals to breaking point. St Andrews Cathedral became a temporary dressing point for the wounded. Natalia and the other nurses were working night and day.

Both Theo and Natalia still had brief interludes at home, to snatch a few hours sleep, bathe and change their clothes, but no longer at the same time. Theo knew she had not yet left, although he saw she had packed two bags in preparation. As January merged into February, and the evacuation of women and children was well underway, he left her a note, beseeching her to get out before it was too late. However, Sir Shenton Thomas was still broadcasting that Singapore was safe and people should stay at their posts, which did not help his case. Quite a few of the European nurses had now left, but those who remained did not feel they should desert their patients just yet.

On Sunday 8th February, there were massive air raids and at the same time Japanese troops crossed the Johore Strait and landed on the north-west coast. Theo and the other volunteers were sent out on night patrols, following each other in line, their faces and hands blackened, passing messages back in a low voice, as whispers carried on the night air. Afterwards, Theo's memories of that final week were quite vague; what stayed with him was the constant fear he had felt and could not show. He recalled just blindly following orders, living from one minute to the next, hoping he would not get killed.

Evacuation orders were issued for naval and air force staff on 11th February and then extended to key service and civilian personnel a couple of days later. Meanwhile, the army was engaged in defending the north but were being pushed back by the enemy forces. On 13th February the Japanese rebuilt the causeway and their tanks rolled across. Residents of Mount Rosie Road were forced out of their homes by the approaching bombardment, as the Japanese advanced on the town. Natalia hastily collected her bags and decamped to the nurses' home. Theo also managed to grab a change of clothing and stuff it into his backpack. After that, he, Edward and

Laurence had to doss down in one of the clubs on the rare occasions when they got the chance for a rest.

Ships were departing with evacuees but many were bombed before they got far. Friday 13th February, later dubbed 'Black Friday', was Singapore's Dunkirk, and a flotilla of ships were waiting to take the remaining civilians to safety. Emma, Jean, Shirley and Natalia finally went to get their documentation at the office in town and joined the thousands of civilians at the water's edge, waiting to embark. Later that day, after a long wait, they boarded one of the ships. It was grossly overcrowded and a far cry from the luxury cruise experience Theo had described. They were crammed six or eight to a tiny cabin, down in the hold, with inadequate sanitary facilities and meagre food rations. They were told it would take eight or nine days to reach Australia and resigned themselves to an unpleasant journey.

"At least we're safe," Emma said. "And we'll be able to get jobs in Australia if we can't get back to England from there."

"As long as we're not bombed and shipwrecked," Shirley commented.

They were. As dawn broke on 14th February, Japanese bombers caught the flotilla in the Bangka Straits. The four girls were amongst those who managed to get onto lifeboats, which headed towards the nearest shore.

Later that day, Japanese troops entered Alexandra hospital and massacred most of the patients and staff. By now, law and order had disintegrated.

On Sunday 15th February at 8.30 pm, the Allied army in Singapore surrendered to the Japanese army. The officers in charge of each platoon had the job of telling their men and the news was met with disbelief. Why? They could have carried on, perhaps even defeated the Japs. They had only just been given the order to counter attack and then it was cancelled.

"This is the end, then," Laurence said bitterly to Theo and Edward. "We'll become prisoners of war. Heaven help us!"

"They've got to follow the Geneva convention and treat us fairly, haven't they?" Edward asked.

"I'm not sure whether they ever signed up to that."

"I don't think they did," Theo said, feeling full of foreboding.

On the night of 16th February, the soldiers were all marched to Changi barracks, a distance of some fourteen miles from the town. The next day, they were followed by the remaining male European civilians, led by the governor, their destination being Changi jail. Two days later, the women and children who were left were also marched to Changi. As they entered the jail, they sang defiantly 'There'll always be an England'.

~***~

Chapter Twenty

The lifeboat carrying Natalia, Jean, Emma and Shirley landed later that morning at a deserted beach on Bangka island. By then the sun was high in the sky and beating down on them. The other lifeboats were also offloading survivors of the shipwreck and they recognised some of their colleagues from the hospital.

"Let's find some shade," Emma said. She was very fair-skinned, with reddish hair, and burned easily.

Many of the others had the same idea and clusters of people gathered under the various trees further up the beach. Several of the younger men, including a doctor from Alexandra Hospital, said they would try to locate the nearest village and get some help, suggesting the rest of them wait on the beach until they returned.

The girls had lost almost all of their possessions. Their suitcases had gone down with the ship and the rest of their belongings had been left behind in Singapore or Kuala Lumpur. Each of them had managed to retain one small bag, either a shoulder bag worn across the body or a backpack. Shirley extracted her cigarettes and offered them round.

"At least I've still got these!" she said lightly.

"You may as well give them up now," Natalia, who did not smoke, answered gloomily. "You won't be able to get any more."

"I'll cut down gradually then," Shirley responded. "It'll be less painful. Although I don't smoke as much as I used to. Arianna didn't like the room being full of smoke, it affected her lungs or something, so I smoked a lot less after she moved in."

"Why on earth are we talking about such irrelevant things when we're stuck here, having lost everything we own, with no idea what's going to happen to us!" Jean exploded.

"I suppose talking about trivial things is a distraction from our predicament," Emma said in a placating tone. "But look at the bright side, at least we didn't drown."

"We might have been better off drowning if this island is in the hands of the Japs, which it probably is, or soon will be," Jean responded crossly.

"Does anyone know where exactly we are? Are we on Sumatra?" Shirley put in.

"I'm not sure, could be Sumatra or maybe Bangka," Natalia answered. "But the Japs are all over this area."

"We don't know for sure that Singapore has fallen, do we?" Emma said. "Perhaps our boys have managed to defeat the Japs and it would be safe to get back in those boats and head back there."

"You wouldn't even know in which direction to head!" Jean said scornfully. "And we wouldn't get far in those tiny boats. Let's wait until the men come back anyway. They may have some information."

A woman from one of the other groups huddled under the trees made her way over to them and they recognised Dr. Marian Bridges from their hospital.

"Hello girls. Are you all right? No injuries?"

"No, we're fine, except for not knowing where we are or what's going to happen," Natalia replied.

"We're on Bangka island, I think, and I believe it's just been taken over by the Japs, which will mean we'll be interned. If we are, then it will be up to us medically trained people to set up a hospital area in whatever camp we're taken to and persuade the Japs that looking after the health of the inmates should be our roles."

Just then, they heard the sound of vehicles approaching from beyond the beach.

"The men are returning, and they've brought help!" Emma exclaimed.

But the vehicles were army jeeps, manned by Japanese soldiers. By means of brusque commands and rough shoving, the women and children were separated from the men and told to march in front of the jeeps, which followed slowly behind them.

"Where are we going?" one woman asked.

There was no answer and she was pushed into line. After a gruelling march of several miles in the stifling midday heat, they arrived at their camp. It consisted of atap huts with thatched roofs -

205

the walls made from atap palm branches woven between slats to form a lattice - which were set in a compound surrounded by a high barbed wire fence. Word went round that this place was called Muntok and the men were being housed in the nearby jail. The Japanese commandant addressed them, in heavily accented English.

"You are all now prisoners of war of the Imperial Japanese Army," he boomed. "You will always bow when addressing a Japanese officer and you will all follow orders without question. I suggest that you appoint a camp leader who can liaise with us on your behalf. Meanwhile, divide yourselves between the huts and find yourselves spaces to sleep."

Dr. Bridges raised her hand. "May I speak please?" She belatedly remembered to bow.

"Yes?"

"I'm a doctor and there are several nurses amongst us. Do we have your permission to set up one of the huts as a sick bay? Some people already have injuries from the journey here and will need medical attention."

"Yes, you can use that one there." He waved his hand towards the end hut.

"And where are the latrines, and the washing and cooking facilities?"

"You will be responsible for setting those up. Your first task will be to dig latrines, over there." He waved his hand again.

"How wonderful!" Shirley whispered sarcastically. "Just what I've always wanted to do!"

"Quiet! No talking amongst yourselves whilst I am speaking!"

They made their way over to the hut next to the one designated as the sick bay, following Dr Bridges' lead. There were nine nurses altogether, including two from St. Andrews Hospital, plus the doctor, and at first they thought they would have that hut to themselves, but others soon crowded in, having found no room elsewhere, and they each ended up with a space to sleep eighteen inches to two feet wide, on top of bare boards raised up from the ground. There were a few thin blankets and Jean pounced on them and gave her fellow nurses and the doctor one each.

206

"That's not fair," someone else protested. "There're none left. You'll have to share. They're big enough to stretch between two people."

After consultation with the women in the other huts, Marian Bridges was elected as camp leader. She was inundated with questions the women wanted her to ask, such as where they could get replacement clothing, as many of them had only the garments they were wearing, and what about laundry facilities?

"I expect all of this will become apparent over the course of the next few days," Marian responded. "Meanwhile, we'd better get digging those latrines as some of us are going to need them shortly!"

Over the course of the next few days they gradually learned what their lives were going to be like for the foreseeable future - and it looked bleak. Twice a day there was a roll call, referred to by the guards as *Tenko,* during which they had to stand in the blazing sun while heads were counted. Food rations were meagre in the extreme, consisting primarily of rice, into which sometimes some vegetable matter was mixed, and bowls of thin gruel.

"On this diet, we're going to get cases of beriberi," Marian forecast gloomily.

Washing was by means of bowl and pitcher, without soap and with no privacy whatsoever, and for a while many of them had no clean clothes until eventually a Red Cross allocation arrived. The Red Cross was also supposed to have provided drugs and other medical supplies but Marian kept asking the Japs for these without success. Punishments for even very minor infringements of the rules, such as forgetting to bow, were draconian and the women learned not to upset the Japanese guards if they could avoid it. There were no mosquito nets and they were constantly bitten, causing the doctor to also worry about malaria.

The huts were filthy and some of the women set about cleaning them as best they could. However, there was little they could do about the infestation of bugs which plagued every building. Some of the inmates were sent out on work parties to be slave labour for the Japanese in the local area, others took charge of the cooking. The nurses and doctor manned the sick bay, and they were soon inundated with minor injuries and cases of dysentery which they had limited means to treat. One woman had arrived with her three month old baby; she was breastfeeding but was concerned that her diet was not providing enough nutrients for the baby and the nurses shared her concern.

Meanwhile, Natalia worried constantly about Theo. Had he survived the fighting? She prayed to God he had. If so, where was he interned? She asked, but no-one knew. Jean, Emma and Shirley were all single with no particular men to worry about, although Emma was concerned about Laurence, having dated him sporadically whenever he was based in Kuala Lumpur. Many of the other women were anxious about their husbands. It was known by now that Singapore had definitely fallen, but there was no information about the military casualties during that last week.

After they had been in the camp a few weeks, Natalia started to feel queasy in the mornings and some days she was actually sick. Then, one morning at *Tenko*, she almost fainted. At first she put it down to an upset stomach from the dreadful food, then Emma asked,

"I don't suppose you could be pregnant, could you?"

Natalia was startled. "No, I always used a cap."

"They're not hundred percent foolproof, though, are they?"

She didn't answer straight away. She was remembering that last emotionally charged night they'd spent together, that final desperate coupling, when she'd been so scared for him. And he'd been scared too. He had not voiced his fear but she'd seen it in his eyes and felt it in the way he clung to her. She had thought only of providing love and reassurance, as well as satisfying her own need, and had given no thought to contraception. Had she inserted her cap that night? She couldn't remember, but it was more than likely that she hadn't. She groaned.

"It is possible. I don't recall using it the last night we were together."

"Which was when?"

"About the middle of January."

"It fits then, doesn't it?"

Natalia sat down heavily. Of all the times to be pregnant! Here, in this filthy, infested place with its limited water supply, no soap, starvation rations and almost total lack of medical equipment. She

208

knew that in any other circumstances she would have welcomed this baby, despite it being unplanned, and Theo would have been overjoyed. A child who was part of both of them, a product of their love. But as it was, she felt only fear and dread.

Emma sat beside her. "Don't worry," she said kindly. "We'll all look after you. We'll try to get you some extra rations, and I've done a midwifery course; I can deliver your baby, if we're still here then."

Natalia managed a wan smile.

At the end of March, most of them were transferred to another camp, near Palembang on Sumatra, which the Japanese had now finally conquered and occupied. They were transported by boat across the Bangka Straits and up the river, a journey from hell which took about twelve hours. Far too many people were crammed into the small vessel and the only protection from the blazing sun was in the hold, which reeked of oil and made Natalia retch. The latrine facility was a wooden board suspended high above the water. The women had to disrobe and perch precariously, relieving themselves in full view of all on board. The only sustenance provided during the journey was a handful of cold rice and a few sips of cold tea.

At Palembang, they were initially housed in a former school building at Bukit Besar, near the centre of town. A contingent of British and Australian soldiers were already there and they had prepared a hot meal for the women, their first proper food in weeks. Natalia asked one of the men if anyone knew what had happened to the Volunteers who had fought in Singapore and was told that they were probably interned at Changi.

After a few days, the women and children were transferred to another camp, formed of abandoned Dutch cottages, enclosed in a guarded compound, surrounded by barbed wire. There was a sentry box at each corner and a guard housed at the gate.

"No chance of escaping from here!" one woman commented.

"No point in even trying anyway," another replied. "How would you get off Sumatra?"

The prisoners had to start from scratch again, making the camp habitable; digging latrines, cleaning, sorting out cooking, washing and laundry facilities and a sick bay. As before, the accommodation was grossly overcrowded and the food rations were no better; that

209

first meal at the school had been a once-off treat and soon became a distant memory.

When torrential rain fell, the ground in the compound became foul with effluent from the flooded latrines. To help prevent this, the latrines had to be emptied regularly by hand, using scoops made of coconut shells and buckets, a singularly unpleasant task.

By now a camaraderie had developed amongst the women. Initial tensions and squabbles had largely subsided and most of them pulled together in adversity, sharing what little they had and pooling their skills. Women who were good seamstresses made over the clothes provided by the Red Cross so that they fit their fellow inmates, sometimes transforming men's clothing into women's. Many of them became adept at using unlikely materials to fabricate things they needed; when their shoes fell apart, they made sandals out of pieces of wood.

The contingent from Muntok were joined by Dutch internees from Sumatra itself. These prisoners had been able to bring some of their possessions, as many as they could carry. Some bartering subsequently took place with those prisoners who had cash buying things they needed from the Dutch.

As Natalia grew larger and heavier, she found the daily grind in the heat and humidity, on so little sustenance, increasingly hard to tolerate. Her fellow nurses tried to shield her as much as possible, taking over some of her chores, but Marian was unable to persuade the Japanese guards to excuse her from the twice daily ritual of *Tenko*. As her due date grew nearer, she became more and more fearful, but at the same time strangely accepting. What will be, will be, she thought. I can't change my fate, whatever it is.

One day in mid October, her labour pains started and, at evening *Tenko*, her waters broke. Marian and Emma helped her to the sick bay and prepared to deliver her baby.

~***~

Chapter Twenty-One

Meanwhile, in Klang, Arianna was having a very different experience of Japanese occupation. Her circumstances were considerably better than the other girls and she should have been counting her blessings, but she was finding that hard to do. She missed Edward keenly and worried about both him and Theo. Had they survived the fighting? Where were they interned? And what about the girls, her sister-in-law and her friends? It seemed impossible to find out anything, she couldn't ask anyone in authority without blowing her cover and giving away her British connections. Radio broadcasts and the press were now controlled by the Japanese military administration. And her grandparents' complacent attitude irritated her.

"We've had the British in charge, now we have the Japs. It probably won't make much difference to us," her grandfather said.

"Well, it might," Khalid replied. "If they wreck the economy and we can't sell our produce."

"People always have to eat and our market is local."

"Aren't you concerned about your grandson?" Arianna asked angrily. "He's either died fighting them or he's now their prisoner, probably being badly treated somewhere. And my Edward too!"

"Theo aligned himself with the British, became a *Tuan,* and fought against the Japs. He has to take responsibility for the choices he's made in life. In fact, Theo is very much an Englishman. I see little of our daughter in him, he's his father's son."

"Don't you even care what happens to him?" Arianna's tone was bitter.

"Yes, of course we do," her grandmother responded. "But there's nothing we can do about it, we just have to hope he survives the war."

Arianna now had no means of earning her own living; she was dependant on her maternal relatives. She tried to earn her keep by taking care of many of the household chores for her grandmother and helping Khalid to market their produce. But such activities bored her, as they failed to occupy her mind, and she felt that she was in a kind of prison herself, albeit a comfortable one. She called herself Arianna *binti* Hassan, taking her grandfather's name. She borrowed some *sarongs* from one of her female cousins who was the same dress size and wore those when she ventured out, along with a scarf over her head. However, she didn't dare go into the centre of town, near the district office, in case she encountered any of her former colleagues, who might just let something slip to the Japanese who were now in charge. She did go past her former school once and saw that it was now closed; Japanese orders had closed all the English and Chinese schools.

She risked a trip into Kuala Lumpur and went to see Natalia's mother to see if she had any news of her daughter and possibly Theo, but she knew nothing either.

"Natalia might have escaped by boat," she said. "Last time we spoke, she was intending to do that. She might be in Australia now, with the English nurses."

She seemed to be clinging to that thought, and Arianna hoped she was right and the girls had got away and were safe. But that had not been an option for Theo and Edward. They would have had to fight to the end, they were now either dead or interned. She couldn't bear to think they were dead, so she told herself they were much more likely to be prisoners of war. Rumours abounded of Japanese ill-treatment of their prisoners, but she had no way of knowing how true they were.

She tried to get the BBC on the radio and sometimes succeeded in getting snippets of news about the progress of the war, but there seemed no sign of it coming to an end soon. And would the end of the war in Europe also mark the end of Japanese occupation here? There was no guarantee of that. No mail was coming through from England and none could be sent; the last time she'd heard from Enid was in November 1941.

After she had been living her twilight life for a few months, one of her former colleagues from the government offices in Kuala Lumpur, Farish, arrived on her doorstep.

212

"I remembered you'd said your grandparents lived in this part of Klang, on a small farm, so I asked a local shopkeeper and this is the third farm I've tried!" he said, beaming.

She was glad to see him. He'd been a friend as well as a colleague. He brought news of life at the secretariat, how it was now under the Japanese.

"They're much harder taskmasters, but they also don't really know what they're doing, so they depend on us."

He told her the Chinese members of staff had been sacked and replaced with Malays. She had already heard that the Chinese were not being well-treated, whereas the Malays were largely left alone to continue their lives as before.

Farish was a Eurasian like her, but much more Malay in outlook than British. His English father had left when he was still a baby and he had been brought up by his Malay mother and stepfather, who were Muslims, and had taken his stepfather's surname. However, he was intelligent and well-educated and Arianna had always found him good company.

After that initial visit, he continued to come to Klang regularly at weekends, bringing news of life in the capital. He told her that the Japanese administration had issued notices threatening anyone who associated with or helped Europeans.

"You're taking a risk visiting me then!"

"You're Eurasian, not British, you're the same as me."

"Hardly! I've been brought up as an Englishwoman and I spent nearly half my life in England. When I was here before, as a child, we lived in the British D.O.'s residence and when I was working in KL, I lived with two English nurses. You know all this. You'd better not tell anyone at the office that you've seen me, it could be dangerous for both of us. As far as the authorities in K.L are concerned, I've disappeared. They probably assume I became a refugee, headed south and then either escaped to England or was interned."

"I expect they do. Don't worry, I've not told anyone at the office about you."

After a few months of visiting her in Klang, he suggested they have a change of scenery and she visit him at his family home next time.

"Have you any Malay clothes you can wear, so that you're less conspicuous on the streets?"

"Yes. But don't tell your family about my British background, will you?"

She wore one of her borrowed *sarongs* and wound a scarf demurely over her head. He met her at Kuala Lumpur station. As they walked to his family home, he said,

"You know, I think you look even more beautiful in Malayan dress."

Arianna had no idea how to reply to this, so said nothing. As they continued on their way, she noted that some of the street signs had now been changed to Japanese and there was a very different atmosphere in the capital than there had been under the British. Everyone seemed to be keeping their heads down, just going about their business, with total lack of *joie de vivre*. They passed the end of the street where she'd lived with Emma and Shirley and she felt a pang of nostalgia.

"I used to live just up there. I wonder who's living in our house now?"

"Japanese officials or army officers, I expect. They've taken over most of the houses formerly occupied by Europeans."

"And I suppose they've also appropriated the things they had to leave behind."

She felt a stab of anger at the thought of the Japanese women using Emma's and Shirley's things. Edward's former home was also not far away and she was suddenly assailed by bittersweet memories of their time together.

"You look sad," Farish said. "What is it?"

"I'm just remembering the good times I had with my English friends, who are probably prisoners of the Japs now."

He made no reply and she then asked, "Is there any way you can find out anything about them? About military casualties in Singapore, for example? I don't even know if my brother is still alive!"

"I could try," he said doubtfully, "but I'd have to be very careful. Did your brother fight with the Volunteers?"

"Yes."

"I don't think there were many casualties amongst them. He's probably in one of the POW camps."

At his home, she was introduced to his mother, stepfather and three younger sisters. When they asked her about her family, she made no mention of Theo or Enid, just saying that she lived with her grandparents and uncle in Klang. As the afternoon progressed, it became apparent what a devout Muslim family they were, and she felt even more alienated from them than she did with her own maternal relatives. It was ironic, she thought, that in England she'd longed for her Malayan identity to be accepted, but here she felt British and hated having to hide that side of her, which she now realised was the greater part of her being. She had little in common with her mother's family and even less with Farish's. She wished now that she'd got on a ship to England before it was too late. She could have been home with Enid now, if she'd done that. She felt a sudden sharp stab of homesickness for her sister, the manor and Oxfordshire. Would she ever get back there?

As they walked back to the station, Farish commented that she'd been very quiet.

"I'm sorry. I was afraid of saying the wrong thing, giving away my British background. I couldn't really relax. And I was feeling homesick. I miss my sister in England a great deal and seeing you with your sisters brought it home to me."

At the station he kissed her hand and said he would see her the following weekend. That pattern continued for the next few months, with him mostly visiting her in Klang but she paying occasional visits to his family in the capital.

Meanwhile, life under the Japanese did not improve. Japanese currency replaced Malayan dollars and inflation resulted, which in turn led to rationing. Arianna's grandparents' became less accepting of the new regime and Khalid grumbled regularly.

After she'd returned from one of her trips to Kuala Lumpur, her grandmother said, out of the blue,

"How do you feel about Farish?"

215

"He's a good friend."

"Is that all?"

"Yes."

"I doubt he sees it that way. He's paying court to you."

She was startled. He had paid her some compliments, kissed her hand, but that was all.

"You see him most weekends, he's taken you to meet his family, that's a courtship."

"Well, in that case, he's going to be disappointed. I love Edward, and when this war is over, we'll be married."

"I see no ring on your finger."

"There wasn't time for that, he was going off to fight!"

"But he did formally propose?"

"Well, no, not exactly. But he said I was the woman he wanted to marry when he was in a position to propose, meaning after the war is over, and I said I felt the same."

"You don't even know for sure that he's still alive. And if he is, he may feel quite differently after the war, after years in captivity. Such experiences change men. And you are not promised to each other."

"I'm in love with Edward and he asked me to wait for him. I don't love Farish."

"Perhaps not yet, but you like and respect him, don't you? And he's a nice looking young man, lovely deep brown eyes!"

"Yes, but that's not enough. I'm not in love with him."

"Being in love is a fleeting thing. Often it can develop into a deep and abiding love, the kind of love which does last, but such a love can also grow between two people who have mutual liking and respect for each other. Your grandfather and I love each other deeply and we have made a good life together, but we were introduced by our families and we didn't even know each other very well when we married."

Arianna suddenly remembered Aunt Mary once telling her, in a rare expansive moment, that she and George had been introduced by their families too and were not in love before they married, but love had grown between them. But that's not for me, she thought. I want to be in love when I marry, I want what Theo and Natalia have, what

216

Enid seems to have with Arthur. Why should I take second best? I love Edward and he's expecting me to wait for him, and I want him, no-one else! God, how I miss him! Out loud she just said,

"This is all irrelevant anyway. Farish hasn't asked me to marry him, hasn't mentioned the future at all. And he's a devout Muslim, he'd never want to marry a Christian girl."

"Hmm. Nevertheless, I think he will ask you, later on, and then you'll have to make a decision."

~***~

Chapter Twenty-Two

Looking back at his time in captivity, long after the war was over, Theo wondered how he had managed to survive, particularly those eight months from hell in 1943.

In Changi barracks, over fifty-thousand men were crammed into quarters designed for a mere ten-thousand. Like the women on Sumatra, they had to sleep squashed up next to each other on hard surfaces and their diet was mainly rice, sometimes mixed with bits of vegetable matter or fruit and occasionally with pieces of snails or snakes - caught by the prisoners themselves - for protein. Being a former army barracks, the sanitation arrangements should have been somewhat better than in the makeshift women's camps, although grossly inadequate in number for the volume of men needing to use them. However, they had suffered extensive bomb damage and the water supply was destroyed. Initially, men had to bathe in the sea and use the swamps at the edge of the sea as latrines. As at the other camps, the Japanese raided the Red Cross medical supplies for their own use, leaving hardly anything to treat sick prisoners.

At first, the main concern of the married men was for their wives and families. Few knew what had happened to the people they loved, whether or not they were safe or even alive, and Theo was no exception. Had Natalia escaped by boat in time? Had she drowned trying to get away or was she interned somewhere? Not knowing her fate was torture.

He had marched to Changi alongside Edward and Laurence and they were in the same hut. All of them wandered around the camp, trying to find friends, and it was Laurence who eventually found Ralph and reunited him with the three of them.

"What happened to you?" Edward asked. "Where were you when the Japs invaded?"

"I was in Kuala Lipis and we retreated south, the same as you. I was also involved in the fighting for Singapore, just in a different unit."

They compared notes and all agreed bitterly that the British high command had let them down badly, had let down Malaya and Singapore, effectively handing the colony to the Japanese on a plate. There had been no need to constantly retreat, sometimes without firing a shot, there had been many times when they could have held off or even defeated the enemy forces. This was a widely held view amongst the Volunteers, and the British officers - now in charge of them all at the camp - were regarded with barely disguised hostility by many.

"What happened to the girls?" Ralph asked. "The three nurses we came over with, and your wife and sister, Theo."

"Arianna escaped to Klang, where she's lying low at her grandparents' place," Edward replied. "I took her there myself."

"And the others?"

"We don't know. They all ended up at Alexandra hospital and we just hope they got away in time by boat."

"I believe some of those boats were bombed and sunk."

"Yes, we know," Laurence said shortly.

"Are the girls good swimmers?"

"Nat is," Theo answered. "She had a good chance of making it to shore if she was shipwrecked off the coast."

No-one knew if that also applied to the others.

Ralph then commented, "If they've been interned, they're quite likely to get raped by the Jap guards, from what I've heard. Young, pretty girls like them."

Theo stared at him, then got up abruptly and walked away without a word.

"That would have been better left unsaid," Edward reprimanded. "He's worried enough about his wife as it is, without having that image put in his head."

It was hard to find anywhere in the overcrowded camp where you could be alone but Theo managed to find a quiet corner behind the block. His mind was churning. Rape had not yet occurred to him, but now he realised that it was by no means unlikely. He couldn't bear the thought of Natalia having to endure that, it tore him apart. But there was absolutely nothing he could do about it, he was totally powerless, unable to protect her. He was filled with impotent rage and frustration which brought tears to his eyes.

Laurence was also mulling over the same unwelcome image. "I hate the idea of that happening to them, especially Emma."

"Are the two of you courting?" Ralph asked.

"Not exactly, but we dated a few times."

"At least you know your lady-friend is safe," Ralph said to Edward. "I'm assuming you and Arianna finally got together? You were as thick as thieves on that ship."

"Yes, we did. And we'll be married when this damned war is finally over."

"Congratulations! But what will your family think of you marrying a half-caste girl?"

"They'll just have to lump it. It's my life, not theirs. Anyway, once they get to know her, they'll realise she's as English as they are, and what's more, higher up the social strata. Her uncle is a baronet."

The prisoners were sent out on work parties, including to the docks where they had to endure hard physical labour for up to forty-eight hours at a time with hardly any rest breaks. The only advantage of such work was that sometimes they could salvage some foodstuff which had fallen out of the crates and supplement their meagre diets. The work broke many of the older men from the civilian camp and some died. Theo watched one elderly man's body being loaded onto a stretcher and felt unbearably sad for him, that his life had ended that way. That feeling was immediately followed by hatred of the Japanese guards who had callously worked him to death.

Discipline in the camp and on the work parties was maintained by the British officers, as if they were still in the army. However, they were ineffective in preventing Japanese brutality. The Japanese view was that prisoners of war were the lowest of the low, the scum of the earth; according to their creed the men should have committed suicide before allowing themselves to be taken prisoner.

At both the military and civilian camps, camaraderie still prevailed and prisoners pooled their limited resources, endeavouring to make the best of things. Some produced camp newspapers, despite the shortage of paper and pencils, and plays and concerts were held.

Others risked torture and death to run illicit radio operations, gleaning news of the progress of the war. For a while two inmates ran a postal service between the two camps, until one of them was caught and tortured. Torture was a common punishment for even minor infringements of the rules, sometimes to the point where the medical officers could do nothing except try to ease the last hours of life for the victim.

At the end of August 1942, all the POWs at the barracks were asked to sign a document declaring they would not attempt to escape and would report any prisoner known to be planning to do so. Everyone refused to sign and, as a punishment, they were all transferred to Selarang barracks, which had been built to accommodate only eight-hundred men. As well as being squashed in cheek by jowl, there was a severe shortage of water and hardly any food, and there were no functioning sanitary facilities. The area was soon foul with human waste. However, morale was high and they continued to refuse until there was an outbreak of dysentery and their commanding officer ordered the men to sign under duress.

Later that year, groups of prisoners, referred to as forces and designated by letters of the alphabet, started to be sent away from Singapore by train. Initially there were rumours that they were going to the highlands to grow vegetables, but it was eventually discovered that many were being sent to Siam to build a new railway link between Siam and Burma. Some forces had also left earlier for camps in Japan, Borneo and Burma. Laurence and Ralph were in the first force to depart for Siam, designated D. Theo and Edward remained at Changi until April 1943, when Theo, who had only just recovered from a serious bout of dysentery, received his orders to depart with Force F. Edward was at that time still in the camp hospital, suffering from a tropical ulcer, so escaped this call up, although many unfit prisoners were included.

F Force consisted of approximately seven-thousand men, roughly half British and half Australian. They were split into battalions, each comprising officers, including medical officers, and other ranks. Only about half of them would eventually return to Changi, the rest losing their lives to a combination of malnutrition, disease and brutality.

The train journey up to Siam took four days and four nights. The men were crammed into sweltering, windowless trucks, too many in each for anyone to be able to lie down. There were no latrines: men urinated out of the doors of the trucks and, at the twice daily stops, rows of POWs could be seen squatting at the side of the track relieving themselves in full view of the native population. For those suffering from diarrhoea, the only way they could relieve themselves en route was to hold onto the handles of the open truck door and stick their backsides out of the train. Theo was glad that he was currently in the dried-up stage which follows acute dysentery. There was very little water to drink and none to wash and their twice daily meal consisted of miniscule portions of rice mixed with boiled onions.

Dehydrated, hungry, dirty and exhausted, they arrived at Banpong, expecting to settle into the camp there, but, to their dismay, they were told that in two days time they would have to commence a march of two-hundred miles to their first long-stay camp. The march took place at night in fifteen stages, interspersed with only occasional nights of rest, and took two and a half weeks to complete. They marched from 7pm to 7am along jungle tracks. Seriously ill men had to be carried on stretchers by their fitter comrades. Most of the equipment which had been brought up from Changi had been left at Banpong and the men took only what they could carry on their backs. As the march progressed, the monsoon period started and they were walking in torrential rain and mud. Most of the staging camps where they spent their days were hardly worthy of the name; there was no cover, no protection from the pouring rain, no latrines. The prisoners were constantly soaked to the skin and living in filth and squalor. Their meals consisted of rice with 'coloured water', occasionally there would be some onion stew. Many of the less fit men died on the way.

They passed through Tasho camp, which was D Force's base camp, where they had a night's rest. Theo looked for Ralph and Laurence and eventually found Ralph. They compared notes: their journey up by train had been almost as bad as Theo's, but they had been spared the lengthy march. Ralph told Theo something of what to expect once he reached his destination and started work on the railway.

"Working on the docks was a doddle in comparison," he warned. "We're worked like slaves here, you're beaten if you don't work fast enough, and it's back-breaking labour, men are dropping like flies."

Theo's heart sank. It was hard to believe that there was worse to come.

"Where's Laurence?" he then asked.

Ralph's face darkened. "He's dead. He died of cholera. I was able to sit with him at the very end and I watched the poor bugger die. At least he's not suffering anymore."

Theo felt sadness sweep through him and a lump rose up in his throat. Poor Laurence, what a way to go. It was hard to believe that such a fit, healthy young man could have died so quickly.

"Some do survive cholera," Ralph continued, "and all the other horrible diseases which abound here. But he wasn't one of the lucky ones."

Eventually, they reached their first permanent camp, Shimo Sonkrai. There were no roofs on the bamboo huts; the exhausted men had to set about making them before they could get shelter from the rain. Ten to fifteen men were packed into each tiny hut, sleeping on ridged bamboo floors. There was a small creek nearby which provided their only source of water, for both drinking and washing.

They had to start work on the railway the next day, despite their exhausted state. The line was to run from Banpong to Kanchanburi, past the Mekon river, skirting high mountains above the valley of the river Kwai, along the Three Pagodas pass into Burma, serviced by a chain of primitive work camps. The track ran on shelves cut out of the rock face, over bridges made of timber with cement foundations, and through the wildest and hilliest country. Theo soon realised that Ralph had not exaggerated the hardship of working on this railway. In fact, F Force, and also H Force which followed behind, were treated even more harshly than the others, as the railway was now in the 'Speedo' stage, where the Japanese engineers wanted it finished as soon as possible and did not care who died in the process. F Force were engaged in blasting and hewing the rock and felling trees to create a pathway for the line and H Force followed behind laying the

223

track. It was hard physical labour which would have taxed fit, well-rested men on good food rations; for the debilitated, half-starved men of F Force it was brutally hard, made worse by the cruelty of the Korean guards, who were themselves being badly treated by the Japanese officers and made sure they passed it on in full measure. When a prisoner was considered not to be working fast enough, he would be beaten with wire whips or bamboo sticks. Many collapsed in the heat and humidity and were beaten mercilessly until they either staggered to their feet or died. The bodies of the dead were burnt on fires.

Disease was rife. Beri-beri from the inadequate food, malaria from the mosquitoes, dysentery, cholera, typhoid, dengue fever and tropical ulcers all abounded. These ulcers could form very quickly in the tropics from even quite minor injuries. Many of the men of F Force had ulcerated feet from the long march. The medical officers did their best but the Japs were either withholding or did not receive medical supplies and the guards would come into the camp hospital and force any man who could manage to stand back into the work parties, despite the protests of the medics that they were unfit to work. To try to stem an outbreak of cholera, a party of men were set to digging proper latrines and eventually a party was sent into Burma to obtain a supply of quinine to treat malaria.

There were draconian punishments for minor misdemeanours, many of them could only be described as torture. A couple of the guards were exceptionally brutal and took sadistic pleasure in trying to break the prisoners.

By July, half the men had no boots as they had disintegrated. They had to live and work in bare feet, resulting in trench foot being added to the list of ailments suffered. Many of the tropical ulcer cases had got to the stage of the bones showing through gaping, suppurating wounds. The treatment for this was for the medical officers to scrape the pus from the wound using a teaspoon, the patient being held down by orderlies as there was no anaesthetic. If this failed to do the trick, the only option was amputation of the affected limb, also without anaesthetic. Few survived this ordeal. When these treatments were carried out, the screams coming from the hospital hut were ear-splitting, and Theo hoped to God he would not have to suffer this fate. So far, he had suffered from one bout of malaria, a further bout of dysentery, and dengue fever, but had managed to recover from all three. At least it had not been cerebral malaria, from which men soon died, screaming in agony.

By September, they were working from 6.30 am to 2.30 am the following day and deaths had escalated to over a hundred a month. Even during their few hours of rest, they still had to endure the daily roll call, which could go on for some time if the guards miscounted. Food was still mainly rice and onions. By then, they had moved to their second camp, Kami Sonkrai.

Throughout it all, what kept Theo going was the thought of his eventual reunion with Natalia. He had long ago convinced himself that she was not dead, he simply could not bear to live with that thought. He had also put from his mind Ralph's comment about rape. In his last note to her, he had suggested that, wherever they both ended up, they should make their way to Singapore at the end of the war, either to their former home, if that were possible, or Raffles hotel, and wait for each other there. He focused on that future reunion, fantasising about it as he fell asleep at night, imagining their lovemaking. Whenever he felt he simply could not endure any more, he conjured up her image in his mind and it seemed to get him through. Otherwise, he just lived from day to day, hour to hour, concentrating on getting through another twenty-four hours without being beaten, getting something to eat and drink and a few hours sleep. When he had a further severe attack of malaria and spent several days in the camp hospital, he put his recovery down to not giving up, to living for Natalia and their future life together.

To reduce the likelihood of getting head lice, many men shaved their heads and Theo eventually did the same. As he watched his thick, slightly wavy, brown hair fall onto the ground, it seemed symbolic of the final shedding of his former privileged life. Looking at himself in a small shaving mirror, his reflection seemed strange, his head distorted. The man who had shaved him commented,

"Good thing there're no ladies here, eh?"

Theo thought of Natalia's shock if she saw him like this. He would have to stop shaving it as soon as they heard that the war had ended and release was imminent. Thinking about the end of the war brought a wave of nostalgia for the cool green fields of England. He would be able to take his long overdue leave then and he and Natalia would go to England. I have to get through this hell, he thought, I have to make it to the end of the war, and surely it can't be much longer now?

Living and working in such appalling conditions, it was hard to maintain a belief in God. There was a chaplain amongst the officers and many men expressed their doubts to him, but his answers failed to convince them.

"If there is a God, then he's taking a holiday," one man declared. "How could he oversee all this and let it carry on?"

Theo was in the doubters' camp. However, others clung to their religion as a source of comfort.

In all the time he had been in captivity, Theo had heard nothing from England. Theoretically it was possible for some mail to get through via the Red Cross and a few men had received longed-for letters from England when they had been in Changi, but nothing had arrived here. Occasionally, he wondered if Enid, George and Mary had any idea that he was a POW. Had they been notified? He hoped Enid did not think he was dead and was grieving for him.

Despite the terrible life they were all living, most of the prisoners still retained their sense of humour. They amused themselves by giving nicknames to their Japanese and Korean tormentors, and managed to make jokes about their situation.

By October, the railway line was almost complete. F and H Forces were due to return to Changi once the line was finally linked and trains ran through. By then, Theo had experienced further attacks of dysentery and dengue fever. He was in the camp hospital when they were told they were to move back to Kamburi camp near Banpong, this time by train. However, there were further delays and then more at Banpong and it was not until the end of November that they finally left Siam, enduring another nightmare train journey back down to Singapore, this time in a much more debilitated state than when they had set off. Their clothes were reduced to rags, they were hollow-eyed, walking skeletons, decimated by disease and malnutrition, many with hardly any buttocks to speak of, as all their fat stores had been used up. Now that they no longer had to summon

226

up super-human resources to do hard manual labour, for fear of the repercussions if they did not, they found that the slightest expenditure of energy utterly exhausted them.

Whilst at Kamburi, Theo had tried to find Edward amongst the H Force men, expecting him to have been sent up in that party, but failed to locate him or find anyone who knew him. Had the lucky devil escaped the fate of being sent to Siam?

Out of the original seven-thousand men of F Force, three-thousand-eight-hundred returned to Changi, but many had to go straight into the hospital section; Theo amongst them, as malaria had set in again on the journey down. When he was released, he finally found Edward, who expressed shock at his appearance.

"My God, Theo! I thought I'd got thin but you are just skin and bone. What happened?"

Theo gave him a brief resume of the horrors of working on the death railway, as it was now being called by the prisoners, and also passed on the sad news about Laurence.

"You had a lucky escape, mate," he added.

In May 1944, The survivors of F and H Force were transferred to Changi jail, where the civilian inmates had been housed, and put on light duties. The civilians were transferred to a camp at Sime Road where they were to be engaged in growing vegetables, in an attempt to supplement the rice diet. F and H Force arrived as the civilians were leaving, and Theo came across his former boss, the Governor of Singapore, who, perhaps not surprisingly, did not immediately recognise him.

It was not until after the war that the survivors of F and H Force became aware that they had experienced the worst conditions, the most severe brutality and hardship, and the most deaths of all the forces sent to work on the railway.

Conditions being slightly better in Changi jail, Theo did not lose any more weight, and his health did not deteriorate any further, but neither did it improve, as the diet was still inadequate. He was sharing a tiny, bug-infested cell with three others but that was an improvement on life in the camps along the railway.

The prisoners heard about D Day through the secret radio operators and it seemed that the war was finally turning in the allies' favour. Hope started to rise. Surely it could not be long now before they were freed? Later, they heard that the allies had bombed the new railway and Theo fervently hoped that there were enough men still up there to effect the repairs and he would not be sent back. Then in November 1944 US bombers attacked Singapore harbour; they could hear the bombs in the distance. Although they were unaware of it, the allies were also dropping supplies to the Chinese resistance in Malaya, and some British men, who had managed to evade capture, were working with them, hiding in the jungle. From early 1945 rumours abounded in Changi, some true, some not, but they all increased the hope that their ordeal might soon be at an end. However, at the same time, conditions were deteriorating, food was becoming even more scarce, and Red Cross supplies were all confiscated by the Japanese.

In May 1945, they heard the news of the German surrender. The war in Europe was over! How long before the Japs caved in? Then rumours started to circulate that in some camps men were being ordered to dig trenches. Were these to be their graves? Were the Japs planning to kill all their POWs? Had they come through all this only to die anyway?

The nuclear bombs dropped by the US on Hiroshima and Nagasaki finally brought the Japanese to surrender, on 15th August 1945. The camp leaders were sent for and they then relayed the news to the men; cheers rang out from one cell after another and someone started to sing "God Save the King." Theo cheered and sang along with the rest of them, giving no thought then to the devastating effects of the nuclear bombs on innocent civilians in Japan. Only long after the war ended would he have some inkling of the price the ordinary Japanese people had paid for his freedom.

After the surrender, Red Cross supplies in abundance arrived in the camp: food, medicines, clothing and cigarettes. Theo did not smoke but took his allocation of cigarettes anyway, as they could be bartered for other things. There were further delays but they were finally liberated on 5th September, the day Singapore was officially handed back. Penang had been first, after the official peace signing, and the retaking of mainland Malaya took place from 9th to 12th, when the British Military Administration headquarters was established in Kuala Lumpur. The prisoners were given medical examinations, issued with further clothing and some money and told they could go home as soon as transport could be arranged. Refugee ships bound for England would shortly start leaving from Singapore. The camp guards and commandants now all became prisoners of war themselves and some of them would later be tried and executed for war crimes, including the most infamous of the guards and officers on the railway project.

~***~

Chapter Twenty-Three

Theo had only one thought occupying his mind when he arrived back in Singapore town - find Natalia. If she had been interned then she should be being released now. If she had escaped to Australia, then it might take a little longer for her to get back. He went first to Raffles hotel, which had been taken over as a refuge for the freed women and children internees. It was full of women milling around. He started asking people if they knew her, holding up the now dog-eared photo he'd carried with him throughout his imprisonment. Heads were shaken. "Sorry, no I don't recognise her" became an oft-repeated refrain. As he wandered around, he came across a suite of rooms taken over as offices by the new British military administration, where women in uniform were processing applications for the refugee ships to England. He asked if she was on their list; no she wasn't.

"You should get your name down," one of the officers advised.

"I can't book a trip home until I find my wife."

"Well, if you book far enough in advance it will give you time to find her, won't it? The earlier sailings are getting booked up anyway."

That made sense to Theo. Natalia would want to spend some time with her family in Kuala Lumpur before they left, so a later sailing would be better. He made a reservation for the two of them on a ship departing in early November, which would get them back to England well before Christmas. Then he carried on with his questioning. He had just about got to the point of giving up, when one woman suddenly said,

"Hold on, let me see that photo again."

Eagerly, he held it out and she scrutinised it carefully.

"I think - I'm not sure, mind - she might have been at Muntok camp on Bangka island, right at the beginning, after we were shipwrecked. Then a lot of them were sent on to Palembang camp on Sumatra. So she probably went there."

Theo thanked her and started asking the women if they'd been at Palembang. Several replied in the affirmative but said they did not recognise her. Then one woman asked,

"Was she one of the nurses?"

"Yes, she was a nurse."

"She looks like the girl who tended to me when I hurt my hand, that was in the early part of our time there. I don't remember her from later on, but there were an awful lot of prisoners in that camp, it was very crowded, especially after the Dutch arrived, and some were later moved to another camp."

"Can you remember the name of the other camp?" Theo asked.

"No, sorry."

Unable to find out anything more after that, Theo left the hotel, feeling despondent. However, it was possible that she had gone to their bungalow, as he had suggested in his note, or even Alexandra hospital. He had no idea whether or not their former home was habitable, whether the Wongs were still there or not, but he would go there and see. Then he'd try the hospital. If he still couldn't find her, perhaps he should go to Kuala Lumpur, to her mother's home, and see if she'd arrived there. He knew that the Japs had rebuilt the causeway, so probably trains were running. He hadn't seen Emma, Jean and Shirley at the hotel either, he realised. Perhaps they were at the hospital? Or perhaps all four of them had escaped by boat and the women who thought they recognised Nat were wrong? In that case, the other three would probably go straight back to England.

He started to walk up to Mount Rosie Road, but he had been feeling ill since early that morning, had been trying to ignore it, and as he walked he started to feel worse and worse. It felt as though a bout of malaria was coming on again. Perhaps he should head to the hospital first and get seen to? But what if Nat was there, in their home, waiting for him? He hadn't much further to go to find out.....

The next thing he knew, he was in a hospital bed with a white-coated doctor and a white-uniformed nurse looking down at him. The nurse's uniform was the same as the one Natalia used to wear and for a split second he thought it was her, then he realised that this woman was Chinese.

"You're back with us then," the doctor commented.

"What happened?"

"You collapsed at the bottom of Mount Rosie Road. Someone found you and brought you here. You have malaria, but we're treating it. Have you had it before?"

"Yes, several times in the last three years."

"Hmm. I don't suppose you ever got adequate treatment for it before. We have the drugs you need in the quantity you need them, so you should recover soon."

"Which hospital is this?"

"Alexandra."

"Do you know Natalia Bradshaw? She's a nurse, she worked here before the invasion. Has she returned here?"

"I don't know her," the doctor said. "I've only just arrived. He turned to the nurse. "Do you?"

She shook her head. "I can ask around for you. Is she a relative?"

"Yes, my wife. I'm trying to find her."

After they had gone, he slipped into a light dose. He slept intermittently over the next forty-eight hours. It felt strange, but also very nice, to be in a proper bed, with clean sheets and a comfortable mattress, wearing hospital pyjamas. The food seemed superb to him, although his stomach had shrunk and he could not manage a full meal. Then he opened his eyes and saw Emma sitting beside his bed.

"Emma!"

"I've been waiting for you to wake up," she said gently.

She looked much thinner and her once luxuriant auburn hair was cropped short and had lost its lustre. Her face was a mass of freckles.

"Were you interned too?" he asked.

"Yes, along with Shirley, Jean and Natalia. We were shipwrecked and landed on the coast of one of the Dutch islands."

"Where is Natalia?"

"That's what I've come to tell you. I was told you were in here and asking for her. I'm just coming in for a couple of hours a day to help out, while I wait for my passage home."

She seemed to be delaying answering his question directly, and her hands were fidgeting with her apron.

"Where's Nat?" Theo asked again, a cold feeling of dread settling in the pit of his stomach.

"There's no easy way to tell you this. Natalia didn't survive the camp, she died at Palembang. She was pregnant when she arrived, although she didn't realise it at first. We delivered her baby - your baby - but he only lived a few hours and Nat died the following day. There was nothing we could do to prevent their deaths; please believe me, we fought to save them, the doctor and I, we did everything in our power, but we had no equipment, no drugs. It was a difficult labour, the baby was in the wrong position in the womb and he tore her apart coming out. She lost so much blood and we couldn't stop the bleeding."

Theo could scarcely take this in. His mind was rejecting her words. Nat couldn't be dead, he needed her, he had longed for her throughout the last awful years. And a baby, a son, whom he would never see.....

"I'm so very sorry," Emma said, and he saw she was crying, tears slowly rolling down her cheeks. "When we realised we could do nothing more, we begged the Japs to let her be taken to a hospital, but they refused. They just didn't care if she died. She called the baby Theo, after you, and he died in her arms. They were both buried there, together, at Palembang, and we held a funeral service for them."

When Theo still said nothing, she went on, "Nat wrote you a letter when she knew she was dying. It's in my handwriting because she was too weak to write; she dictated it to me. She asked me to deliver it to you after the war."

She passed him a dog-eared, stained envelope, with his name on it. "Sorry about the state of it, but I expect you know how difficult it is to keep anything pristine in the camps."

He took it from her, but found he couldn't speak. There were words in his head but he couldn't voice them.

"I'll leave you to read it, and I'll come to see you again before I sail back." She kissed him lightly on the forehead and left.

Theo just lay there for a while, not knowing how to deal with the grief which was threatening to tear him apart. Then he opened the letter:

233

October 1942, Palembang Camp, Sumatra.

My dearest, beloved Theo,

I am writing this to you because I am dying. I know that, they can't keep it from me. I'm slowly bleeding to death. I've just given birth to our son, conceived that last night we were together. No child could have been conceived in more love, but it didn't save him. He was so beautiful, he looked so perfect, but he didn't live long. I called him Theo, after you. Soon I will be with him in the afterlife, if there is one; I hope there is.

My love, the short time we had together was the happiest period of my life. Just over three years, but three such wonderful, magical years! I love you more than I ever thought possible and I know it's the same for you. We are true soul-mates, aren't we?

Don't grieve for me too long, my darling. You are still young, you can find happiness with someone else one day and have more children. I give you my blessing in that.

I wish I could be with you one more time before I go. I yearn for your arms around me, your lips on mine, just as I have ached for you ever since we were taken captive. I hope your own captivity is bearable and you will survive to read this letter, know how very much I love you and that I died loving you more than words can describe.

Your Natalia,

XXXXXXXXX

Theo let the letter fall onto the bedcover and turned his face to the wall. The grief inside him was unbearable but he could not express it, could not cry. It was like an iron vice gripping his chest, a searing agony which he was unable to release. The nurse came in with his lunch, but he left it untouched.

"You must eat," she scolded. "You won't get better if you don't and if you lose any more weight you could die, you have no fat reserves left."

"I don't care. My wife is dead, I have no reason to live."

"I'm very sorry for your loss, but you still have most of your life ahead of you, she surely wouldn't want you to give up?"

Theo just turned his head away.

Later that day, Edward arrived at his bedside. "Someone told me you were in here, I've been looking for you."

Theo looked at him with deadened eyes.

"What's the matter with you? Malaria?"

"Yes."

"Well, you'll get proper treatment this time, they'll soon have you sorted, then it's back to dear old Blighty for us both. And Natalia and Arianna of course. I'm off up to KL tomorrow and then to Klang to collect Ari; I've booked us both on a ship sailing in ten days time. Meanwhile, I'm staying at your bungalow, hope you don't mind. The Wongs have got it all shipshape again and they told me to tell you that they managed to salvage some of your personal possessions and keep them in storage at their quarters. Good news, eh? I'm hoping I might find the same at my former place in KL. Oh, and guess what, the banks are open and I was able to get money out; my final month's salary was in there! You'll find the same." He paused for breath then went on, "I'm thinking about a spring wedding, if Ari agrees, what do you think? Will you be my best man?"

Theo just looked at him for a moment and didn't answer immediately. Edward suddenly realised that he hadn't reacted to anything he'd just said. Then Theo said simply,

"Natalia's dead, she died in the camp."

Shocked, Edward's exuberant mood immediately subsided. "Oh, Theo, mate, I'm so very sorry! I did wonder where she was, the Wongs hadn't seen either of you, then I assumed she would be here."

After that, there was little more to be said. Edward kept thinking of things to say then dismissed them as being too trite or clichéd. But neither did he feel that he could just get up and leave. Theo was his friend, soon to become his brother-in-law, he couldn't just desert him in his grief. Then the nurse arrived with his supper.

"Make sure he eats this, will you?" she said to Edward. "He refused his last meal. He says he doesn't care if he dies - which he soon will if he doesn't eat. He's got no spare flesh to lose."

When she had gone, Theo pushed the plate away. Edward pushed it back.

"Don't be silly, old chap. You've survived the war and everything the Japs threw at you. You haven't come through all that only to

235

starve yourself to death now. Look at this grub, it looks delicious. Just think how we'd have killed for a meal like this in the camps!"

"You eat it then, and let her think I have!"

"No way. I'm not going to aid and abet you in killing yourself. You've got the rest of your life ahead of you. And Nat wouldn't want this, would she? And what about all the people who care about you? Think of your sisters at least. Am I going to bring Ari back here to find her brother dead? Do you really want that for her?"

Theo said nothing but he took up the fork and ate a couple of mouthfuls.

"There, does that satisfy you?"

"Well it might prevent your imminent death, but it's not going to get you your health and strength back. You need to eat more than that."

"My stomach's shrunk."

"So's mine, but I can still manage more than that!"

Theo took one more mouthful then decisively pushed the plate as far away as he could on the bed-table.

"Well, I'll be back in a day or two with Ari and we'll see if she can get you to eat properly. Meanwhile at least eat something each mealtime. If you don't, they may decide to force feed you by tube."

After he had left, Theo thought about what he had said. He didn't much like the idea of being force fed, but it was probably nowhere near as bad as many of the ordeals he'd endured in Siam. It was the mention of his sisters which gave him pause for thought. He didn't want Arianna to arrive and find him dead or dying. There were other ways to end one's life apart from starvation. He would wait until she had returned to England. She and Enid would still grieve for him but at least they would be thousands of miles away and would have each other for support, as well as Arthur and Edward.

He was wallowing in a deep, black pit of despair from which he could see no escape. He felt as if there was a big gaping wound in his heart which could never be repaired. An image of Natalia bleeding to death kept flashing into his mind; how she must have suffered. And his baby son; had he felt pain as the life drained out of him or had his death been peaceful? He realised he had no idea what their baby looked like, was he light or dark skinned, had he brown or blue eyes?

He supposed it didn't matter, but perversely he wanted to know. When Emma came back he'd ask her. To make the pain easier to bear he tried to focus on images of Natalia in happier times, to remember their life together, but the knowledge that he would never, ever know those times again kept intruding and breaking his heart anew.

Edward arrived in Kuala Lumpur late the following day. He went first to his former home, to see if anything could be salvaged but found it trashed and half-empty. None of his belongings were still there and his houseboy was nowhere to be found. Oh well, never mind, he thought philosophically, they're only things, things can be replaced. He then headed for Klang.

Arianna's grandmother opened the door and recognised him immediately, despite the weight he had lost.

"Hello. How are you all?" he asked politely. "Is Arianna in?"

"No, she's not here."

"When will she be back?"

"Come in please, and I will explain."

A sense of foreboding began to infiltrate Edward's mind. What needed to be explained? Had something happened? She should have been safe here.

Inside, he was offered tea, which he accepted. Then the old lady sat down opposite him, just as her husband entered the room.

"Arianna's married now, with a baby. She lives in the capital."

The bottom dropped out of Edward's world. For a minute he just sat there, gaping at them.

She went on, "Her husband is a former colleague of hers at the government offices; he started visiting her here not long after the Japanese occupation started. They married in April last year and her little daughter was born in February."

Edward's mind was reeling. Like Theo with Natalia, thoughts of Arianna and their future life together had kept his spirits up throughout the darkest days of captivity. Now all his hopes and dreams had been demolished with one sentence. He wanted to just get up and leave, go away from here and try to forget her, but he had promised Theo he would bring his sister to him. He couldn't let his friend down and Arianna needed to know urgently the state Theo was in, that he was contemplating suicide.

As if reading his thoughts, Arianna's grandfather said, "Have you news of our grandson? Was he interned with you? Is he still alive?"

"Yes, he is, but he's in hospital in Singapore. I did tell him I'd bring Arianna to see him. He's just found out that Natalia died in the camp."

"Oh, I'm so sorry to hear that," the old lady exclaimed. "She was a lovely girl!" Her face registered shock and grief.

"Indeed she was," her husband agreed. "That's very sad news."

"I need Arianna's address in KL from you. I have to tell her about Theo and hopefully take her to see him. He's in a bad way."

"He's not dying?" the old man asked, his voice full of concern.

"No, but he's taken the news of his wife's death very badly and he's hardly eating anything. He's already like a walking skeleton, much worse than me, because he was one of those prisoners sent to work on the Burma-Siam railway. They endured brutal conditions; many of them died. I'm hoping Arianna can persuade him to eat properly and get better, instil in him the will to live."

"I'll write down the address for you. When you see Theo again, please give him our love and tell him we hope to see him before he goes back to England, if he has time. I assume you will all be returning there?"

"Yes, for at least six months."

The old man finished writing the address and passed it to Edward.

"I'm sorry if you are disappointed that Arianna didn't wait for you. But her husband is a good man, a Eurasian like her, and he takes good care of her."

Edward didn't comment, just bade them farewell and left.

By the time he got back to the capital, it was quite late and he decided to find somewhere to stay the night and see Arianna in the morning. He was in luck; the cadets' mess was up and running again, being used by personnel from the new military administration who had just arrived prior to the formal handing back of Kuala Lumpur. They offered him a camp bed for the night.

After breakfast, he set off to find the address he'd been given. It turned out to be an upper apartment in one of the many shop-houses which lined the streets of the capital. The street door was unlocked and he made his way up the dark, narrow staircase. Arianna answered his knock.

"Edward! Oh, you're still alive, that's wonderful!" She flung her arms around him.

He resisted the instinct to hug her back, and stiffly disengaged himself, holding her at arms' length. Suddenly realising the gulf that her changed circumstances had created between them, she stepped back and said, more formally,

"Please do come in."

He entered a small, but welcoming kitchen cum living room. A baby of about six months old lay in a cot in one corner, kicking her legs in the air and cooing. Arianna was wearing a *sarong*, she looked very Malayan.

"Gosh, you are thin, Edward, and so sunburnt. Was it terrible in the camps? I've heard some awful stories. I suppose my grandparents gave you this address and told you everything?"

"About your marriage, yes. Where's your husband?"

"He's left for work."

"I had hoped you might have waited for me, but that's not why I'm here. I'm here about Theo."

"Is he all right? I've been trying to find out but no-one could tell me anything and the phones don't work, the Japs destroyed the network. Please don't say you've come to tell me that my brother is dead!"

"He's alive, but only just." He briefly outlined the situation.

"Oh, no, how dreadful! Poor, poor Natalia! And Theo must be devastated. How did she die?"

Edward realised he didn't know, he hadn't asked Theo for any details. "I don't know. Can you come back with me today to Singapore? You can stay at Theo's bungalow."

Arianna made a split second decision. Farish would be furious if she just took off, but if Theo needed her....

"Yes, just give me time to pack a bag. I'll have to bring my baby with me, though."

"Yes, of course. What's her name?"

"Sakirah. Would you like some refreshment while you wait?"

239

"Just a glass of water will do."

She poured it out then disappeared into another room. When she returned she carried two bags and had changed into European dress.

"I just need to change Sakirah and then we can go."

Edward watched her as she changed the baby's nappy. Misery rose up anew inside him; in his fantasies he had often imagined her looking after the children they would have together. When she had finished, she put the baby into a sort of sling which she wore across her body, so that the child was carried facing her.

"I'll just leave a note for my husband."

Wondering how much of an explanation to give, she just said that Theo was very ill in hospital in Singapore and she had to go to him. She hoped to be back in a few days time. He was going to be angry whatever she wrote.

On the long train journey to Singapore, they sat opposite each other, the atmosphere strained. Sakirah fell asleep, lulled by the motion of the train. Arianna knew he was owed an explanation, but how to start? Especially when seeing him again had brought all her old feelings flooding back.

"Edward, I'm so sorry. I did wait for you at first, for quite a long time, but as the years went by our romance seemed more and more remote, and I didn't know whether you were dead or alive and, if you were alive, whether you would still feel the same at the end of the war. Farish was there, he made me feel safe and he kept asking me to marry him....."

Her voice tailed off, she was not explaining it well, she was making herself sound shallow. Edward just looked at her and she felt chastised by his steady gaze. She had let him down. He had been in captivity all this time, doubtless enduring considerable hardship, looking forward to resurrecting their relationship once the war ended, and she had deserted him. And she would have been so much happier with him! But it was too late. She had Sakirah now and Farish was her father. She regretted a great deal but she could never wish that her child had not been born.

"I did hope that you would wait for me, I'm disappointed that you haven't, but it's done now, isn't it? There's no point in having a post mortem on it."

His tone was cold and that told her just how much she had hurt him. And he was the last person she wanted to hurt; she loved him, she still loved him. What a mess she had made of everything!

She changed the subject. "I can't believe Nat's dead, it's so awful. I shall miss her too, we were good friends. And you say Theo won't eat? Is he trying to die too, to be with her?"

"It seems like it, yes. He's lost the will to live. He's grieving terribly and he's not thinking straight. And he has no spare weight to lose, he's all skin and bone as it is, much worse than me."

"Is that why he's in hospital?"

"He collapsed with a recurrence of malaria. He had it several times in Siam."

"Siam?"

"He was sent to work on the railway the Japs were building between Siam and Burma. Conditions were appalling there, disease was rife and they were worked like slaves, worked to death in many cases. Only half of Theo's force came back. And Laurence died up there. Ralph was still alive when Theo left, hopefully he survived. I expect he was sent back direct to England at the end of the war."

"But you weren't sent there?"

"No, I was lucky. Changi was no holiday camp but it was never as bad as that."

Arianna fell silent, humbled by the realisation of what they had all been through, while she had been cocooned safely in Klang.

"What happened to Emma, Shirley and Jean? Do you know?"

"No. But it may have been one of them who told Theo about Natalia. I didn't ask him how he knew."

After a while, Sakirah started to grizzle.

"I need to breastfeed her. Do you mind?" There was no-one else in their compartment.

"I'll turn my head away."

And he did, despite being tempted to look. There was no point in desiring a woman who was married to another man, but how did he turn off his feelings? Only time and distance would do that.

When they finally arrived in Singapore, weary from the long, hot journey, it was late evening, too late to go to the hospital. At Theo's

241

former home, the Wongs welcomed Arianna and Lian exclaimed over Sakirah.

"What a beautiful baby! We will make up a cot for her, there's one in the garage, left by another family who used to live here years ago."

Edward told Arianna to take Theo and Natalia's room, he was in the guest room. He then bid her a curt goodnight.

The next morning at breakfast, when she was spoon feeding the baby some pureed food that Lian had prepared, he said he would leave her to make her way to the hospital on her own.

"You know where it is, don't you?"

Arianna nodded. She had visited Theo and Natalia here before the invasion and had once gone to the hospital with Natalia.

"I can look after the little one for you, while you are there, if you like?" Lian offered.

Arianna hesitated, then said yes, and thanked her. It would be best to see how see Theo was before bringing her baby to see him, and she also had to explain!

~***~

Chapter Twenty-Four

For a second or two she almost didn't recognise him. Could this gaunt-faced man with hollow eyes and sunken cheeks really be her brother? His eyes were closed and his head turned slightly to the side, and she stood stock-still for a moment at the foot of the bed, taking in his skeletal frame, shaved head - stubble just beginning to grow back - and skin burnt nut brown by the sun. His pyjama jacket was open and she could count his ribs. He was barely thirty but looked middle aged.

She let out a little murmur of distress. "Oh, my poor, dear brother, what have they done to you?!"

Hearing her voice, he opened his eyes and turned his head in her direction. "Ari!"

She came up to his bedside and wordlessly reached out to him. Theo let himself sink into her embrace. Hers were not the arms he had longed for throughout the long years of captivity, but they were still dear and familiar arms, and her scent evoked memories of his childhood, that idyllic time before the fire when he had scarcely known what bereavement was. Suddenly, the grief, which had been lying inside him like a heavy stone weight on his heart, rose up and erupted outwards.

Arianna just held onto him and let him cry. When his sobs finally subsided, he sat up, fumbling for his handkerchief.

"I'm so sorry. I haven't seen you for four years and then I go and blub all over you!"

"I think you needed that, *sayang,* and you don't have to put on a stiff upper lip with me. I'm so terribly sorry about Natalia."

"Edward told you?"

"Yes, but he didn't know what happened. How did she die?"

"She was pregnant and she died in childbirth. The baby died too. It was a boy."

"Oh my God, how awful. I'm so very sorry. How did you find out?"

"Emma told me. She was there with her."

"Emma's here, in Singapore?"

"Yes, but she's sailing back to England soon."

"What about Jean and Shirley?"

"I don't know. Emma said she'd come and see me again before she sailed, I can ask her then. I want to ask her other things too, about Nat and the baby. I was too shocked to think of them before."

There was a moment's silence, then Arianna said, "Edward told me you're not eating, that you want to die. That's not the answer, Theo, she wouldn't want that. I know it feels like the end of your world right now, but you know that grief subsides eventually, with time. You'll never forget her, but you'll learn to live without her and you will be able to enjoy life again one day."

He didn't answer and she tried another tack. "Don't do this to us, to me and Enid. We've lost our mother and father, don't let us lose our brother too."

"That's emotional blackmail."

"I don't care what it is. I'll pull out all the stops to get you to eat again, so that you get better. You're my only brother and I love you and I want you well again. I spent the whole of the occupation not knowing whether you were dead or alive, and now that I know you are alive, I'm going to damn well keep you that way!"

He smiled, despite himself. "Actually, I have been eating a little bit, the last couple of days."

"Good, well make it more still now. When your lunch arrives, I will watch you and make sure you eat it!"

"You always were bossy!"

"And you never let me boss you about before, but you will now!"

As if on cue, his lunch did arrive then and under her watchful eye he ate about half of it.

"And the rest!"

"No, I'm full. My stomach still has to adjust. I've been on starvation rations for three and a half years."

Her face clouded over. "Yes, I can see you have. Edward said you'd been sent to work on a railway line in Siam and that conditions there were even more terrible than in Changi?"

244

"That's an understatement. It was a living hell. But let's talk about something pleasanter. I gather you and Edward are sailing back to England in about a week's time?"

Now she had to tell him. She took a deep breath.

"No, I'm not going with him. I can't. I'm married, Theo and I have a baby girl. You're an uncle!"

He just stared at her, then he looked down at her hand and saw the gold band on her finger.

"Does Edward know?"

"Yes."

"He'll be heartbroken. He was planning a spring wedding."

"Don't make me feel any worse than I already do!"

"Tell me all about it."

She told him about Farish finding her in Klang and starting to visit regularly.

"At first we were just friends, as we'd been at work, then he took me to see his family and it was grandma who pointed out that he was courting me. I didn't really believe her at first and for a long time he was very respectful and did no more than kiss my hand upon greeting and farewell. I knew I still loved Edward, but Farish's company partly alleviated the boredom of my life. I know I have no right to even seem to complain after what you and the others have been through, I know I was living a life of luxury in comparison, but it was a dull life, stuck with Mama's family; you know how limited their conversation is. And I felt I was in a sort of limbo, and I worried constantly about you and Edward and the girls, not knowing what was happening to you all. I looked forward to being able to talk to Farish once a week. Then, after about fifteen months, he asked me to marry him. I said no, that I didn't feel that way about him, but he asked again a few months later and then again. And that time he gave me an ultimatum, saying that if I refused him again it would be the end of our friendship, I wouldn't see him again. I didn't want that, and by then my romance with Edward seemed such a long time ago, rather remote, and I didn't know if he was even alive and if he was, whether he would still feel the same at the end of the war. And grandma said being in love does not always last, and provided I liked and respected Farish and found him attractive, that would be

245

enough. She said love would grow through being together in marriage."

"And did it?" Theo interjected.

"Yes, of course it did."

But her eyes belied her words and he said, "Ari, you can't fool me. I know you too well."

She said nothing for a moment then burst out, "All right, I made a mistake. A bloody huge mistake! I don't love Farish, I don't think I ever will, and I'm still madly in love with Edward; as soon as I saw him again I knew that. But it's too late! I'm not only married, I have a child. She's nearly seven months old and she's beautiful and I adore her. Whatever else I regret, I can't regret her existence and Farish is her father."

Theo sighed. "What a mess! But you're right, you're stuck now, you can't take her away from her father. You've made your bed and now you'll have to lie in it - literally!"

"Yes, all right, Theo. There's no need to rub it in!"

"Is he a good husband at least?"

"Yes, I suppose so. He provides for us and he adores Sakirah."

"That's a pretty name."

"It was his choice, but I like it too. Her middle name is Alya, after Mama. That was my choice."

"Both Malay names."

"Farish is very Malay. He's Eurasian like us but his father left when he was a baby, he has no memory of him and thinks of his stepfather as his father. They are a devout Muslim family, always at the mosque and praying. He'd like me to convert to Islam but I've refused. However, I had to agree to our children being brought up as Muslims. He likes me to wear Malay dress too. I did that anyway during the war, whenever I went out, so that I blended in with the natives, but now I can wear my European clothes again, and he doesn't like that. He likes me to behave like a good Malay wife."

Theo observed drily, "That's not really you, is it? Malay wives are subservient to their husbands and you've never been subservient to anyone in the whole of your life!"

Arianna shrugged. "Well, I try to meet him halfway, it makes for a more peaceful life." Then she added, "I'll have to go now, Sakirah will need feeding. But I'll be back in a couple of hours and I'll bring her with me, to meet her uncle."

"Who's looking after her?"

"Lian Wong. I'm staying at your home."

"Is Edward still there too?"

"Yes."

Not long after she had left, Edward appeared back in the ward.

"Has she told you?" he asked, without preamble.

"Yes. I'm so sorry, old chap. If it's any consolation, she regrets not waiting for you, she still loves you."

"I don't think it is any consolation, it almost makes it worse," he answered gloomily. "Anyway, I came to tell you that I've established we're entitled to up to a year's leave, starting from the day we dock in England. The first six months on full pay and the rest on half."

"Will you come back afterwards?"

"I don't know. I think I'll come back, after all this is supposed to be my career, but I might feel differently later on. What about you? Assuming you've decided to continue living!"

Theo wasn't sure whether he had decided that or not, but it seemed to have been decided for him. His plan to wait until Arianna had gone to England was null and void now that she was not going. He couldn't inflict his suicide on her and neither could he do the same to Enid once he was back in England. Answering Edward's question, he said,

"I'm not sure either."

"Well, we don't have to decide for a long time, do we? When are you sailing, by the way, or have you not booked a passage yet?"

"I booked for early November. I thought Natalia would want to spend some time with her family in KL first." Even speaking her name was painful.

"You might be able to bring it forward."

"Yes, perhaps, but I could also spend some time with Ari and my grandparents. I suppose I ought to get to know my new brother-in-law, although I'd much rather it were you!"

"That reminds me, your grandparents asked you to come and see them before you sail, if you can, and they send their love and best wishes for your recovery. Oh, and guess who I bumped into this

247

morning in Raffles; Emma, Jean and Shirley. They all looked a bit the worse for wear, it seems their camps were just as bad as Changi. Emma said she'd seen you. It was she who told you about Nat, wasn't it?"

"Yes. She said she'd come back before she sailed. There are things I want to ask her, about the baby especially."

"The baby?"

"Didn't she say? Natalia was pregnant with our baby when she was taken prisoner and she died giving birth to him. He died too."

"Oh, Theo, that's dreadful! No, she didn't say, perhaps she thought you'd told me. I'm so very sorry."

Edward had left by the time Arianna returned. Theo had slipped into a light dose - he seemed to be always dosing off since he'd been in here - and was awakened by the sound of the baby. He sat up and Arianna rearranged his pillows behind his back.

"This is your uncle Theo, Sakirah," she told the child as she lifted her out of the sling she carried her in and sat her on Theo's lap. "Say hello to him and give him a big kiss!"

Sakirah looked up at this strange man and reached up a hand to touch his face. She smiled.

"She's lovely, Ari, and she looks a lot like you." He wondered again what his baby son had looked like and felt a fresh stab of grief.

Their talk centred on the baby for a while and then Arianna asked, "Have you booked a passage home yet? Edward said he's sailing in a week's time."

He told her he wasn't sailing until November and explained why.

"Oh, that's good. When you're well enough you can come back to KL with me. Stay with us and visit the family in Klang."

"Thanks. But will your husband not mind?"

"No, of course not, you're my brother and he's very family minded. And we have a spare bedroom. Have they said when you can leave hospital?"

"No, but I can ask the doctor when he comes round tomorrow morning. They can't want to keep me in much longer, and I can convalesce at the bungalow." As he spoke, he wondered how he was going to bear being back there without Natalia.

"I'll stay here in Singapore with you until you're well enough to travel up to KL."

"Thanks. I'll go and see Nat's mother when I'm there. I wonder if she knows yet?"

"We should send Enid a telegram letting her know that we're both alive. She'll have been worrying all this time. I'll do that on my way back to the bungalow."

"She should have already had one about me. The lady at the military admin office asked me for my next of kin's details in England. But you'll still need to tell her that you're all right."

"I wonder if she's been carrying on writing to us all these years and her letters have just been piling up somewhere? Maybe they'll arrive eventually."

"More likely they'll just be lost."

"I bet she has a child by now as well. They were getting married in forty-two."

After a pause, Theo said, "It's strange thinking of you both as mothers now, especially Enid. The last time I saw her, she had only just left school."

The next morning, the doctor pronounced Theo fit to be discharged the following day, provided he had somewhere to go and someone to look after him. He also said that he should be fit to travel by train up to Kuala Lumpur a few days after that. Theo wanted to see Emma again before he left the hospital so he asked one of the nurses to get a message to her. She turned up later that day, accompanied by Jean and Shirley. There were hugs all round between the three girls and Arianna, and they all exclaimed over Sakirah, who was passed from one to the other.

"This is a surprise," Shirley said. "You married, with a baby!"

"You know you've broken Edward's heart?" Jean commented, with a disapproving tone to her voice.

"She's also broken her own," Theo put in. "She still loves him."

"Then why on earth did you marry someone else?"

"It's complicated." Arianna replied. She didn't want to have to go through the explanation all over again.

"Emma," Theo said, "There're things I've thought of that I'd like to ask you about Nat and the baby."

249

She pulled up a chair at the side of his bed, and he asked her the questions that had been preying on his mind. She hesitated for a minute or so before replying.

"Nat did suffer a lot of pain during the birth. There was no pain relief available and it was a difficult labour. But afterwards she just gradually became weaker and eventually lost consciousness."

"And the baby?"

"I don't think he felt much pain, if any. He didn't cry much. He was very weak from the start. He was quite light-skinned and his eyes looked as if they might become brown later on, but at birth a baby's eyes are often an indeterminate light colour and they change later. He had dark hair, but again that can change."

There was little more she could tell him and after an hour or so, the three girls left. They were all sailing home in two days time and they left their addresses in England.

"Do come and see us, Theo, and please write, Ari."

The next morning, Arianna arrived to collect Theo and accompany him to Mount Rosie Road. She found him sitting on the edge of the bed, fully dressed, waiting for her. She felt a fresh stab of pity at the sight of his stick-like legs protruding from his Red Cross issue shorts. She gave him her arm and they headed outside. There were trishaws waiting - bicycle rickshaws which had been introduced by the Japanese - and they took one.

"It would be a good idea to start going for short walks," Arianna said. "Build up your strength gradually."

At the bungalow, the Wongs gave Theo an effusive welcome, and expressed their sorrow at Natalia's death.

"She was such a lovely lady, so gracious."

"You look to be in sore need of my cooking," Lian said. "I'll be making all your favourite dishes while you're here."

They brought out the two suitcases full of Theo's and Natalia's personal belongings which they had managed to save.

"The Japanese Officer and his wife who lived here said to throw everything out, but we hoped you'd be back one day. The *Mem* took two bags with her to the ship, so there are more of your things in there than hers."

250

After she'd left the room, Theo opened one case. He found quite a lot of his clothing, both tropical wear and a couple of outfits suitable for England. His framed photographs were also there, for which he was profoundly grateful as they couldn't be replaced. One was of their wedding and his eyes filled with tears as he looked at it.

"There was a whole album of wedding photos as well, but that's not here."

"Maybe Natalia took that with her?" Arianna said.

"Then it's at the bottom of the sea!"

In the second, smaller case there were a few of Natalia's things. He took out a silk robe, which she always wore in the house at the beginning and end of the day, and lifted it to his face.

"It doesn't smell of her anymore!" he said, disappointed.

"Well, it's been three and a half years," Arianna commented.

"Yes, I know it's been three and a half bloody years," Theo suddenly exploded. "I've lived through them, three and a half years of hell which felt like twenty years! And what kept me going all that time was dreaming of Nat and our future life together. If I'd known she was dead, I'd have given up and died long ago. Why didn't I know? Why didn't I feel it here?" He beat his hand against his heart. "And now I don't know how I'm going to carry on without her. I feel as if I've lost a part of my soul."

"Just take it one day at a time," Arianna suggested. "Don't think ahead to the future, not yet. Right now it will be like looking into a dark abyss. Later on you'll feel differently."

Lian Wong came back in. "I've changed the sheets in the guest bedroom for you, *Tuan*. *Mem* Arianna and the baby are in your room and there's more room for the cot there. I'll make up a bed on the settee for *Tuan* Edward."

Theo was glad not to be sleeping in his old room, it held too many bittersweet memories.

At lunch, Han Wong asked them how long they were planning to stay.

"Perhaps until Monday?" Arianna said, looking questioningly at Theo. "Do you think you'll be well enough to travel then?"

"Yes, I'm sure I will."

"I ask because we received this yesterday." He showed Theo an official looking document which notified the occupants of the bungalow that it would shortly be requisitioned to house personnel from the new administration. This could happen any time from next Wednesday.

"Well, that's all right," Theo said. "We'll leave on Monday and Edward sails Tuesday."

"Where will you stay in November before you sail?" Arianna asked.

"I'll find somewhere, it will only be for one night. Maybe I'll take the steamer down the coast overnight instead of going by train."

That afternoon, Theo walked down into town, to get some exercise, and, while he was there, went to the bank and found that Edward was right, his last salary had been paid in. He withdrew most of the available funds, just leaving a few dollars to keep the account open. Then he went to the train station and bought two tickets for the morning train to Kuala Lumpur on Monday. By the time he returned, he was tired, hot and sweaty and decided to take a cool bath. As he came out of the bathroom, with just a towel round the lower half of his body, and turned to go into his room, Arianna was just coming out of her room.

"Theo! Your back! How did you get those scars?"

He'd forgotten about the scars. All the survivors of F and H force had them.

"On the railway, from being whipped by the guards. We were all beaten regularly, to get us to work faster."

"That's utterly barbaric!" Arianna's face registered shock and horror.

"Well, they are barbarians. But they don't hurt anymore and I expect they'll fade eventually."

On Monday morning they said goodbye to Edward and he and Theo exchanged addresses and telephone numbers in England. Edward lived in Surrey, so they would not be too far apart.

"Give me a ring when you get back," Edward said. "Laurence is dead and God knows what's happened to Ralph, but you and I can keep in touch, eh? And maybe visit the girls, they're all from the

252

home counties. Perhaps we can all have a get together in the New Year."

Arianna felt excluded from their conversation and their plans. Edward was ignoring her, just as he'd done ever since they arrived in Singapore. She couldn't blame him, but it made her feel thoroughly miserable. She was never going to see him again. If he did return to Malaya, he would give her a wide berth and that would not be difficult as she no longer went anywhere near the places where the Europeans congregated and socialised. She felt like an exile.

Han Wong drove them and their baggage to the station and wished them a good trip.

"Thanks for everything," Theo said to him. "I hope you get some nice people moving in next week."

"Well, they're bound to be better than the Japanese!"

~***~

Chapter Twenty-Five

The journey was long, hot and exhausting. Theo dosed off intermittently and Sakirah, usually a happy baby, was being grizzly. Feeding and changing her in a crowded train was well-nigh impossible, but at lunchtime Arianna spoon fed her some of the pureed food Lian had packed, along with their sandwiches, and gave her some water. After they stopped at Gemas, in the early afternoon, the passengers thinned out and they had the compartment to themselves. Arianna breast-fed Sakirah and then changed her, cleaning her with a damp flannel she had brought with her and then putting it and the dirty nappy into a rubber lined bag. Theo watched the proceedings, marvelling at how domesticated his sister had become.

After that, Sakirah fell asleep, cradled in Theo's lap. Arianna looked down at her daughter and said suddenly,

"I love her so very much, but I wish Farish wasn't her father. I wish that by some fluke she could be Edward's."

"Did you and Edward ever...?"

"Sleep together? No, we never quite got that far. We were heading in that direction, but then the Japs invaded and Edward had to go and fight. I wish we had! I wish I'd known what it's like with someone you really love. When I was with Edward, I felt desire like I've never felt for Farish, and seeing him again brought it all back. Lying in that bedroom, with him the other side of the wall, all I wanted to do was go and make love to him. I know I can't begin to compare my situation with yours; Edward's not dead and it's all my own fault that I'll never see him again. I'll save you the bother of telling me that! But you know that dark abyss I mentioned the other day? I feel that if I look into my future with Farish."

Theo looked at her sympathetically, but didn't know what to say to make her feel better. And she was right, it was all her own fault and Edward was suffering too. And she was short-changing her husband who had married her in good faith and presumably loved her.

They arrived in the capital in the early evening and took a taxi from the station. As they alighted, Theo said, surprised,

"You live in a shop-house?"

"Yes, on the top floor. The people who run the shop live on the first floor."

There was no sign of Farish inside.

"He must have gone to his mother's to have dinner," Arianna said.

She showed Theo their spare bedroom, which was small but pleasantly furnished.

"The bed's made up and I'll get you a towel and fill the water jug." A jug and bowl stood on a washstand. "I'm afraid the bathroom and lav are downstairs at the back and we share them with the other family. The quickest way down is by the back stairs." She showed him the door to the fire escape stairs at the end of the corridor and pointed out the two outbuildings. "Shanghai jar and thunderbox style, like at grandma's. There's a pot under the bed if you need it in the night. We're hoping to move to a better place soon, if Farish gets the promotion he's aiming for, now that the British are back in charge."

"It's fine, Ari. It's a nice cosy little apartment."

She went to look in the larder and found it virtually empty.

"I'll just pop down to the shop and get some provisions for our supper and for breakfast, then I'll go to the market tomorrow."

She came back with some cold meats, bread, fruit and other things which required little or no preparation.

"I'll cook properly tomorrow," she said.

After they had eaten and Sakirah had been fed and changed, she put her into her cot, where she cooed and gurgled happily. They were just clearing the table when they heard the outer door open.

"So, you've finally decided to return home," was Farish's greeting to his wife. His tone was cold.

"Farish, this is my brother, Theo. I've invited him to stay with us for a few weeks until he sails back to England."

Farish put out his hand and shook Theo's. His tone immediately became courteous. "You are most welcome, brother-in-law. I believe we met before. Weren't you at the Treasury for a few months about seven years ago?"

"Yes, that was my first job over here. I thought you looked familiar."

"I was just a lowly clerk then. I have a more senior position now."

They made polite small talk for about fifteen minutes, while Arianna was washing up in the scullery. Then Theo asked if they minded if he turned in.

"I'm very tired."

"But of course. I understand you've been ill?"

"Yes, malaria."

"And you've been a prisoner of war these last few years?"

"Yes."

"How did they treat you?"

"Badly. I'm not usually this thin!"

"He's had a terrible time," Arianna put in. "They were starved and beaten and I don't know what else. He hasn't told me much detail yet."

"I expect you want to forget about it," Farish commented.

"I wish I could!"

He said goodnight and left the room. Farish waited until he'd heard Theo return from downstairs and close his bedroom door, then he firmly shut the door from the hall and also the one leading to the scullery, which was opposite Theo's room.

"Right, now I want an explanation from you!" His tone was coldly furious.

"I explained in my note."

"You said you'd be back in a few days, it's been a whole week."

"Theo's only just become well enough to travel."

"You could have returned earlier, as soon as he was out of danger, and he could have travelled up on his own."

"I was worried about him. He'd just learned of his wife's death in the camp and he was in very low spirits. I was afraid he might do something stupid."

"How did you get the news about him?"

"A friend of his came to find me."

"That wouldn't be the same friend you dated before the invasion, would it?"

256

She hesitated. She had never told Farish about Edward.

"Don't bother to lie! Your grandmother told me. And I often saw you meeting him after work."

"Yes, it was the same man, but we were only ever friends, and there's nothing between us now."

"And where did you stay in Singapore?"

"In Theo's bungalow. The Chinese couple who look after it were still there."

"And where did he stay, this man?"

"He stayed there too."

"Very cosy!"

"We slept in separate rooms! And I hardly saw him, I was at the hospital all day. And Theo was discharged on Thursday so we were all three there after that."

Farish looked at her speculatively for a moment, then said, "You're wearing European clothes."

"Yes."

"You know I prefer you to wear a *sarong*, and a scarf over your head when you go out. But I suppose you've been flaunting yourself around Singapore dressed like that."

"I haven't been flaunting myself as you put it. I'd have stood out more there in Malayan dress."

"Well, as from tomorrow you will dress modestly again. And don't you ever go off again like that, without a word, with a strange man and taking my daughter with you."

"He wasn't a stranger, and of course I had to take her with me! I'm her mother and I'm still feeding her. And Theo's my brother; would you not have gone to one of your sisters if they were ill in hospital?"

"How did you feed Sakirah on the train journey down?"

"We had the carriage to ourselves after a while and Edward went out into the corridor while I fed her." It was a lie, but he would never know.

"Well, if I ever find out that you and this Edward resurrected your love affair, you'll wish you'd never been born!"

"We didn't have a love affair to resurrect! I was a virgin when I married you, you know that!"

257

He just looked at her for a long moment, then said, "How you have conducted yourself is not appropriate behaviour for a Muslim wife."

"I'm not a Muslim!"

"You are the wife of one and you will behave accordingly in future."

Theo, lying in bed, heard the rise and fall of their voices and guessed they were having an argument, although he couldn't make out the words, just the tone. He hoped Farish wasn't giving his sister a hard time. Should he get up and go in, try to mollify Farish, take the blame for Arianna's sudden departure? Or would it be better not to intervene between husband and wife? He tried to imagine being in the same situation if Natalia had had to leave suddenly to visit a sick member of her family and had just left a note. Would he have been angry? No, of course he wouldn't, he would have completely understood. Why couldn't Farish?

The next morning Arianna went to the market and he went with her. He watched in amusement as she wound a scarf round her head, hiding her hair. She was already wearing a *sarong*.

"You really look the part of a native Malay woman!"

She pulled a face. "Well, I might just bump into my mother-in-law in the market and if I'm wearing western dress she's bound to report back to Farish. And I'm in his bad books as it is."

"I'm sorry. I assume that's because you came to Singapore? Shall I say something to him tonight, take the blame?"

"No, better leave well alone. It'll blow over. And it's not your fault. I'd do it again in similar circumstances, and he ought to be able to understand."

In the afternoon, Theo left Arianna doing domestic chores and went to see Natalia's mother, taking some of the things she had left in Singapore. He found that she already knew of her daughter's death, and her eyes were red with weeping.

"I received a notice from the British Military last week. But it didn't say how she died. Do you know?"

He told her, his voice cracking as he recounted the details Emma had given him. She shed further tears, dabbing at her eyes with her handkerchief. He noted that she had aged significantly these last few years; her hair was now completely grey. He asked her how the occupation had been for them.

"Not good, although obviously nothing like it was for you. You are all skin and bone, what happened to you?"

He recounted the gist of his years in captivity, glossing over a lot of the gory detail, particularly during his time on the railway. However, she seemed to be able to read between the lines and when he stopped speaking she put out her hand and clasped his.

"Those barbarians! I hope they are now getting their just deserts. I've heard they are all now prisoners themselves."

"Indeed. But we observe the Geneva convention, so they'll receive better treatment than they meted out to us. But I believe some of them will be tried for war crimes."

"And you are still suffering, grieving for my Natalia. I know how much you loved her. But she wouldn't want you to grieve for ever, one day you will find happiness again."

"I can't imagine that. No-one could ever replace her."

The following day, they went to Klang. Theo received an ecstatic welcome from his grandparents, although they were shocked at his appearance. They expressed their sorrow about Natalia's death, then his grandfather started to ask questions about his time in captivity. He managed to answer them without going into much detail, not feeling ready to do that yet, if he ever would.

"Do you still think that he deserved his fate, Grandpa?" Arianna asked, startling Theo with the question.

"I never said that!" the old man protested.

"You said that he'd become a *Tuan* and fought against the Japs and therefore had to accept the consequences of his actions."

"Perhaps I did say something like that," the old man conceded, "but I never dreamed that those consequences would be so disproportionate. You can't believe I wanted him to be starved and beaten and God knows what else, and for his wife to die!" His tone was indignant but his voice also shook a little. "Please believe me, Theo, I never meant that!"

"It's fine, I know you didn't."

But Arianna hadn't finished. Her grandfather's words had rankled at the time and she was not going to let him off lightly. "You also

259

said that you could see little of Mama in Theo, that he was entirely English."

"Well, that's probably true," Theo said, unperturbed by this. "But it's also true of Ari, despite her colouring, and Enid. It's how we were all brought up. Having said that, Enid is actually the one of us who is most like Mama, not in looks, but in personality and tastes and talents."

"It's a pity then that we shall probably never see her again," his grandmother said, with a sigh. "We don't even get letters from her, just messages at the end of her letters to Ari, which she translates for us."

"That's because she can't write the Malay language," Arianna said patiently, having explained this before. "She was only at school in Klang for a short time and she soon forgot what little she'd learned."

On the way back on the train, Arianna said, "It's true what you said about us all being more English than Malay, even me. It's ironic that when I was in England I felt a misfit and thought I'd fit in better here, but as soon as all the English people I mixed with here had gone, I felt like a fish out of water. And I really miss England!"

Arianna had started a long letter to Enid, filling her in on the last three and a half years, regarding both Theo and herself. There was a lot to say and she kept running out of time and had to put it to one side. She asked Theo to keep it with his belongings, as she had written things she did not want Farish to read.

"I plan to finish and post it a week or two before you sail, then it will get there before you."

On the Sunday after Theo's arrival in the capital, they all went to Farish's family home for curry *tiffin*. It was a pleasant meal and they were all very courteous to their guest but Theo could understand why Arianna felt she did not fit in; she had nothing in common with them. The three sisters were all very demure, deferring to Farish and their father in everything they said. He tried to imagine Arianna behaving like that with himself and Jim or George and almost laughed out loud.

A couple of weeks later, Theo started to have nightmares in which he was back on the railway. In some of the more bizarre dreams, Natalia also featured, incongruously giving birth at one of those camps with a Japanese medical officer in attendance, yelling 'Speedo' at her. He would wake, drenched in sweat and take several minutes to realise where he was. Such dreams usually happened in the early morning, when Arianna was already up attending to Sakirah and she heard him muttering and groaning in his sleep. After a few days of this, she told him she knew he was having nightmares and suggested he speak about the detail of his time in captivity, especially on the railway.

"It might help to put a stop to those dreams."

"But I don't want to relive it, I want to forget."

"But you're not forgetting, are you? It's coming out in dreams so it must all still be festering inside you."

"The details aren't very pretty, they're not for feminine ears."

She snorted. "Fiddle! This is me, not some delicate flower who faints at the thought of anything earthy! I don't know how any woman who's given birth can still be squeamish."

He gave some thought to her words and the next afternoon he began, hesitatingly, to tell her what had transpired following the British surrender. He started with the march to Changi and described conditions there, then progressed to his departure for Siam. At first, he was telling it as if it had all happened to someone else, dispassionately and in an almost toneless monologue. But once he started to relate the dreadful journey up to Siam, he began to relive it. He was back there; he was marching those two-hundred miles again in the monsoon mud, watching men die en route; he was living in the dreadful makeshift camps, enduring the appalling conditions and the starvation rations; he was slaving on the railway track, being beaten by the Korean guards whenever he was too ill or exhausted to continue, or simply not working fast enough; he was being dragged out of the hospital tent still weak from malaria or dengue fever and forced back to the railway track once more; he was suffering the misery and humiliation of having acute dysentery when the latrines were a long distance from where they slept; he was once more witnessing some of his fellow prisoners being tortured to death. When he finally faltered to a halt, he became aware of his sister's shocked expression. She said shakily,

"I don't know what to say to you. Anything I came out with would seem trite and meaningless. I just hope that talking about it has helped."

And it did seem to, the dreams lessened. As the weeks went by, his hair grew back, now flecked with silver, and he was slowly putting on weight, although he still had a long way to go. Arianna was making it her mission to fatten him up as much as possible before he sailed.

"Then Enid can take over, or Cook if she's still there and you're staying at the manor. You'll get better cooking from them!"

"I don't know about that, your cooking's improved no end!"

"Farish doesn't think so, he's always comparing my dishes unfavourably with his mother's."

Theo wondered why Farish always had to put her down. Why couldn't he pay his wife compliments?

Sakirah was now crawling and into everything. Theo played baby games with her and had her squealing with delight. A bond was forming between uncle and niece, but every now and then he would feel a sharp pang of grief at the loss of his own child, whom he had never seen. His grief for Natalia was still at the forefront of his mind, and although he had put aside suicidal thoughts, he believed he would never be really happy again.

It was his thirtieth birthday a few days before he was due to sail. A celebration was arranged at his grandparents' home in Klang and many of the aunts, uncles and cousins were also there. Farish did not go with them, as the date fell on a Friday, when he spent his spare time at the mosque. Their grandmother had baked a cake and decorated it with three candles and a festive meal was laid out. It was also a farewell gathering for the family in Klang, as they would not see him again before he sailed. They all wished him a safe journey and hoped he would enjoy his long leave.

"When we see you next, you will have your health and strength back and there will be more of you!" his grandfather said.

But Theo was by no means sure that he would return. All he could think of was the cool green landscape of England, he longed for that, needed it as a salve to his soul, and couldn't see any further ahead. He said as much to Arianna on their way back to her home.

She made only a minimal comment in response, but a few days later, when they were on their way to the port where Theo would catch the local steamer to take him to Singapore overnight, she suddenly burst out,

"Please come back at the end of your leave! Enid's life is settled in England now and mine has to be here, we will probably never see each other again, but you can bridge the gap between us, spending your leaves in England and your working life here."

"We don't need a bridge, Ari. There's a strong bond between the three of us which can never be broken and letters will help to keep it alive. And commercial air travel is developing fast, the rich can already fly between the two countries. Well within our lifetimes, we'll probably see reasonably priced flights become available, so that you can holiday in England and we can visit here."

"Yes, perhaps." But she was thinking that Farish would never agree to their taking a holiday in England, nor allow her to go alone.

They reached the port and Theo joined the queue to embark.

"I wish I was going with you. I'd give anything to be able to go back to England. I miss it so much now, not only Enid, but the manor, Oxfordshire, everything!"

"Is there no chance that Farish would ever consider emigrating and getting a job in England? His English is excellent, he'd have no trouble."

"No chance at all. He actually hates the British although he hides it well when he's with them. I think it's because of his father, who just left his mother high and dry when she was expecting him. He didn't even leave money for his education, like Nat's father did, his stepfather paid for that."

"Strange then, that he chose to marry a girl who's half British!"

"He married the Malay half of me! He doesn't much like the other half, but unfortunately for us, that's the dominant part."

Theo looked at her, rather startled by her words. She had made it clear she wasn't very happy with Farish and wished she had waited for Edward, and Farish did often seem offhand and rather cold with her, but it seemed things were even worse than he had thought. Still, she had a child and there could be no turning back now.

263

He was now nearing the front of the queue. "Thanks for everything you've done for me these last weeks, Ari. Your sisterly care and affection has got me through, set me on the road to recovery. Perhaps you may even have saved my life!"

"You'd have done the same for me!"

They hugged each other as best they could with Sakirah sandwiched between them, then he kissed the baby.

"Bye-bye little one."

To his sister he said, "Take care of yourself, *sayang*, and try to make the best of it with Farish."

"You take care too. And give Enid a massive great bear hug from me!"

Her voice broke on the last words and tears started to cascade down her cheeks.

"Don't Ari, please don't, you'll start me off!"

Sakirah caught her mother's mood and also started to cry. Theo was now right at the front of the queue. He quickly hugged them both again, walked up the gangway and disappeared inside the ship. Arianna turned and walked back to the train station, tears running unchecked down her face, Sakirah wailing in sympathy. She was not only crying because she missed England and Enid, and would now be missing her brother too, but also because she was now going to be alone again with Farish.

~***~

Chapter Twenty-Six

Theo docked in Liverpool on a cold, grey December day. He was very glad of his Red Cross issue greatcoat as he disembarked and made his way past bomb-damaged buildings to the railway station. On the lengthy train journey down to Oxfordshire he saw further evidence of Hitler's bombs whenever he passed through towns and cities. He had already heard about the post-war austerity still being imposed upon the beleaguered people of Britain. There were severe shortages, particularly of housing, and rationing was still in place. Unemployment was high and Britain was broke, in debt to other nations because of the cost of the war. He had also heard about Hitler's treatment of the Jews, the concentration camps and the gas chambers. Was there no limit to man's inhumanity to man? he wondered. He knew that a labour government had now taken over from Churchill's conservatives and were promising nationalisation of rail, fuel and other industries, also much improved pensions and benefits, and, best of all, a national health service, free for all at the point of delivery. In Theo's present state of mind he was inclined to be cynical as to whether much of this would ever happen, but he would be glad to be proved wrong. It was time the ordinary working people had a better deal. The wealthy had had it too good for too long. I'd better not voice that opinion to Uncle George though, he thought. He's probably cursing the result of the election!

Alighting at Great Pucklington station and making his way to the bus-stop, he saw that there was little change here and the sleepy Oxfordshire town had escaped being bombed. From the window of the bus, he drank in the Oxfordshire countryside, with its fields and hedgerows - how he had missed it! The village, when he reached it, looked exactly the same. Before heading up to the manor, he made a detour via the churchyard.

"Hello, Mama. It's been a long time," he said out loud, squatting at the side of her grave. "Were you watching over me when I was working on that infernal railway? Is that why I survived when others didn't? Were you my guardian angel?" Once, in the height of

265

malarial fever, he had imagined she was there, soothing his brow, telling him it would be all right. "Why didn't you watch over Natalia too?" he asked now. "I don't even have a grave to visit for her."

He noticed there were fresh flowers on both graves. Enid, he thought. He didn't look too closely at the family plot where Jim was buried, didn't see the additional name on the headstone.

Entering the estate grounds, he wondered whether to go straight to the Estate Manager's house to see his sister, or go first to the manor. He longed to see Enid, but did not want their reunion to be short-lived. Best to go first to the manor, greet George and Mary and those of the staff who were still there, dump his luggage and then spend the evening with Enid and Arthur. He no longer had a key to the kitchen door, so he rang the bell at the main entrance. After a couple of minutes, the door was opened by a much older looking Mr Hughes, now completely bald.

"Mr Theo! How good to see you! Come inside."

Theo asked if George and Mary were home.

"Oh, of course, you don't know, there's been no communication. I'm very sorry to have to tell you that Sir George died last year. It was a heart attack, very sudden and very quick, he didn't suffer. But it sent Lady Mary over the edge. She'd been losing her memory for a few years and getting confused, but after his death she deteriorated significantly and Sir Albert had to put her into a nursing home. He's the Baronet now, of course, but he and Lady Violet divide their time between here and London."

Theo was busy absorbing the news of George's death. He had not expected that. Somehow, he had thought that everything would be the same here. Sadness swept over him at the loss of the man who had taken over the job of bringing him up, finished what Jim had started. He recognised now that George had guided him through the transition from boyhood into manhood and had done it with discipline, yes, but also with kindness, tolerance and generosity. He'd been looking forward to seeing him again and he knew he would miss him.

"I expect it's a shock," Mr Hughes said kindly. "Do you want to see Sir Albert? He's here today."

Theo nodded.

"I'll just go and announce you. After you've had a chat with him, do come and see us all down in the kitchen. There's just me and the missus and Cook left from the old staff."

He disappeared into the drawing room and returned by the time Theo had taken off his coat.

"Do go in."

Bertie rose from his chair and shook Theo's hand. "Welcome back! Would you like some tea?"

Theo declined the offer. He saw that Bertie's hair had thinned and he had developed a paunch.

"How did you get on as a POW under the Japs? I assume that's what happened to you? I hope they didn't treat you too badly."

"It was rather a test of endurance," Theo said drily.

"Yes, you look to have lost a lot of weight, and you've aged a bit, old chap."

"You should have seen me a few months ago! I'm very sorry to hear the news about your father."

"Yes, sad business, but at least it was quick."

"And your mother's in a home?"

"Yes, it's not far from here. You can go and visit, although she probably won't recognise you. A lot's changed here, as you'll realise if you're sticking around for a while. We lost staff during the war, Dave, Millie, Daisy. And the Hughes' and Cook are all due to retire soon and I shall have to find replacements. It's rather a headache running this place, especially as I'm still on the board of the bank and have to spend at least a couple of days a week in London. And Violet prefers to stay in London, although she comes down occasionally at weekends. Papa's death lumbered the estate with crippling death duties; I'm going to have to do a deal with the National Trust and open part of the house to the public. There'll be a lot of building work to separate the two parts and create tearooms and so on. Although we had a taste of what that will involve during the war; during forty-two and forty-three the manor was requisitioned as a school and the family were confined to one wing, with children running amok around the rest of the house. Could well be the stress of all that which led to Pa's heart attack." He paused for breath and then said, "You're welcome to re-occupy your old room if you want

267

to, but I understand Enid's expecting you to stay with them. Have you seen her yet?"

Theo shook his head. "I'll go down there as soon as I leave here."

"There's some of your stuff here still, I believe it was packed up. I'll have it sent over later. Oh, and your little old car is still in the garage. You might be able to get it going again. Dave now works at the garage in town, I expect he could sort it for you. By the way, where is your wife? Did she not return with you?"

"She's dead. She died in captivity."

"Oh, I'm terribly sorry to hear that, old chap."

There was an awkward pause then Bertie said, "At least you escaped having to fight, eh?"

Theo stared at him for a long moment, then said levelly, " I did fight for a few weeks and I'd far rather have been fighting for the rest of the war. I'd have had a much easier time of it and been in no greater danger of death."

"Is that so? You do rather look as if you've been through the mill."

"Yes, it was hell. Probably not much different from the concentration camps I've been hearing about, but at least we were not sent to the gas chambers. Death for us was the luck of the draw, we did have a chance of survival."

There was a short silence, then Bertie said, "And what news of Arianna? Is she still over there?

"Yes. She escaped internment by staying with our maternal relatives and she's now married with a baby."

"Oh, right. Enid and Arthur have a child too, a little boy."

Theo absorbed this bit of news with pleasure.

"Did you have to serve in the forces," he enquired of Bertie.

"No, I was over the age limit. Did my stint in the home guard."

"And Charlie?"

"He did a spell in the RAF. Ground staff."

"Are you and he reconciled?"

"No, not really. I saw him at Pa's funeral of course."

Has war not taught you anything? Theo thought. Such a senseless estrangement between two brothers and he knew it would not be Charlie who had kept it going.

He rose. "I'd better be going. I promised to pop down to the kitchen before I head over to Enid's."

Bertie rose too. "Keep in touch while you're here, won't you?"

Down in the kitchen, Theo received an effusive welcome from Mrs Hughes and Cook.

"Look at you, you're so thin!"

"You should have seen me a few months ago," he said for the second time.

"Didn't the Japs feed you?"

"Not much. Barely enough to keep us alive."

Mrs Hughes surveyed him closely, observing the grey in his hair, the lines around his eyes and mouth. He still looked older than his thirty years, despite the time which had elapsed since his release.

"You've had a bad war, dear, haven't you? And Miss Enid told us a couple of days ago about your wife. She'd just had a letter from Miss Arianna. We're all so very sorry for your loss."

"Thanks."

She brought him up to date on the changes at the manor. "Dave's been demobbed and he's got a job at the garage in town; Sir Albert drives himself so there was no job for him here. He still lives in the village, as does Daisy. She got married in forty-three and she has a little girl now, about the same age as Enid's little boy; they sometimes play together. Millie left to work in a munitions factory, we don't hear from her any more. We have a woman from the village comes in daily to help clean and another who comes when Sir Albert and Lady Violet are entertaining at the weekend. Otherwise, it's just us."

"Yes, I have the whole top floor to myself!" Cook put in.

"That'll probably change when the house is converted," Mr Hughes commented. "Did Sir Albert tell you about his plans?"

Theo nodded. They chatted a bit longer then he got up to leave. "I'd better get over to Enid's now."

"Yes, she's expecting you. She's got their guest room all ready for you and she can't wait to see you again!"

As he turned to go, he saw a strange cat stroll into the kitchen. "Where's Felix?" he asked. Old Humphrey had died before he left for Malaya but Felix had still been his usual frisky self.

269

"He died, dear, end of last year. He was a good age for a cat."

After all the human deaths, he should not be affected by the death of a cat, but he felt a wave of sadness that Felix was no longer there to greet him.

Enid must have been looking out of the window, because she was out of the house and running towards him as he approached. She flung her arms around him. He dropped his case to the ground and hugged her back fiercely. When they broke apart, he held her at arms' length, took a good look at her and, in a voice thick with emotion, said,

"My baby sister, all grown up!"

"And you've changed too, my dear, but I know why. I got Arianna's letter a few days ago. I'm so, so sorry about Natalia. I'd been really looking forward to meeting her."

They linked arms and went on into the house. When he had divested himself of his greatcoat, she also exclaimed at his thinness. "Although Ari said you were literally just skin and bone when she first saw you so you've obviously put some weight back on."

"She did her best to fatten me up and we were also well fed on the ship, although, being a refugee ship, it was not the luxury cruise experience we had on the way over."

The house had a very similar layout to the one they had occupied before the fire. As they entered the living room, he saw a toddler in a playpen looking at him with curiosity.

"This is our little son, Jimmy," Enid said proudly, plucking him out of the pen and transferring him to Theo's arms. "He's just coming up to twenty-one months old and he's a handful!"

"Hello, Jimmy!"

"This is your Uncle Theo," Enid told him. "He's going to be staying with us for quite a while." Then she added, "You are going to base yourself here for the whole of your leave, aren't you?"

"If it's all right with you and Arthur. I'm being paid so I can contribute to the housekeeping."

"It's more than all right, I shall be upset if you stay anywhere else! It's seven and a half years since I've seen you!"

"Is Jimmy named after Papa?"

"Yes. His full name is James Frederick, after both our fathers. Arthur will be home soon and he's really looking forward to seeing you again."

She went to put the kettle on and when she returned with the tea, Theo told her he'd seen Bertie and the Hughes' and Cook.

"You went there first?"

"Well, I wasn't sure where I'd be staying. And I didn't know about Uncle George."

"Ari didn't get my last letter? I posted it a few days after we heard that Malaya and Singapore had been liberated."

"Not by the time I left, no. I expect she has now."

"And all our letters during the Japanese occupation must have gone astray. Arianna got none of mine and I don't suppose you did either. I wonder where they all are?"

"Well, I had no chance to write once we were interned and Ari wasn't able to post letters to England. The last letter I sent you was in December forty-one. Did you get that one?"

"Yes, I did. You'd just been mobilised in the army full time and everyone was worried about the Japs invading."

"Not worried enough as it turned out. The British defences proved to be woefully inadequate."

When Arthur arrived home, there was another joyous reunion, the two friends shaking hands enthusiastically and clapping each other on the back.

"It's really good to see you, mate," Arthur said. "Enid's been so worried about you, she didn't know whether you were dead or alive until she got Arianna's letter a few days ago. She wasn't sure about Ari either, whether she'd have been interned or not."

He picked up his small son who had toddled over to him and gave him a hug in greeting. Theo looked on a little enviously, thinking of his own son, born in forty-two. He would have been three now.

"Did Ari tell you how Nat died?" he asked Enid.

She nodded, her face clouding over. "Yes, I know about the baby. It's dreadful Theo, I can only guess how much you are grieving for them both." She reached out her hand and clasped his.

Later that evening she told him more about George's death and funeral and Mary's subsequent decline.

271

"It was such a shock and so unexpected. He'd been doing the rounds of the estate with Arthur a couple of hours earlier and he was fine. Then he apparently just dropped down dead! Only Aunt Mary was actually with him when it happened and it was difficult to get a coherent story out of her, but when the ambulance men came they pronounced him dead and said it was probably almost instantaneous. The post mortem basically said it was a massive heart attack, although it was put in fancy medical language. There was a large turnout at the funeral, practically all the village as well as the bigwigs from town, the church was packed. Charlie was there of course, but Bertie and Violet and Aunt Isobel and her lot hardly gave him the time of day, poor chap. I don't think Aunt Mary really knew what was going on; once she asked me whose funeral it was, then she seemed to realise and started crying. Aunt Isobel and I tried to help her through it, but it wasn't easy. Afterwards, she went downhill fast, wandering around the house and the estate at all hours of the day and night, often dressed only in her nightie - or even less! - and often forgetting the way to the bathroom and wetting herself. Then every now and then it was as if her mind cleared for a short while and you could have a normal conversation with her. But it became too much for Mr and Mrs Hughes and Cook to deal with. They're not getting any younger, they'll all be retiring soon. And Bertie and Violet weren't there all the time and anyway Violet has no patience with her. Aunt Isobel came down a few times and she seemed better when she was there, but that wasn't a long-term solution, so Bertie found her a place in a nursing home. It's a nice place, just the other side of town. She's got a lovely room and the gardens are beautiful, she likes to sit out there in the warm weather. She seems a lot calmer since she went there - maybe they give her sedatives - but if you visit you may find she doesn't recognise you. She doesn't always recognise me, sometimes she calls me Alice. One time I visited with Jimmy and she must have thought he was Bertie or Charlie and I was his nanny. She told me I could go now and she'd ring for me when she needed me! It's all very sad but she's not really aware of her condition so she's not unhappy."

Over the course of the next few days, they were all busy preparing for Christmas, Theo's first proper one for four years.

"Did you celebrate Christmas in the camps?" Enid asked him.

"Yes, as best we could. We sang carols and so on but our Christmas dinner wasn't up to much!"

"Ari said in her letter that you'd had an absolutely terrible time when you were working on that railway line."

"Yes, it was much worse than Changi and that was bad enough!"

He did not feel ready yet to go through the detail again, but on New Year's Eve, Arthur opened a bottle of whisky which one of his agricultural suppliers had given him as a Christmas gift, and he and Theo polished off the bottle between them, Enid not having any taste for hard liquor. The alcohol loosened his tongue and also Arthur's inhibitions about asking searching questions, and he found himself once more reliving that terrible time. His tale shocked Arthur into sobriety and tears streamed down Enid's face.

"I can't bear to think of you going through all that!"

Arthur said slowly, "Why isn't this known over here? We've heard about Hitler's extermination camps but no-one seems aware of what our own countrymen suffered under the Japanese. People seem to be assuming that the colonials were lucky to escape the fighting in Europe and were just languishing in some holiday camp in the sun for the duration!"

"Yes, I know. I think the British people at home simply don't want to know. Now the war has ended they want to look forward, not back. There's been enough bad news, they don't want to hear any more. And the powers that be are probably embarrassed at how they let their colonials down militarily."

"That's no excuse. Perhaps you should talk to a journalist from a newspaper or the BBC? Let them know how the Japs behaved so that it can be publicised."

"No, I'm not ready to do that yet. It's one thing to tell people I'm close to, but I can't talk about it to strangers, not yet anyway. The Japs who ran the camps are all now prisoners themselves and many will be tried for war crimes, there was talk of some being executed. That's enough for me for now."

"I feel so guilty," Arthur said. "I was in a reserved occupation, I didn't even fight!"

"Well, I'm glad you didn't," Enid declared.

A couple of weeks later, Theo went to visit Aunt Mary. He found her sitting in a chair in her room, looking out of the window.

"Hello, Aunt Mary."

She turned, but there was no sign of recognition.

"It's Theo."

"Theo? Who's Theo?"

"I'm your nephew, Enid's brother. I lived with you and Uncle George for several years, until I went out to Malaya."

She still looked blank. He sat down beside her. "Are they looking after you well here? Are you happy?"

"Well, you can't get the staff now you know. This stupid war."

"The war's over now, Aunt Mary."

"Have you come for the chauffeur's job? You'll need to speak to my husband."

He gave up and just sat beside her for a while. She fiddled with her skirt, pulling it up to an almost indecent level then pulling it down again. He was just about to take his leave of her when the door opened and Charlie came in.

"Theo! You're back! How good to see you, old chap."

They shook hands vigorously and clapped each other on the back. Charlie stood back and surveyed his cousin.

"My, you've aged a bit, old fellow! You look nearer my age now!"

"Thanks a lot!" Charlie was fourteen years his senior.

"No offence meant, old friend. How was it as a prisoner of the Japs? Doesn't look like they treated you very well."

"No, they didn't."

"When I've had a little chat with Mama, shall we go to a cafe in town and catch up?"

"Yes, I'd like that."

Mary did seem to recognise her younger son, although she appeared to have forgotten about his sexual inclinations and kept asking him if he had a sweetheart and when was he going to get married. He stayed with her for about fifteen minutes, then kissed her goodbye and they left.

In the cafe - which reminded Theo of the one in the next town which he and Clare had frequented all those years ago - they caught

274

up with each other's news. Charlie told him that life in the RAF had been uneventful.

"I was ground staff, being too long in the tooth to learn to fly. I just kept my head down and got on with the job. The chaps were a nice lot and no-one knew anything about my background, so it was fine. What about you? The last letter I got from you, you and your wife were in Singapore and you were training with the Volunteers."

"Yes, we were mobilised full-time eventually, but the war against the Japs was a disaster, all over in a couple of months, and then I was interned."

"Yes, I guessed you would be. What about your wife, and Arianna?"

"My wife was interned too and she died in the camp. I found out what happened at the end of the war. Arianna hid out with our maternal relatives for the duration."

"I'm very sorry for your loss," Charlie said, putting his hand briefly over Theo's. "Is Ari still out there?"

"Yes, she's married now, with a baby girl."

He went on to give Charlie a brief resume of life in captivity and the horrors of working on the death railway, also touching on the immediate aftermath of the war and Arianna's disastrous marriage decision.

"No wonder your hair's going grey! I'm so sorry you had to go through all that. And it doesn't sound as if Arianna is set for a happy life."

"No, but she's stuck now. She'll have to try to forget Edward and make the best of it with her husband."

Arianna had poured her heart out to her sister in her letter and Enid and Theo had discussed her situation at length, but could see no way out for her because of Sakirah.

After an hour or so they parted, promising to keep in regular contact, and Charlie suggested he come and stay with him for a weekend, perhaps when the weather got better. As the first signs of spring appeared, he took up Charlie's invitation, and also got together with some of his university friends who were working in London. He later spent a weekend with Edward in Surrey and they met up with the three nurses. Emma and Shirley said they had decided not to return to Malaya but Jean said she was thinking of going back.

"Despite the heat and humidity and the dreadful insects, I've become attached to the country."

Edward said he was also planning to return. Theo was still unsure and said so.

Now that the weather was better Theo thought about driving again. He contacted Dave who came out and got his little old car going again, although he warned Theo it might not do too many more miles and it would be better not to take it on any really long journeys. After he'd paid him, they adjourned to the pub and spent a couple of hours exchanging notes on their wartime experiences. Like Arthur, Dave was shocked to hear how bad it had been for the prisoners of the Japanese, and thought it ought to be publicised.

By now, Theo had also renewed his acquaintance with Daisy, who often came over to see Enid, bringing her little girl with her, who was just a month or so younger than Jimmy. He was forging a bond with his small nephew, playing games with him and taking him out into the estate grounds. He showed him the tree house and told him that he and his Mummy and Daddy had played there when they were children. Jimmy wanted to climb up, but his legs were far too small and if Theo had climbed up holding him, there was always the danger he might miss his footing and drop him.

"When you're a bit bigger, you'll be able to play there," he promised him.

One Saturday evening in early May, Theo, Enid and Arthur were invited over to the manor for dinner with Bertie and Violet. Isobel was also staying there that weekend. Daisy came over to babysit. Fairly soon, the talk got on to Mary's slide into senility and Bertie said to his wife,

"Do you remember that time we had the National Trust chap to lunch and she wandered in looking for the lavatory?"

"I'm not likely to ever forget it, but that's not a suitable topic for over dinner!"

Undeterred, Bertie continued, "I expect you can guess the gist of it. Took ages to get the stain out of the carpet, I believe. The National Trust chap didn't know where to look! "There was some laughter but both Theo and Enid felt uncomfortable that poor Mary's loss of dignity had become a subject for dinner party jokes. Theo felt a surge of pity for the once proud and dignified lady and thought how mortified she would have been to know her son was making jokes about her decline.

Once he started driving again, he became aware that his distance vision was not as sharp as it had been, and he went to see the optician. He was told he had become a little short-sighted and would need glasses for driving, cinema, theatre and so on. He asked what had caused it and was in turn asked about his wartime experiences. After he said he'd been a prisoner of war under the Japanese and had been fed starvation rations for years, the optician replied,

"Then that's undoubtedly the cause. Malnutrition can affect the eyesight. You're lucky to have got away with such a small deterioration."

Something else to thank the Japs for! Theo thought. Enid commented that the tortoiseshell-framed spectacles made him look very learned.

He drove to Bristol and spent a happy few days with Harry, Dorothy and their two children, a boy of six and a girl of four. Harry had served in the army during the war, coming out as a sergeant, and they compared notes on their very different wartime experiences.

"Are you going back out there?" he asked Theo. "Or are you going to find a job in England? If you decided to take up teaching, with your degree you'd only need to do a short training course."

"I'm not sure yet whether I'm going back. I have a few more months to decide. If I don't, I'm not sure know what else I'll do, I'll have to look into my options. I suppose I ought to start thinking about it fairly soon."

By now he knew that Edward was definitely returning. His passage was already booked for the end of October and Jean was sailing on the same ship. Theo wondered idly if romance might develop there. Edward tried to persuade him to go back. The British Military Administration had ended in April and the colonial service was once more in charge. Experienced civil servants were needed to guide the new recruits and take the more senior posts, so he would almost certainly get an immediate promotion upon his return. Malaya and Singapore were now being slowly guided towards eventual independence, with Singapore being administered separately. However, there were problems brewing with the Chinese communists, who had formed a resistance movement during the occupation, working with those of the British army who had escaped internment and others who had been parachuted in, to form Force 136 as it was called. They had operated out of the jungle organising guerrilla attacks on the Japanese. Now, these Chinese, along with some Malays, were clamouring for independence without delay. Theo couldn't help wondering just how long his career would last if he did return. India was becoming independent; it would not be too long before Malaya followed, surely? Arianna wrote entreating him to come back, while Enid tried to persuade him to stay, so he was pulled in opposite directions by his sisters.

As summer drew to an end and the first signs of autumn were appearing, he knew he could not delay a decision much longer. If he were going to return, he would have to sail before Christmas. But he was feeling more and more disinclined to leave England. He wasn't entirely sure why; it was not really because of his experiences in captivity, as the worst of those had been in Siam, not Malaya, and only partly because of Natalia's death and the fact that Malaya and Singapore were full of memories of her. It was just a gut instinct. He didn't much like the idea of teaching, so started looking into other options. He applied to join the civil service in London and attended an interview. They offered him a job, but at a fairly low grade initially and his pay would be considerably less than he was used to. Charlie, whom he met for lunch after the interview, offered him his spare room rent free until he got a pay rise, but he was still unsure. At the same time, he had applied for some jobs in local government and a week or so later, travelled up to Leeds for an interview with the city council. He was offered that job, which was at quite a senior level and at a good rate of pay, and they also offered to find him lodgings. When he discussed it with Enid and Arthur, they encouraged him to take it.

"Leeds is not too far and quite quick on the train, you can come to visit us some weekends."

He bit the bullet and accepted the job, at the same time sending off his written resignation to the colonial service. Their reply expressed regret at, but also understanding of, his decision, bearing in mind his wartime experiences. They did say that he would be welcome to rejoin at a later date, so he had not totally burnt his boats.

He was due to start his new job on the first Monday in November and he travelled up on the Friday, so that he would have the weekend in which to settle into his new lodgings, which were with an Anglo-Indian family who owned a three story town house on the outer edge of central Leeds and let the top floor rooms. Enid and Jimmy saw him off at Great Pucklington station. As the train approached, he kissed the little boy goodbye and turned to his sister.

"Thanks, Enid, for looking after me so well. Between you, you and Ari have put me back together again. I'm very lucky to have such wonderful, caring sisters."

"Well, you always looked out for us when we were children. It was our turn to look after you. Good luck with the new job and we'll see you again at Xmas."

His new landlord and landlady, Mr and Mrs Dexter, turned out to be an Englishman in his late fifties who had retired after running businesses in India, and his Indian wife who was somewhat younger. They had a daughter aged twenty and a son who was just sixteen and still at school. The daughter, Ayesha, worked in a department store and had just been promoted to second in command of the ladies' fashion department, a very responsible job as her mother proudly told Theo. They let two rooms with a shared bathroom on the top floor, and the two lodgers took their meals with the family downstairs. Theo's room was spacious and nicely furnished and had a dormer window. He learned that the other lodger was a young teacher named Richard who only occupied his room during weekdays in term-time, spending weekends and holidays at his family home in North Yorkshire.

"He's engaged to a girl up there," Mrs Dexter told Theo. "When he's saved up enough for a deposit on a house, they will get married and she will move to Leeds."

Theo met Ayesha and her brother at supper that evening. Jayant plied Theo with questions about what he had done in the war, but

279

when Theo said he had been a prisoner of the Japanese, his father told him not to ask for any more detail. "He may not want to talk about it." Apparently, Mr. Dexter was less ignorant of what had gone on in South East Asia than the general population of England. Ayesha was an attractive raven-haired girl with light coffee coloured skin. She didn't say a great deal that first evening, apart from asking him where he was to be working. On Sunday evening, Richard returned. He was a likeable young man in his mid twenties and he and Theo hit it off from the start.

Theo found his job congenial and interesting. He had a lot to learn and needed to learn it quickly, so applied himself diligently and often stayed a bit later than the official office closing hours. His offices were not far from Ayesha's store and they regularly travelled in on the bus together. After he'd been there about ten days, as the bus was passing the Odeon cinema, Ayesha commented that there was a film on which she would like to see, starring Bette Davis.

"Richard might like to see it too. We sometimes go to the cinema together. Would you like to come with us?"

So the three of them went and Theo subsequently made a habit of joining them whenever there was a good film on which they all wanted to see. As Richard was engaged to be married, he did not feel he was being a gooseberry and Ayesha's parents seemed happy for her to be accompanied by their lodgers, regarding her as being in safe hands. At weekends, Theo and Ayesha sometimes went alone and once or twice they went to the theatre or to a dance. Although she seemed very young and inexperienced to him, she was funny and clever as well as being lovely to look at, and he found himself enjoying her company.

However, their evenings out were soon to be curtailed by the weather. December had been bitterly cold but was followed by a milder spell in early January. Then from the third week in January to the middle of March, the whole of Britain was in the grip of the severest winter in living memory. The snowfall was the heaviest on record and snow fell somewhere in the country on every single day. Temperatures were down to minus twenty-one degrees centigrade, drifts of more than fifteen feet high blocked roads and railways, and icicles hung from gutters. Frost even formed on the inside walls of houses. Transport was severely affected, which had a knock-on effect on supplies of food and fuel. There was a shortage of coal, which most people used to heat their houses and food rations were cut. The Leeds to Liverpool canal froze solid and the station roofs at Wakefield and Grantham collapsed under a blanket of heavy snow. Horses were brought out again as transport and people used sledges to pull goods. Telephone and power cables were brought down by the weight of the snow and the electricity supply was also affected by the lack of coal. Power cuts were imposed in London and other cities. In the countryside, villages were cut off and farmers despaired for their crops. In places, the sea froze over up to a hundred feet from the shore.

During it all, Theo, Richard, Ayesha and Jayant trudged along icy roads, with snow piled high on the pavements, in order to get to work and school, and once home had no inclination to go out again, even if anywhere had been open. Theo felt the icy cold even more than the others, having returned so recently from the tropics. Many weekends Richard was unable to get back to his home town because no trains or buses were running. The household huddled around the sitting room fire in the evenings, playing cards or board games, reading or listening to the radio. Richard had his marking to do and Jayant his homework, but it was far too cold for them to stay long in their inadequately heated rooms, so they sat at the dining room table and the others tried to speak quietly in the adjacent room, so as not to disturb their concentration.

Enid wrote to Theo saying that Arthur was very worried about the crops on the estate but could presently do nothing except keep the estate roads cleared. Only Jimmy was enjoying it, making snowmen, sledging and throwing snowballs.

When the thaw finally set in, the volume of melting snow caused massive flooding, resulting in more hardship for the beleaguered population. Spring, when it finally arrived was welcomed even more than usual and Theo managed to get down to Pucklington for the Easter weekend.

~***~

Chapter Twenty-Seven

Meanwhile, Arianna's relationship with Farish was going from bad to worse. He had become quite controlling and hard to please before she had gone to Singapore, but, after Theo had left, it became clear that he had never forgiven her for taking off in Edward's company. He started to pick arguments about the slightest thing, and she had to tread on eggshells around him. He showed her no sympathy when she turned to him for comfort after receiving Enid's letter telling her about George and Mary. They had been her surrogate parents since she was twelve and she was upset to hear the news of George's death and Mary's descent into senility, but he just brushed the matter aside as of no consequence and certainly of no interest to him.

"You would never have seen them again anyway," he said cruelly.

In an attempt to retrieve something of their earlier relationship and to avoid disagreements, she started bending over backwards to please him and refrained from retaliating when he came out with unjust and hurtful remarks. She didn't much like the person she was becoming; subservient, a doormat as she thought of it. It went entirely against the grain with her to constantly defer to another person, and, moreover, it didn't seem to be getting her very far. He was at best cool and distant towards her, at worst angry and spiteful, no matter what she did. The more she tried to make things right, the more he seemed to despise her, but standing up to him just made his mood worse. He had stopped showing her any affection, his physical attentions towards her were purely sexual and she was starting to dread those nights. When they were first married, despite not being in love with him, she had found him quite attractive and he had made some effort to give her pleasure. Now, she no longer felt any desire for him and he made no attempt to arouse her, just getting his own satisfaction whenever he felt like it and then rolling over and going to sleep. She could scarcely recognise the man she'd known as a colleague and a friend. How could he have changed so much? Was it somehow her fault? She tried to get him to talk about it, but he refused.

The only times he was nice to her was when they were in the company of others, usually their families. Her Klang relatives all thought he was a lovely man, her grandmother positively doted on him. Once she tentatively tried to talk to two of her aunts about the problems she was having but they seemed incapable of understanding and even went so far as to suggest that the fault may lie with Arianna and her English ways. She felt alone and friendless, unable even to confide in her siblings and friends in England because Farish had started opening and skim-reading her mail. The first post arrived before he left for work and if they responded to anything adverse she had said about him, he would see it. Luckily, Enid's letter, replying to her first long one sent after the liberation, arrived in the second post. She kept it hidden and eventually destroyed it, to play safe.

Her European clothes were all now consigned to the back of the wardrobe and she wore sarongs all the time, covering her hair when she went out. She dressed Sakirah in pretty little English frocks and he allowed that for now, but had commented that, when she was older, that would have to change. He was planning to send her to a Muslim school, where she would be instructed in the Islamic religion as well as learning her numbers and letters. Arianna wasn't too keen on the idea but supposed it was no worse than Sunday school in England. He complained that Arianna spoke to her too much in English.

"I don't want English to become her first language."

When she heard from Jean that she was planning to return to Malaya, she was overjoyed, although she had not been as close to Jean as to Emma and Shirley, but as she read further on in her letter, she realised that she was going to be working in Singapore, not Kuala Lumpur. She may as well still be in England, she thought despondently. I'll have no chance of visiting her there.

In the summer of 1946, Farish started going out more in the evenings and not to his mother's home, as she eventually realised when his mother complained at one Sunday *tiffin* that she rarely saw him nowadays. Afterwards, she asked him where he was going and received the terse answer that it was none of her business. She wondered if he was having an affair and dared to ask him that. His lip curled in disgust.

"No. You're the unfaithful one, not me."

"I've never been unfaithful!"

He ignored that and continued, "I'm meeting some people, a group I've joined, it's political."

"What do you mean, what group?"

"People who are concerned for the future of Malaya and want a speedy end to British rule; the Malay Communist Party."

She was dismayed, but said nothing. She had learned through bitter experience that voicing pro-British views was guaranteed to incur his anger.

In October, she realised with dismay that she was pregnant again. That was the last thing she wanted but perhaps Farish would at least be nicer to her now. She told him one evening after supper when he was in a relatively benign mood. He smiled.

"That's good news. Let's hope we have a boy this time, eh?"

The atmosphere between them did improve for a few weeks and she started to let down her guard and become herself again, speaking her mind. But one evening, when they were discussing politics, she made the mistake of taking a directly opposing view to his, which triggered a sudden furious reaction in his part. She should have shut up then, but the devil in her continued to argue her point. His fist smashing into the side of her face took her unawares and she staggered back, tasting blood.

"That'll teach you to disrespect me!" he said and strode out of the room.

In shock, she put her hand to her face and it came away covered in blood. She went to the scullery sink and bathed her face in cold water, pinching her nose to stop the bleeding. The next morning she had a black eye and her nose and lip were still swollen. Farish, who had ignored her totally the rest of the previous evening and then turned his back on her in bed, said coldly.

"You'd better stay home today. You can't go out looking like that."

"Aren't you even going to apologise?" she dared to ask.

"No. You drove me to it, you pushed me too far, made me lose my temper."

She was speechless.

At the weekend they were due to have Sunday *tiffin* with her grandparents. Most of the swelling had subsided but her eye was still discoloured.

"If they comment on it, we'll tell them I left a cupboard door open and you walked into it," he instructed her.

Please see through his lies, she silently implored her grandparents and uncle, but they just laughed and said she should be more careful. Farish then told them about the baby and they expressed their delight at the news.

"I expect you'd like a boy this time," Khalid commented.

"Indeed."

Arianna wondered how he was going to react if she had another girl. He would probably blame her, although she knew from school biology lessons that sex was determined by the male sperm.

Having hit her once seemed to have broken a barrier and it happened several more times, although he always took care to cause bruises where they did not show.

In January, not long after Christmas - which she had not been allowed to celebrate - they were both at her grandparents' house when Aunt Rania popped in for a brief visit.

"You'll never guess who the new D.O.is!" she said to Arianna.

"Who?"

"That friend of yours and Theo's, the one who came here with you sometimes before the Jap invasion."

"You mean Edward?" her grandmother asked.

"Yes, he's the new *Tuan* in Klang."

Farish's face darkened. Arianna's feelings were mixed. She'd known from Theo's letters that Edward was on his way back but had not thought that he might be posted to Klang. Not that it made any difference, he was lost to her now. However, she wished Rania had not come out with her news in front of Farish.

On the way home, Farish warned, "Don't get any ideas about contacting him. If I find out you've been anywhere near the D.O.'s office or his house......" He left the rest of the sentence unvoiced.

"I've no intention of contacting him and he wouldn't want to see me anyway. He's still Theo's friend but he's no longer mine."

That evening, Farish seemed to be brooding about the news and determined to pick a fight with her. His mood made her nervous. Some months previously, Sakirah's cot had been moved into their spare room, which was now her bedroom. She was now nearly twenty-three months old and into everything. She did not seem tired that evening, having had a longer than usual nap that afternoon in Klang, and Arianna delayed her bedtime, knowing Farish would not lose his temper violently in front of her. When she did finally put her to bed, she took a long time about it, singing her a lullaby and then, after she fell asleep, just looking at her, drinking in her little face, so angelic in sleep. Farish appeared at the doorway.

"Are you planning to stay in here the rest of the evening?"

She followed him out of the room. Keenly aware of his mood, she was trying to avoid an argument, but nothing she said or did was right. He complained about the evening meal she served and told her she was a lousy cook. Afterwards she could no longer remember exactly how it had got to that point, but, angry at something she'd said, he advanced on her and she was sure he was going to hit her again. Something snapped in her.

"If you hit me again, I'm going to leave you!"

"Go by all means," he taunted her, "but Sakirah stays with me. Under Islamic law, fathers have all the rights."

Her blood ran cold. "That can't be right," she dared to say. "This is still a British ruled country."

He laughed. "They don't interfere in domestic issues concerning Malay families."

"But I'm British, and so are you for that matter."

"No I'm not, not officially. There's no father's name on my birth certificate. And the British rulers have enough on their plates, they're not going to bother about one Eurasian woman."

She had no idea whether he was right or not but was not going to risk it. But he hadn't finished.

"Go on then, go." He started pushing her towards the apartment door. She fell against it. He pulled her to her feet and opened the door, pushing her out. She resisted. He gave her an almighty shove and she staggered back so far that she was almost at the edge of the stairs.

"Careful," he warned, jeeringly. "Don't fall down the stairs!"

She turned, but somehow missed her footing and fell headlong down the first flight of stairs. Farish, for once, seemed concerned for her welfare and leapt down the stairs after her.

"Are you all right?"

"I think so."

But she wasn't. Stomach cramps set in an hour or so later and then she realised she was bleeding. I'm losing this baby, she thought, almost fatalistically. When Farish realised, he was furious.

"I told you to mind the stairs! Now you've killed my son!"

Even knowing him as she did, she could scarcely believe that he was taking no responsibility for what had happened. He had pushed her out of the apartment, but he seemed to be totally forgetting that.

After a painful and unpleasant night, during which her body expelled the foetus inside her, she set off for the hospital with Sakirah, as soon as Farish had left for work. The English doctor she saw confirmed that she had indeed had a miscarriage.

"You and your husband should refrain from marital relations for a couple of weeks, give your body a chance to heal. And it would be best if your husband took precautions for a month or two after that, so that you don't become pregnant again immediately."

When Farish got home that night, she told him what the doctor had said, but extended the times she had been given so that she would be spared his attentions for six weeks and would not risk becoming pregnant for a further three months. Farish grumbled, but acquiesced, perhaps feeling some belated remorse. Now, I have to plan my escape, she thought, and go before that time is up. I can't take any more of this.

However, that was easier said than done. To be out of Farish's reach entirely and to keep Sakirah safe from his clutches, she had to go to England, and that was also where she now longed to be. It was no good turning to her Klang relatives for help. They would be likely to condemn her for even thinking of leaving her husband and might well tell him of her plans. They would never believe he was violent towards her, that was too at odds with the side of his character he displayed to them, and she knew it was also quite rare in Malay marriages. The wives were deferential to their husbands, yes, but they were also cosseted by them, and the Islamic religion abhorred violence. Her family would probably think she was lying because she wanted to return to England. She had not yet heard from Theo about his plans; if he was on his way back she would wait until he arrived and enlist his help. She had a little saved from her housekeeping money but it was not enough for the fare. She would be able to pay Theo back once she arrived in England and could access her trust fund money. However, when a letter finally arrived from Theo, a few days after her hospital visit, Farish opened it as usual, skimmed the contents and then tossed it to its intended recipient.

"Your brother's not coming back to Malaya," he announced, almost gleefully. "He's started a new job in England."

And doesn't that suit you! she thought. No-one around to protect me. You know he wouldn't be so easily fooled as my Malay relatives. She had mixed feelings about the news. If she succeeded in getting back to England it would be good to have both her siblings in the same country, but now she had to manage her escape on her own. Either borrow some money from someone else - but who? - or somehow get money transferred from England without Farish knowing. She knew little about the banking system, but assumed she would have to provide an address when opening an account and making a transfer from England. If only Jean was in KL instead of Singapore, she could be her post box. She'd only have to show her the bruises to get her on her side. She wondered briefly if showing them to her grandmother would have the same effect and enable her to use the Klang address for her mail without Farish becoming aware, then dismissed the idea. Farish would be confronted and would just say she had tripped and fallen and they would instantly believe him. She could just see him being hurt and sorrowful that she would accuse him, and then making her pay for it afterwards.

Then she remembered Edward. She had no right to ask anything of him, but he had loved her once and he was Theo's friend, and he was also a gentleman through and through. Provided he believed her, he would surely help her, he would not turn away a damsel in distress. By now it was February and a weekend was coming up

288

during which she could do nothing, but she decided she would go and see Edward on Monday. Then Farish received a message from his mother. She had fallen and badly sprained her wrist. Could Arianna come over each day for a while to help her in the house? Farish went to see her and returned having promised Arianna's attendance for several hours each weekday until the wrist was healed, which could take several weeks.

"She's got three daughters, why can't they help some of the time?" Arianna ventured to ask.

"As you well know, one's at school, one's at work and the other has her hands full with twin babies. You only have Sakirah and you can take her with you to play there. Don't be selfish."

So she was trapped and it was early March before she was able to go to Klang to see Edward. It was with considerable trepidation that she climbed the few steps to the District Office, struggling to lift Sakirah in her pushchair. She hoped Edward was in his office and not out around the district. As she entered the Reception area, she noted with relief that the girl behind the desk was new, not someone she'd worked with in her time there, although her former colleagues might well not recognise her dressed as she was now. She asked for Edward. The girl enquired who she was and she gave her maiden name. She noted the girl's puzzled look at the incongruity of the English surname with the Malay woman in front of her. She told Arianna to take a seat and she would see if he was free. Arianna's heart was thumping and her palms were sweaty. How would Edward react to her visit? Would he refuse to see her? She was suddenly beset with doubts about the wisdom of coming here and almost got up and left. Then the girl returned.

"He says to come through to his office. I'll show you the way."

Arianna knew the way but said nothing and followed the receptionist, pushing Sakirah ahead of her. Her heart was racing and, as she got through the door and saw Edward rising to greet her, for a few seconds she was afraid she might faint.

"Arianna! Please sit down. My, this little one's grown, hasn't she?"

He offered her water from the iced flask on his desk and she accepted gratefully. Her mouth was dry, but not from the heat. Her heart gradually returned to normal speed.

"What can I do for you," Edward asked.

"I've come to ask for your help. I know I have no right at all to ask anything of you, but there's no-one else I can turn to. Theo's not coming back. I have to get out with Sakirah, back to England, but without my husband knowing."

"Why?"

She started haltingly to explain, then her words gathered momentum and it all poured out, the misery of her marriage, the violence, the way Farish had fooled her Malay relatives.

"He's a Jekyll and Hyde character. I married Dr Jekyll, but now I only see Mr. Hyde when I'm alone with him. I've saved up some money towards the fare home but it's not enough. Please could you lend me the rest? I can pay you back as soon as I arrive in England. I have money in a bank there, my inheritance from my father, but I can't access it from here without Farish finding out. He reads my mail."

"Yes, of course I'll lend you the money."

Relief flooded through her. "Thank you, thank you!"

"I'm also tempted to go and confront your husband and give him a taste of his own medicine."

"No, please don't! That would make everything far worse and you might get into trouble. And I have to get away without him knowing or he'll take Sakirah from me and I'll never see her again."

"He can't do that!"

"He says he can. We were married under Islamic law and fathers have all the rights."

Edward frowned. "But the British still rule this country and our laws take precedence."

"But they wouldn't interfere in a domestic dispute between Malays."

"Not normally perhaps, but you are British."

"Only half. I can't risk it. Even if the law did take my side, it could take months to settle the matter and meanwhile he'd take Sakirah to his mother's house and refuse to let me see her. I can't lose her and she's only two, she needs me." Her voice ended on a half sob.

Edward badly wanted to go and put his arms around her, but resisted. "All right. Have you considered the logistics of getting away?"

"I plan to pack up the day before I sail, travel to the port later that day and stay the night there. If I sail from Singapore, I can stay with Jean, but if it's Penang, I'll need a few extra dollars for a cheap hotel room. But I'll pay everything back as soon as I get to England; the bank will be the first place I go to, I promise."

"I'm not worried about how quickly I'm paid back, Ari," Edward said gently. "What about your passport. Is it up to date?"

"No. I'll need to have Sakirah added, won't I? I brought it with me and also her birth certificate. Can it be done here?" She scrabbled in her bag and handed him both documents.

"Not here, no, but I can sort it for you. We may need a photo of her, but I have a camera here, I'll take one before you leave. I could book your passage for you too, if you like. Would that make it easier?"

"Yes it would! Oh, thank you Edward!"

They continued to discuss the plan and he suggested he come with her to the port. " It will make it easier if I drive you and you'll be able to take more luggage. I take it you'll want to leave on the first available ship?"

She nodded. "But I'll have to leave during the week, when Farish is at work."

"Of course. He's not planning to take any days holiday is he?"

"Not that I know of and he's never off sick."

She had a sudden cold feeling in the pit of her stomach. What if he suddenly did decide to take a day off on that day?

As if guessing her thoughts, Edward said, "If something crops up last minute, then hopefully we can transfer the sailing date. But you'd need to contact me urgently, to prevent me turning up!"

"I could find an excuse to go down to the shop and use their phone."

"Then I think we've covered all bases. How can I let you know the sailing date?"

291

"It would be best if I came here again."

"Give me a couple of weeks then, to sort the passport and get the ticket."

She reached into her bag and handed him an envelope. "That's the money I've saved so far."

"Keep it. You'll need some cash on the voyage. I'll pay the passage and the hotel and you can pay it back as soon as it's convenient after you get to England. No rush."

"Would you keep the cash for me meanwhile? It will be safer with you. And keep hold of my passport once it's been amended. It would be awful if Farish decided to confiscate it! But please, if you take it home, don't put it where Aunt Rania might see it!"

"Don't worry, I'll keep it here, in a locked drawer in my desk." He took out his camera and turned to Sakirah. "Now, young lady, let's have your picture!"

"I'm so very grateful for your help, Edward. How can I ever thank you?"

"No thanks needed. I still care about you and even if I didn't, you are an Englishwoman in distress!"

"I still care for you too."

Two weeks later, he showed her the updated passport and a ticket for a passage on a P and O liner departing from Penang on Thursday 17th April. They agreed he would come to collect her at 4pm on the previous day, and they would drive to Penang, arriving late evening. He had booked a small hotel near the port.

"I booked two rooms. I won't want to drive back without a night's rest and it means I can help you to the ship with your luggage and see you off."

"Thanks so much. I don't deserve all this help from you, I know, and I'm really, really grateful."

"We all make mistakes in life, Ari, and you've paid pretty heavily for yours."

From the following day she started surreptitiously putting some things into her trunk, which was stored in Sakirah's room, taking care not to noticeably deplete her cupboards and drawers. The trunk was used for storage anyway and already contained a lot of Sakirah's things. On the morning of the 16th, she was in luck; Farish said he had to be at work early for an important meeting and left an hour earlier than usual. She left the washing up undone in the sink and got on with the rest of her packing. She was more or less finished when Edward arrived and just had to change into the European dress she'd left out ready. She left all her sarongs in the wardrobe and her headscarves in the drawer. Besides the small trunk, she had one large and one small suitcase, plus Sakirah's pushchair. She had written a note for Farish saying that her grandmother had been taken ill and she may stay the night in Klang. That should ensure that he did not start to look for her until after she had sailed.

On the long car journey, at first the atmosphere between them was a little formal, but gradually their old easy friendship returned and they chatted about various things.

"Does Theo know about Farish's behaviour?" Edward asked.

"No, not the violence. That all started well after Theo left. He and Enid knew I wasn't happy with him, but when it all got worse, I didn't dare write about it in case they responded and Farish read their letters."

"You could have asked them not to respond on that issue."

"I couldn't risk them forgetting or hinting at it obliquely, and I was also afraid Theo might take it upon himself to play the heavy big brother and write to Farish telling him to lay off. That would have had the opposite effect!"

"You've been living in fear, haven't you?"

"Yes, I suppose I have."

He reached across and squeezed her hand. The comforting gesture brought tears to her eyes and also made her long for more of his touch. She knew she was as much in love with him as she had ever been, but there was no chance of them ever being together when she had to be in England and he here.

When they arrived at their hotel, tired, hot and weary, they found there had been a mix-up with the reservation. Instead of two rooms, one with a cot, a twin bedded room with a cot had been allocated. The hotel was full so it could not be changed.

"It doesn't matter," Arianna said. "There are separate beds, we can share the room."

"I hope you don't think I did that deliberately," Edward said. "I assure you I booked two rooms!"

"I know you did. Really, it doesn't matter."

Once in the room, Arianna took Sakirah to the bathroom and got her ready for bed. Edward watched her tuck the sleepy little girl up and carefully draw the mosquito net around her cot, making sure there was no gap. Then she adjourned to the bathroom and returned wearing a thin cotton nightdress. When he too returned, wearing pyjama shorts, she was not yet in bed but fiddling with things in her case. As he headed up the narrow space between the two beds, so did she and his bare arm and leg brushed against hers. With the desire they were both suppressing, the effect was electric. They turned and the next minute they were in each other's arms, kissing passionately, bodies pressed together. Edward broke away first.

"This is madness! We can't do this. From tomorrow we are going to be thousands of miles apart with no hope of being together for years, if ever!"

"Please, Edward, let's just have this one night together and to hell with the future. I want you so much and I can feel you want me too!"

He groaned. " Of course I want you, more than anything. But I'll have to get some rubbers, we can't risk making a baby."

He threw on his trousers and a shirt and went out to the barbers shop he'd noticed next door. It was still open and he returned with a packet of three condoms. She was sitting on the edge of the bed. He tore off his shirt as she unbuttoned his trousers. Lifting her nightdress over her head, he exclaimed at the bruises on her ribcage and upper arms.

"That bastard! I'd like to kill him! Thank God I've got you away from him!"

Their first coming together was frantic and soon over, both of them climaxing quickly. The second was slow, languorous and very loving.

"I never stopped loving you," Arianna said afterwards, stroking his face tenderly.

"It was the same for me. I managed to push you to the back of my mind but you always came back into it whenever I dated another girl. No-one ever came near you!"

294

They were both determined not to think of tomorrow, their inevitable parting. They fell asleep in each other's arms, crammed together in the single bed and, when dawn broke, made love again, using the last condom.

"It would have been a shame to have wasted it," Arianna said laughing.

On the way to the port, Edward suddenly said. "You know you said you had an Islamic marriage? Did you also have a civil ceremony?"

Arianna shook her head. "No, but the Imam issued a certificate. Farish has it."

"Well, I'm not sure that would be legal under British law. You can check the position with a solicitor when you're back in England, but you may not need a divorce and I believe Farish can divorce you just by saying it in front of witnesses, but that's his problem, not yours."

"Right, well, my cousin is a lawyer so I'll ask him to check it out. But would that make Sakirah illegitimate?"

"I don't know. Perhaps technically, under British law, but no-one needs to know, do they?"

But Arianna remembered Theo feeling that there was a stigma attached to his illegitimate birth, despite his subsequent adoption by her father.

As she queued to embark, having checked in her trunk, the reality of losing each other again set in for both of them and they clung together desperately.

"I've no idea what the future is going to bring," Edward said miserably. "I think it's better if we don't write to each other, don't make promises which we may not be able to keep. We're going to be apart for several years at the very least. I'll be on leave again in about three and a half years time, but if you still can't risk returning to Malaya......."

"I don't see how I could. Even once he's divorced me he still has the right to claim Sakirah and he might find us, especially if we were living in KL. She's the only person I would ever put before you, my darling, but I have to!"

"I understand."

As she neared the front of the queue, her tears started to flow and she saw his eyes were wet too.

"I love you," he said thickly. "I probably always will, whatever the future brings."

"So will I!"

She disappeared inside the ship, tears still rolling down her cheeks. With a heavy heart, Edward turned and set off on his long drive back.

Farish was annoyed when he saw Arianna's note, but took it at face value. When she was still not back the following evening he assumed her grandmother must be really ill and did not particularly want to turn up at a house of sickness in case he caught something. On the Friday evening he went to the mosque as usual and then to his mother's for dinner and by the time he got home and found she was still missing, it was too late to go to Klang. So it was Saturday when he made his way over there. He was taken aback when the old lady herself opened the door.

"Oh, you're better. So Arianna can come home?"

She looked bewildered. "What are you talking about?"

He followed her inside where it quickly became apparent that she had never been ill and Arianna had not been there at all this last week. A cold fury setting in, he turned and left, leaving the old couple wondering what on earth was going on. He headed straight for the D.O.'s house. If she was there with her lover, he'd make them both pay! And if she had left him, she was not keeping Sakirah.

"Yes, what can I do for you?" Edward asked politely, when Farish was shown in by his houseboy.

"Where's my wife?" His tone was belligerent.

Edward feigned ignorance. "Your wife?"

"Arianna, as you well know."

"Ah, you are Arianna's husband. How is she? I've not seen her for a couple of years and I can't imagine why you think she would be here!"

Farish looked uncertain, then said. "I know you were lovers before the occupation and I know you were together in Singapore two years ago. She's now disappeared, lied to me about where she's gone. Where else can she be but here?"

"We were not lovers, only friends, and I escorted her to Singapore to see her brother, that's all. And, I repeat, she is not here. Search the house if you like!"

"So where else could she have gone?"

Edward was sorely tempted to tell Farish that his wife was on her way to England with his daughter, he would never see either of them again and it served him right for the way he had behaved. But he resisted. It would be better if Farish did not find that out for a bit longer, until Arianna was well on her way towards European waters. There was a remote possibility that he might somehow get on a flight to Colombo, intercept the ship and try to abduct his daughter. Better to send him on a wild goose chase to gain time.

"One of her friends from England is now working in Singapore, at the Alexandra hospital. Perhaps she's gone to see her?" He gave Farish Jean's name. He would have to apologise to her later, but there would be plenty of security staff at the hospital to protect her if Farish got difficult.

Farish headed back home. Should he go to Singapore? But if she'd only gone for a visit, she might be back in a day or two. He recalled her asking if she could visit Jean and he had refused. However, when he got back to the apartment, for the first time he looked in Arianna's drawers and cupboards and in Sakirah's room and realised how much was missing. This was no brief visit, she had left him!

He caught the next train to Singapore, arriving late evening. After finding somewhere to stay the night, he arrived at the hospital the next morning only to find Jean was not on duty that day. He asked for her home address but the staff refused to divulge it. He had to be back at work the next day but he now had no option but to stay another night and telephone the office with an excuse in the morning.

When he finally saw Jean, both her surprise at him turning up and her denial that she had seen Arianna rang true.

"Perhaps she's gone back to England?" she suggested.

Farish then headed to the port office and enquired whether she had sailed from there. He gave both her married name and her maiden name. The clerk searched the lists back to Wednesday but came up with nothing.

"Perhaps she sailed from Penang," he suggested.

"Can you check?"

"Not from here, no. You'd have to go there. But if you know where she booked her ticket, they'd have records."

That must have been in KL, Farish thought. By the time he got back, all the travel agents were closed and he had to go to work the next day and also work through his lunch breaks for the next couple of days to catch up. He couldn't tell his boss that his wife had left him and he needed to find her, that would make him a laughing stock. On Friday he forfeited his usual lunchtime visit to the mosque in order to try one travel agent but they had no record of her. On Saturday he was committed to spending the whole day on Communist Party business so it was Monday lunchtime before he could try another agent, but this time he was lucky. A Miss Arianna Bradshaw, accompanied by a small child, had been issued a ticket for the P and O departure from Penang on 17th April. He asked the destination, already knowing the answer. England! He asked the first port of call.

"Colombo."

"When does it dock there?"

The clerk consulted a schedule. "Yesterday."

Farish ground his teeth in impotent rage. It was highly unlikely that he'd have been able to get to Colombo if he'd found out sooner, but now she was totally out of his reach. She'd gone and she'd taken his daughter with her. Damn and blast the bitch to hell!

~***~

298

Chapter Twenty-Eight

Meanwhile, in England, Theo and Ayesha had resumed their social life now that the long harsh winter was finally over. Theo found himself enjoying her company more and more, although he still thought of her as very young and lacking life experience. He felt rather world weary in comparison. Her family had lived in India until she was thirteen and she often talked about her childhood there. He in turn shared something of his life in Malaya and Singapore, although he steered clear of his wartime experiences. Once or twice she had mentioned a childhood friend of hers, Rajeev, who was the son of friends of her parents. One Saturday evening in late April, they had returned home from a dance and were having a nightcap in the living room, the rest of the occupants of the house having gone to bed, when she suddenly said,

"Rajeev is coming to England next summer for a few months, between finishing his studies and starting work in his father's business."

"That's nice," Theo said politely. "I expect you're looking forward to seeing him again."

"Yes, I am. His parents and my mother want us to marry. They are hoping we will become engaged by the end of his visit."

He was startled. "You mean an arranged marriage?"

"No, nothing like that. We will only marry if we both want to. My father says I should not agree to it unless I fall in love with him, but my mother says it will be enough if I still like him, that love will grow within marriage and being in love does not always last."

Where have I heard that one before! Theo thought. Out loud he said, "I know it's none of my business, but your father's right. There's no guarantee that love would grow. My sister was given the same advice and she's not happy in her married life."

"Your sister in Oxfordshire?"

"No, the other one, in Malaya. Enid did marry for love and she is happy."

After a moment, she said, "But Rajeev and I played together as children and by the time he left we were both thirteen and starting to become a bit more than friends. I really missed him when I first came here and we've written to each other ever since."

"Then perhaps he is the one for you," Theo conceded. "But if you don't still feel the same, if you're not in love, you should think twice about going ahead with the marriage. And remember, you will both have changed in the years since you last met."

She nodded. "Perhaps you're right. My father would agree with you. But if I do marry him I will have a good life out there. His family are very rich and he'll be a partner in their business eventually."

"Then I hope it works out for you. But don't be tempted just by his wealth, money doesn't buy happiness."

He felt rather sad at the thought of her going back to India. He would miss her vivacious and undemanding company.

Ayesha then said hesitantly, "You're a widower aren't you?"

"Yes."

"Were you very much in love when you married?"

"Yes, head over heels."

"And did it last?"

"It certainly lasted for the short time we had together, just over three years, and I believe it would have lasted for ever."

"Did she die during the war?"

"Yes. In a prisoner of war camp."

"Do you miss her still?"

"Yes, all the time." However, as he said it, he realised it was no longer quite true. He had got to the stage of not thinking of her for long periods, but when he did the familiar pain was still there and it often took him unawares.

A few weeks later, he received a telegram:

Arriving Liverpool Tuesday 27th May. Arianna.

He phoned Enid that evening, as soon as long distance calls were on the cheaper rate.

As soon as she heard his voice, she said, "I was just about to pick up the phone to call you. Have you had a telegram from Ari?"

Enid's telegram had exactly the same minimal wording.

300

"Are they all three coming?" Enid wondered, "or just her and Sakirah?"

"I don't know. But I imagine just her and the child. She told me he hated Britain and the British."

"Do you think that means she's left him for good? Or she's just persuaded him to let her have a long holiday in England?"

"No idea. But I rather suspect the former. I can't see him letting her come to England for months when he made such a song and dance about her going to Singapore for a few days to see me."

"It will be best if she stays here with me," Enid said, already planning ahead. "She's probably expecting to do that anyway, as you're in lodgings there. And we haven't seen each other for nine years. I can't wait to see her again!"

"She's bound to have loads of luggage though. It'd be best if she stays up here until Friday when I can come down with her and help her with it on the train journey. She'll have to change trains and stations in London. It might be possible for her to stay in this house. My fellow lodger's room will be empty as it's half-term. I'll speak to him and my landlady and let you know."

"Will you meet her off the ship?"

"If I can get the morning off work, yes."

Mrs Dexter and Richard were both accommodating and said Arianna could stay in Richard's room. It had a small double bed so if Farish was with her, that would not be a problem.

"How old is her daughter?" Mrs Dexter asked.

"She'll be two now."

"Then we'll get our old cot down from the loft and the high chair."

"Thanks very much. Let me know how much rent I'll owe you."

"Oh, we won't charge any rent. The room would be empty anyway. Just give me a bit extra that week to cover their meals."

Theo thanked her again, thinking not for the first time how lucky he was to be lodging with this family.

He was able to get that Tuesday morning off work and also the following Friday afternoon. Enid said he could share Jimmy's room for the weekend.

"We have a camp bed we can put up in there. Ari and Sakirah will be in the room you usually occupy. Jimmy will think it great fun to be sharing a room with his Uncle Theo!"

Theo checked the arrival time of the ship and got there in good time. On the train on the way there, he had time to think about the situation and, for the first time, look at it from Farish's viewpoint. Despite his shortcomings as a husband, he loved his daughter, and if Ari had left him for good, she had taken his child away from him. He found that difficult to condone. He thought of his small son, whom he had never known, and imagined how he would feel if he had known him and he'd then been snatched away.

He saw his sister before she saw him. Coming down the gangway, carrying Sakirah, a porter following behind with her luggage. He waved madly and she spotted him and waved back. They made their way towards each other through the throng of people and embraced. The porter dumped her luggage at their feet and Theo tipped him.

"I'm so glad to see you!" Arianna said.

"Likewise! Farish is not with you then?"

She shook her head. "I'll tell you everything, but first I need to go and sort out my trunk. Shall I have it sent down to Enid's?"

"Yes. We're going down there on Friday."

They went to redirect the trunk after Theo had first re-introduced himself to Sakirah. He squatted beside her and she looked up at him shyly, her eyes dark pools.

"I knew you when you were a little baby," he told her. "Haven't you grown!"

On the train on the way down he asked bluntly," Have you left him?"

"Yes. It became intolerable."

He frowned. "But you've taken his daughter from him by coming here. How can he ever see her now?"

"I had no option. Had I stayed in Malaya, he'd have taken her from me and made sure I never saw her again. He has all the rights under Islamic law."

"But Malaya is under British rule."

"Yes, I know that," she said tiredly, "but the powers that be probably wouldn't interfere in what they would view as a native

302

marriage, and I couldn't risk it. Don't judge me, Theo. You don't know everything yet and I'm not going to tell you in a crowded train carriage."

He shut up for the time being. After they had arrived at his lodgings, had lunch with Mrs Dexter - who was enchanted by Sakirah - and Arianna had settled the child in her cot for a nap, she came into his room.

"Are you going to explain now?" he asked.

"Yes." She sat down beside him and described how her marriage had deteriorated after he had returned to England; the increasing control, the coldness and verbal cruelty, eventually escalating into physical violence. When she described the night she lost the baby, tears coming into her eyes as she relived the scene, Theo exclaimed,

"My God, the bastard! I wish I could get my hands on him! But why didn't you tell us what was going on?"

"Because he read my mail."

"I can't believe our grandparents would have taken his side if you'd told them what was happening."

"You don't know what he was like with them. He had them eating out of his hand, they thought the sun shone out of his backside. With them, he was charm personified. And I did once try to talk to Aunt Rania and Aunt Irdina about how he was behaving, although that was before he got violent, and they just said it was probably my fault for being too English!"

"How did you get away without him knowing?"

She told him about contacting Edward, how he had helped her.

"That was good of him, considering."

"Yes, I know. But he still loves me. He was really angry when he saw my bruises."

"Hold on. I thought you said Farish only hit you where it didn't show?"

She looked away and said nothing.

"Did you and Edward....?"

"Yes. That last night in Penang."

"Well, that was bloody stupid, wasn't it? You might have sailed away with another baby inside you, given birth to another child with a father thousands of miles away!"

"We took precautions!" she snapped. "And don't take such a holier than thou attitude! Don't tell me you never give way to your feelings; I know you and Nat slept together, before you were even engaged and without taking any precautions, because she told me. You have no right to judge me!"

"I suppose not. I'm sorry. But what a mess, Ari. Edward will be in Malaya at least another three years and then he'll have to go back again after his leave is over. Will you be able to return with him then?"

"I don't see how, not without risking losing Sakirah. And he'll probably have found someone else by then anyway."

It was suddenly all too much; reliving her ordeal with Farish while missing Edward desperately, just as she'd missed him the whole time on the ship. Tears escaped and trickled down her cheeks.

Suddenly contrite, Theo said, "I'm sorry, I didn't mean to upset you."

"I'm not upset because of anything you said. I'm miserable because after a life from hell with Farish I finally found Edward again, only to lose him the very next day! I so want to be with him and he wants that too, but I don't see how we can ever be together."

The next day Arianna went to a branch of the bank where her trust fund money was held and competed the formalities to access it. She then arranged to transfer to Edward the amount she owed him and also withdrew some cash to tide her over for a while.

When they arrived at Great Pucklington station late Friday afternoon, Enid, Arthur and Jimmy were all there to meet them. Enid and Arianna flew into each other's arms and held on tightly for a long time, cheek pressed to cheek, tears of joy mingling. Theo and Arthur offloaded the luggage and Theo lifted Sakirah down from the train. He introduced her to Jimmy and the two children eyed each other warily.

"How old are you?" Jimmy asked her.

She didn't answer, so Theo said, "She's two."

"I'm three," Jimmy said proudly.

"Yes," Arthur said, "and as you're older, you should look after your little cousin and make her feel welcome. She's come from a very different country - much hotter for a start! - and everything's going to be strange to her."

Jimmy took hold of Sakirah's hand. "I'll show you my new train set when we get home and you can play with it if you like."

Sakirah still said nothing but she smiled.

Over supper, Arianna said that she'd have to look for a job and somewhere to live. "I can't impose on your hospitality indefinitely. Perhaps I can find myself a live-in housekeeper's job, where I can have Sakirah with me."

"Well, that might not be necessary," Enid said. "When Bertie heard that you were coming back, he asked me about your qualifications and work experience, and he's asked you to go up to the manor to see him next week."

"I think he might be looking for an assistant," Arthur said, "to liaise with the National Trust people about the division of the house when he's in London and to act as his secretary when he's here. They deal with me about the grounds but I can't get involved with the house as well."

"That would be marvellous!" Arianna exclaimed. "But what will I do about Sakirah?"

"Well, I daresay I could look after her for you most days while you are working," Enid said. "She'd be company for Jimmy. And on the days I can't do it, I expect Daisy would oblige if you paid her something. She has a little girl about Jimmy's age."

"Thanks, Enid, you're an angel!"

Enid then told them she had passed her driving test a few days ago.

"Well done!" Theo said. "I supposed that means you'll be whizzing around everywhere in my little old car and wearing it out!"

"I'll only be going shopping in it," Enid replied laughing. "And it needs to be used sometimes."

"I wouldn't mind learning to drive," Arianna said. "Who taught you, Enid?"

"Theo to start with, when he was here last year. Then Arthur took over."

Arianna looked hopefully at Arthur.

"All right! I'll give you lessons. But in Theo's old car, not in mine."

"It will wear out even sooner then, with yet another learner mistreating it!" Theo said.

"Well, I expect you gave it a hard time when you were learning," Enid retorted.

On Sunday, Charlie came to lunch and Arianna asked him about the legality of her Islamic religious marriage. After asking her several searching questions, he said he thought it might well not be valid here, but he would check it out with someone he knew who was more of an expert in that field and let her know.

On Monday, a letter arrived from Farish, addressed to Arianna care of Enid. It was filled with vitriol, without a word of contrition or admission that he might have played a part in driving her away. Towards the end, he told her that her Klang relatives were disgusted with her and had all disowned her. She read some of it out to Enid.

"What a dreadful man he is! You are well shot of him."

"I wrote to our grandparents from the ship, apologising for not saying goodbye and explaining in detail exactly why I left. They might not have got it yet, but when they do, Farish will have some explaining to do. I wonder if he'll manage to convince them I'm lying?"

"If he does, perhaps it would be a good idea for Theo to write to them, backing up your story? I'd do it but I can't write in Malay."

"Perhaps. I might ask him. I don't want them to continue to think badly of me. However, I did say that the D.O. at Klang - Edward - helped me to get away and they might go and speak to him. Aunt Rania works at his house."

"Let's hope that he doesn't mention seeing your bruises," Enid said, "seeing as they were in places he wouldn't have seen if you hadn't spent the night together!"

Arianna spent the rest of that afternoon writing out her qualifications and work experience. Bertie was due back at the manor on Wednesday.

She treated her visit to see him as a formal interview and dressed accordingly, in her smartest and least flamboyant outfit. Bertie was in the room which had been George's study. He pecked her on the cheek and welcomed her back to England. Mr Hughes brought tea and biscuits and they chatted informally for a while. She told him she'd been to see Aunt Mary the previous day and that she'd not only not recognised her but had been quite rude to her.

306

"Sorry about that," Bertie said. "But she doesn't really know what she's saying or doing. She's not herself anymore, so you mustn't take it personally."

"Oh, no, I didn't. It's just so very sad."

"Indeed. Now, I understand that you're back for good, that your marriage in Malaya is over?"

"Yes."

"You'll be getting a divorce?"

"It may not be necessary." She told him about the doubtful validity of her Islamic marriage.

"So, you'll need to support yourself and your child? Or will your husband send money for her?"

Arianna laughed. "There's as much chance of getting blood out of a stone! And I don't want anything further to do with him."

If Bertie had the same thoughts as Theo about taking a child away from its father, he kept them to himself.

"Right, let's get down to why I asked you to come here. I expect Arthur and Enid have told you about the plans for the house? That a large part of it is to be transferred to the National Trust and open to the public?"

She nodded.

"These are the plans." He spread them out in front of her and went through them, clarifying.

"The central part of the house with all the main rooms, drawing room, dining room, library and so on, together with the large bedrooms above and the kitchens and pantries below, will all be taken over by the Trust and the public will be taken on guided tours around them. There will be a tearoom created on the ground floor of the west wing and the first floor rooms above that will be used by the Trust. The family will retain the east wing in its entirety, plus the rest of the second floor rooms. A new and more modern kitchen will be installed in the basement of the east wing, the two smaller ground floor rooms will be knocked together to form a large drawing room and the other main room will be the dining room. This study will remain, as will the ground floor cloakroom. We will have to do without a library, although we will still have access to the original one when the house is closed to the public. The bedrooms and bathrooms on the first and second floor of that wing will serve the family. They include the nursery and the rooms you and your brother and sister occupied when you lived here. Most of the toys in the nursery playroom will be transferred to an exhibition room on the first floor of the west wing. If you and Enid want to take some of the more modern, smaller toys for your children, then you're free to do that before the Trust do an inventory. My daughters have already taken a few things. But don't take the large doll's house and the train set, they will have pride of place in the exhibition."

"Thanks. I'll tell Enid." Arianna interjected.

"That's the gist of it as far as the house is concerned," Bertie went on. "In the grounds there will be a car park constructed, an outhouse with WCs, and a gatehouse where tickets will be issued. The agricultural land will all be fenced off as will the fields with livestock - all that land and the farm itself will remain in my ownership, as will the three cottages. But you don't need to concern yourself with any of that, that is Arthur's province."

This was the first time he had specifically indicated there was a job he was considering her for. She asked carefully,

"So, you're looking for an assistant are you, to help you deal with the National Trust in the conversion of the house?"

"Exactly. From what Enid said about your qualifications and experience, you seem to be just the person I am looking for, with the bonus of being a relative, someone I can trust."

Arianna handed him the resume she had written out and he scanned it quickly.

"Yes, that looks fine, confirms more or less what Enid said. I'll need you to be my eyes and ears when I'm in London, liaise with the Trust and the builders and so on, and act as my secretary when I am here. I envisage the job continuing, albeit in a revised format, once the transition of the house is complete. I imagine it will be more or less a full-time job. Will that be a problem with regard to your child? I understand she's still a toddler."

"Enid's offered to have her most days. She can play with Jimmy."

"Capital," Bertie beamed. "Well, if you want the job, it just remains to discuss salary and hours of work."

"Yes, I do want it. Thanks very much. But I'm out of touch with the cost of living in England and I don't know yet how much I'll have to pay to rent somewhere."

"Oh. I was rather assuming you'd be staying with your sister?"

"In the short term, yes, but I can't impose upon them indefinitely."

"Right, well, if it would help, you could live-in here. I and my family are not going to need all the bedrooms in the east wing, let alone the rest of the second floor, and we're not here half the time. To start with, you could re-occupy your old room if you like and your little girl could have one of the two rooms opposite and the other can be refurnished as a small sitting room. That bathroom would be mainly yours and you would have the use of the kitchen. How does that sound?"

Arianna's smile said it all. "That would be marvellous! I'd be near Enid and Arthur without living on top of them."

"Yes, and I would have someone living in to keep an eye on the place. At the moment there's only Cook sleeping here when I'm in London and she is retiring at the end of this year. So are the Hughes. That's something I forgot to mention. We will have to advertise for replacements and you could carry out the initial interviews and prepare a shortlist for me. I'm thinking of engaging just a married couple; to be cook-housekeeper and butler-handyman. They will occupy the Hughes' cottage."

"What is proposed for our old cottage?" Arianna asked.

"I haven't decided yet. I may just demolish it or I may rebuild and let it out."

They agreed a starting salary and the amount to be deducted for board and lodging and Bertie said he would look into increasing it in six months time if she proved to be an efficient assistant.

"I will," she promised him. "When do you want me to start?"

"On Monday?"

That was agreed and the hours of work settled on as nine to five, Monday to Friday, with the occasional Saturday morning if required. Arianna returned to her sister's house in jubilant mood.

~***~

Chapter Twenty-Nine

June 1948

Arianna was sitting at her desk in the office she shared with Bertie when there was a tap on the door.

"Come in," she called, assuming it to be the builders' foreman. She kept her head down, concentrating on finishing adding up a column of figures.

"One of the builders let me into the house and showed me to your office," a familiar voice said, a voice she had longed to hear again. She looked up and saw him standing there, a boyish grin on his face.

"Edward!" she shrieked, leaping out of her chair and hurling herself into his arms.

He swung her up and around and then kissed her passionately.

"What are you doing here? Have you taken leave early?"

"No, I'm back for good. I've left Malaya and resigned from the colonial service."

Joy flooded through her. "Tell me everything!"

"There's not much to tell. There's a lot of unrest in Malaya now. A state of emergency was about to be declared and I've since heard that it has been. It won't be many years before Malaya becomes independent and then there wouldn't be a job for me. I don't want to start again in another part of the empire and anyway, India is already independent and others will follow. So I resigned and came back. I've been back a few weeks actually."

"A few weeks! Why didn't you phone me or come here sooner?"

"Well, I wasn't sure what your situation was until I'd spoken to Theo and then I wanted to have a job lined up, so I wasn't coming to you as an unemployed man with no income. I've just been for an interview in Oxford, for a job in local government; they've offered it to me and I've accepted. Theo told me you were working and living here and as far as he knew there was no man in your life, so I came straight here afterwards."

"There has never been anyone else in my heart! And I wouldn't have cared if you were unemployed!"

"Well, I now have gainful employment, along with temporary lodgings in Oxford. Have you got a divorce from Farish now?"

"I didn't need one. You were right. The marriage wasn't valid in England."

"So there's nothing to stop us being together?"

"Not as long as you accept that Sakirah and I come as a package."

"Yes, of course. I never thought otherwise. I could adopt her if you like, become her official father....Oh, I'm rather jumping the gun, aren't I? I haven't asked you yet."

He got down on one knee and took hold of her hand.

"Darling Arianna, I have loved you for almost ten years, since we first met on that ship. My love has survived our separations and everything else life threw at us and now I'm finally able to ask you to do me the honour of becoming my wife."

"Yes, yes, of course I will!" She flung her arms around him.

Bertie chose that moment to wander in through the partly open door. Seeing the scene in front of him, he cleared his throat loudly, then said,

"Shall I go out and come in again? I seem to be interrupting something!"

"No, Bertie, it's fine. This is Edward and we've just become engaged to be married. You can be the first to congratulate us! Edward, this is Sir Albert, my cousin and also my boss."

"Congratulations to you both, and I'm pleased to meet you, Edward. But isn't this rather sudden?"

"Not at all sir," Edward said. "We've known each other since 1938 but events have conspired to keep us mainly apart since '42."

"I see," Bertie said, although he didn't entirely. "Does this mean I will lose my very efficient assistant?"

"Not necessarily," Arianna answered. "Not for a while anyway. Edward's just got a job in Oxford."

"Yes, if we can find a house this side of Oxford, I daresay she could still come here, especially if it's on a direct bus route."

311

"No need for the bus route," Arianna put in. "I passed my driving test a few months ago."

"You could live here to start with if you like," Bertie offered. "After you're married, I mean. Until you find the right house. Arianna has a small suite of rooms upstairs and I believe her bedroom has a double bed in it. There's a good train service to Oxford from the town and a bus to there, if you don't have a car."

"Thank you sir, that's a very generous offer. And I will have a car. I'm borrowing my father's at present, but he's about to get a new model and he says I can have this one."

"Perfect!" Arianna exclaimed. "Then we could get married as soon as the arrangements can be made, couldn't we?"

"I'd marry you tomorrow if it could be done! When do you finish here for the day? I'll wait for you and then perhaps you can introduce me to your sister and I can meet Sakirah again."

"I finish at five."

"Fine, I'll take a walk in the grounds meanwhile, if I may sir?"

"No need for that. Just finish off those figures quickly, Arianna, and then you can call it a day. It's not every day you become engaged and you'll want to celebrate with your sister."

"Thank you, Bertie. You're the best boss ever!"

Their wedding was arranged for late August, in the village church, with a small reception in the upstairs room of the village pub. Enid donated some of her clothing coupons, as did Violet and Isobel, and they had enough to buy a length of cream satin, which Enid, who was an excellent seamstress, made up into a wedding dress. Arianna asked Theo to give her away and Enid to be her matron of honour, with Sakirah as a bridesmaid and Jimmy a page boy. Apart from their families, they invited a few friends each, including Emma and Shirley and their new husbands, and Arianna's old school friend, Rosa. Edward asked his brother to be best man.

A week or so after their engagement, Arianna had gone to meet her future in-laws. She had been quite nervous but Edward had prepared the ground well and she was warmly welcomed into their family. If his parents were dismayed that their son was marrying a mixed race woman who already had a child, they hid it well.

On the day, Charlie was detailed to drive Theo and Arianna to the church, while Arthur took Enid and the children. The two men waited at the foot of the stairs for Arianna to appear.

"Gosh, Sis, you look stunning!" Theo said admiringly. "Edward will be bowled over!"

In the car, Arianna said she'd had a disturbing dream that night.

"You know the bit where the vicar asks whether anyone knows of any impediment to the marriage? Well, I dreamed that the door to the church burst open and Farish stood there and said I couldn't marry Edward because I was still married to him!"

Theo laughed. "Have you been re-reading Jane Eyre lately? Don't worry, if he does, Edward and I will throw him out and tell the vicar he's an escaped lunatic from the nearest asylum!"

Charlie chuckled. "No need for that. I'll just stand up and tell him I'm your lawyer and your marriage in Malaya was definitely not legal in this country. Not that it's going to happen, it was just a dream."

"Yes, just a stupid dream, Ari," Theo said. "Put it out of your mind and relax and enjoy what should be the happiest day of your life. You and Edward have waited a long time for this!"

Nevertheless, as they stood at the altar and the vicar came to that part of the service, she held her breath, but the church door remained firmly shut and the proceedings continued without a hitch.

At the reception, Theo gave the speech normally made by the bride's father and, after making the audience chuckle with some tales of Arianna's wilder childhood escapades, he struck a more serious note, saying that Arianna and Edward's love for each other had prevailed over adversity, surviving lengthy separations and they deserved every happiness now they were finally together. Edward, in a voice thick with emotion, said he had loved his beautiful bride for ten years, thoughts of her had got him through his years in captivity during the war, but he had then lost her, found her again and lost her a second time before they were finally able to be together. After that, the best man wisely confined himself to cracking a few light-hearted jokes at his brother's expense.

After the newly-weds had departed on their honeymoon and Sakirah's tears at her mother's departure had been dried, Enid slipped her arm into Theo's and said,

"Just you left now, my dear, to marry and settle down."

"I already did. And no-one can ever replace her."

"Someone will, one day. What about that half-Indian girl in Leeds, you mention her quite a bit?"

"Ayesha? She's just a friend. She's years younger than me and anyway she's more or less promised to an Indian boy who's come over to visit this summer."

He had seen little of Ayesha since Rajeev had arrived. He was staying with some relatives of his who also lived in Leeds and Ayesha had been spending more time there than at home. Rajeev had taken supper with Ayesha's family on a couple of occasions and Theo found him a pleasant young man. He didn't understand why it was that he felt rather depressed when he saw the two of them together. Was it because they reminded him of himself and Natalia? But he didn't have that reaction seeing Enid with Arthur or, more recently, Arianna with Edward. He was simply happy for his sisters and glad that they had both ended up with two of his best friends.

Theo took some of his annual leave and spent the week after the wedding with Enid and Arthur and the two children. Sakirah was missing her mother and, to cheer her up, he took the two children to a fair which was based in Great Pucklington for the week. The children enjoyed themselves on the merry go round and the dodgems and he bought them both ice creams. Sakirah attracted some curious stares from the crowds and some of the older children pointed at her. Four year old Jimmy eventually noticed and asked,

"Why do people keep staring at Saki?"

"Well, it's probably because she's darker skinned than most English people and they're not used to that round here."

Dark skins were starting to become more prevalent in large towns and cities, as workers were being imported from the Caribbean, but this trend had yet to penetrate into rural Oxfordshire.

Jimmy asked, "Why is she a darker colour? And Auntie Arianna too?"

"Well, Mummy's told you about your Malayan grandmother hasn't she?"

He nodded.

"Malaya is in South East Asia where people have darker skin. Auntie Arianna takes after our mother in her colouring and Sakirah has a double dose of Malayan heritage. You, on the other hand, look like your father."

Jimmy was red-haired with light skin, prone to freckles.

When Theo got back to Leeds, the house was quiet, all the family being out. Then Richard arrived back, as it was the end of the school holidays. When they had both finished their unpacking, they adjourned to the kitchen and made themselves a pot of tea.

"Any news on Ayesha and that Indian chap?" Richard asked. "Are they engaged now?"

"Not as far as I know, but I've been away for ten days."

"He's supposed to be going back early September, isn't he? Not much time left for him to pop the question. Mind you, if he doesn't, I think Pa Dexter will be pleased, he doesn't want her to marry him and go to India."

Theo made a vague response. He couldn't help hoping that Ayesha wouldn't become engaged and go off to India. He told himself it was because he didn't want to lose his congenial social companion. But if she left, perhaps it would be the prod he needed to bestir himself into asking other women out occasionally. Normally, attractive women of his age would all be spoken for, most of them married with children, but the war had created quite a few widows and many more had lost their sweethearts. He told himself he would have far more in common with women like them than with a young girl like Ayesha. There were several pretty young women working at the council offices; he would just need to find out which of them were unattached and then pluck up the courage to ask one out.

Ayesha was taking her annual leave from the department store so he travelled in on the bus on his own for the next week and only saw her in passing. It was the following Friday evening that she next appeared at the Dexters' supper table. He could tell there was rather an atmosphere when he walked into the room. Richard had gone back home for the weekend so he was the only non-family member present. Mrs Dexter had a displeased look on her face as she served the meal and she made very little conversation, which was unusual. Her husband seemed more or less his usual self as did Jayant, but

Ayesha was quiet and downcast and seemed to be avoiding addressing her mother directly. Later that evening he found her alone in the sitting room.

"Not seeing Rajeev tonight?" he asked.

"He's gone back to India. He left earlier today."

He looked at her ring finger, it bore no adornment. "You're not engaged then?"

"No."

His curiosity got the better of him.

"Did he propose?" he asked, then added, "I'm sorry, it's none of my business, is it? Forget I asked."

"It's all right. Yes, he did, a few days ago, but I said no. My mother is quite annoyed with me, she says I'll never get the chance of such a good marriage again."

Theo felt elated. "You didn't fall in love with him, then?"

"No. I liked him a lot still and maybe love would have grown, but I wanted to feel more than that to start with, I wanted to be in love. My mother says I have silly ideas based on romantic fiction and I don't know what love is, but that's not true. I do know what it's like to have your heart beat faster when a particular man walks into the room. I wanted to feel that with Rajeev, but I didn't."

He had to ask. "Have you felt that with anyone else?"

She nodded.

"Someone at work?"

She didn't answer directly. "It's someone rather older than me and I don't think he feels the same way at all. It's rather silly of me, really, wishing he were more than a friend."

He asked again, conflicting feelings rising up inside him, "Is it someone you work with? A married man, perhaps?"

"No, it's not a work colleague. And he's not married, not anymore."

She had been looking away from him as she spoke, but now she turned her head and looked him full in the face, willing him to understand, hoping against hope that he might feel the same, afraid to come straight out with it for fear of making a fool of herself. Finally realising that she might mean him and for the first time admitting to himself that this was what he wanted, Theo asked hesitantly,

"Is it me, Ayesha?"

She blushed and looked down again. "Yes. Stupid of me, isn't it? Of course you could never feel that way about me, I'm just a silly little girl to you."

"That's not true!" he exclaimed. He came over and sat beside her. "I've only just fully realised it myself, but I've been slowly falling in love with you for some time."

Her face lit up. "Really?"

"Yes, really, my love. I didn't want you to marry Rajeev and go to India, I was hoping you wouldn't."

He reached out to her and they kissed, slowly, gently and tenderly. Then she snuggled into his arms.

Theo felt happiness suffuse through him. She was not Natalia, she would never be Natalia, and he would probably never experience that depth of passion again. Perhaps such a love was a once in a lifetime experience. But Ayesha was sweet-natured and bright and funny, and there were many different kinds of love. He could see them having children and growing old together. She would never replace Natalia, and his first wife would always occupy a piece of his heart, but there was room in it for Ayesha too; his love for them both could reside side by side. Like him, Ayesha was half Asian and, as with Natalia, the two halves of his heritage would not be in conflict. As he held her in his arms, kissing and caressing her, while contemplating their future together, he felt a profound sense of peace and serenity, as if, after a long and arduous journey, he had finally come home.

~****~

Epilogue

Theo and Ayesha married the following spring, bought a house on the outskirts of Leeds and went on to have three children, two boys and a girl.

Theo later talked to a journalist about his experiences as a POW of the Japanese, as did others, and the world eventually became aware of the atrocities which had taken place.

In 1972, accompanied by his eldest son, he flew out to Singapore and, after showing his son the places he had lived in Malaya and Singapore and visiting some of their Malay relatives, they went on to Jakarta to visit the Commonwealth War Cemetery, where Natalia's remains and those of his baby son had been reinterred in 1961. As he laid flowers on their grave and stood for a few minutes in silent contemplation, he fancied he heard her voice telling him she was happy that he had found love again and had a good life, but it may just have been his mind playing tricks.

Theo died in 1982, aged 66, from an aggressive form of skin cancer, which almost certainly had its origins in the relentless sun exposure he'd experienced while in captivity.

*

Arianna and Edward went on to have two more children, a girl and a boy.

In 1967, Farish came to England to visit his now grown-up daughter. He showed her photos of her half-siblings and suggested she come to Malaya for a holiday and visit them. Afterwards she told her parents that she might take him up on his offer, but that she could never think of him as her father; Edward would always be her Dad.

Arianna died in 1976, aged 57, from lung cancer, despite having never smoked. The doctors were non-committal about the cause but Theo and Enid were convinced it was the long ago smoke damage she had suffered during the fire and that yet another murder could be attributed to the arsonist, who was now a free man.

*

Enid and Arthur never succeeded in having any more children, Enid suffering several miscarriages. She outlived both her siblings and also her husband and died peacefully in her sleep at the ripe old age of ninety-one.

*

Charlie did live to see homosexuality legalised in 1967. By then, he had a long term partner and they were able to live out their last years openly sharing a home.

~*****~

Author's Note

Malaya finally gained independence in 1957, after peaceful negotiations with the British. It was renamed Malaysia in 1963. In 1965, Singapore separated from Malaysia and became an independent state.

Great Pucklington, Little Pucklington and Pucklington Manor are entirely fictional places, but I imagined the town to be along a rail line which was closed in the 1960s. All other specific place names mentioned are real, both in England and South East Asia, but some names have changed since colonial times, e.g. Port Swettenham is now Port Klang and Siam has become Thailand.

In chapter two, a child character uses a racist word which is not normally put into print nowadays. However, this was 1928 and such words were in frequent use then. I hope that no offence will be caused to any of my readers. Similarly, in chapters thirteen and fourteen, some homophobic expressions appear, which were in common usage in the 1930s.

Readers of 'Voyage To Venning Road' will probably realise why Theo never found his biological relatives. That novel was based on a true story and a blend of fact and fiction. Theo's natural father and his family were real people and to have the fictional Theo connect with them in the 1930s or 40s would have been blurring fiction with reality too close to the present time. The people referred to in the book are all now dead, but their descendants, born in the 1940s, are still alive.

~***~

Sources for Historical Background

Tales of the South China Seas by Charles Allen
Out in the Midday Sun by Margaret Shennan
The Burma-Siam Railway by Robert Hardie
Secret Letters from the Railway by Charles Steel, edited by Brian
Best
1930s Britain by Robert Pearce.
Plus Google and numerous websites.
Some inspiration was also gleaned from the TV series Tenko, the
film The Railway Man and the novel Tanamera by Noel Barber.

~***~

Acknowledgments

Jonathan Moffat, Malayan Volunteers Group
Bob Bartlett and John Stone (police procedure)
Roy Parsons (military operational detail)

~*****~

Printed in Great Britain
by Amazon

82988317R00190